THE AEON OF ERIS

A Tale of the Nepheleid

By Marisol Charbonneau

ARCANA ELEMENTS

*Dedicated to the memory of Jan (John) Stychalkowski,
uncle (sort of), friend, neighbour, Holocaust survivor,
and the most bad ass motherfucker who ever lived.*

You were loved, and you are missed.

Hail the traveller!

Chapter One

Time to go and say goodbye to all my relations, Junia thought as she gazed upon the sunlit ocean planet beneath her feet. Autumn had dawned this very morning upon the Northern Hemisphere and it would not be long until the City-ship Nephele, Junia's home in low Earth orbit, unmoored from its tether to the ground below and set out to fulfil its noble mission in the decades and centuries to come. Five years from today, the Nephele will reach the Asteroid Belt between Mars and Jupiter to rendezvous with its sister vessel, the mining station Corona, and build a spacefaring fleet destined to seed the Cosmos with Earthly Life beyond the outermost reaches of the Heliosphere. But today, Junia would take her last trip to the surface of the Earth, and formally bid farewell to the only home world she and her crewmates had ever known.

Junia crossed into the vestibule separating the Nephele's lowest deck from the Hesperides Autonomous Station, the permanent home of the CARINA ALSESTIS Laboratories. Tasked with providing life support systems for City-ships under construction in space, the station also provided a verdant buffer between the cold sterility of the Hub, the massive space elevator linking the Nephele to the CARINA Polaris station in the High Arctic, and the ambulatory citadels that vessels like the newly completed Nephele were meant to become.

Like a placenta. That's what Mom used to say, Junia mused, recalling something her eldest brother told her about how their mother once likened the Hub to an umbilical cord linking the Earth to her mechanical children beyond the boundary of the Sky. Junia bit her lip, realizing that by this logic she was, in a way, returning to the womb, albeit for the last time. At least it was fitting that she would make the journey alone. It would be like the heroes of old setting out on their quests before overcoming insurmountable obstacles and becoming full-fledged gods.

Speaking of which, I should probably take my frailty pills while others are looking.

Stepping into the lift, Junia reached inside her jacket pocket for a pack of vacuum-sealed candied ginger. She made certain that the other travellers congregating at the thick doors of the airlock saw her rip the seal open and take a piece, before tucking away the rest of the candy for the long descent back to Earth. It was very important for Junia to be seen taking the preferred prophylactic against microgravity-induced nausea for Junia was no mere mortal. In the previous Winter, Junia's last attempt to leave the Nephele was accomplished by leaping from the airlock and landing squarely on terra firm with only her clothes singed off during re-entry. That removed all doubt that she was as nigh indestructible as the gods of Olympus were before they consumed the herb of invulnerability when they waged war against the Giants long ago, far from the gaze of mortals.

Before Junia was born, Prometheus, forever the benefactor of humanity, rallied Hera, the Queen of Olympus and the wife of his arch-nemesis Zeus, to his cause. Prometheus was working to ensure that mortals could thrive beyond the confines of the broad-pathed Earth by building great City-ships to allow their fragile kind to survive the journey through interstellar space. That was fifteen years ago.

Shortly thereafter, Hera found out that Zeus murdered her first husband, the Giant Eurymedon to whom she bore Prometheus, then erased her memory and gave her son to her handmaiden Klymene. Having had her memory restored, the Queen left Olympus with Prometheus, and with the newly conceived Junia in her womb. When Zeus found his errant wife years later, he compelled her to return to Olympus with their young daughter in exchange for a promise that no harm would come to Prometheus, nor his learned mortals of the Nephele whose very existence he considered an insult to the supremacy of the gods. As a show of goodwill, or perhaps hubris, Zeus wagered to his Queen that Junia would choose to remain on starry Olympus and dwell among the gods once she came of age. If Junia chose instead to remain with the crew of the Nephele, Hera would be free to join the learned mortals in the wandering citadel beyond the Heavens over which Zeus rules.

In the years that followed, Zeus grew so confident in his preferred outcome that he allowed Hera and Junia to spend parts of the year on the Nephele. It was during such a sojourn six months ago that Junia decided to pay her Olympian kin a visit by leaping out of the airlock. Though unharmed from her Earth-dive, Junia unwittingly set into motion a chain of events that almost led to the annihilation of the human race. Mortals were spared from extinction when Hera challenged Gaia, the primordial Earth-Goddess herself, in a battle of wills. It was a contest that would have ended in a stalemate had Zeus not come to rescue his oft-estranged bride and brought her back once again to starry Olympus. Significantly weakened from her clash with the angry, sentient biosphere, Hera remained on Olympus ever since, biding her time. Once Junia returned to the abode of the gods to declare her intent to remain with the learned mortals of the Nephele, thereby releasing her mother from her infelicitous union with Zeus for all Time.

"To all Earth-bound passengers," said an unseen voice somewhere through the walls. "Hold on to the railings while we open the doors beneath you. You may feel lightheaded for a few hours even after the cabin starts moving. This is perfectly normal. If you are inconvenienced by microgravity, we strongly advise that you induce sleep during the descent with a dose of our patented Hypnos mist."

Junia ignored the rest of the recorded message and curled her legs beneath her in a tight ball. With a practiced hand, she pulled herself all the way down onto the boarding platform of the Krios Khrysomallos, the Hub's luxurious passenger cabin. It was especially equipped for the voyage from low Earth orbit to the planet's surface at a much reduced speed than its cargo conveyances, so as not to further sicken its delicate mortal occupants. Once she reached the opening to the Krios proper, she spied a familiar figure waiting for her on the other side. He was floating in microgravity with his legs aligned as if he were standing tall on the ground, in much the same way as he did when flitting about on starry Olympus.

"Hermes?" Junia said. "What the – I thought Mom forbade you from setting a winged, sandaled foot on the Nephele!"

"That is technically correct," the messenger of the gods answered in his usual cagey manner. "However, the Nephele is exactly one waystation from this very spot, and I am on this side of the opening to the Hesperides, which means I am, strictly speaking, on the Hub. As far as I know, which is quite a lot, the Hub remains under Canadian jurisdiction, or whatever country mortals have determined lies at the very bottom of this contraption."

"The United Territories of Turtle Island," Junia replied. "Just exactly how many months did you spend on Earth and spying on Mom, when we all lived at the CARINA stations? No one calls it Canada anymore. Not even Greater Canada, after they annexed the United States following the great plague of 20–"

"Isn't it funny," Hermes remarked, visibly shuddering when Junia mentioned the year of reckoning, "that mortals have not updated their corpus of Space Law ever since the last Dark Age, even after they almost bled themselves white fighting over the resources on the Moon, while their lowlands on Earth vanished beneath the waves?"

"Is this the part where you tell me that Zeus was right to oppose Prometheus and Hera for building this City-Ship and the ones yet to come?" Junia asked sullenly, as if she this were not the first time they argued about such matters.

"I have no opinion on that, little one," Hermes answered. "My orders are solely to bring you safely home... back to Olympus, that is."

"You could have waited for me on the Polaris," Junia replied, slowly making her way to the narrow opening into the Krios. "They still have that heated lounge in the lower deck for visitors."

"And how would you have made it to Olympus from there?" Hermes asked.

"I would have taken a ride on a flying canoe!"

Hermes threw Junia a sideways glance.

"I have people waiting for me down there," Junia answered. "Pretend mortals, like – What the hell, Hermes!" she exclaimed when the messenger reached out to put a hand on her shoulder before she could cross into the cabin. Hermes then pulled her aside to let the passengers in the queue behind her board the Krios first.

Junia quickly calmed herself and took a breath, remaining mindful not to get overexcited and accidentally cause Hermes to lose consciousness and lie breathless for the duration of a full year, as per the penalty of those who perjure against an Oath by the Holy River Styx.

"I am not here to kidnap you, Princess," Hermes said, half facetiously, though a shadow of terror momentarily crossed his countenance. "I thought I would spare you the very long descent in the vertical hamster tunnel and bring you home at once."

"They track all people coming in and out of the Hub," Junia answered flatly. "They counted you coming up, under an assumed name, no doubt. It would look weird if we both did not show up on the other end.

It would look as though we vanished into the vacuum of space somewhere halfway back to Earth!"

"There are ways to circumvent that protocol," Hermes replied with a coy smile.

Junia raised an eyebrow. "Eris is not here," she said. "And I think the mortals have gotten better since then at counting heads..."

"You really do favour your mother when you look vexed," Hermes retorted. "Besides, do you truly believe that Eris is the only deathless one capable of confounding mortals as to your presence on the Krios? Some of us took notes, after that little stunt you pulled last Winter when you jumped out of the airlock up there to land on Olympus."

"I did that only once," Junia answered calmly.

"I know, thanks to that clever trinket on your finger. I hope you've grown into it? Your mother did say you were due for a growth spurt after your school uniform disintegrated somewhere in the troposphere."

"You mean this ring?" Junia inquired, emphatically extending the middle finger of her right hand where an ornately gilded ring loosely bedecked her childlike digit. "This glorified tracking device that's too big, yet somehow I can never take off while I am up here?"

"That is a temporary measure," Hermes told her calmly, as if chiding a fractious child. "You will be able to take it off your finger once you come of age and decide your fate."

"Yeah," Junia grumbled. "Until then I can't practice opening portals on my own through space-time like Mom and Eris do all the time, not without setting off every security alarm on the Nephele *and* the Hesperides!"

"So I suppose we will not be taking a shortcut to Olympus from here," Hermes said.

"Not unless you want to be the cause of a major inquest on the safety of every airlock on this side of the Hub!"

"You have made your point," Hermes replied somewhat dejectedly.

"It's not all bad," Junia told him as she wriggled her way back to the end of the quickly moving queue. "The view is amazing. Just don't stare straight into the Sun."

"Hephaestus will be pleased that your ring almost fits you," Hermes retorted, keeping pace with Junia as she swiftly pulled herself all the way down to the bottom of the Krios, presumably to be among the first to exit when they reached the Polaris.

"I'll tell him myself," Junia said, almost out of breath. "When I see him on the Nephele once I get back."

"You truly believe Hephaestus will leave Olympus with Prometheus and his learned mortals to sail the stars?" Hermes asked in an almost mocking tone. "Or that Prometheus will allow such a thing? It was he who chained Prometheus to his rock!"

"Hephaestus is as much a victim of Zeus' malice as Prometheus was," Junia answered calmly, deftly deflecting the provocation. "Prometheus is wise enough to know this. And it's not just Hephaestus who will join us. Ares and Eris already have jobs up there. Hebe and Herakles don't yet, but they've practically sworn to never leave Mom's side. I don't know about Eileithya, though. She is best buddies with Aphrodite, and Mom pretty much told her that Aphrodite will never be welcome aboard the Nephele, ever."

"And yet," Hermes said, pushing Junia gently into her seat and buckling her harness in place as if she were a toddler. "I do recall Hera uttering her battle-cry to all the immortals gathered atop the Polaris all those years ago, after Herakles and I found you both in the Kingdom of Hades. Hera *practically swore* she would welcome anyone who wished to join her in her great quest to sow Earthly Life among the stars if they so desired, no matter what transpired between them. You were probably too young to remember."

"I was there, Hermes," Junia protested, resisting the urge to slap his hand away from her seat buckle. "I definitely remember."

"So Hera's words hold true for all immortals, except Aphrodite?" Hermes asked as he took his seat and bucked his own harness.

"And Dionysus," Junia added.

"And Dionysus," Hermes agreed. "Although that one still requires an explanation."

"Mom said that here is no room for harlotry on the Nephele," Junia answered. "So Aphrodite will not have a place among the crew."

"And here I thought the Cosmos was infinite," Hermes retorted sarcastically.

"It is," Junia answered. "But the network of City-ships and waystations that are yet to be built are definitely not. Think about it! They can never be infinite in the vacuum of space!"

"And yet Hera is of the mind that both of her trueborn sons will follow in her footsteps in her voyage to the stars without Aphrodite trailing in their wake?"

"Yes, Jesus! We've been through this!"

Now it was Hermes' turn to raise an eyebrow. "And what of Dionysus, who brings joy to mortals?" he asked.

"What about him?" Junia asked dismissively.

"Your mother was never fond of him, I ought to know, and yet she has long since reconciled with him, as she does with all the demigods she never succeeded in killing."

"My Mom never killed anyone, *ever*," Junia replied defensively.

"I suppose not," Hermes retorted. She usually lets others do the dirty work for her."

"Like you do for Zeus?" Junia spat back.

"*Touché*," Hermes conceded, though a faint smile began curling upon his lips.

"And Dionysus is a thug," Junia pontificated. "He has a history of driving mad all those who refuse to recognize his divinity. And those who do, he makes soft and indolent."

"And what is wrong with softness and indolence once in a while?" Hermes asked. "Even the most stalwart immortals deserve to let loose and have a bit of fun every now and then."

"Mom said that Dionysus is a god for mortals who feel powerless and trapped by their circumstances. He and gods of his ilk become ascendant at the moment societies begin to collapse. Just look at what happened to Old Rome!"

"Again, *touché*," Hermes retorted.

"Dionysus won't be needed up there either," Junia continued. "Mom told me that the learned mortals on the Nephele, as well as all the immortals who will dwell at the farthest boundaries of the known Cosmos, will want for nothing after we set out. They will have no need for liberators, for their will be no slavers of any kind, not while my mother watches over them."

Hermes heaved a theatrical sigh. "I sometimes forget how young you are," he told Junia facetiously.

"No you don't!"

"When you're right..." Hermes trailed off, momentarily distracted by the recorded message announcing the Hub's imminent departure from Hesperides Station.

"I noticed you are travelling light," Hermes said, trying to change the subject.

"I'm not, Junia answered. "My luggage was sent earlier through the cargo shipment. It's probably already on the Polaris. Hey, I have to ask, since you're here... when we land, can we go to Uncle Hades' Kingdom before we go to Olympus? I'd like to see my Mama in Elysium for the last time before the Nephele leaves Earth."

Hermes gave Junia a quizzical look, before remembering that Hera's handmaiden Klymene, to whom Zeus gave the infant Prometheus to raise as her own son, remained with Hera to help her raise Junia when they hid for many years on Turtle Island. That Junia considered Klymene her second mother always annoyed Zeus a great deal, even though the King of the gods never begrudged Klymene for remaining a loyal servant to her Queen. When Hera wrangled Gaia the previous Winter, the dastardly King Kronos and his Titan brothers, long imprisoned in Tartarus after losing the war for ascendancy over the Cosmos to Zeus and his siblings, came to the aid of their former enemies to help them find the embattled Queen of Olympus. Hermes recalled that at the time Kronos had given Junia his storied sickle, with which he castrated and dethroned his own father, the Sky-King Ouranos.

With this fabled weapon, Junia opened a portal that led to the Garden of the Hesperides – Hera's nuptial garden at the boundaries of the Earth and not its namesake waystation between the Hub and the Nephele – where all the gods found Hera bound at the tree of the golden apples and caught in a gridlock in her battle with the Earth-Mother. Hermes lost sight of the sickle shortly thereafter, for Prometheus quickly spirited Junia away to the Nephele when Zeus became distracted with rescuing Hera, while Hermes was preoccupied with bringing the blessed gods back to Olympus. To thank the Titans for their assistance, Zeus released his former foes from Tartarus and they became the lords of Elysium, where the shades of the mighty dead dwell. As far as Hermes knew, the sickle remained in the Garden of the Hesperides or, knowing Hades, the Lord of the Underworld took the sickle back with him to his infinite Kingdom for safekeeping.

"Hermes? *Can* we make a quick pit stop at Uncle Hades'?" Junia asked again, bringing the messenger god back to the present moment.

"I'm afraid not, little one," Hermes answered diplomatically. "Not today. Perhaps later, after you've spent some time on Olympus. Father would be most displeased if we dawdled in the Underworld, where Time slows to a crawl…"

"But you can synchronize Time in the Kingdom of Hades with that on the surface of the Earth!" Junia protested. "I've seen you do it!"

"That is true," Hermes conceded. "As I said, perhaps later. Right now, Father awaits your return. He is quite eager to see you again."

"I doubt that very much," Junia muttered under her breath as she reached to press the button above her seat to release a generous dose of Hypnos mist, deliberately leaving Hermes without a conscious travelling companion for the long descent back to Earth.

This might be my last chance to sleep for a while, she thought as the world around her faded into blessed darkness.

Nepheleid

Chapter Two

At the Thunderer's behest, fair-haired Rhea graced the banquet hall where the blessed gods gathered on starry Olympus to await the return of swift Hermes with the young Junia. Standing beside her favoured son, Rhea felt ill at ease for the errand she knew Zeus soon would entrust her. Longing for the halcyon days when all her children heeded her counsel without question, Rhea knew that the King of Olympus would task her with a most onerous endeavour. It would fall on her to persuade his Queen to remain by Zeus' side should Junia decide to leave the Earth's embrace on the City-ship Nephele with Prometheus and the learned mortals under his care. There was no need for Rhea to consult her sister, Themis, for her wondrous oracular gift. The Mother of the gods already knew that she would fail to coax her youngest daughter to remain amongst the gods, unlike the time when she convinced gentle Demeter to return to Olympus after her daughter Persephone was returned to her.

Swaying the goddess of the furrows to put aside her anger at Zeus for giving their child away in marriage without her knowledge or consent had been no easy task. So great was her outrage at having her daughter stolen by Hades and taken to the Underworld to be his Queen that Demeter refused to rejoin the families of the gods on starry Olympus. This was even after Zeus decreed that Persephone would henceforth spend one-third of the year in the Underworld with her bridegroom and the remaining two-thirds with her mother. Still, cajoling Demeter to return to Olympus would prove rather effortless when compared to attempting the same with Hera, the reigning Queen of Olympus and Rhea's true heir in every conceivable manner. Unlike Demeter whose forbearing nature rendered her easy to beguile with words, golden-throned Hera was unfathomably difficult to deceive having spent a veritable eternity matching, and often surpassing, wits with her King.

A supremely competent ruler in her own right, Hera was as formidably combative as she was proud, possessing both qualities in abundance. She also carried a smouldering grudge against her mother for favouring

Zeus above all her other illustrious offspring. The Titan-Queen never knew the degree to which her youngest daughter held her in contempt until the day Themis hosted a banquet in Hera's honour, one year before Junia was born. On that occasion, Hera outright accused her mother of being wilfully daft for arbitrarily waiting for her sixth child to be born in order to spare him from the cannibalistic fury of her husband, the Titan-King Kronos. At the time, the goddesses gathered in Themis' palace and blamed their Queen's outburst on the presence of the uninvited Eris, the goddess of chaos, confusion, and discord. Eris was Hera's youngest daughter then, but Rhea knew that even Eris could not have moved Hera's heart to such displays of righteous fury without a suppurating wound festering deep inside her very core.

With the conviction that she could never accomplish that which Zeus would ask of her, Rhea turned her thought to persuading Zeus undertake a different course of action. Perhaps Zeus could renew his efforts to coax Hera back into their marriage bed, lest the Queen's disgust at her King doom all of Olympus to a fate worse than oblivion.

"How fares your bride?" Rhea asked Zeus, though she already knew the answer.

"Still picking apples with Eris in the Garden of the Hesperides," the Cloud-gatherer replied unhappily. "As far as anyone knows, she has done nothing else since Winter turned to Spring."

"Has she not once shared your bed since she awoke from her long rest?" Rhea asked him casually.

"Tread lightly, Mother," Zeus answered in a low voice, as a roll of thunder reverberated around the lofty peaks of starry Olympus.

Rhea remained silent for a moment, knowing full well how inordinately prickly her favourite son became whenever she meddled in his private affairs. The Thunderer also never forgave his mother for forbidding him to marry as he came of age and began pursuing the ill-fated Metis, daughter of Okeanos and Tethys, and mother of grey-eyed Athena. Centuries later, with Metis firmly embedded inside his head and counselling him on all matters, Zeus set his sights on marrying his beautiful sister – against Rhea's wishes and Hera's better judgment. Predictably, Rhea objected to this union. She was fearful that Hera would end up swallowed up for a second time, but Zeus placated Rhea by swearing an Oath that Hera would never meet Metis' fate, nor dwell in

Tartarus or fade from the living world into oblivion. As far as the Mother of the gods knew, Hera remained ignorant of this Oath and of the role the Titan-Queen continued to play in upholding her ascendancy among the blessed gods who dwell on high Olympus.

"You already know," Zeus said after a long pause. "Bloody hell, all of Olympus knows..." He turned his gaze away, as if it pained him to utter the words.

"That Hera has not joined you in love since she recovered from wrestling with the Earth-Mother at the Tree of the golden apples?" Rhea voiced Zeus' thoughts to allay his unease. "What of her nuptial bath?" she continued. "Your steward Ganymede told the Horai, who then told Hermes, that Hera bathed in the waters of the Kanathos Spring upon her return to Olympus. Did you not renew your love then?"

Zeus said nothing, though the darkening clouds gathering around the heavenly ramparts of high Olympus gave an ominous yet eloquent answer.

This is an ill omen, fair-haired Rhea thought. Long ago, when the gods were young and the nations of mortals younger still, Hera considered it her utmost duty to uphold the marriage bond. It constituted one of the only means by which the goddess initiated young maidens into adulthood, as young men achieved maturity in service to their *polis* through martial pursuits. Maidens who refused to marry were often viewed with contempt and derision, as were the fifty daughters of Danaus who refused to wed the fifty sons of King Aegyptus. All but one of the Danaids slaughtered their husbands on their wedding night, a heinous act which condemned the sisters to the pit of Tartarus. Here, they must serve their penance carrying water to fill a huge, perforated cauldron, therefore never bringing their futile task to completion. The Titan-Queen now feared that Hera, in her lassitude at preserving her vexing union with her deceitful and lecherous husband, finally and unequivocally decided to unburden herself of her sacred union with the Thunderer, as unequivocally as the Danaids refused their unions with their doomed bridegrooms. This, Rhea knew, meant that Hera would relinquish her Queenship among the blessed gods to pursue her everlasting glory among the mortals bound for the stars, no matter what choice the young Junia would make in the days to come.

This eventuality disquieted fair-haired Rhea more than she cared to say. Her daughter's imminent and final departure meant that the uneasy peace that the gods enjoyed on starry Olympus would soon unravel when more than half their number joined Hera and Prometheus in their voyage across the Cosmos. Most of all, the Mother of the gods feared what Hera would do should Zeus thwart her from leaving. At the banquet hosted in Hera's honour all those years ago, Hera asked her fellow goddesses in attendance how the Centaur Chiron could have granted immortality to Prometheus, not knowing that he was a demigod and her son by Eurymedon, the mortal King of the Giants. Alarmed that Hera would unwittingly compel the goddesses into revealing an ancient secret, Rhea berated her daughter for allegedly seeking the means to bequeath her own immortality to a worthy mortal to free herself from the thankless chore of being Queen of the gods. This predictably led to Hera's spectacular outburst where she questioned her mother's intelligence while praising her dastardly father for being the source of her own acumen. Rhea's accusation against her daughter, though transcendentally ludicrous at the time, seemed far more plausible an outcome should Hera not get her way. She obviously no longer cared about the Earth, her marriage or her reign as Queen of Olympus.

"What troubles you, Mother?" Zeus asked, to Rhea's great surprise.

The Titan-Queen considered her words carefully, hoping that wise Metis would heed her counsel in tandem with her royal son.

"I worry about Hera and her state of mind," Rhea replied diplomatically.

"All of Olympus fears she has gone mad," Zeus said without derision, in a way that gave Rhea hope that it was Metis who now addressed her. "Especially since she has taken to keeping the company of Eris in Junia's absence. This does not bode well."

"You think Eris is manipulating Hera?" Rhea inquired. "What in the world could she possibly have to gain from doing so?"

"Eris foments chaos and confusion because she wishes to upset the balance of power on Olympus," Zeus replied calmly. "And when she has done and finished her work, she will aim to be the one who whispers in the ear of the next sovereign among the gods."

"Eris will not be the one who steals the throne of Heaven," Rhea said. "The Fates have not decreed it so."

"Hera has made it abundantly clear that she considers Zoe her heir,"

Zeus replied, emphatically calling Junia by her true name. This name was revealed to all gathered in the Garden of the Hesperides when Apollo probed Hera's mind during her struggle against Gaia. "And Eris loves Zoe like a daughter. Perhaps she got it into her head that Zoe will supplant me, especially since the girl is somehow in possession of my father's sickle."

"Junia – Pardon me, *Zoe* is only a child. She will not replace Hera as Queen of Heaven," Rhea declared. "Your father knows it to be so."

Zeus turned his gaze towards his mother. "Does he, now?" he said, raising an eyebrow in a most uncharacteristic manner.

Tread carefully.

"You should not concern yourself with what your daughters may or may not do," Rhea answered, attempting to change the subject. "What troubles me is what Hera might do-"

Zeus furrowed his brow at the mention of his Queen's name.

"What Hera might do to herself if Junia, I mean Zoe, chose to stay," Rhea continued.

"What the hell do you mean?" the Thunderer asked bluntly.

"Hera is... quite motivated to bring all her designs to completion," Rhea said cautiously. "My fear is that she might do away with her immortality if she considered Junia's choice unsatisfactory to her plans."

"*How*," Zeus asked pointedly, "is such a thing even possible!?"

"Do you remember how Chiron met his end?" Rhea asked.

"That was not fated to happen," Zeus replied dolefully.

"No, my son. Sometimes the Fates cannot foresee the random whims of Chaos, and that was what ultimately did him in. But Chiron was immortal, and to end his suffering from the poisoned arrow, he had to bestow his deathless nature on a mortal, or someone who was not quite as deathless as we are."

"Hera can never taste death," the Cloud-gatherer said flatly. "She is far too powerful, and I swore an Oath that such a fate would never befall her. Your worries are for naught, so enough of this foolishness."

15

Nepheleid

"And yet the young Junia, despite her pedigree as the daughter of two deathless Olympian gods, was born after the great Deluge," Rhea added. "Therefore, she ought to be mortal, unless she has tasted nectar and ambrosia in years since Hera returned to Olympus, before the Nephele was complete."

"You know full well that Hera forbade Zoe from partaking of the food and drink of the gods until she comes of age," Zeus griped. "Are you insinuating that Hera has been preserving Zoe's mortal nature to bestow her immortality upon the girl as a final insult to us all if she failed to convince her to leave on the Nephele?"

Rhea nodded slightly, afraid of further upsetting her royal son.

"That will never come to pass," The Thunderer decreed. "I swore an Oath, and so long as I am the reigning King of Olympus, my word remains Law. Now, Mother, do these words alleviate your fears?"

"They do," the Titan-Queen answered truthfully, gladdened that she would not likely lose her youngest daughter once more to an uncertain fate. "But *you* must bring her back to Olympus," she continued. "You must go to her. You must find her in the Garden of the Hesperides and compel her to return by your side. I cannot do this on your behalf, for she will not heed my counsel. She is not fond of me, but you already knew this, of that I am certain. You must win her back by love alone, not by force or threats. Oh, I know about the Oath she swore to you at the ramparts of Troy, when you granted her the satisfaction of destroying the city dearest to your heart, in exchange for you to do the same to a city dear to hers. And we all heard you release her from that Oath when you held her at the Tree, but my son, that will not be enough. You must prove your love to her if you mean for her to stay willingly. You must prove yourself worthy, in a way you never have before!"

"Hera knows I love her," Zeus said dismissively as a grimace crept upon his countenance. "I'll have you know, I've got Aphrodite's unfailing assistance in this endeavour. What –"

"Aphrodite holds even less sway over Hera than I do," Rhea replied. "Do you not remember how your Queen forbade her, as well as Dionysus whom I raised as my own child, from joining the company of Oceanides, boundary-dwellers, and other immortals who would set forth towards the stars aboard the Nephele if they so choose? Hera is wary of Aphrodite's tricks, and they no longer have any influence over her, if they ever did. You must be the one to sway her! If Hera begins to pick off immortals one by one, whether it be here on Olympus or on distant stars, then the future generations of mortals are doomed before they set forth and mould the worlds yet to come!"

"Aphrodite will not trouble Hera," The Thunderer told his mother is a confident voice. "Hermes assured me that Aphrodite means to concentrate her considerable efforts on the young one, whose virgin heart has yet to erect the sorts of defences against love that Hera has developed over the course of millennia."

"Are you saying that Aphrodite means to compel Junia to stay by making her fall in love with a denizen of Olympus?" Rhea asked with alarm. "Would it not be wiser to simply let the child go forth on the Nephele with Prometheus and his learned mortals, where she will blossom into a great Goddess-Queen someday to the generations of mortals yet to be born, while Hera remains here on Olympus as your Queen?"

"Truth be told, Mother, I would rather they both stay on Olympus," Zeus answered.

"Surely you do not mean that!?"

"I never jest about such matters," the Cloud-gatherer replied.

"I hope you do not linger in your presumption that she will wed Apollo," Rhea said pointedly. "My grandson all but refused to entertain the notion when Junia leaped out of the Nephele and landed on Olympus last Winter!"

"Apollo refused the union because she was still a child," the Father of gods and men said. "She will soon come of age and make for a more suitable bride. She has grown in beauty in much the same way her mother has. And, to be perfectly frank, I would welcome my son's attention being drawn away from my wife. These two have been thick as thieves since the night... since Hera learned the truth about Prometheus being her son."

"Junia must not choose to stay on Olympus," Rhea stated.

Zeus raised an eyebrow once more. "Why the hell not?" he asked. "You already assured me that she is not a threat to me or my throne. Why can she not stay here, especially if she decides this of her own free will?"

Nepheleid

Rhea took a moment to answer. "Junia might not be fated to become the new sovereign among the gods," she said at last. "However, it is in her power to choose the one who will next sit upon the throne of Heaven. Your father has foreseen this the first time he laid eyes upon the child. He continues to say as much, even after you released him and his Titan brothers from the pit of Tartarus."

"My daughter is not a threat to me," Zeus replied indignantly.

"That would be true, my son, only if she boarded the Nephele and set sail towards the stars – far away from Olympus, with her brother Prometheus, the benefactor of humanity."

"Are you saying that Zoe might name Prometheus as the next Sky-King, if only to spite me?" the Thunderer asked with some measure of vexation. "That is preposterous! Prometheus is very much as –"

"As a father to Junia," Rhea said. "That is true. She would never wed him because she would never fall in love with him. Apollo, on the other hand, constitutes a real and present threat, even if he has sworn fealty to you after he, Hera, and Poseidon failed to end your reign millennia ago."

Zeus took a moment to ponder Rhea's words but said nothing.

"If Junia were to wed Apollo," Rhea added, "then he would come by the throne of Heaven honestly, as Junia has never sworn fealty to you. And as you well know, he has earned Hera's admiration and respect time and again through his valiant and glorious deeds. Hera might eventually soften her heart at the thought of him becoming her son-in-law. Surely you grasp why it would be best to let the child go on her merry way towards the farthest reaches of the Cosmos?"

"I will consider your words," Zeus said placidly.

"You are plotting to have Junia wed Apollo upon her arrival, are you not?"

Zeus gave no answer, his silence speaking his assent.

"Do you really believe for a second that Hera would allow her daughter to become betrothed to the son of Leto?" Rhea asked irritatedly. "Even if Junia herself somehow threw all caution to the wind and became besotted with him?"

"This would render her pliable to our will," Zeus answered casually. "Then perhaps Hera would choose to stay, if only to help our daughter navigate the vicissitudes of married life."

"You are aware that Junia despises you as much as Hera hates me, do you not?" Rhea asked sharply. "Unlike the hero Bellerophon, whom you struck down with your lightning bolt for his hubris of riding Pegasus to Olympus to dwell among the gods, Junia wants to stay as far away from the abode of the gods as possible. You must be aware of this! And if not you, then Metis surely must know!"

Zeus shook his head, prompting a mild tremor to shake the hallowed halls of starry Olympus.

"Zoe was only a child the last time she set foot in the throne room," he said finally. "Little girls may grow up, yet they always remain fond of their fathers. We shall welcome her this evening when Hermes brings her home from that damned mechanical abomination at the boundaries of the Earth. And you will go to the Garden of the Hesperides to summon Hera to Olympus. She will not spurn you, as she will be overjoyed to be reunited with our daughter. Now go – the Krios is soon to land on that damnable floating fortress. Do not return without Hera. Eris may remain in the Garden if she so chooses. That is of no concern to me."

Once her son had uttered these words, fair-haired Rhea gave Zeus an obedient curtsey and headed towards the boundaries of the broad-pathed Earth, to greet her ingrate of an heir and warn her of her King's designs. Should all else fail, then perhaps Rhea would join her kin on the Nephele and raise her granddaughter as she raised Dionysus in the shadows of the mountains, shielded by the Curetes who protected Zeus in his youth.

Or perhaps not, as this would surely give Hera true cause to hate me, the Mother of the gods pondered ominously as she sped Westward towards the golden light of Sunset and its garden of wonders.

Nepheleid

Chapter Three

"There is another cluster up there... a little to your left! Fly out a bit, there you are!" golden-throned Hera instructed Eris, standing on the firm ground some distance away from the foot of the Tree of the golden apples.

The goddess of chaos and discord obeyed her mother's command, quickly setting off to pick the ripe fruit off the very top of the Tree, her wings beating at an almost imperceptible speed like a giant, frantic hummingbird. Ares lifted the heavy baskets of golden apples off the ground and placed them in the cargo hold of the Henokhie, the mortal-made chariot his mother flew across the skies when she dwelled on Turtle Island. Hera inspected the wondrous harvest bound for the Nephele – these golden apples were no ordinary treasure. For millennia, white-armed Hera believed these to be merely an eccentric gift that Gaia, the Earth-Mother, bestowed upon her on the occasion of her marriage to loud-thundering Zeus. At the time, Hera thought it wise to hide the Tree of the golden apples in her Garden at the boundaries of the world, tended by the Hesperides nymphs and protected from prying eyes and thieving hands by the serpent-dragon Ladon. After Herakles slew Ladon during one of his Labours, the Pleiades, the seven daughters of Atlas, stole the golden fruit from the Tree, leaving it completely bare and slowly dying for centuries.

On the evening that Junia leaped off the Nephele and retrieved Kronos' sickle along with Eris, Hera returned to the Garden of the Hesperides to await her daughters. Hera had been steeling herself to cut down the moribund Tree to salvage its still-living roots and replant them somewhere high above the Earth. She had not yet decided then whether to enroot what remained of her treasure Tree on Hesperides Station, or on the Nephele itself, bound for the stars in aeons to come. In the end, her cogitations proved futile, for Gaia intervened to protect the Tree and ensnared Hera, binding her with fleshy bonds at the base of the trunk and reaching into the goddess' belly. Predictably, the Queen of Olympus retaliated, drawing up much of the ubiquitous miasma that remained on the surface of the broad-pathed Earth long after mortals gave up poisoning their world at the pleasure of their masters' greed. Hera only discovered the true purpose of the golden apples shortly thereafter, when she awoke from her long slumber in her garden on starry Olympus, between her palace and that belonging to her King, with winged Eris by her side.

Having slept for a fortnight after Zeus ended her stalemate with Gaia, Hera awoke to the sound of her husband loudly bedding another in his palace. For some reason, someone – most likely Aphrodite – placed a stunted golden apple in Hera's hand while she slept. The apple had the same inscription as the prize that Aphrodite won in the beauty contest at which the ill-fated mortal Paris unwisely served as the sole judge. Angered by this double insult, Hera threw the apple far into the Sky, unwittingly opening a starry tunnel at the end of which she thought she saw, if only for a moment, distant worlds ready for seeding with Earthly Life. Hera then decided that she would no longer fall prey to the anger that Zeus' indiscretions habitually stirred within her heart and set out to bring to completion the task she gave herself the last time she left her King. She would henceforth endeavour solely to help Prometheus and the learned mortals under his care seed the Cosmos with Earthly Life and uphold the light and memory of the gods among their descendants in worlds yet to come.

Most of all, Hera was determined to never again share Zeus' bed, even if he unexpectedly desisted from his amorous ardour after she fell fast asleep in his arms in the aftermath of her virginity bath upon her return to Olympus from the Garden of the Hesperides. She cared not a whit what the blessed gods who dwell on starry Olympus thought about her newfound purpose, or her uncharacteristic chastity. She knew, however, that the Cloud-gatherer would redouble his efforts to thwart her from leaving the Earth forever, especially after Junia witnessed the unspeakable debauchery that customarily befalls the Olympian Court whenever their Queen sets upon her journeys at the time appointed by the Seasons, before Winter turns to Spring.

On the night Junia dove to Olympus, Zeus vehemently refused to accept her choice to join the crew of the Nephele under the pretext that she was still a child and therefore unsuited to choose her fate. The Thunderer, Hera knew, had long planned for Junia to wed Apollo, and in his hubris decreed it so before all the gods who dwell on Olympus. Fortunately, Apollo had the good sense to decline the betrothal, for his sake as much as for Junia's. Yet Hera knew that this would not be the end of the matter, for her youngest daughter was soon to return to Olympus as her fourteenth birthday drew near, an age Zeus still considered adequately marriageable for maidens.

"Mother!" Eris called out as she slowly floated back down from the crown of the Tree of the golden apples. "Mother, I sense a stirring in the Heavens. Someone is headed for the Garden!"

Ares, standing ready to receive the remainder of the golden apples from Eris, drew his sword in anticipation for battle.

"Put that away, Ares," Hera chided him. "No mortal or deathless trespasser would dare tread upon my Garden while I am here. It's probably Hermes, come to announce Junia's return from the Nephele. Come now, take the apples from your twin and put them in the Henokhie."

"It's not Hermes," Ares said as he put his sword back in its sheath and helped unburden Eris. "Father would most likely have sent him to fetch Junia atop the Hub."

Hera raised an eyebrow. "You are probably correct," she said, slightly impressed at her son's unappreciated cleverness – very much like her own at the best of times. "But that does not matter," she continued, "since he cannot take her anywhere unless she allows it. Still, there is much work to be done before she sets foot on Olympus. Ares, I think we have enough cargo for now. Take the Henokhie to Polaris. Iris will have a team at the ready to take the delivery *up there*. Breathe not a word of this to Hermes when you see him, for I suspect that Junia will have made him travel back to Earth via the Hub. If he asks what you are doing there, tell him that you have orders to bring Junia to Olympus. Leave the Henokhie at Polaris, Iris will know what to do. I will see you on Olympus shortly."

"Aye, Mother," Ares replied as he headed towards the Henokhie. When he reached the front of the vehicle, he turned around and gave Hera a questioning look.

"The launch passcode is 'Pomegranate'," Hera said before Ares could ask. "And yes, Iris knows this as well."

Ares nodded, then stepped into the cockpit. Seconds later, the Henokhie soared above the Garden of the Hesperides and headed North towards the Polaris, near the very top of the Earth. Once the craft disappeared into the perpetual incoming night of the Garden, where time forever remains at a standstill, Hera turned her gaze towards Eris, whose cleverness was also perennially misunderstood and underestimated in equal measure.

"Do you think Iris will leave a few golden apples in the freezer vault in the other Garden of the Hesperides, *up there?*" Eris asked with the most innocent expression she could muster.

Hera smiled. "I certainly hope not," she answered. "At least if she does, then my hope is that they will never need to take them out."

"But you think the seeds within can bring Earthly Life to worlds that are... not alive."

"Not *yet* alive," Hera corrected Eris. "And breaching the skin of the apples to reach the seeds requires a great deal of force, much like the impact of a small meteorite hitting the planet's surface. The impact alone from an apple cast off from Hesperides Station could take out an entire country, so long as it does not land somewhere in the Sea."

"Are the apples not small enough that they would simply gravitate around the Earth forever?" Eris asked innocuously. "Or burn up upon re-entry, like Junia's clothes did when she jumped-"

"You know full well these are not *apples*, Eris," Hera interrupted. "If one needed to take out a golden apple and cast it upon the Earth from the Hesperides *Autonomous* Station, that would mean that mortals failed to restore Earthly Life to the Land and Seas. The world would have to start anew, with all this entails from those among us who have seen their foolish kind repeat the mistakes of their forebears. Truth be told, I am quite done playing nursemaid to generations of dunces who refuse to learn, especially to their so-called heroes whose exploits mortals celebrate in story and song, each one dastardlier than the next!"

Eris gave Hera a genuine, mildly bemused look, but said nothing. She sensed that her mother needed to rant to maintain her otherwise tenacious sanity intact.

"Heroes are miscreants," Hera continued. "The whole lot of them. Long gone are the days when mortals sought my favour and blessings through great deeds, by willingly renouncing their lives for the glory of a short season in the service of their fellow human beings. Those were *true* heroes – not those hypocrites who, by sheer happenstance, were begat by your father's unholy union with my own priestess, Io, to which he returned time and again to water the garden planted by his own seed! My own priestess, Eris! Her progeny should be the ones called the cloud-born, not my little Junia, for Zeus visited Io in the guise of a cloud *on the grounds of my very own temple*! He could not have insulted me more, as a goddess and as his Queen, other than by fornicating with another in our marriage-bed. Something which he all but swore to me he would never do! And yet, he did!"

"I know, Mother," Eris said casually. "I was there with you when you awoke last Spring."

"So you know what a duplicitous cad your father truly is!" Hera replied ardently. "Just like the so-called heroes of his line. What heroic deeds have they ever done, really, except to embolden men to claim and lay waste to the Earth with their hubris. All in the name of taming the wild and unknown places to bring the light of *reason* and *civilization* to the world? Hubris is, without a doubt, the only trait they inherited from Zeus, as well as being no friend to women and to all those who bring forth and sustain Life upon the broad-pathed Earth. Think about it, Eris! What has Perseus, the first notable among Zeus' many inbred whelps born of the line of Io, ever done except murder a hapless gorgon? The poor wretch Medusa never wronged anyone in all her mortal life, yet she ran afoul of Athena for getting herself raped in her temple – by Poseidon, no less! And what of Herakles, whom Zeus forced me to adopt as my son upon his mortal death? It was he who slew Ladon, which emboldened Hermes' thieving whore of a mother and her sisters to rob me blind, with no regard for that which belongs to their Queen! Just like that wench Aphrodite, and Athena, who both brazenly claimed the prize of the golden apple at Thetis' wedding, when in truth that apple always belonged to me, for it came from my Garden, by then already in ruins.

"Oh, they all pretend to admire and respect me, the deathless gods who dwell on high Olympus, but I know they secretly mock me and hold me in the utmost contempt, especially the goddesses! I know exactly what they say about me when they think I cannot hear their vicious gossip. To Tartarus with the lot of them! The only goddesses worthy of my consideration were present at the banquet Themis hosted in my honour upon my return from my journey all those years ago. You remember… You were there! All of them I would bring with me when I set out on my journey towards the stars. All of them, save perhaps for Rhea. Her presence aboard the Nephele would make the journey rather unpleasant. Besides, she would never agree to leave the Earth, and I shall never ask her to do so."

"What of my brothers?" Eris asked innocently as she withdrew her wings under her dress. "They were not there."

"Ares, Hephaestus, and Herakles were not there because Themis invited goddesses exclusively," Hera answered. "But you know full well that your brothers will be there with us when the Nephele unmoors from the Hub and the Station – even Herakles. It should not be long now. We are awaiting the few remaining mortal youths who attended school at Borealis, and whose parents declined to leave when given the chance. The Inuit Jewess, Jennifer Cohen-Tugaalik, already decided to leave her village even though she is only barely older than Junia. Fortunately for us, her community agreed to let her take her leave. We are now waiting for the young man, Paul Red Buffalo, to make his decision now that he is eighteen years old."

"What of Apollo?" Eris inquired in a childlike voice, in a futile attempt to ingratiate herself to her mother while bringing up a subject she knew irritated Hera to no end. "Will he be joining us in the City-ship beyond the heavens?"

"We've already discussed this, Eris," Hera replied with undue patience. "I bloody well don't expect that he will *leave* Olympus, as he is unlikely to ever leave his mother and his twin sister behind, no matter how fond he has grown of Prometheus' learned mortals and the potential they represent. Neither Leto nor Artemis would ever dare to leave Olympus to dwell in a world high above the Heavens where I shall rule as uncontested Queen. Besides, the worlds we will seed across the vast Cosmos will be very different from the one in which you and Apollo and Artemis were born; there will be no separation between the wild places and civilization, for we will have both, simultaneously, for the untold centuries that our fleet of City-ships will travel across the expanse between the stars. That is why so many of the children of Turtle Island already feel right at home on the Nephele and on the Hesperides Autonomous Station. The plants and fruit trees that grow the food that will nourish future generations of travellers grow well within the habitable tiers, with small beasts and insects to sustain the balance of life, much like the garden forests that once covered the coasts of Turtle Island. The people there once knew how to uphold the Earth-Mother's sovereignty without damaging her beyond all hope of repair, as their descendants learned again after the Sea swallowed the lands across the world.

"No, Artemis would not feel at home on the Nephele or the fleet of City-ships of its ilk, absent wild game to be hunted for sport, far from the gaze of men. At least not until the progeny of the learned mortals land upon a suitable wanderer and bring back the great Earthly animals frozen in their vaults as they make these new worlds their home. And before you ask, I will not invite Athena or Aphrodite to join us on the Nephele either, for I expect them to find themselves ill at ease in any world where I am ascendant. They are both far too accustomed to serve the interests of men while belittling those of women, albeit for vastly different reasons. Especially women who are wives and mothers, which means most women throughout all ages and nations. No, the worlds yet to come will not repeat the mistakes of the past, the first and foremost was allowing my brothers to rule the Cosmos while my sisters and I were left with no kingdoms of our own-"

Hera suddenly grew quiet. "Wait, that is not quite fair," she said, shaking her head slightly. "Fate did favour Hades when he drew to rule the Underworld, and yet he has proved himself a superb ruler, magnanimous and just, and a good husband to his Queen, which is far more than I could say about Zeus or Poseidon. He will be the only one among my brothers that I will miss, really. The entire Cosmos would have been a far more virtuous and just place had he drawn the lot to rule over the Heavens, even if he never chose me to rule by his side. I wonder if I will ever choose another Consort once we set out towards the stars, to which I will grant the glory of a short season in exchange for glory and, perhaps, godhood. Perhaps I will have no need of such, should we land upon a wanderer tidally locked upon its star, and therefore unbound by the Seasons.

"What wondrous worlds await us, Daughter! There are planets so richly different from our own that even the cleverest among mortals cannot yet fathom! It is they, who have boarded the City-ship Nephele, and the Corona a few years earlier, who are the true heroes among mortals! They who are willing to leave all that they have known so that their kind may have a future in worlds beyond this one! They are truly worthy of my love and favour, and that is why I must dwell among them, and protect them as my own children. How wonderful that mortals have become so awakened that such things are even possible! How fortuitous for Junia to have been born at this Aeon, when endless possibilities are open to a brilliant girl child! That is why we must do all that is within our power to protect her from Zeus' scheming. I know he is plotting with Aphrodite to have her remain on Olympus, even now as she travels on the Hub back to Earth. He will try again to yoke her into marrying Apollo, if only to compel her to stay. If this comes to pass, I will have to admit defeat and stay as well, leaving the learned mortals aboard the Nephele and the Corona, and all the City-ships yet to be built, vulnerable to the random whims of Chaos in the expanse beyond the heliosphere. Do you understand what I am telling you, Eris?"

"Yes, Mother," Eris acquiesced, her gaze fixed on a faraway point of light growing brighter on the horizon.

"You must do all that you can, by any means that you see fit, to thwart Zeus and Aphrodite's scheming to compel Apollo and Junia to fall in love. I am not so concerned for Apollo, though. I admit, he would make a worthy son-in-law, even if he has brought more youths to his bed than I have before I wed loud-thundering Zeus. And *they* were legion, I'll have you know. That was before Zeus yoked me into marriage, without abdicating any of the freedoms he compelled me to renounce once he brought me to the nuptial bed. No, we must put an end to his machinations against Junia's freedom – as well as our own. There is no room in the endless Cosmos for tyrants who would limit our sovereignty, which has been withheld unjustly for far too long. Do you understand what I ask of you, Eris? Speak quickly, before our uninvited visitor arrives."

"Yes, Mother," Eris replied with an impish grin curling upon her otherwise placid features. "I understand completely."

"Good. Now make haste, quickly, before they land," Hera said, raising her hands to open a starlit portal.

"You will still get an earful on Olympus, Mother," Eris replied as she took a step into the luminous portal.

"Oh, I know," Hera retorted as fractal eddies began to swirl around Eris. "But I am in no mood to hear her chiding me for going against the will of Phanes and behaving in a manner anathema to Life. Now go, I will be right behind you."

As Eris disappeared in the tunnel of light, Hera cast a final glance at the perpetual dusk of the Garden of the Hesperides. Just as fair-haired Rhea landed upon the long-fallow soil of the sunset garden at the very boundaries of the broad-pathed Earth, the Queen of Olympus looked her mother in the eye, then stepped into the swirl of stars that promptly collapsed into a pinpoint of light, leaving a deafening echo in its wake.

Nepheleid

Chapter Four

Junia knew she was dreaming. She found herself treading upon the familiar starlit meadows in fields of twilight, awash in the reflected light of distant rivers crisscrossing the nighttime skies in all directions. Junia knew that this place was not of the Earth, nor of any physical object orbiting in space, whether in the vast heliosphere or anywhere else in the realms made of atoms and other exotic matter. This was the place where she first encountered Apollo and it it was the night Hera dreamt of her forgotten first husband Eurymedon who had been slain by Zeus in a fit of jealous rage. Hera also dreamt of the long-lost son she bore the gentle Giant in the Underworld before Zeus cast her in the River Lethe to end her grief.

In the naiveté of her fleshless, unborn form, Junia failed to appreciate the tremendous majesty and beauty of the divinity standing before her. She did she understand Apollo's awe upon encountering what he saw as a traveller, come from unknown parts, to be conceived within the holy womb of the Queen of Olympus. For many years, and long before Hera left Turtle Island to return to the abode of the gods with her exiled progeny, Junia habitually met Apollo in these fields of twilight. She becoming accustomed to his presence as children do with older siblings, and trusted adults, in familiar settings. At eight years old, when she met the Archer in person, she was secretly overjoyed to learn that he, along with several gods of Olympus, would join Hera on Turtle Island. He would help Hera bring to completion her undertaking among the learned mortals under her care. Since then, Junia felt little need to continue her encounters with Apollo in fields of twilight. This was even after Hera decreed that the two could not be in the same room together without the presence of a guardian to mind her young daughter's innocence.

Now, while she lay strapped snugly in her seat aboard the Krios Khrysomallos, her unchaperoned mind was addled by enough Hypnos mist to lull a herd of bison to sleep for a full Season. Junia felt her unrestrained adolescent libido running amok in these very same, long-neglected fields of twilight. Without a care for propriety or her mother's sternly enforced admonitions against being left alone with Apollo, Junia bore witness to her dream self unabashedly seeking out the Archer's gorgeous form, not knowing what she would do once she eventually found him. Then again, her conscious self would probably know what to do in theory having aced her lessons in anatomy during the long Summer months spent aboard the Nephele.

Remembering Apollo's powerful prophetic gift, as well as his ability to poke his golden head in the fields of twilight whenever he felt the call, Junia turned her thoughts instead to her memory of the last time she dreamt of her long-time friend and blameless mentor while on her way back from low Earth orbit. Though the recollection was hazy at best, when Junia last dreamt of Apollo, he appeared to be warning her of a matter of some urgency but she couldn't hear his voice in the dream. Shortly thereafter, her classmate Derek poked her awake after the Krios landed at the bottom of the shaft of the Hub. For a fraction of a second, she wondered if Derek and the Archer were one and the same. She remembered looking up at the lad whose attractive features and blond hair were backlit by the bright sunlight against the high window of the Krios. Since that day Junia found herself wondering, every now and then, whether Derek was a son or descendant of Apollo, even if the boys' mortal family hailed from Iceland.

Perhaps, Junia pondered, Derek's people hailed from Hyperborea, the mythical land where Apollo wintered each year, only to return in the Spring among the company of the blessed gods. This would be much like Hera when she used to journey across the broad-pathed Earth and return to Olympus at the time appointed by the Seasons. On second thought, Junia thought it unlikely that Iceland, or Thule as it was once called, harboured Hyperborea. Iceland remained uninhabited well until into the Viking Age, whereas Hyperborea was known to the mortals of Hellas since ancient times. Truth be told, Junia still did not know where to find Hyperborea on a map of the world, even those from centuries past, before the Sea swallowed the low-lying regions of the Earth. Some learned mortals speculated that this ancient and mythical land lay somewhere beyond the Danube, yet such tales told of a land sheltered from the hardships of boreal Winter, under the yoke of eternal Spring. This led Junia to believe that perhaps Hyperborea lay somewhere beyond the Russian steppe, perhaps near Crimea, where the climate closely resembles that of the Mediterranean in the time before the lands bordering the inner Sea turned almost to desert.

The Oceanid Klymene, Junia's second mother now reunited with her Titan husband in the Elysian Fields, once told her that Apollo and Artemis' mother, Leto, hailed from Hyperborea. Though she knew her as one of Zeus' many concubines, and one of the many denizens of Olympus whom Hera disliked, Junia never gave much thought to Leto. Still, Junia did not find it strange that Leto ought to hail from such a faraway place as Hyperborea. Both her mothers came of age in the House of Okeanos and Tethys at the boundaries of the Earth, while Junia was born and raised on the shores of Turtle Island, half a world away from starry Olympus.

Ugh, Olympus. Junia thought aloud in the safety of her dreamscape.

I guess I'll have to wake up and get this done and over with. I can't believe Zeus is having me come all this way just to tell him that there is no chance in Tartarus I'll ever choose to stay! At least he can't force me or Mom to stay, otherwise Hermes will be in trouble. He has absolutely nothing to gain from his messenger suffering the penalty of those who perjure against the Oath of the Holy River Styx. That means he'll probably cook up some kind of cockamamie scheme to keep us from leaving.

I wonder if Apollo knows anything about this. Maybe he'll be kind like before, when he kept our whereabouts on Turtle Island secret for several years and help us out! I do hope he'll choose to come with us in the end. He's so pretty...

No! Stop! Don't think of him like that. He's my brother-cousin, and he's like three thousand years old! Derek, on the other hand, is about to turn eighteen next April. And I'll be fourteen in less than a month. He's not too old. Okay, it might get weird for a few years in-between until I turn eighteen, but he'll be twenty-two by then... It won't be weird or frowned upon. Assuming he doesn't hook up with one of the older girls by then.

Ugh. Emotional transference sure is a lot of work!

Junia heaved a heavy sigh, fully aware that Hermes could see her on the other side of her consciousness – assuming he was also awake.

Okay, time to wake up. No matter what happens in the next few days, at least I'll see Apollo again in the flesh, even if it might be for the last time. If he stays, I wonder if he'll still want to meet in the fields of twilight once the Nephele unmoors. This should not to be limited by astronomical physical distances. I mean, he is, literally, a god! But no more wet dreams about Phoebus. I have a way better chance with Derek than with Apollo, even if Zeus got his way and –

"Oh, bloody hell... wake up already!" Hermes griped with a hint of amusement in his voice.

Junia opened her eyes and turned her gaze towards her travelling companion.

"Have we landed?" Junia asked groggily. She glimpsed at the high, Earth-facing window, and saw that Krios was still above a thick canopy of churning clouds.

"No, but your virginal ramblings were getting to be a bit much!" Hermes replied casually.

Junia bit her lip, embarrassed that she had let herself voice her thoughts while under the influence of the Hypnos mist.

"Here is some unsolicited advice, Princess, for when we reach Olympus," Hermes said. "Keep your lustful thoughts to yourself, otherwise Zeus might declare you unready to decide your own fate and marry you off despite your mother's protests!"

"Wait, so let me get this straight," Junia replied. "I'm too young to decide what I want to do when I grow up, but not too young to get married? Where's the logic in that?"

"We are speaking of the workings of the mind of almighty Zeus, the Father of gods and men," Hermes answered. "Zeus cares not for logic, only for that which will uphold his supremacy. And you, Princess, have proved yourself quite the little menace, especially when you waggled Grandfather's sickle at Zeus back there in Garden of the Hesperides."

Junia answered with a sullen stare.

"Good thing Ares stopped you as swiftly as he did and pulled you out of harm's way," Hermes continued. "Hera was wise to name him as your minder. He is much better suited for the task than Eris, in my humble opinion."

"You're not humble," Junia said flatly.

Hermes gave Junia an amused look.

"Clever girl," he said after a moment. "Baiting me to brag about my humility. That almost worked! You ought to save all that cleverness for

Olympus though. Heaven knows, you will need it!"

Junia said nothing for the remainder of the descent, which mercifully ended less than an hour later as the Krios touched down on the topmost platform of the Polaris.

The rain was falling in sheets by the time Junia and Hermes exited the base of the Hub. Hermes walked beside Junia, who insisted on carrying her own oversized luggage crate despite the messenger's offer to help. Somehow, both remained completely dry as they entered the vast lounge on the upper tier of the Polaris. This was converted into a waiting room of sorts for travellers shortly after the CARINA Polaris crew and their equipment relocated to the Nephele high above the Earth. Before Hermes could say anything further, Junia made a beeline towards a familiar figure loafing alone on a comfortable chair, looking rather dejected as he read something on a screen he held in the palm of his hand.

"Derek!" Junia called out cheerfully. "Hi!"

The young man looked up at the shrieking girl, all trace of woe vanishing from his comely features.

"Junebug!" Derek said with a genuine smile. "Hey..."

"What are you doing here?" Junia asked a little too chipperly.

"I, ah... I was supposed to pick up Paul and accompany him on the Hub," Derek answered. "He's decided to leave with us on the Nephele so I volunteered as his orientation guide for the next couple of months."

"Yeah, I heard about that," Junia said. She bit her lip, wondering if Derek knew whether Paul continued to dislike her as much as he did when they were still schoolmates on Turtle Island. "That's... great, right? I mean, you guys are pals –"

"Yeah, I'm happy he's coming with us," Derek replied, "except that he can't fly in today from Borealis. There's a big hurricane and all air traffic is grounded for at least 72 hours."

Hermes cleared his throat. Junia gave him an annoyed look, as she knew that he only did so to get her attention. The deathless gods who dwell on starry Olympus do not produce phlegm under any circumstances after all.

Nepheleid

"Derek," Junia said sedately, "you remember –"

"Hey, Zippy!" Derek interrupted with good humour.

Hermes nodded politely, pretending not to mind the irreverent nickname that the children of Junia's school gave him while he dwelled briefly among the learned mortals at Borealis.

"Well that's a shame about your friend," Hermes said. "There was a time when tropical hurricanes did not reach the circumpolar regions."

"That was *before our time*," Junia muttered emphatically, reminding Hermes to behave as if he did not remember the era before the Sea flooded the Earth after the polar ice caps all but vanished.

"Yeah," Derek continued," which means I'm pretty much stuck here until Paul is able to travel. And I don't know for sure how long that will be! I don't want to go back up without him only to go right back down again, then go back up. The trip is kind of –"

"Excruciatingly long?" Hermes offered. "Yes, we are well aware having just arrived. Now, not to cut this pleasant conversation short, young Derek, but we must be on our way."

Derek looked up at Junia questioningly.

"I'm spending a few days in the place where my moms used to live before they started working at CARINA. Like a farewell visit."

"I'm sorry to hear about your mothers' break-up," Derek said sincerely to which Hermes reacted with an undignified snort. "I liked Ms. Klymene. She was nice."

"Yeah... I know," Junia said with a slight strain in her voice. "Hopefully I'll be visiting her soon," she added, throwing Hermes a sideways glance.

"There you are!" said a stentorian voice at the opposite end of the cavernous lounge.

Junia, Hermes, and Derek spun round and saw Ares, clad in the CARINA fleet uniform worn by the Nephele's security team, quickly jogging towards the trio at an enthusiastic pace.

"Oh, I didn't realize your big brother was picking you up," Derek stammered, as the colour drained from his cheeks.

Junia looked upon Ares with a mixture of gladness and confusion, realizing that she also had not known that the god of war planned to greet her in the travellers' lounge of the Polaris.

"Ares," Junia said at last. "I thought Iris was the one picking me up down here."

"There has been a slight change of plans," Ares answered truthfully, "so Mother sent me instead. Well, shall we?"

"Let's," Hermes agreed. "It is unwise to keep Father waiting for too long."

As Junia turned to say goodbye to Derek, she noticed that his features had grown even paler than a moment ago. Was he remembering the time he met Zeus briefly after Hera cast him off her high-rise office window at the old CARINA-ALSESTIS headquarters in Borealis five years prior? Junia could never forget the look of utter shock on Derek's face after Zeus rose from the ground unscathed, then told Junia, Ares, and Eris that he would agree to their mother's terms in exchange for her return. When Derek finally mustered the courage to ask Junia whether the indestructible man was her father, Eris promptly proceeded to confound the boy, until Derek could no longer tell whether what he saw had been real. At times like these, Junia questioned the extent of Eris' ability to permanently alter the perceptions of mortals – she was clearly capable of doing in the spur of the moment. Even if Eris' prodigious gifts often went under appreciated by the deathless gods who dwell on high Olympus, Junia reckoned that there must be ways to sidestep her power to sow chaos and confusion, as well as infix specific thoughts in the minds of her victims.

"Junia, are you all right?" Derek asked, pulling her out of her reverie.

"Uh, yeah... Listen. Why don't you come with us for a couple of days?"

"What?" Hermes and Ares replied in unison.

"Yeah," Junia continued. "This way you don't have to be alone while the weather clears up and Paul gets here."

"Uh, that's really sweet of you to offer, Junebug, but how are you guys going to travel to your moms' hometown?" Derek inquired. "I mean, there are no aircraft allowed in or out of the region. The hurricane made it too dangerous for air travel! You guys are pretty much stuck here too, just like I am."

Nepheleid

"We have other means of travel, young one," said a female voice originating from somewhere behind a tall potted decorative shrub. The lady stepped aside to let herself be seen, all the while giving Hermes the most caustic of smiles. Turning her gaze towards Ares, she said, "Mother thought you lot were taking too long, so she sent me to bring you back... with our young guest, I suppose."

Hermes did not reply, and everyone, including Derek, thought rather odd.

Ares shrugged. "If it's all the same to you, I'd like to be on my way," he told Hermes, picking up Junia's large luggage crate with one hand and nudging her towards the exit with the other. "Derek? Are you coming with us, or what?"

Junia looked at Derek, who was now staring straight into the eyes of the interloper.

"Hi, Eris," Derek mumbled with a goofy smile as he rose to his feet and grabbed his satchel. "Okay, sure," he said finally, sounding more like himself. "I don't know exactly where you're going, but if it's just for a couple of days, as long as I'm back when Paul gets here."

"I will personally see to it that you are returned safe and sound to this place when your friend arrives," Hermes said crossly, giving Eris an icy stare.

"Marvellous!" Eris proclaimed giddily as she headed towards the exit with Ares and Junia, while Hermes followed her closely, as if watching her every move. "Oh, what fun we will have!"

Chapter Five

In centuries long gone by, the turn of the Seasons from Summer to Autumn, began in the torrid month of Karneios and ended when shorter days gave way to lengthening nights. This heralded the time when mortals gathered to pluck the grape from the vine and harvest the grain from their fields for the long Winter that lay ahead. Demeter, who brings forth gifts, taught mortals how to extract sustenance from the bountiful Earth. Mortals also sacrificed the sacred ram to Apollo each year to praise him for protecting their fields against rot and their flocks against pestilence. By these benefactions, the mortals grew stronger and more prosperous with each passing generation, until they became too numerous for the land to sustain. During such times, the bravest of mortals set forth to colonize new territories across the Mediterranean, reducing the pressure upon their native soil to nourish their unmanageable numbers. For those who chose to remain, the Archer often reduced their numbers through plagues, while spear-brandishing Ares, Stormer of city walls, continued the cull with perennial wars.

Two millennia after their ancestors abandoned the gods of their homelands to embrace the faiths of the Book, mortals in all the nations of the world multiplied exponentially. They turned the wild places of the Earth into croplands, dedicating them to the everlasting cycle of sowing, planting, ripening, and harvesting. Their numbers grew so vast that almost no forests, wetlands, or meadows remained for wild beasts, fish, and fowl to fill the Earth with Life. The Sea rose and slowly devoured the land to rid the Earth of the blight of an overabundant humanity. Meanwhile, mortals waged endless wars among themselves as diseases, uncovered from the vanishing wild places of the Earth, reduced their numbers even further. When the worst of the slaughter and sickness had passed, survivors wisely chose to put aside the short-sightedness, greed, and foolhardy fratricidal impulses of their forebears, and gathered in cities far from the shores.

There, they began growing their food throughout the year within palisades of steel and glass, irrespective of the movements of the heavenly bodies. There were also resurgent indigenous peoples whose ways of being, long thought extinguished by centuries of conquest and scorn, reclaimed their ancestral lands in all the remaining habitable recesses of the broad-pathed Earth.

A few decades had come and gone since the mortals in the steel and glass fortresses began venturing out again beyond their cities, heeding the medicine of their neighbours in a way their ancestors never had. In the aftermath of this welcome truce, mortals began flourishing again, albeit in much smaller numbers. The ascendancy of the indigenous gods rebounded with the strength of the resilient mortals under their care.

Gladdened that the Earth would remain well tended long after the world's most learned mortals left aboard the Nephele with Prometheus, Apollo pondered his future in the aeons yet to come. Sitting among the blessed gods in the banquet hall of starry Olympus, the Archer tried not to stare at his Queen who sat alone. Hera was deliberately distant from her King, by a high window overlooking the broad stairway leading up into the throne room. Apollo thought it strange that Eris was not by her side, as the goddess of Discord had followed Hera like a shadow throughout the entire Summer. The Archer closed his eyes whenever Hera's gaze happened to cross his own, lest the Queen surmise that he was hard at work seeking the right words to announce to her, without arousing her famously spectacular ire, his intention of joining the roster of immortals on the Nephele.

This would prove no simple task, for the Lord of the golden bow knew that Hera fully expected him to decline the invitation to join the crew of the City-ship. She believed the Archer was loath to leave behind his beloved twin, fleet-footed Artemis, who had shown no interest in leaving Olympus for worlds unknown. Apollo understood why Hera harboured such thoughts, as the Queen usually divined the intentions of others by ascertaining how their decisions affected their familial bonds. Although Hera was seldom proved wrong in her otherwise sound reasoning, this time she evidently underestimated the deep affection Apollo felt for the Nephele. He perceived it as the epitome of scientific achievement, the very embodiment of the triumph of civilization and rationality over the uncontrolled chaos of the natural world.

Apollo fell in love with the idea of sailing the stars long before the magnificently self-sustaining Nephele and its predecessor, the mining-ship Corona, were built, when he first paid a visit to the CARINA installations at Borealis on Turtle Island long ago. This happened several years before Hera encountered Prometheus in the lonely woods and mountains near Borealis, only to become thereafter her son's most ardent ally and advocate, as well as the Director of Operations for CARINA's ALSESTIS division. Tasked primarily with overseeing the reliability of the life support systems in vessels yet to be built, and burdened with the duty of sparing the Nephele's learned mortals from Zeus' displaced anger at Prometheus for absconding with his Queen, Hera may have failed to notice how much the CARINA venture's fleet of City-ships suited Apollo's innate affinities.

Like Hera, Apollo often left Olympus for months on end, preferring to spend the long Winter in storied Hyperborea. Or, dwelling for years among the mortals he believed most worthy to receive his light and blessings, until Zeus declared that the time came for him to return to the abode of the gods. Unlike Hera, Apollo did not harbour any resentment towards Olympus or its King, even though he had more than once clashed against his father's judgment as well as rebelled against his rule. Even though he was the Thunderer's eldest son, the first to have lived past infancy after the ill-fated Zagreus was devoured by the Titans, Apollo knew he could never become King in his own right so long as Zeus sat upon the throne of Heaven. After his last failed rebellion against Zeus, after which he was condemned to guard the flocks of King Laomedon as well as build the walls of Troy with his co-conspirator Poseidon, Apollo abandoned his pursuit for kingship. He focused instead on cultivating the minds of mortals by bestowing the light of reason upon those able to receive it. But now that wise Prometheus found a way for the deathless gods to expand their influence far and wide across the Cosmos, Apollo felt renewed hope that his days as a vassal prince, to a King whose Queen no longer considered him a worthy ruler and Consort, would soon come to an end.

By leaving Olympus and joining the crew of the Nephele, Apollo knew that he stood a fair chance of one day becoming King in his own right. If this meant serving at Hera's pleasure for a few more decades, until another vessel like the Nephele was built with the metals mined in the fields of space rocks between the wanderers Mars and Jupiter, then so be it. By that time, he hoped that Hera and Prometheus would find him tenable of commanding his own City-ship, and that they would rule jointly the expanding fleet of learned mortals as part of a triumvirate, much like the three priest-kings once ruled over Hyperborea. Just as Hyperborea, the land of eternal Spring, was bordered to the North by the great River Okeanos, the City-ship under Apollo's dominion would mark the farthest boundary of the known and inhabited Cosmos. And like the Hyperboreans who remain forever sheltered from the ravages of war and disease, so too would the learned mortals under the Archer's rule be spared from unnatural death. The latter would be artificially preserved in sleeping chambers during their long voyages across interstellar space, until the time came for them to settle worlds that could sustain Life for aeons to come.

Apollo hoped that he could spend the next decades, or possibly centuries, gaining Hera's affection and trust until she acknowledged his true worth as potential King, and lifted her prohibition against him courting a matured Junia. Truth be told, since the last turn of the Seasons, Junia had revealed herself to a far more suitable bride-to-be than Apollo could have anticipated. Apollo could not help but smile at Hera's whimsy for giving her youngest child a purportedly secret name which, in the old tongue of Hellas, meant "Life", all the while proclaiming for years her intent to bring Life to the stars. As he remembered the young Junia back in the Garden of the Hesperides and, armed with Kronos' might weapon, and standing resolute against Zeus with the Titans by he side, Apollo chuckled. And this instantly drew the attention of his Queen.

Hera said nothing as she set out to penetrate the depths of the Archer's mind with her wide, ever-vigilant eyes. Apollo deflected her probing by affecting the most innocent look he could muster, causing the Queen to let out a loud, throaty laugh, startling all the blessed gods gathered in the banquet hall on high Olympus. Zeus looked at his wife and son, confused and annoyed in equal measure, while fair-haired Rhea, newly arrived from the Garden of the Hesperides, glowered at her youngest daughter with the look of one who deeply regretted her life choices. Hera ignored her husband and mother, stifling her laughter as she turned her gaze back towards the stairway to the throne room. Her watch was brief, as moments later swift Hermes suddenly appeared alone in the throne room, his demeanour betraying a sense of urgency that caused all the blessed gods to immediately forget the tense and giddy exchange between Apollo and their Queen, her King, and the Titan-Queen.

"Why are you alone?" Zeus asked crossly before Hermes could utter a single word. "Has something happened to Zoe?"

Hera rose to her feet slowly, though her countenance showed no sign of alarm.

"No, Father," Hermes answered as he caught his breath. "They are here... Eris and Ares were there to meet up with Junia... Ah, thank you my dear," Hermes said as he accepted a cup of nectar from Hebe.

"Have they not all returned with you?" Zeus asked while Hermes took a long, calming draught.

"Yes, Father," the messenger replied, his voice steady at last.

"Then why in Tartarus are you such a nervous wreck?" Zeus retorted irritatedly. "Do not tell me she thought you were abducting her and used her power against you –"

"No, that is not what happened," Hermes interrupted. "Junia brought a guest, or should I say, a hostage, from Polaris."

"She did *what*?" Athena asked, more surprised than daunted.

"Who did she bring?" Apollo inquired with genuine curiosity.

"The mortal boy Derek," Hermes replied. "From the Nephele," he added when Zeus gave him an inquisitive look.

"Why did she bring him here?" Apollo asked, voicing the question on the minds of all the blessed gods gathered in the banquet hall.

"I think Junia felt sorry for the lad for being stranded at Polaris," Hermes explained. "Derek was waiting to escort another mortal to the Nephele, but a hurricane grounded all air travel overland between Borealis and Polaris, so his companion could not fly in until the storm had passed. Junia took pity on the boy and invited him to join her for a few days so he would not be alone. Although, truth be told, I suspect that Eris planted the idea in her mind without her knowledge."

"Where are they now?" Hera asked calmly.

"They should be coming up the stairway at the moment," Hermes answered. "The mortal was still reeling from the voyage when I ran ahead to warn you. Eris had him believe he was in a submersible the whole way! I have no idea how she will explain how or why we are surrounded by mountains –"

"As long as Eris hasn't confounded the boy to the point of causing permanent brain damage!" Apollo said in a low voice, certain that Hera alone heard him. "It took him long enough to recover the last time, when he was still a child!"

The Queen nodded, stifling a smile.

"Father, must we take on the guise of mortals while he's here?" Hebe asked.

"No, we will absolutely not," the Cloud-gatherer decreed. "Let Eris confound him when the time comes for him to leave. Until then, he shall remain a guest of the Princess of Olympus. And of Eris, I suppose."

"Mom!" Junia exclaimed as she stepped into the banquet hall. She was followed closely by Ares, Eris, and a very confused-looking Derek.

Hera predictably walked towards Junia and embraced her, then nodded at her twins. When Derek's gaze fell upon the Queen of Olympus, his cheeks flushed slightly, and the pupils of his pale blue eyes dilated visibly to all the immortals gathered.

"Hello Derek," Hera greeted him warmly. "I am told you've decided to spend a few days with us?"

"Uh, hello Dr. Argosi," Derek replied timidly. "Yeah, uh, Paul couldn't make it to Polaris for a couple of days, so Junebug – I mean Junia – asked me to tag along here..." He leaned closer to Junia and whispered, "Um, Junebug, where *are* we, exactly? I mean, all those mountains... Are we in Switzerland? If we are, how did we get here in a submersible if we're in Switzerland?"

"Never you mind where we are," Hera answered in a reassuring manner. "This is a small mountain principality you've probably never heard of, in the backwoods of the Old World. I could tell you the name of this place, but you probably will not remember it," she added, looking straight at Eris, who answered with a knowing smile and an almost imperceptible nod.

"I believe you already know some of the others," Hera continued. "There is Dr. Weiss," she said, gesturing at Athena, who stood between Demeter and Apollo. "And of course, you remember Dr. Summers and Dr. Archer, and..." she paused when Derek's gaze fell upon Zeus, who stared at the young man with an inscrutable expression.

Hera looked at Apollo briefly, then turned her attention back to Derek.

"That is Mr. Diaz, my ex-husband," Hera said. "I think you might have met him briefly when we all lived at Borealis, did you not?"

Apollo bit his lip, trying not to laugh at Hera introducing Derek to the King of Olympus by his contemporary Hellenic name, in much the same way she introduced herself to the mortals of Turtle Island by using an Italian-sounding variant of her seat of power in ancient Hellas.

Derek gave Hera a blank look.

"I, uh, don't really remember, I'm sorry." he replied.

"That's quite all right," Hera told him benevolently, while Eris took a step back. "That was many years ago. I wouldn't have remembered either. Now..."

Hera paused as golden Aphrodite appeared before the newcomer, smiling coyly as her form took the entirety of the mortal's field of vision. Apollo sometimes wondered whether she used this very trick on the mortal Paris when the time came for the poor wretch to decide who among the three goddesses – Hera, Athena, and Aphrodite – was the fairest.

"Oh, what a handsome young man you are!" Aphrodite tittered at the lad, reaching out her hand for the mortal to kiss. "I do hope you enjoy your stay while you are here. Perhaps you will decide to cast your lot among us and remain here as another cupbearer. We can never have too many, of those, can we?" she mused aloud, to which Ganymede answered with a visible pout, and Hebe with an upraised middle finger as she feigned scratching the bridge of her nose.

"Wait, what?" Derek said, his eyes growing wider.

"You did not hear that, mortal," Eris growled.

Derek shook his head slightly, then turned his gaze back to Hera. In the span of a mortal heartbeat, his cheeks began to flush once more, until he remembered to breathe. Then he grew pale as Zeus furrowed his brows, after which a tremor shook the gilded halls of starry Olympus.

"What was that?" Derek asked, as if awaking from a strange dream.

"He does that sometimes," Junia answered, taking Derek's hand and leading him in the direction of the Queen's palace.

Nepheleid

"Where do you two think you are going?" Zeus thundered at the pair.

"To get him settled before dinner?" Junia replied bluntly, to which Zeus answered with another frown. "What? He just got here!" Junia protested.

"Father, if I may," Hermes interjected. "I believe it would be best if Derek were to stay in my palace, since he is a traveller, and therefore under my protection."

"I think not," Hera interjected. "Young Derek is a crew member on *my* City-ship. He will surely feel more comfortable surrounded by those most familiar to him. It would be best if he stayed in the guest quarters at my palace."

Apollo looked at Derek, who appeared somewhat bewildered that the lady he knew as ALSESTIS' Director of Operations, and the man who spent almost a year following her everywhere she went, should squabble over who ought to put him up in their homes. As far as Apollo knew, Derek had no idea of the danger in which he would find himself should he choose to stay with Hera. Mortal men past the age of puberty who spent some time on starry Olympus as guests had the unfortunate tendency of falling deeply in love or in lust with the Queen, as did the mortal Endymion, beloved by the Moon-goddess Selene, and Ixion, the father of Centaurs, respectively. Only Ganymede, abducted by Zeus from the ramparts of Troy as a princely youth, was spared this fate, and to this very day he had yet to know a woman's touch.

"He will do no such thing!" Zeus decreed. "Besides, it is highly improper that a young man ought to dwell under the same roof as our virgin daughter."

And your beautiful wife, who just now introduced you as her former spouse, Apollo thought, biting his lip to stop himself from laughing. That Zeus ought to consider the boy a threat to the integrity of his marriage bed, after Hera herself publicly repudiated her King in front of their guest, was absurd.

"You're right, he is a young man," Hera retorted, "of military age, and yet too young to be a husband or father. Do you not recall that in Old Rome, such young men were called *juniores* because they fell under my protection until they came of age?"

"Then perhaps it would be best if young Derek stayed with me," Apollo said at last. "He is a young man, as you say, and he and I are well acquainted. Are we not, Derek?"

"Uh... sure Dr. Archer," the lad stammered in agreement, though visibly unsure of himself and still quite confused.

"Very well," Hera acquiesced. "Besides, all this bickering is making our guest uncomfortable. I, for one, need to catch up with Junia. We shall retire for now, until the evening banquet."

"I'll see you later," Junia told Derek as Eris took her hand and bade her to follow their mother to the Queenly palace.

Derek instinctively began to follow them, however Apollo caught him by the arm before he took a step. Hera turned around, her gaze fixed upon Apollo, then told Eris in a low voice that she had in her palace a substantial reserve of mortal food, enough to feed both Junia and her mortal guest for many days if need be. She then kept silent for a moment, allowing Apollo to understand her meaning that Derek ought to dine in her hall before this evening's banquet, lest the famished boy unwittingly render himself immortal by ingesting ambrosia and nectar, the food and drink of the gods.

As Hera resumed her trek back to her dwelling, Apollo began to form a theory as to why Eris compelled Junia to bring Derek to Olympus. If, as Eris expected, Derek should fall in love with Hera, Zeus would be honour-bound to smite him for befouling his sacred law of hospitality. Should this come to pass, then Junia would surely repudiate her father and Olympus, and perhaps dethrone Zeus to avenge Derek, with or without the aid of the Titans, then depart forever on the Nephele.

"Dr. Archer?" Derek said hesitantly. "Can you let go me? You're hurting my arm."

"My apologies," the Lord of the golden bow replied, laying his hand upon Derek's arm so that the nascent bruise immediately vanished. "I will show you to your room, then we shall dine with Dr. Argosi and Junia."

And then, I shall see to it that you do not run afoul of loud-thundering Zeus, and share the fate of Endymion and Ixion, or even Bellerophon, whose hubris spelled his doom at the end of a lightning bolt.

Nepheleid

Chapter Six

"Did you *see* that?" golden Aphrodite griped indignantly at the blessed gods gathered in the banquet hall on high Olympus once Apollo and Derek were out of earshot. "The mortal barely reacted when I smiled at him, as if he was under some sort of spell!"

Doughty Ares, Saviour of cities, turned his face away from his former lover to hide his creeping smile in anticipation for the spectacle about to unfold. Fortunately, his lovely and gracious sister Hebe divined his mood and promptly handed him a full cup of nectar to bring to his lips, so that he could better conceal his amusement at the goddess of love's imminent tantrum. Had Aphrodite deigned to spend more time among the learned mortals who used to dwell at Borealis before they ascended to the Nephele all those years ago, she would have understood the cause behind Derek's failure to swoon at her considerable womanly charms.

It took Ares quite some time to grow accustomed to the extent to which most of the youths – and some maidens – who attended the school run by the CARINA venture at Borealis lusted after white-armed Hera. Even in the sparsely populated villages dotting the hilly woodlands surrounding the CARINA-ALSESTIS Headquarters, tales were told among the Indigenous storytellers, albeit in a tone of utmost respect, of the beautiful stranger who fell out of the Sky to live with the People and bring Life to the Stars. Though initially appalled that Junia's older classmates thought of his mother in her mortal guise as more than the Director of Operations of CARINA's ALSESTIS Division, Ares took comfort in the fact that most of these adolescents possessed enough good sense and self-discipline to never admit their shared libidinous obsession to their elders.

"I have warned you of this for *years*!" Aphrodite continued, turning her ire towards loud-thundering Zeus in a manner only his Queen ever dared when other gods were present. "I've warned you time and again that Hera intends to turn the future generations of spacefaring mortals into eunuchs! Now do you see? The boy did not even blink when I entered his field of vision!"

Nepheleid

The Cloud-gatherer did not reply, though the frown he affected earlier, when Junia addressed him with her usual brazenness, answered Aphrodite's whining with undue eloquence.

"My dear, I think Eris had more to do with the poor lad's stupefaction than whatever it is you think Hera did to him and his ilk," Hermes answered diplomatically in Zeus' stead, to which the Thunderer nodded in assent.

Aphrodite turned to face the messenger, who kept a calm demeanour despite her wrath.

"You heard it straight from the horse's mouth," Hermes continued, undaunted. "He thought he came here in a submersible and that he's now in the Swiss Alps! Really, you ought not to concern yourself with one extremely confused mortal's lack of arousal after gazing upon your... ahem, beauty."

"The boy probably lost more than a few brain cells on his way here," Dionysus slurred cheerfully. "When he returns later, give me a few minutes alone with him and my brew and I will sort him right out!"

Ares chuckled at Dionysus' absurd solution for placating Aphrodite's unwarranted conniption fit. In another lifetime, Ares would also have done everything within his power to soothe her anger and satisfy her capricious whims, if it meant that he would ultimately find her in his bed when starry Night shrouded the Heavens. In recent years, or more precisely right after Hera withdrew from Olympus to dwell among Prometheus' learned mortals on Turtle Island, Ares divested himself of his once boundless longing for Aphrodite. He finally realized that the goddess of love manipulated everyone, including loud-thundering Zeus, in much the same way she repeatedly manipulated him for her own ends. Ares now also felt sorry for his brother Hephaestus, to whom Hera gave Aphrodite in marriage, for adding to his troubles by becoming the one who cuckolded him repeatedly and without remorse.

Hera, Ares knew, took no pleasure in arranging the union between Aphrodite and Hephaestus. However, that marriage was the only means by which the smith god would agree to deliver his mother from the snare he placed upon her golden throne as retaliation for being cast off Olympus at his birth. Aphrodite never forgave Hera for striking that bargain, even though she knew full well that the Queen did so under extreme duress. What made the whole sordid affair even more egregious was that Aphrodite also knew that it was Zeus who decided upon that marriage to restore peace on starry Olympus. It was Zeus after all that discarded the newborn Hephaestus after refusing to recognize the child as his progeny. Nevertheless, Aphrodite chose to make Hera pay for her imagined misdeeds by enabling Zeus in his many infidelities throughout the centuries, and more recently by trying, and failing, to compel Hera to return permanently to her King's untended marriage-bed.

The god of war was glad that his mother finally abandoned her hypocritical, disloyal, irresolute lecher of a husband, and took great delight in Hera's triumph over Aphrodite's previous sloppy attempts to bring her back to Olympus. In his estimation, Hera should have left Zeus in a blinding whirlwind of stars long before discovering the truth behind her kinship with Prometheus. Like his mother, Ares often felt as though he should have left Olympus centuries ago to begin anew amongst mortals, even if today their reduced numbers, scattered haphazardly across the broad-pathed Earth, rendered wars functionally obsolete in all the nations of the world. This state of affairs mattered little to Ares, for he possessed many other qualities – such as his indefatigable strength and his boundless courage – that made him a useful asset among mortals.

While Ares delighted in war and carnage, having been conceived with his twin sister Eris in the wake of the War against the Titans, he was also a stalwart, albeit under appreciated, defender of Olympus against all manner of Giants, monsters, and other assorted abominations. At times, his dauntless fury against his enemies cost him dearly, such as when the Giants Otos and Ephialtes, sons of Poseidon and a mortal woman, stormed the heavenly Citadel to abduct Hera and Artemis as their brides. Before the pair were defeated by fleet-footed Artemis, Otos and Ephialtes bested Ares in battle and trapped him in a bronze jar for thirteen months. Artemis managed to defeat them by taking guise of a doe and jumping between the brothers, causing them to stab each other. The god of war would have remained imprisoned for years had it not been for Hermes who found him after the brothers' stepmother alerted the messenger of the gods to Ares' whereabouts.

This was not the only indignity Ares endured in service to Olympus. When Hephaestus ensnared Hera upon her golden throne, the god of war was the first to volunteer to bring his brother to the abode of the gods and force him to free their mother from her bonds. Hephaestus proved a worthy adversary, keeping Ares at bay by slinging fiery stones at him – of which the smith god possessed an inexhaustible supply. Ares did not bear Hephaestus any ill will for besting him in battle then, nor for the time his brother humiliated him by trapping him and golden Aphrodite under a net while in a tryst. Truth be told, Ares empathized with Hephaestus' plight a little more each day, knowing full well that he deserved his brother's wrath for profaning his oft-defiled marriage-bed. What Ares could no longer forgive was Aphrodite's cavalier attitude towards him after she intermittently grew bored with his affections and sought the bed of other lovers. The bitterness Ares suffered whenever Aphrodite scorned his love also gave him a keener appreciation for the constant affront his mother sustained whenever Zeus strayed from her bed.

Ares had little affinity or patience for his father, given that the Cloud-gatherer held him in utmost contempt despite his unwavering loyalty to Olympus, going so far as to claim that he was his most hated son. As for Hera, Ares long believed that his mother considered him a disappointment. That is, until she entrusted him with Junia's protection and care when he and Eris joined her on Turtle Island. When Hera expressed her admiration for the way Ares unfailingly protected his mortal children, especially his daughters the Amazon warriors of old against those who would do them harm, the god of war was almost moved to tears. Hera also confessed to Ares of how proud she felt when he slew Hallirhothios, another dastardly mortal son of Poseidon, when the whelp tried to rape his daughter Alkippe. When Poseidon cried foul and demanded that Ares be punished for murdering his son, Hera stood out as one of Ares' most enthusiastic defenders upon his subsequent trial, during which the god of war was acquitted of the deed.

Though Hera never spoke of the incident again, during the trial she let all who dwell on starry Olympus know that Ares ought to be lauded for smiting the evildoer instead of denouncing his victim. When Ares joined his mother and siblings on Turtle Island, Hera told him, albeit far more privately, that she considered him a far better father than Zeus was to his own children, especially those born of her womb. Humbled by his mother's long-unspoken admiration, Ares resolved to henceforth always take her side in her disputes against the Thunderer. This was even if he risked arousing his father's wrath in the same way Hephaestus did when he came to Hera's defence millennia ago, on the night Zeus chained her to the Sky upon her failed insurrection. The god of war had long since regretted not coming to his mother's rescue, as this terrible incident further secured Hephaestus' place as Hera's favourite child. That is, until Junia seemingly materialized out of Chaos from whence emerged Gaia, the Earth-Mother, and Eros the Elder, known to immortals as Phanes and to the mortal people of Turtle Island as the Great Spirit.

If Hera proved to be an imperfect mother at the best of times, she never once abused the great power bestowed upon her by Eros the Elder when she reigned as Mistress of all Life during the long centuries before she wed the Thunderer. Eros was and will forever remain the most powerful force in the Cosmos, ascendant over even the King and Queen of Olympus, whose union he endorsed and blessed, as witnessed by all the gods of Earth, Sea, and Sky. As Queen of Olympus, Hera never debased her prerogative of brokering partnerships of all kinds by using her subjects' innate propensity for love and longing, as was Aphrodite's preferred weapon in her arsenal by which she conquered the hearts and carnal desires of gods and mortal men. Hera customarily arranged unions for primarily pragmatic reasons, never outright manipulating her subjects, whether mortal or otherwise, by compelling them to fall in love. If Hera once found herself in the unfortunate position of having to arrange a marriage between the goddess of love and her estranged son in order to regain her freedom and dignity within the Olympian Court, at least she had the decency not to require either party to swoon over the other. As far as Ares knew, Hephaestus became enamoured with his reluctant bride of his own volition, which the god of war suspected to be Aphrodite's handiwork for reasons known only to herself.

As Ares contemplated the merits of divesting himself of his fealty to Olympus and its King, Hebe pulled him out of his reverie with a swift and efficient poke between his unarmored ribs.

"What the –" Ares grumbled in a low voice, almost dropping his cup of nectar upon the gilded floors of the banquet hall.

Hebe caught the cup with a practiced hand, in such a manner that not a single drop spilled from the vessel. The cupbearer then answered her brother by tacitly and unsubtly throwing her gaze towards golden Aphrodite. At some point during Ares' meditation, Aphrodite began elaborating her ruse to convince the mortal boy Derek to remain among the gods who dwell on starry Olympus.

"Even *you* must admit," Aphrodite told Hermes, as the messenger emphatically rolled his eyes when he saw Ares looking in his direction. "He would make a fine manservant to at least one of us! If I enchant him now, in the full bloom of youth, mortal boy though he is, surely I can convince him to live forever among our blessed kind!"

"You forget yourself, my dear," Hermes replied. "The mortal is to remain among us only for a few days, until the storm passes over Turtle Island, and his friend can finally make his way to the Polaris. I gave Derek my word that he would be returned safe and sound – and I intend to keep my promise. And I'm fairly certain Apollo spirited the boy away to give him mortal sustenance so that he, like Junia, does not become bound to Olympus –"

"Unless he chooses so!" Aphrodite interrupted excitedly. "Can you imagine if Derek agreed to remain with us, and then Junia *somehow* fell in love with him, and decided to stay among her kin on high Olympus for all time? Then Hera would have no choice but to stay, and Love will have prevailed after all!"

"Hera would rip your lovely throat asunder with her immortal teeth," Hermes answered, "if she even suspected you of trying to manipulate her child."

"I would not die!" Aphrodite huffed, her cheeks draining of colour at the thought of her beauteous flesh becoming marred, even momentarily, until Apollo healed her wound.

"Besides," Hermes continued, "I assume Hera will be watching over the boy even more so now. I doubt very much that you will find any opportunity to catch the boy unawares to beguile him, as well as Junia, in the span of a few days!"

"Then we shall make these few days last, as an interminable, how do mortals say, *long weekend*?" Aphrodite mused, turning her attention towards loud-thundering Zeus. "Surely our King will allow it, if it should grant me a fair chance of obtaining his heart's desire?"

Zeus pinched the bridge of his nose in exasperation. "I would rather not," he answered after a moment.

"And why not?" Aphrodite asked in a shrill voice. "It is in your power as a child of Kronos to slow the passage of time! Heaven knows you've done that more than once, on your wedding night, when you prolonged it for three hundred years, and on the night you conceived Herakles upon the mortal Alkmene, which you dragged on for the length of three nights!"

"Hera will immediately know if I do so," the Father of gods and men replied, visibly losing patience. "She is also a child of Kronos, and far more attuned to his power than I will ever be. If I do as you ask, she will know, and denounce the ruse before Zoe, who will then choose to leave us forever. If you wish to slow time while the mortal dwells among us, then another must do the deed."

Ares turned his gaze away from Aphrodite when he heard his father utter these words, for he knew immediately that the goddess of love would ask him to perform the trick. Centuries ago, when the mortal Kadmos and his companions trespassed upon a pristine forest belonging to the god of war, to slay the dragon guarding its sacred spring, Ares demanded that the mortal expiate his offence by working as his bondsman for a full year. In order to punish the impious wretch in a way he found satisfactory, Ares prolonged Kadmos' year of service into an everlasting year, amounting to eight years in the mortal realm. When Kadmos' service was done and the debt repaid, Zeus decreed that Ares ought to forgive Kadmos, and allow him to wed Harmonia, his daughter by Aphrodite and a mortal for having been born after the Deluge. Ares only reluctantly agreed to the union to placate his father. In hindsight he should have refused. Hephaestus, who was still sore at his wife's infidelity that begat Harmonia, gave the bride a cursed necklace as a wedding gift. The necklace ensured that whoever inherited the jewellery would be cursed as well.

Despite their splendid nuptials, Kadmos and Harmonia suffered throughout their mortal lives many misadventures and innumerable hardships. When the the time came to leave the mortal realm, as appointed by the Fates, Kadmos and Harmonia were turned into serpents. The symbol of perennial life, they were then carried off to the Isle of the Blessed in the Kingdom of Hades. Their daughter Semele, beloved by the Thunderer, was the first to suffer Hephaestus' curse. She was consumed by Zeus' thunderbolt before she could give birth to Dionysus, who had to be sewn into his father's thigh so that he could be born full term. Ares' heart never truly softened towards Kadmos for what the mortal did to his dragon, in much the same way as Hera still mourned her slain pet Ladon, guardian of the Tree of the golden apples in the Garden of the Hesperides. However, he felt that both Kadmos and Harmonia deserved better than to spend eternity as reptiles, even if they dwelled in Elysium among the Mighty Dead. Derek also deserved better, for that matter. The first time Ares met the boy years ago, he thought the mortal an impudent little shit. However, since that time

Nepheleid

Derek had grown into a kind, clever, and above all genuinely innocuous young man. He made Ares smile whenever he used to accompany him on the upper deck of the Polaris at sunset when the god of war led the local women in their outdoor yoga classes.

His back resolutely turned to Aphrodite, Ares drained his full cup of nectar in one swallow, handed the empty vessel to Hebe, and quickly exited the banquet on high Olympus. If the goddess of love wished to slow down time to devise an opportunity to bewitch Derek, then she would have to find another accomplice among the children of Kronos, or among those of Zeus and Hera. In the meantime, Ares would do all within his considerable power to do right by Hera and Junia, and ensure that Derek returned to the Polaris on time, unharmed, to accompany his friend Paul to the Nephele.

I will make you proud, Mother. I will be the son you always deserved.

Chapter Seven

The cargo door of the Henokhie slid shut soundlessly as mighty Hephaestus helped Prometheus remove the last basket of golden apples from their mother's shuttle. Once the harvest was safely delivered, the smith god took a teetering step towards the lift at the far end of the station's loading bay – his attendants caught him quickly to steady his gait. Hephaestus created these attendants long ago from the forge he kept on starry Olympus. This was far from his preferred Earthly home on the Island of Lemnos, where mortals once believed him to light the mountains with fire and flame whenever he and his Cyclops endeavoured to build all manner of wondrous weapons for the deathless gods, and the heroes who brought them glory through illustrious deeds. Hephaestus crafted these attendants in the shape of beautiful maidens, with limbs fashioned with gold, gifted with strength and intelligence. They were spared the frailty of mortal flesh and never left their master's side, except to run errands at his command.

Upon Hera's orders, the loading bay was deserted save for Hephaestus and his attendants, swift Iris of the rainbow wings, as well as Prometheus and Asia, given the highly sensitive nature of their current undertaking. Unbeknownst to the learned mortals of the station, and of the Nephele above, the deathless gods dwelling in their midst intended to use the golden apples harvested from their Queen's nuptial garden. These would be the very means by which they would begin the long and painstaking process of terraforming empty worlds devoid of Life and orbiting distant stars.

Last Spring, an angry Hera threw a stunted apple that had been plucked too soon from her treasure Tree into the night Sky. She had awoken to the din of Zeus loudly fornicating in their wedding bed, if Eris was to be believed. The Queen discovered that, even unripe fruit from the Tree of golden apples could be cast across vast distances in the vacuum of space, without coming to harm. This serendipitous revelation prompted Hera to spend the long Summer months tending her garden, pruning the Tree, and picking its fruit without stripping it bare, so that it would continue to thrive long after its mistress left the Earth.

Hera pondered for days on how to explain the origin of the golden apples to the learned mortals under her care. It was an eventuality that would undoubtedly yield unexpected results. In the end, Hera wisely decided to leave this task to immortals. They could transform these into a payload delivery system to seed faraway wanderers with Earth-born bacteria, and other life-sustaining materials. More specifically, Hera tasked Hephaestus with optimizing the golden apples for their newfound purpose and change their outer appearance so that they could be safely wielded by mortals. The mortals, in turn, would store the world-seeders in the deepest recesses of the Nephele until the time came for the City-ship to set out towards interstellar space. Hephaestus was grateful for being assigned the task, which he could complete in the privacy of his workshop high above the Earth. It presented a welcome distraction from the insanity that he knew would soon unfold on starry Olympus.

In only a few short years, barely half the span of a mortal heartbeat for the deathless gods of Olympus, Hephaestus learned to feel quite at home aboard the Nephele. He took great delight residing among the most competent mortals of their age, and countless immortals who once dwelt at the boundaries of the Earth – the sons and daughters of Okeanos and Tethys, the Father and Mother of Rivers, as well as other sea-gods who fled the ravaged Earth to make new homes in ocean worlds across the stars. On the City-ship, well beyond the reach of Heaven, Hephaestus felt as though he was finally free from the constant humiliation of Aphrodite's scorn. He was also free from the palpable loathing he knew Zeus harboured for him, despite having built the ramparts of lofty Olympus, and providing the forge where the Cyclops had crafted the Thunderer's lightning bolts.

Unlike the blessed gods who dwell on starry Olympus, the learned mortals of the Nephele and their deathless comrades earnestly appreciated Hephaestus for his considerable skills. The sincere admiration they held for him indubitably facilitated Prometheus and Hera' decision to grant the Lord of the Forge command of the Nephele's sister-ship, the Corona. The Corona was a mining vessel orbiting the Asteroid belt between the wanderers, Mars and Jupiter. Strangely enough, the the ship was named after the constellation bearing the likeness of Ariadne's crown, an exquisite jewel Hephaestus crafted by his own hand to give to Aphrodite as a wedding gift. For reasons known only to herself, Aphrodite never wore this beautiful diadem and chose instead to gift it to Ariadne upon her marriage to Dionysus – an upstart demigod who more than once shared Aphrodite's bed, much to the amusement of the blessed gods who dwell on starry Olympus.

At times, Hephaestus thought it a cruel jest that his eventual kingdom ought to be named after yet another symbol of Aphrodite's rejection. However, he chose to see it as a portent from the Fates that he was never meant to dwell on Olympus, a sentiment he shared with his mother, and hopefully, his youngest sister Junia. Truth be told, Hephaestus would have liked to be present on Olympus when Junia declared her choice to leave the Earth and become a permanent crewmember of the Nephele. Most of all, the god of the forge would have felt inordinately vindicated the moment Zeus, at long last, suffered a warranted defeat after centuries of lording over his Queen and her legitimate progeny. Like his half-brother Prometheus, Hephaestus proved unlucky in his dealings with Zeus, and for this reason he reluctantly dispatched one of his attendants to remain among the blessed gods of starry Olympus to attend his mother and sisters – Hebe, Eileithya, and Junia – until the time came for them to take up residence within the Nephele for all time. As for Ares and Eris, Hephaestus figured that the pair could easily handle matters in their own peculiar ways in the unlikely eventuality that Zeus ought to show resistance to their desertion from the Olympian Court.

As Hephaestus and his attendants quickly made their way towards the exit doors of the loading bay, swift Iris caught up to them and landed gracefully before the lift doors.

"Why the haste, Lord Hephaestus?" she asked in her usual diplomatic manner, folding her rainbow wings around her shoulders like some eerie, enchanted shawl.

"I may be a cripple with a limp," he answered, "but I've never trudged like one."

"Oh, of that there never was a doubt," Iris replied with a smile. "Prometheus and Asia were simply curious as to why you are leaving so soon. We were all hoping you would accompany us to the Nephele to enjoy some refreshments for a job well done."

"There is still much work left to do," Hephaestus said.

"True," Iris replied. "Yet the learned mortals have barely begun manufacturing the terraforming compounds in the laboratories above, as Hera willed it. There is little work left for us to do until they have done their part. Wouldn't you rather enjoy the company of your kin in the meantime, or do you feel compelled to flee Prometheus' presence because guilt lingers in your heart for the part you played in his captivity all those centuries ago?"

Hephaestus winced very slightly at these words. He knew Iris was right about his culpability for having forged the chains that bound Prometheus to his rock while Zeus' eagle devoured his liver each day, until stalwart Herakles delivered him from his ordeal.

"You know full well he bears you no ill will for that," Asia said, having caught up to Iris and Hephaestus by the exit towards the lift. "For he stole fire from Olympus from your forge. It is a mercy indeed that Zeus did not find you as culpable for the crime as he did my husband. No matter; as it is with Prometheus and I... you, your mother, and the sons and daughters of Okeanos and Tethys are all of the same mind – we would rather see mortals strive to achieve the fullness of their potential than wallow in rank ignorance. And, we all agree that achieving the next step in their collective evolution requires that they make their homes beyond the confines of the broad-pathed Earth, in the farthest reaches of the Cosmos. For this reason, my Lord Hephaestus, are most welcome aboard the Nephele, as are all the immortals who dwell at the boundaries of the Earth, and the blessed gods who find themselves as refugees from Olympus, such as our dear, brave Iris."

"I know", Hephaestus replied, his gaze fixed upon Prometheus dallying towards them at a leisurely pace. "If you must know why I tried to leave with such haste," he continued when Prometheus was well within earshot, "it is only because I wanted to link up with Galatea, my attendant on Olympus, to see that our young sister made it safely there."

"She has," Prometheus said confidently, closing in on his companions. "However, it appears that Eris has created a... complication."

"And how is this news?" Asia replied in a way that was not truly a question.

"It's not the *how*, my darling," Prometheus answered, "so much as the *what*. Our fractious minx of a sister decided to compel Junia to invite the mortal boy Derek to join her on Olympus for a few days. I can only guess at Eris' true intentions for the lad, as her mind is as opaque and impenetrable as the atmosphere of the planet Venus."

"She did *what?*" Hephaestus almost shrieked, his eyes growing wide in surprise.

"It is as I said, and nothing else so far," Prometheus replied. "If you don't mind, Brother, I would also very much like to see what your handmaiden Galatea has to report on that account."

"We all would," Asia added, to which Iris nodded in assent.

Hephaestus took a deep breath. "If Derek does not make his way back to the Nephele," he said after a moment, "then young Paul Red Buffalo might change his mind about joining us. I need him, *we* need him on the Corona once he becomes a specialist in his craft –"

"I am well aware, Hephaestus," Prometheus said, raising his hand in an appeasing gesture. "I wanted to be the one to deliver the news, so that I could stop you from leaping to Olympus to bring him back, along with Hera and Junia and everyone else to whom Mother promised safe passage to the stars. Your past history of landing upon the Earth from great heights is not quite as stellar as that of our little Junia, I'm afraid."

"Perhaps that was beginner's luck," Hephaestus scoffed. "I'll have you know, I was not a cripple after my *first* fall from Olympus, when I landed in the Sea at the very threshold of Thetis' palace. That happened later, after I came to Mother's aid on the night Zeus bound her to the Sky."

This time, it was Iris' turn to wince in disgust at the terrible recollection of seeing her Queen, and oldest friend, so mistreated after Zeus accused Hera of instigating the failed insurrection against his rule, even though all the denizens of Olympus – all save for Hestia – took part in the coup. Hephaestus said nothing, remembering only his seemingly endless fall that night from the heavenly citadel, after Zeus caught him attempting to rescue Hera from her bonds. Hephaestus did not recall his first fall from Olympus, for he was cast off moments after his birth – an event which few deathless gods can recall. It took centuries for Hephaestus to make his peace with the role he believed his mother played in his first ejection from Olympus. For all Hephaestus knew, Hera might have allowed Zeus to throw him off the ramparts of his royal palace while she lay in childbed but he also realized that she likely had no say in the matter. As Thetis, his nurse and foster-mother, told the tale, Zeus never claimed Hephaestus as his son to spite Hera for her jealous rages against his many lovers. At least the Cloud-gatherer never dared to accuse his Queen of bearing an offspring from an illegitimate union during their marriage – that would have made him look weak before the Olympian Court. Instead, Zeus claimed that Hephaestus was the child of Hera alone, conceived without male seed.

Hephaestus bit his lip as he recalled Junia's reaction when he first told her the tale, when she was a small child dwelling at Borealis in Turtle Island. Even at her tender age, Junia thought it preposterous that anyone of sound mind could have believed that Hera bore a son without biological input from a male donor. Hephaestus was much amused when the little girl explained to him, in excruciating scientific detail, how only male donors could provide the SRY gene that contributes the required Y chromosome to produce a male offspring. If Hera had conceived a child without male seed, Junia argued, then Hephaestus would have been born female, either as Hera's identical clone, born of her alone, or as the offspring of another female, who would have contributed another X chromosome in providing the second pair of genes required to produce a viable offspring.

Then, with a triumphant glimmer in her eye, the child exclaimed, "I bet no one ever confused you for a girl, right? So that says it all. Zeus is either a liar, for telling people that you were born from Mom and no one else, or he's a poop-head who doesn't understand where babies come from."

From this glorious moment, Hephaestus decided that the wondrously clever little girl deserved his full loyalty and devotion. He swore to himself that Junia would never come to harm so long as he drew breath.

"You will find no quarrel on that matter, Brother," Prometheus said emphatically, as if divining Hephaestus' thoughts. "We are of the same mind and we would rather not have Zeus cast off our young sister from Olympus when her choice will eventually be made known, even if she has proved herself quite resistant to the vicissitudes of gravity when cast from a great height."

"Unlike ourselves," Asia interjected, "Junia may yet prove mortal after all, though this possibility grows less likely with each passing day. Yet it is Hera's will that the choice on the matter of immortality be hers alone."

"Unless Demeter has Junia taste the barley brew she bestowed upon mortals when she instituted the Mysteries at Eleusis," Iris mused. "The *kykeon* relieved mortals of their fear of death, granting them a glimpse beyond the veil that separates the mortal world from the totality of the

Cosmos. The Vision was so rapturous that those initiated into the Mysteries were never the same afterwards."

"Hera would never allow that, despite her sisterly affection for Demeter," Hephaestus replied. "And like Herakles, Junia has so far travelled twice to the Kingdom of Hades while still alive. She has no further need to glimpse beyond the veil that separates mortal life from death, unless she were to somehow pay a visit to the Primordial Gods of the Cosmos who were already ancient when the Earth-Mother begat Ouranos, the Father of All," he continued, turning towards the exit to the lift.

Anticipating his intent, swift Iris flew towards the double doors of the lift, followed closely by Hephaestus' attendants. The messenger goddess pressed the summoning command sequence, giving Asia, Prometheus, and Hephaestus ample time to reach the heavy double doors before the cabin reached the loading bay floor. When the doors finally slid open, Hephaestus entered first, while his attendants placed their hands on the sensors to give their master and his retinue enough time to step inside without the doors shutting too quickly.

"If you will all follow me," Hephaestus said once the doors slid shut and he was alone with his deathless brethren, "we can view what Galatea has seen from my quarters."

"I thought you'd never ask," Asia replied, half in jest.

"Promise me you will not jump from the airlock if you see something that alarms you," Prometheus said.

"We are about to view live footage filmed on location from Olympus," Iris scoffed. "Of course, some of it will be alarming by anyone's standards!"

"Junia is well protected by my mother, my brother, and sister," Hephaestus declared. "I am certain that Eris will find the most inventive ways to take matters in her own hands should Zeus fail to honour his promise when Junia makes her decision known."

"And if she does not?" Prometheus asked.

"Then I will go there myself, jumping straight down from on high, holding my forging hammer with both hands, to crack Zeus' head open in much the same way you did on the day Athena was born!"

"In that case we should requisition nanocarbon-fibre parachutes from the shuttle bay for you and your handmaidens, just in case," Asia said. "There is no need to break your leg a third time if we can help it at all!"

"We are already equipped with these devices, my lady," said the handmaiden standing to Hephaestus' right.

"Our Master carries one on his tool belt at all times," said another.

"It seems that you are not alone among Hera's children to have been gifted with foresight," Iris told Prometheus, to which he, Hephaestus, Asia, and the handmaidens replied with hearty laughter.

"Let us hope Junia shares that gift," Hephaestus said at last as the lift reached the landing at the bottom of the Nephele.

Chapter Eight

Gazing upon the starry firmament from the high ramparts of holy Olympus, swift Hermes beheld a seemingly endless stream of space debris reflecting the light of the Sun in a pale imitation of starlight. Viewed from the surface of the broad-pathed Earth, this parade of metallic confetti would have looked beautiful. On high Olympus however, the spectacle was often ruined by loud-thundering Zeus' incessant gripes against the mortals who dared to litter his once pristine Skies with the detritus from their hubristic pursuits. Though more than two centuries had passed since the most powerful nations of the world raced each other towards the boundary beyond the Heavens, Zeus never quite forgave their learned kind for their unmitigated gall of crossing the very edge of his Kingdom, and more recently for their sheer audacity of claiming his Queen as one of their own. The Cloud-gatherer particularly loathed these learned mortals for having successfully made a home beyond the Sky, from whence they could look down upon Olympus in the same way one looks down upon the tunnels and sewers that crisscross the underbellies of the once great cities of the mortal world. And now, to make matters even worse, Eris incepted the idea in Junia's impressionable adolescent mind to invite one such learned mortal to the abode of the gods – doubtlessly to sow chaos and confusion among her deathless kin.

Though clever by anyone's measure, Derek was still a boy. An inoffensive, guileless boy for whom Hermes found himself utterly responsible, and a boy whose very life might be in danger by virtue of his unwitting familiarity with golden-throned Hera. Even if Derek had no idea whom he addressed earlier that day when he sought the nurturing guidance of one Dr. Ella Argosi, Director of Operations of CARINA-ALSESTIS and the mother of his little school friend, Hermes knew that Zeus would not soon forget the provocation of his informal demeanour with his Queen. If the Fates proved merciful, perhaps Zeus would look kindly upon the boy, and take pity on him for falling under Eris' spell of stupefaction until he could be returned to the shores of Turtle Island. Hopefully, Eris' mischief would not overly muddle Derek's otherwise keen mind, and leave him only with vague recollections of being spirited away by elves to a magical mountain kingdom in Europe, where some of his future colleagues spend their idle time clad in bedsheets and little else.

This will not end well, Hermes thought to himself as the blessed gods gathered cheerfully in the gilded banquet hall of starry Olympus. *Not unless I keep the boy as far away from Father as possible, and then get him back home safely before anyone notices, tropical hurricanes in the Arctic be damned!*

As Hermes tensely held his breath, he heard Apollo say, "Let us hope that all will turn out exactly as you anticipate... for both our sakes."

Hermes spun around and saw the Lord of the golden bow standing a few paces away from him inside the banquet hall, flanked by fleet-footed Artemis and wise Athena.

"I take it you saw the lad fed and watered with mortal food and drink?" the messenger replied, only mildly annoyed that he let his guard down just enough for Apollo to hear his harried thoughts at a distance. "And you made certain he had a bathroom break in the shed behind the garden before he set foot in Hera's palace?"

"Of course," the Archer answered with an amused smile. "Had I done otherwise, our Queen would have hanged me by the balls in her parlour next to her chandelier."

"I very much doubt that," Athena said. "Hera has grown quite fond of you in the last few years – about as much as I have fallen out of her favour."

"Some of us never had the luxury of her favour," Hermes quipped under his breath, though it seemed that his siblings did not hear his impudent words.

"I can pinpoint the exact moment, *to the day*, when she started taking a shine to you," Artemis interjected. "It was when this whole sordid business with Prometheus and the Nephele began! You two have been rather familiar since then. Do not think that Father has not noticed!"

Apollo threw a sideways glance at his twin. "Is it not yet time for you to leave on your Moon-lit stroll?" he asked her.

"Why yes, it is," Artemis replied good-naturedly, taking the hint without delay.

"Good hunting, Sister," Apollo said in his usual manner, ignoring the inadvertent bite in his habitual nightly farewell to his twin.

Hermes nodded a silent farewell to Artemis, who disappeared through the open door the very moment that Hera, Eris, Ares, Junia, and the mortal boy Derek arrived. A shiny, sentient automaton Hephaestus had left behind on Olympus also entered the banquet hall. Neither Hera nor Artemis acknowledged each other in passing, given their lingering mutual dislike. At times such as these, Hermes wondered whether Artemis counted the days until Hera left the Olympian Court to join the crew of the Nephele once Junia inevitably declared her choice to do the same. With Hera gone, there would be no one left among the deathless gods to enforce the Queen's ban on hunting for sport across the broad-pathed Earth for mortals and immortals alike. This would free the Huntress to resume her preferred pursuit in the few wild areas left in the world where Life recovered as if humanity never waged a devastating war against the natural world.

"I thought you accompanied Derek to Hera's palace to see him fed," Hermes said as he grabbed a full cup of from a very annoyed-looking Ganymede.

"I did," Apollo replied, grabbing his own cup as Athena took hers. "He and Junia dined on a Turtle Island feast of corn on the cob, pumpkin soup, and Eris' favourite... something she called 'bun-less hot dogs'."

"It sounds like Hera wishes for Derek to feel at home," Athena said. "The poor lamb must feel so disoriented. My only hope is that Eris' tricks haven't ravaged his brain too much by the time he is returned among his kind."

"I made certain Derek's mind cannot be addled any further," Apollo replied. "He should be completely back to normal by the time he sets foot on the Polaris. He will think it was due to jet lag, so there will be no harm done."

"How will he explain to himself all that he has seen so far?" Athena asked.

"Hera assured me she would handle that when I left Derek at her table," Apollo answered.

"Were you not with him the entire time?" Hermes asked.

"That was my intention," Apollo answered, "however, once the meal was well under way Hera told me that she would like to spend some time with the children, and asked me alert her when the banquet started, so I took my leave. Ares saw me out and assured me that he would also keep an eye on the boy."

"You left him with *Ares*?" Hermes asked, stifling a laugh. "Do you wish the boy ill?"

"Absolutely not," the Archer said. "Derek and Ares have had an understanding ever since the Sceptred King of Manliness became Junia's minder and put the fear of, well, *us* in Derek and the other boys at the school in Borealis. Ares made certain no one ever dared to tease Junia for being the daughter of one of CARINA's most high-ranking executives. I assure you, both he and Derek will be on their best behaviour this evening."

"Well, I certainly hope you are right," Athena said. "Though one of us ought to warn Hera not to let Derek out of her sight, as Aphrodite fully intends to beguile him as a ploy to compel Junia to change her mind and stay here on Olympus forever."

"One of us?" Apollo asked, raising an eyebrow. "You mean –"

"You, specifically, yes," Athena told Apollo bluntly. "Hera will not listen to me, as you well know. She has not sought my company nor listened to my counsel in the last four years! She still blames me for masterminding her return to Olympus with Junia when all the learned mortals ascended to the Nephele!"

"You did mastermind her return," Hermes said flatly. "We only facilitated your master plan to appease Father's wrath against the mortals bound for the Nephele –"

"And against the Nephele itself," Apollo agreed. "And for this I have no regrets – especially since Zeus subsequently released Hera from the Oath she swore to him at the ramparts of Troy, allowing him to one day destroy a city dear to her heart."

"Father would never –" Athena protested.

"Whether or not he would have destroyed the Nephele in retaliation for Hera's desertion from Olympus is no longer a concern," Apollo interrupted. "What worries me is whether the City-ship will thrive once it unmoors from the Hub, should Hera find herself unable to join the crew."

"So you think Father will challenge Hera if Junia declares her intention to leave?" Athena asked them both.

"Of course he will," Hermes and Apollo answered almost in unison.

"Why do you think he tasked Aphrodite with changing Junia's mind, albeit in the most byzantine way imaginable?" Hermes retorted.

"Junia's mind is already set," Apollo said. "Aphrodite's efforts will come to naught. Junia will absolutely choose to leave on the day of her fourteenth birthday."

"So, you've foreseen this," Athena said.

"Our brother's gift of foresight need not be called upon to predict the outcome, my dear," Hermes answered in Apollo's stead. "Junia never took to Olympus, and she is as fond of Zeus as he was fond of Kronos, and as Kronos was fond of Ouranos. Do you see a pattern here?"

"I have the inkling," Apollo added, "that Father would gladly let Junia take to the stars if he could somehow compel Hera to stay here and remain as Queen of Olympus."

Hermes and Athena answered the Archer's words with silent, surprised stares.

"Were Hera to stay," Apollo continued, "many immortals already aboard the Nephele might change their minds about leaving the broad-pathed Earth without their Queen to guide them in their voyage across the Cosmos. If that were to happen, then Prometheus' plans would become compromised… chaos could ensue within the City-ship itself."

"And do you count yourself among those immortals who would rather not leave without their Queen?" Hermes asked Apollo.

"Yes," Apollo said after a long silence, eliciting a gasp of surprise from Athena.

"Do not let Father hear you say such words!" Athena exclaimed in a hushed voice. "Or let him know that you consider leaving at all! It's bad enough that he must contend with Hera's imminent desertion – he will not be able to bear yours as well!"

"He already knows that some of us would rather follow our Queen to the stars than remain with our King on Olympus," Apollo explained as calmly as he could, almost whispering the words so that no one else could hear beyond the din of joyful voices in the banquet hall. "Like Hera, I have long known that lingering here, in these gilded halls, means remaining bound to serve at Zeus' pleasure. That is why Hera took the opportunity to break free from him as soon as she learned the terrible deceit at the very foundation of her union with our King. Like our Queen, I am also of the mind that, until we also break free from Olympus and make our own way in the Cosmos, *we* will remain forever children at Father's mercy. And since Hera extended her invitation for all immortals to join her in her endeavour to spread Earthly Life to the stars, I think it would be foolish to remain here when the opportunity presents itself to carve out one's own realm in worlds yet unknown."

"I see," Athena said finally, her mien aghast and engrossed in equal measure.

"Others among our kin are also of the same mind," Apollo continued, his gaze turned to Hermes. "Is that not so, Brother?"

Hermes took a sip of his nectar to gather his thoughts. "That all depends on how things play out on Junia's birthday, doesn't it?" he asked instead of answering after a moment.

"But there is still a chance that Father might reject Junia's decision to leave, is there not?" Athena asked sharply. "He might declare her unready to make such a decision until she is older, say, eighteen or twenty-one years old, as is the fashion of mortals. Or until she has spent a satisfactory span of time among the company of the blessed gods who dwell on high Olympus."

"Father will have no choice but to honour his part of the bargain he made with Hera as a condition of her return with Junia," Apollo retorted. "Proceeding otherwise would weaken him in the eyes of the Olympian Court. If his word no longer holds meaning, then his Kingship can be lawfully challenged by anyone without risking the libel of treason. He knows this all too well."

"Not to mention that I would lie breathless somewhere far from Olympus for a full year, then exiled nine years more, if that were to be Father's course of action," Hermes agreed.

"And Father knows that he can suffer your absence far less than he has suffered Hera's many withdrawals," Apollo added, addressing Hermes. "In other words, he needs you more than you need him, and he also knows this well, which is why he will have no real recourse to keep Hera from leaving Olympus, lest he somehow sway her heart otherwise."

"Which is not bloody likely to happen," Athena said.

"What I do know for certain is that Father will once again send me away to bring her back," Hermes continued, "but by the time I catch up to her, the Nephele will have set it course towards Mars, and I will be exiled nonetheless."

"There is another solution to your quandary, Brother," Apollo said. "But you might not like hearing it."

"You mean that I would have to find our gracious and pragmatic Queen before Junia's birthday," Hermes retorted, "and beg her for mercy so that she may lift her admonition against my boarding the Nephele or any other City-ships of the CARINA fleet."

"I think you would like it on the Nephele," Apollo replied. "As I know you do," he then told Athena. "Judging from the few weeks we spent up there, five-odd years ago, when Hermes and Herakles went searching for Hera and Junia in Hades' Kingdom."

"That was a welcome respite from Father's insufferable grousing after Hera had been gone for more than nine years!" Athena agreed, nodding in assent. "That was when Hera still spoke to me as to her favourite step-daughter," she added sullenly.

"Then, you both know that without Hera, Olympus will become unlivable – far more so than it was during the few years she took refuge among the learned mortals on Turtle Island," Apollo said. "It is perhaps a mercy that this state of affairs will come to an end in little more than a fortnight, when the young one declares her choice. My only regret is that I did not have enough time to strengthen her resolve when she sought my counsel on the evening she dove to Earth from the Nephele. That was the only time I ever heard her express doubts about leaving the Earth for good."

"Then Father made a fool of himself when Hera came to fetch Junia,"

Nepheleid

Athena recalled.

"Which allowed Junia to set her mind to leaving forever with the Nephele," Apollo replied. "Ironically, Father did the work for me!"

"But what of your mother, or your twin?" Athena asked. "Would they follow you aboard a City-ship where Hera will rule as de facto sovereign?"

"If they did," Apollo answered, "and I certainly hope this is so, I expect they will enjoy a long overdue truce with Hera, as the source of their enmity is unlikely to follow them on the Nephele."

Athena bit her lip, looking uncharacteristically unsure of herself.

"What is the matter, Pallas?" Hermes asked. "Are you reconsidering your stance on staying?"

"It's not as if either of us have a choice," Athena answered. "You are forbidden from setting foot on the Nephele –"

"At the moment," Apollo interrupted.

"At the moment," Athena continued. "And I am no longer in our Queen's good graces."

"Hera always forgives, eventually," Apollo said.

"Give or take a few centuries," Hermes griped. "Unless Father manipulates her somehow to forget her anger..."

"I suppose you're both right," Athena said. "Just remember the time Father almost repudiated Hera in favour of Thetis! Hera did return to his marriage-bed shortly after Father abandoned the pursuit of the Nereid and betrothed her to the mortal Peleus!"

Apollo cringed at these words, almost dropping his cup of nectar upon the polished marble floor.

"What is the matter with *you*?" Hermes asked him. "You're not picturing Zeus and Hera in bed together, are you? Because I'm fairly certain such a thing will never happen again!"

"I suppose not," Apollo whispered, as his cheeks slowly began to regain their colour.

Athena threw a startled glance at the Archer, perhaps understanding at long last the cause behind his reaction at her mention of Zeus and Hera's questionable long-ago reconciliation, which in turn catalyzed the sequence of events that led to the Trojan War.

"Which is why," Apollo said, his gaze fixed upon the Virgin Warrior, "I intend to see to it that Junia and Hera break free from Olympus along with those who have already left or intend to do so."

"Then you might want to remain close by while Father and Aphrodite try to sway the children's minds," Hermes suggested, taking a step towards Hera and her retinue as loud-thundering Zeus did the same. "I have an inkling that young Derek is about to get quite the education."

Nepheleid

Chapter Nine

"My dear lad, placing those cameras behind your golden handmaiden's eyes was pure genius," dark-robed Mnemosyne, Mother of the Muses, told Hephaestus as she took her seat before the viewing screen in the smith god's living quarters aboard the Nephele.

"Don't be so surprised," Asia said before Hephaestus could answer. "He and Prometheus have the same mother. It stands to reason that he ought to be at least half as clever as my husband."

Mnemosyne gave Asia a look of mild horror, however Hephaestus took the jest in the spirit in which it was intended and answered with a good-natured chuckle.

"If you think I am only half as clever as Prometheus because Zeus is my father," Hephaestus told Asia, "then how do you explain how Junia, who is undoubtedly his child, may yet prove the cleverest of us all?"

"Perhaps it is as Zeus told it when Junia fell to Earth," Iris answered in Asia's stead. "Since Apollo shared a mind with Hera on the night Junia was conceived, perhaps the Archer unwittingly became as her father in spirit."

"That would explain why he has so far declined every opportunity Zeus granted him to claim the girl as his bride," Asia added.

"I doubt this very much," Mnemosyne retorted. "And I think you lot are quite foolhardy for underestimating Zeus' innate cleverness, even if Prometheus outwitted him once, and our Queen far too many times for anyone to keep count. I was married to the Thunderer briefly and bore him nine daughters, I'll have you know. Our bridal may not have lasted three hundred years, but I spent enough time with him to know that anyone who belittles him does so at their own peril."

"Your glorious daughters clearly take after you, venerable one," Asia replied.

Nepheleid

"And I would very much like for them to follow Apollo and I to the Nephele when Junia declares her choice before the Olympian Court," Mnemosyne replied.

"We would all prefer that outcome," Prometheus said.

"And yet," Mnemosyne continued, "persuading a small number of specific immortals to join us in our voyage also requires persuading the many loved ones they would leave behind to join us as well. That is why we need to convince all the gods of Olympus, even the ones who are of the same mind as Zeus, that they are welcome among us."

"Even Aphrodite?" Hephaestus grumbled.

"Even Aphrodite," Mnemosyne agreed. "Hera cannot thwart her, nor Artemis and Leto, or Dionysus, or even Hermes for that matter, from boarding the Nephele – not if we all agree that their presence would be a boon and not a bane for our endeavour."

"This will prove quite the challenge," Prometheus replied. "Especially since Hera asked Eris and Ares to hold the battle lines on high Olympus while she fends off those who would conspire for Junia to stay."

"Like Aphrodite," Hephaestus said.

"Like Aphrodite," Iris agreed. "And perhaps even Dionysus, if he gets his hands on the mortal boy Derek and turns his temperament to hedonism, and also offers Junia perennial, drugged-out bliss in exchange for repudiating her upbringing. Say, Hephaestus, have you instructed your attendant on high Olympus to run interference against those who seduce Junia and Derek to a life of indolence?"

"I commanded Galatea to remain kind and forbearing in her dealings with my mother and siblings, to the point that Zeus will think her completely harmless," Hephaestus answered.

"That may yet yield the outcome we hope for," Prometheus said. "Shall we look through her eyes and join her in the melee at the evening banquet?"

"It is still early," Iris quipped. "Melees and orgies usually begin much later on Olympus, long after Hera has retired for the night."

Asia bit her lip, resisting the urge to comment on melees and orgies of a different sort following Hera to her marriage-bed.

"If our plans come to fruition," Prometheus told his bride after reading her mind effortlessly, "then those days are long behind for our Queen."

"Here we are," Hephaestus said brusquely, drawing everyone's attention to the viewing screen.

"Does Galatea know that we can see through her eyes?" Iris asked.

"She does," Hephaestus answered. "And she will hear us if I allow it, so be mindful of your words," he added, glancing at Asia as if warning her to keep her indiscrete thoughts to herself.

"Galatea is holding the rear guard behind Mother and her entourage," Hephaestus continued, "And it appears that Hera has taken Junia and the boy into the banquet hall. I suppose there is a first time for everything, as she never allowed our little sister to taste nectar and ambrosia while she resided among the gods."

"She likely fed the children, stuffing them to the gills so that they would not be tempted to partake of the sustenance of the immortals," Asia said, her eyes scrutinizing the scene displayed before her of the comings and goings of the gods dwelling below their feet.

"Derek does have a sluggish gait to him," Mnemosyne retorted. "He was never one for gluttony. I ought to know, he's been a pupil at my school for almost as long as Junia's been alive!"

"He follows Hera like a puppy!" Iris remarked. "That would be darling if it did not put him in mortal danger in his dealings with Zeus."

"Look closer," Prometheus replied. "Ares is at his heels, trailing him like a shadow. I would bet my new liver graft that Hera tasked him with his protection during his stay on Olympus."

"Hera knows the boy's worth and is willing to afford him the protection she would give her own child," Mnemosyne said. "Like a lioness protecting her cub, as it should be."

"Or perhaps Hera wants to keep the boy close so that she does not have to pay much heed to Zeus," Asia commented, artfully dodging Hephaestus' caustic glare.

"Wait a minute," Iris said. "Did...did Aphrodite just dash off? Without saying a word of welcome to Derek? That is so unlike her!"

"Galatea reported earlier that Aphrodite tried to beguile the boy upon his arrival on starry Olympus," Hephaestus related unhappily. "Luckily for Derek, Eris had him so confounded that he scarce noticed her at all. Perhaps that is for the best. He will not last for long if he falls prey to her wiles, not while Ares is entrusted with keeping him alive."

"Look, Zeus just asked Derek to sit with him," Asia said, as the viewing screen displayed the image of Derek taking a tentative step towards the Cloud-gatherer. Ganymede handed Derek a full cup of nectar with his countenance displaying his utmost displeasure at the mortal guest.

The screen then showed Hera grabbing the cup and emptying the contents in a nearby flowerpot, which subsequently exploded in a shower of glittering leaves and petals. For some reason, by the time the debris settled upon the polished floor, Ganymede was nowhere to be found.

"Well, that was different," Prometheus commented. "Though I suppose there is a reason why the cupbearer would try to murder young Derek?"

"Aphrodite," Hephaestus and Iris answered almost in unison.

"Ah," Prometheus replied. "Is there a way to hear what they are saying to each other?"

"Yes, hold on a minute," Hephaestus mumbled. "Galatea, broadcast, please! There we are."

The previously silent viewing screen came alive with the din of cheerful immortal voices laughing at what they believed to be a rare practical joke orchestrated by Ganymede.

"And that is why we stopped inviting mortals to dwell among us on Olympus," Dionysus whispered off-screen, to which Hera responded with the most threatening glower she could muster.

As Derek took his seat before the Thunderer, Hera and Junia remained nearby, flanked by Eris, Ares, Hebe, and Herakles. Athena, Apollo, and Hermes were sidling up behind Zeus at a respectful distance, yet well within Galatea's line of sight. Without being instructed to do so, Galatea inched closer until she stood directly behind Junia, slightly craning her neck so that she could acquire a good view of both Zeus and the mortal boy, without making herself overly conspicuous to others who became curious as to what would soon transpire.

"Derek," Zeus said at last once the lad stopped staring at Hera and turned his attention to his host. "I take it you've settled in Apollo's quarters?"

Derek answered with a look of momentary confusion.

"Well then," Zeus added. "Speak up!"

"Uh, yes sir, Mr. Diaz," Derek stammered. "It's all – to be honest it was all kind of a blur."

"Leave it to Eris to put a spell on the boy so that he only hears the names of the gods he knows under their assumed mortal names," Prometheus commented.

"Derek is quite jet lagged, are you not?" Hera said, giving the mortal a sympathetic look.

"Uh, yeah, jet lagged," Derek acquiesced. "But, I mean, yeah, Dr. Archer has a really nice... vacation home? Is this what this is? A resort? Is this a resort town?" he continued, looking at Hera inquisitively.

"Something like that," Hera answered, before Zeus made a gesture to command the boy's attention once more.

"So, Derek," the Thunderer said. "I was told you've known my daughter since you were quite young. Is that so?"

"Junia? Yes sir, I've known Junebug pretty much since she was a baby," Derek answered more confidently than before, which elicited a smile from Apollo and Hera. "My Mom and Dad started working for Dr. Argosi pretty much since she, uh, *landed* at Borealis. Junebug and I went to the same daycare run by Miss Klymene, and then we went to school together. So I guess, yeah, I've known her my whole life."

"And this school you speak of, at Borealis," Zeus continued, "it leads its pupils straight to the employ of the masters of the City-ship Nephele, does it not? They who expect their young to follow them blindly into the void of space, never to return?"

"Uh, yes?" Derek replied tentatively.

Nepheleid

Somewhere beneath Galatea's line of sight, Junia could be heard breathing tensely, despite the newly arrived Demeter reaching out to lay a calming hand on the girl's shoulder. The goddess of the grain held in her other hand a frothing cup of something that looked suspiciously like beer, but was definitely not beer.

"Then tell me, young one," Zeus said, ignoring Junia's escalating annoyance, "have you ever had a thought for a different kind of life, here on Earth, where your days would assuredly not be cut short by the chaotic whims of the Cosmos?"

Derek looked at Junia briefly before answering. Hephaestus and his guests did not need for Galatea to glance upon the child's face to guess at her current state of displeasure for witnessing one of her oldest friends being ruthlessly interrogated by the one she hated the most.

"We get to choose," Derek replied sheepishly. "We are told of the risks involved in signing up to join the crew of the Nephele, and most of us chose to join up. The school has counsellors who make sure everyone knows what they're in for, so I don't think anyone actually makes that decision blindly. At least I didn't."

"Very well," Zeus said, his tone softer, perhaps from having sensed the brunt of Junia's enmity. "Tell me, Derek, what do you mean to do once you join the crew of the Nephele? What will be your profession there, if they even allow you to choose one?"

"I want to be a doctor," Derek answered meekly.

"All senior staff of the CARINA Venture hold the rank of doctors," Zeus sneered.

"Did you mean a physician," Demeter asked the boy, before taking a sip of her suspicious brew. "Like Apollo?"

"Well, sort of," Derek replied. "But mostly a doctor of the mind."

"A head shrinker?" Zeus replied disdainfully.

"And *what* is wrong with that?" Junia blurted out angrily.

"That is a career better suited for women," Zeus answered without taking his eyes off Derek.

Before Junia could reply with the full force of her ire, Derek said calmly, "Some women, yes, and also some men. It's a profession best suited for those who have empathy and patience, and those who want to unravel the mysteries of the mind." Glancing up a Junia, he added with a smile, "It's definitely not for everyone."

"Tell Mr. Diaz what it is you wish to accomplish in your future career as a *head shrinker*," Hera told Derek, pantomiming air quotes in the mortal fashion for emphasis.

"I want to be one of the first to study how humans adapt psychologically to long-term space travel," Derek replied sanguinely, as if Hera's words robbed him of his doubts.

"But you would not be the first," Athena said, surprising everyone gathered. "There have been studies on the long-term physical and psychological effects of space travel on humans ever since the dawn of the Space Age more than two hundred years ago,"

"True," Derek replied, "but we as a species have never spent entire lifetimes away from Earth. I'm talking about *generations* of people living in purely artificial habitats, floating in space, taking turns staying awake to fly ships through interstellar space! And doing this voluntarily! That is truly a first in human history!"

"How so?" Zeus inquired.

"I mean, in the past," Derek answered, "the people who left their homes to colonize other lands on this planet did not always do so willingly, or if they did, it's because they didn't have much choice. Unlike us. The reason why so many of us decide to pursue a career with the CARINA Venture is because this constitutes the pinnacle of opportunity available to anyone alive today."

Zeus raised an eyebrow. "Interesting," he conceded after a moment. "I admit, boy, that you have given me much to think about, and I have little reason to believe that you are a blind fool who will follow your Masters to your death."

"Uh, thanks?" Derek replied uncertainly.

"Before I dismiss you," Zeus continued, "I would like your professional input about your chosen field of inquiry..."

Nepheleid

"Sir?"

"I mean a matter of the mind," Zeus answered.

"I'm not – I'm not yet..." Derek said.

"I know you are still a young apprentice in your craft," Zeus replied. "However, you certainly must possess at least *some* rudimentary knowledge on the subject matter since you intend to dedicate your life and career to unravelling the mysteries of the psyche."

"Okay," Derek answered dubiously.

"So tell me, Derek – in your opinion – what would cause a woman who is intelligent, mature, well established, and happily wed, to undergo a complete reversal and leave behind her husband, children... everything and everyone she has ever known and held dear, after *someone* she trusts coaxed her to take a sip of water under the pretext that it will cause her to recover lost memories?"

"Oh look," Asia told Mnemosyne in Hephaestus' living quarters. "He's talking about *you*!"

"Good thing Derek has no idea he's also talking about Hera," Prometheus said.

"Be quiet!" Mnemosyne chided her kin. "I want to hear what Derek has to say!"

"Well," Derek ventured uneasily. "Assuming the patient has not been clinically diagnosed with a mental or personality disorder, I would say that this person was probably extremely susceptible to suggestion to begin with. I mean, if she genuinely believed that she drank from a memory potion – and that's really not a thing. That alone sounds like an extreme example of the nocebo effect. That's like the flip side of the placebo effect, where the patient is given a sugar pill but then experiences all the negative side effects she was warned against. In this case, the patient might have been triggered to remember repressed memories by just sipping the water, leading her to question all her life choices and act to correct her perceived mistakes. And that *can* look like a breakdown from the outside looking in. But my gut tells me that this person probably wasn't as happy and secure and established as others believed her to be, and that she took the so-called memory potion as an opportunity to turn her life around under the guise of ingesting questionable medicine."

Zeus furrowed his brows at these words. Fortunately for Derek, and all the blessed gods gathered in the banquet hall on starry Olympus, the Earth did not quake at the Thunderer's displeasure.

"Wait a minute," Derek said after a moment. "Are we talking about that pretty blonde lady that just left a couple of minutes ago? The one that looked like she was flirting with me when we got here this afternoon? She looked like –"

"That pretty blonde lady," Hera interrupted, "believes that our geneticists on the Nephele intend to turn your descendants, and by that I mean *all* the children yet to be born to the crew of the entire CARINA fleet, into organisms that will eventually reproduce asexually."

"Be quiet!" Mnemosyne almost shouted as Hephaestus, Prometheus, Asia and Iris burst into laughter on the Nephele high above the Heavens.

"Galatea cannot hear us," Hephaestus replied as soon as he caught his breath. "I've put us on mute for the moment."

"Hold on, the boy is about to speak." Asia said.

"Reproduce asexually?" Derek asked incredulously. "Like amoebas?"

"More like clones, I would think," Hera answered.

"But, no... that's so wrong!" Derek added.

"I know," Hera agreed. "Not everyone understands that our use of incubator and cryostasis chambers are exclusively for the protection of living foetal tissue against cosmic radiation as we travel through interstellar space, and until we find planets suitable for colonization, with adequate magnetospheres."

"But... We as a species won't be in space long enough to evolve asexual reproduction!" Derek added.

"Not through natural means, anyway," Hera answered.

"Should we tell her?" Derek asked innocently.

"Tell her what, exactly?" Hera replied. "That it is absurd to even consider co-opting humanity's most brilliant minds to destroy nature's perfect work by de-sexing humankind, given that the whole purpose of off-world colonization is to ensure the continuity of Earthly Life and human civilization? My dear boy, you would be wasting your breath. Some people are inordinately resistant to facts and reason, even when they stare them right in their pretty face!"

"All right," Zeus interjected, his tone weary. "You have both given us quite a lot to think about and – *where* has Zoe gone?"

Derek turned around, his eyes searching for Junia.

"I though I saw Junebug standing right behind…" he stammered.

Hera took a step back and looked straight into Galatea's eyes. Hephaestus wasted no time whispering a command into an unseen microphone from his living quarters, presumably to Galatea who stood at the ready.

Seconds later, the viewing screen showed Hera fishing for a device from a fold within her robes, then perusing it briefly. Looking at Galatea once more, the Queen nodded almost imperceptibly in acknowledgement for her son's unspoken assistance, then tapped Eris on the shoulder to show her the screen of her device.

Eris bit her lip, looked at Hera once, then nodded in assent and withdrew from the crowd without uttering a word.

Hera then turned her gaze towards Apollo, who now stared at his Queen emphatically.

"The hour is late," the Archer said at last, looking straight at Derek. "you must feel very tired. This has been a long and eventful day…"

Derek suddenly began to look as though he would fall asleep where he sat. "I guess so…" he said meekly, as his lids grew heavy, and his speech became slurred.

"If you will excuse us, Father, my Lady," Apollo told Zeus and Hera, "I must accompany young Derek back to my palace. Morpheus, Hypnos, please help carry him to his chambers! And I don't want him bruised."

Zeus nodded his assent, then turned his gaze towards Hera, who continued to ignore her spurned bridegroom.

"Good night," the Queen told Derek, who did not resist when Apollo lifted him effortlessly from his seat, flanked by Morpheus and Hypnos, summoned from the crowd by the Archer's command.

"Go find Eris and Junia, my dear," Hephaestus said aloud to the viewing screen.

Moments later, Hephaestus' guests saw Galatea's line of sight exiting the banquet hall on high Olympus. The handmaiden took one last look at Apollo and his entourage as they left the premises before heading out towards the muted lights of Aphrodite's palace.

"Well then," Iris told the others gathered in the smith god's quarters on the Nephele high above the Earth. "I know one young man who will sleep well tonight!"

"And one little girl who will likely not sleep for many days," Prometheus added sombrely, to which Hephaestus and Mnemosyne nodded in earnest accord. "It's truly a mercy that she forgot to remove her ring when she arrived at Mother's palace."

"You've welcome," Hephaestus replied. Looking at Asia, he added with a wink, "not bad for your half-wit brother-in-law, eh?"

"You are absolutely an improvement from Epimetheus," Asia answered with a smile.

"Let us hope Junia forgets to say as much to Klymene when she visits her in Elysium," Prometheus said, looking at Iris.

"Right," the messenger goddess replied, taking her leave from Hephaestus and his guests. "I shall see you lot in a fortnight or perhaps sooner, depending on the whims of Eris, I suppose."

"Give my brothers and your twin sister our regards," Mnemosyne told Iris as the messenger goddess vanished from the room, leaving a faint rainbow shimmer in her wake.

"Aglaea," Hephaestus told one of his handmaidens. "See to it that Paul Red Buffalo knows not to board the Nephele via the Hub at Polaris once the storm clears. Tell him that Mr. Smith will send him another conveyance, and that on his way here he will have to make a detour on a mission of goodwill to a small principality in Europe as youth ambassador of the United Territories of Turtle Island. He will understand soon enough."

Nepheleid

"Right away, My Lord," the handmaiden replied as she left Hephaestus' quarters.

Prometheus rose to his feet, then turned his attention to the remaining handmaiden. "Keep the Henokhie at the ready," he told her. "Iris will return much sooner than she believes."

The handmaiden gave the benefactor of humanity an obedient nod and followed her mechanical sister out of the room.

"Should we not wait until the outcome becomes fixed before we take further action?" Asia asked Prometheus.

"The Fates' decrees are never completely sealed, dear child," Mnemosyne answered. "Not unless Eros the Elder has a say in the outcome."

"And Lord Eros will invariably take the side that favours Life," Prometheus said. "That is how we know that our labours will not be in vain."

I certainly hope you are right, Brother, Hephaestus thought before giving Galatea the command to retire for the night.

Chapter Ten

With a terror-stricken leap, winged Eris flew across vast Olympus towards Aphrodite's gilded palace, hoping to intercept Junia before the child came to actual harm by confronting the goddess of love for her sempiternal hostility against Hera's determination to leave Olympus. If the signal received by Hephaestus' mechanical handmaiden proved accurate, Junia now lurked somewhere behind the rose bushes framing the floor-length windows outside laughter-loving Aphrodite's abode, hidden from view by the occupants within. Knowing Junia, Eris fully expected to find her young sister skulking in the shadows, like a tiny lioness preparing to pounce upon her unsuspecting prey.

No wonder Mother calls her 'kitten', Eris pondered as she soundlessly closed in on her quarry. *Even the smallest, sweetest house cats are born with needle-sharp claws and milk teeth, ready to devour the entire world as soon as soon as they open their eyes. This fierceness will serve her well once the Nepheleid lands upon new worlds ripe for the taking, but first she must survive the next few weeks on Olympus with her resolve intact...*

With a soft ruffling of her feathered wings, Eris landed directly behind Junia, using her power to remain undetected by the child's keen ability to perceive the unseen and the unknown. She would reveal herself soon enough, though hopefully without eliciting a loud cry of "What the hell, Eris?" she now fully expected from Junia whenever she successfully surprised the child by eluding her while hiding in plain sight. Like the crouching kitten before her, Eris took a step closer towards the high open window of Aphrodite's sumptuous parlour, where she spied the goddess of love idling lazily upon a ludicrously overstuffed, heart-shaped divan. She was flanked by a low table holding a rather large open jar of wine to her left, and Eileithya seated on another couch to her right. Eris saw Junia clenching her little fists upon seeing their older sister fraternizing with their mother's *bête noire*. The goddess of discord said nothing as a pang of guilt assailed her for never disclosing to Junia that Eileithya had been a friend and companion to golden Aphrodite for as long as the goddess of love had been wed to their brother Hephaestus.

Nepheleid

Hera arranged the friendship partly as a ruse to keep abreast of the Sea-Born's scheming, However, since Aphrodite's latest machinations against the Queen of Olympus resulted in the unplanned conception of Junia, Hera covertly redoubled her efforts to neutralize the very real threat her rival presented against her and the CARINA Venture, even if very few immortals believed Aphrodite's mad ramblings about Hera's efforts to unsex humanity out of spite. Hera also knew that, despite cultivating a well-crafted reputation as a frivolous, vapid tart among those who knew her only superficially, Aphrodite had revealed herself unfailingly as a scourge to mortals who neglected to give the goddess her due.

Such was the fate that befell Tyndareus, King of Sparta, who upon sacrificing to the gods forgot to include Aphrodite's share in the feast. As punishment for this impiety, Aphrodite promised the King's daughter Helen, then married to Menelaus, to the Trojan prince Paris if the latter declared her to be the fairest amongst the goddesses. Tyndareus' other daughter Clytemnestra, wed to Menelaus' brother Agamenon, murdered her husband when he returned victorious from the Trojan War, and was herself murdered by her son Orestes for the crime. Menelaus also incurred Aphrodite's ire when he failed to deliver the hecatomb he promised the goddess upon his marriage to the uncommonly beautiful Helen. This prompted Aphrodite to single out the hapless mortal bride as incentive for Paris to declare her as the fairest of them all, causing Helen's jilted husband, and her ambitious brother-in-law, to wage a storied ten-year war against Troy.

Eris herself once came to Aphrodite's aid in exacting revenge against the women of Lemnos for a similar, albeit deliberate, neglect. When Aphrodite retaliated by cursing the Lemnian women with a foul stench, their husbands repudiated the lot of them and instead took the captive women of neighbouring Thrake to their beds. Eris then rallied the betrayed wives, driving them to a murderous rage, to repay this insult by killing all the men on the island. With the slaughter complete, Aphrodite's vengeance was fulfilled, and by the time the Argonauts landed upon the island in their quest to acquire the Golden Fleece, no men remained on Lemnos. This was a situation the Argonauts dutifully rectified by bedding the Lemnian women and seeding their wombs with sons. Aphrodite's failure to credit Eris' role in her victory against her impious mortal foes contributed to the Nurse of War's decision to use a golden apple from her mother's garden as a device of disharmony at the wedding of Thetis and Peleus on Olympus. Though emphatically uninvited to the event by Zeus' decree, Eris knew full well that Aphrodite's vanity would compel her to claim the title of the fairest among the immortals, even if the goddess of love risked brawling with goddesses who were far more skilled in the art of war – such as Athena and Hera – in order to win the prize.

If Aphrodite believed that the crew of the Nephele, and of City-ships of its ilk yet to come, were bound to renounce her worship in favour of Hera, then perhaps the mortals under Hera's care could find themselves in mortal danger from the spurned goddess of love and harlotry. For this reason alone, Hera saw to it that her own sons by the Thunderer would join her in her voyage to the stars. Once, they fought so fiercely over Aphrodite's affections, but they have since grew disenchanted and realized that a world absent of meretricious manipulation was possible among the empty wanderers yet to be discovered. Convincing Junia of the same would prove a much easier task, Eris thought, for the child's demeanour as she spied upon Aphrodite and Eileithya betrayed her displeasure at her mother's most egregious slanderer.

Eris quieted her thoughts, drawing her attention to the voices of the goddesses inside Aphrodite's parlour. She tried her best to eavesdrop above the steady rumble of Junia's loud, calming breaths, a technique for delaying the moment of battle taught to her by a bevy of mortal martial arts teachers since she was a toddler. Eris smiled, imagining the long-ago conversation between Hera and Klymene, her Oceanid handmaiden with whom the Queen of Olympus co-parented her youngest child. How feisty Junia must have been as a nursling for her mothers to so readily agree that she ought to learn self-control in war and in life from the wisest of mortal teachers as soon as she learned to walk.

"Yeah, well, I'm really glad they did that," Junia whispered to the winged goddess lurking behind her. "And before you ask, no I didn't *see* you, but your thoughts are as loud as ten thousand flocks of Canada geese heading South for the Winter so... there."

All right then, Eris said wordlessly in the recesses of her mind. *What did I miss?*

Junia nudged her head towards the open window, beyond which Aphrodite loudly complained to Eileithya of all the methods Hera employed of late to make a fool out of her.

Nepheleid

"That *ingrate!*" the goddess of love bemoaned. Does she not remember all the times I helped her ease her way back into the Thunderer's bed when their union barely hung by a thread? Still, she repays my *kindness* and daughterly piety by forsaking her marriage-bed, just as she mocked me by cursing my son Priapos with an enormous –"

"Insult of the so-called filial piety you conveniently defiled when you conceived that son after sharing a bed with Zeus," Eileithya interrupted. "Perhaps you should not have done that, my dear. You know full well that although Father desires you – as he does everyone and *everything* upon the Earth, Sea, and Sky. He has no appetite to replace Hera with you as his Queen."

"It was I who facilitated her union with her King in the first place!" Aphrodite protested.

"A union Mother never wanted," Eileithya retorted. "If Mnemosyne told it true, then you acted at the behest of Zeus alone. For centuries Hera resisted his ceaseless advances until you counselled him to ravish her in the woods of Mount Thornax, disguised as an injured baby bird so that her maternal instinct would override her otherwise well-honed senses, warning her that something was terribly amiss. That alone absolves Hera of any pretence you might have to her *gratitude*."

"I was also acting at the behest of the Primordial Gods of the Cosmos, I'll have you know!" Aphrodite objected indignantly. "And don't forget the other immortals who dwell at the boundaries of the broad-pathed Earth, who unanimously agreed that it would be in the best interest of all for Hera to be crowned Queen of Olympus, enthroned at Zeus' side, if only to provide a tempering influence on the Thunderer! Why do you think Phanes himself, the one whom mortals and deathless gods alike also call Eros the Elder, drove Hera's bridal chariot upon her nuptials to the King of Olympus? He wanted to be certain that she appeared at her own wedding, so that the Fates could seal her union to Zeus for all Time!"

"And yet, here we are," Eileithya said.

"But that's not all!" Aphrodite continued, ignoring the midwife goddess' subtle plea to stop her tirade. "Not only does Hera openly mock the sacredness of her union, sanctioned by Eros the Elder, the most powerful being in the Cosmos, after whom I named my firstborn son by Ares, she also disdains all for which it stands by picking clean the golden apples

90

of her nuptial garden, a wedding gift from the Earth-Mother herself!"

"Well, actually," Eileithya interjected, that's not quite –"

"And with *Eris* at her side for the entirety of the long Summer months!" Aphrodite interrupted, her usually mellifluous voice rising at a pitch most unpleasant to mammalian ears. "Do you think Hera is also under Eris' spell, like that beautiful idiot boy they brought back from Turtle Island?"

"Eris?" Eileithya replied, stifling a laugh. "Beguiling Hera, her own mother, and the only goddess clever enough to outwit Zeus and Metis combined? *Really?*"

"What if Eris had planned this all along?" Aphrodite continued, unconvinced. "What if Eris arranged for Prometheus to find Hera on that lonely mountaintop near Borealis all those years ago, triggering a sequence of events that would lead our Queen to sow chaos and dissension after leaving her husband? Such schemes are not unknown to her! Do you not remember the time Eris disguised herself as the Titan-Queen Rhea, riding upon her lion-chariot, and appeared to Dionysus to goad him to wage war against Deriades, the King of the Indians? No... Hera is surely under an evil spell, and must be brought to heel in her marriage-bed, for her own good, before the very fabric of the Cosmos folds upon itself and all Life is snuffed from the broad-pathed Earth!"

"Do you not think it more likely," Eileithya scoffed, "that Hera needed Eris' help *and her wings* to better care for her neglected and oft-plundered treasure tree of the golden apples? The same you have also helped yourself to, on occasion, to grant boons to mortals seeking your aid in winning their lovers' affection? Perhaps you ought to leave Hera be, even if she does wish to return to her old ways as a Maiden Queen or metamorphose into whatever would have become of her had Zeus never murdered her first husband Eurymedon, the King of the Giants, and given her firstborn son to Klymene to raise as her own. Or perhaps, my dear, you seek to find fault with the way your Queen chooses to spend her last days on the broad-pathed Earth because you fear becoming irrelevant in the worlds she seeks to create. Worlds where Hera would be once again ascendant, emboldening women to choose their lovers as freely as she once did. Worlds where she will not suffer fools so gladly, nor allow love and sex to become commodities to be traded as favours when supplicating powerful men. In my estimation, such worlds would be most propitious for her young daughter to thrive, as would all the mortal women and men of all the nations of the Earth. Would it not therefore be best for you to abandon your fruitless quest to sway young Junia's heart to remain here on starry Olympus?"

At long last, Aphrodite paused before replying. Her frown conveyed her troubled thoughts far more eloquently that her words ever could. "Whose side are you on?" the goddess of love asked Eileithya with an edge to her voice as sharp as Kronos' sickle.

"I am on the side that would rather not rouse my mother's ire," Eileithya answered coolly. "And as my mother invariably acts in the interests of preserving Life, so do I, regardless of the means by which she chooses to pursue her ends. You will recall that I also had my doubts about the way in which Junia came to be born, however after spending some time with my brothers on the Nephele, and on its daughter-station named after Mother's sacred garden, I do believe that Hera remains true in her pursuit to spread Earthly Life across the vast Cosmos."

"I fear what kind of Life would take root across distant stars and wanderers if our Queen personally rebukes the yoke of marriage and sex," Aphrodite retorted sharply. "What kind of example is she setting for those poor, hapless mortals, if she would have them multiply through bloodless means, and remain for centuries frozen in their icy vats, floating aimlessly through Time like the lost souls in the Holy River Styx, forever adrift, searching for the shores of Hades' Kingdom? Would you truly suffer your young sister to live in such a world, even if immortals alone remained awake during the monotonous and lonely crossing between the stars? You would have this fate befall your own mother? Where is *your* filial piety?"

"To be honest, I do not particularly wish for Hera to leave the Earth," Eileithya answered, eliciting a gasp from Junia, which Eris managed to stifle with a swift motion of her hand before the goddesses inside detected their presence. "I would rather see Mother reconciled of her own volition with her husband, and for Father to prove himself worthy to be her Consort. Failing that, I would prefer to see her take to the stars than endure whatever trickery you wish to impose upon her and Junia. You are no match for Hera's cleverness, and Junia appears to take after Mother in all respects. If you continue to antagonize either of them, I fear you will be brought low in a way from which you might never recover!"

"If you find me so inept before Hera's obstinacy and powerless before Junia's insolence," Aphrodite retorted, "then perhaps the Primordial Powers of the Cosmos ought to have a say in the outcome of Zeus' wager with his Queen."

"You cannot mean –"

"I will go forth and supplicate Phanes," Aphrodite said triumphantly. "I will seek out the most powerful force in the Cosmos, known to some as Eros the Elder, and I will compel him to bring low our seditious Queen! As I've said before, to our fellow blessed gods who dwell on holy Olympus, I shall see to it that Love conquers all!"

Ensnared in Eris' arms, with the goddess of discord's hand still covering her mouth, Junia twitched to break free, but her older, winged sister held fast.

Not this way, child. Aphrodite is far more powerful that you realize. Do not believe the tales told about her lack of prowess in battle. They are as slanderous as the ones proclaiming Mother's disagreeable nature.

With a sharp intake of breath and a dizzying swirl of light and colour expanding in all directions at once, Eris transported Junia to the steps outside her own dwelling. From from Junia's perspective, this took the form of a derelict ice cream truck at the centre of starry Olympus yet hidden from view by most with abundant ambient shrubbery. Once safely out of earshot from Aphrodite's neighbouring palace, Eris released Junia from her embrace and gave her young sister a few seconds to regain her composure.

"What the hell, Eris!?" Junia cried out irritatedly.

Ah, there it is, Eris thought, momentarily forgetting that Junia could hear her regardless.

"You're just going to let Aphrodite seek out the Primordial Gods of whatever to humiliate and defeat Mom further than she has already done? Whose side are *you* on, Eris?"

"If you must ask," Eris replied with mock haughtiness, "I am on the side that always breaks stagnation and clears the way for the future to unfold. Mother tasked me with your protection against Aphrodite's assaults on your higher mental faculties. And now, more than ever as your flower is about to bloom, I intend to see that your will, whether to leave or to

93

stay, shall be respected and enforced when you are brought before Zeus when you come of age in a few weeks."

"You know damned well that I don't want to stay!"

"And Mother will be most pleased."

"So, what do we do now?" Junia asked. "Just wait here until Phanes shows up to zap Mom with his magic fairy sex-dust, then punch him in the primordial dick?"

Eris let out a laugh but said nothing.

"Because I don't have Grandpa Kronos' sickle anymore, Eris," Junia continued. "I left it in the Garden of the Hesperides, just when Ares yanked me out of there the moment Zeus showed up to humour Mom at the Tree... You didn't happen to see it while you were there, did you?"

Eris shook her head. "It was long gone when Mother and I returned there in the Spring to tend the Tree. If I am not mistaken, Lord Hades brought it back with him to the Underworld, presumably for safekeeping."

"So, we get it back and then bobbitize Phanes when he comes for our Mom, like Kronos did when Ouranos came for his?"

"No child, we will do no such thing," Eris answered. "We will instead seek the aid of *Elder Gods* of our own. Remember that, like Mother you also have a great number of friends in low places, many of whom remain grateful for what you did last Winter that resulted in their release from their prison in the gloomy pit of Tartarus."

"So... we're going to the Underworld? For how long?"

"As long as it takes to ensure our victory, but less than the time it would take for us to return before your coming-of-age banquet."

"What about Derek?" Junia asked after a few moments. "I know that Apollo is supposed to protect him and all from his carnal impulses –"

Eris stifled a laugh to let Junia continue speaking.

"But I don't think we're supposed to bring mortals to the Underworld unless we have someone else to trade him for," Junia said finally.

"It gladdens my heart, Princess, that you remember the laws governing our Uncle's Kingdom, despite your repeated and unwise intrusions into the realm of the dead," Hermes said, leaning against the hood of Eris' enchanted ice cream truck dwelling.

"AH, F–" Junia shrieked artlessly.

Nepheleid

Chapter Eleven

"I swear," Hermes told Junia with an impish grin, "your use of profanity grows more colourful by the minute. Why, I had no idea you spoke German!"

"That's nothing," Eris said. "You haven't heard colourful profanity until you've visited the French-speaking people of the vast Saint Lawrence River Valley region of Turtle Island!"

"You forget, Eris – I spent a year shadowing our Queen across all of Turtle Island," Hermes retorted. "I've had quite an earful in the old New France. I might even have lost a bit of sanity every time I restrained myself from laughing out loud whenever someone cursed their ancestors' liturgical paraphernalia as they slipped on ice or dropped their keys in puddles of slush."

"How much of that did you hear?" Junia asked flatly.

"Before or after the 'flying baby caca'?" Hermes inquired.

"I asked you first," Junia replied.

Hermes cocked his head to the side ever so slightly, his playful mien intact, but said nothing. By now, Junia knew the messenger god well enough to realize that Hermes had not, in fact, heard anything beyond vague notions of visiting Hades' Kingdom. His uncharacteristic muteness was nothing more than a subtle method of interrogation, a non-threatening enticement for Junia to fill the silence by confessing what he wanted to know.

His gaze fixed on Junia, Hermes failed to notice Eris' smile.

He knows nothing, Junia heard Eris whisper in her mind. *But he might prove useful.*

"Ah, well," Junia told Hermes with mock resignation. "Since you're here, there is no point in denying that Eris and I intend to pay a visit to our kin in the Underworld. But you already knew that. I mean, I *told* you when we boarded the Hub that I wanted to see Klymene one last time. And you told me you would take me there later, after I've spent some time on Olympus. Well, it's later so... can we go now?"

"You arrived on Olympus barely three hours ago!" Hermes protested.

"It's still later!" Junia retorted.

"And you brought an unexpected guest!" Hermes continued. "To leave him here alone, when you know full well that Aphrodite intends to corrupt him in every conceivable manner, would prove most unwise, not to mention bloody *rude*. Wouldn't you agree?"

"That is why we need *you* to take us there," Junia replied.

"Since when do you need *me* to travel between the realms, when you've got a perfectly capable harbinger of Chaos at your beck and call?" Hermes scoffed, gesturing at Eris.

"You possess a skill that I have yet to master," Eris answered. "Unlike I, you can synchronize Time as it is experienced on Earth, on Olympus, and the Underworld all at once. All of us deathless gods know this. Some mortals know this as well."

"Yeah," Junia agreed. "I mean, we have to be back by morning before anyone notices we're gone – otherwise Zeus will freak! And since we can't take Derek with us, what with him being mortal and all, we have to leave now while he's safely tuckered in Apollo's palace for the night. So, can we go? Pretty please? I really want to say goodbye to my Mama."

Hermes furrowed his brow, his countenance leaving no trace of his earlier sprightly grin. Junia doubted whether he took her plea seriously, however she also knew that he could not deny her request, especially not after he swore an Oath before Hades by the Holy River Styx to never hold her captive on starry Olympus against her will.

"All right," Hermes said after a long moment, looking at his surroundings as if to confirm that they were well and truly alone in the vicinity of Eris' enchanted dwelling. "I will take you to Elysium, and nowhere else, to greet Klymene. After you've said your goodbyes, I will take you back to your mother's palace. But we *must* return before sunrise, as Zeus and Hera are both early risers, and they *will* notice that something is amiss if you fail to fetch Derek for breakfast in your mother's parlour."

"If Eris can come too then you've got yourself a deal," Junia replied.

"I will be on my best behaviour," Eris quipped when Hermes predictably groaned.

"You'd better…" Hermes griped as he reached out and put his arms upon their shoulders. In the span of a mortal heartbeat, the starlit gilded halls of high Olympus turned to cloudless noontide skies under the Underworld's mysteriously unbounded firmament. This realm was too lofty and vast to be interred within the recesses of the broad-pathed Earth – something that Junia had observed long ago.

"Stay close," Hermes warned when they landed upon the hallowed grounds behind Kronos' tower, at the very heart of the White Island, known to mortals as the Isle of the Blessed. "For even Lord Hades would be loath to turn this visit into a search party, should either of you decide to explore his nigh endless realm, as the little one did when I found her the first time."

"Where else would we go," Eris asked, her voice barely audible above the joyful sounds of Elysium, "if the ones we seek dwell here among the shades of fallen heroes and the virtuous dead?"

"You would go where other immortals do not dare to tread," Hermes answered, "because there is always more than one reason as to why you go about your business as you do."

"We are here exclusively because Junia has matters to settle before the Nephele unmoors," Eris replied. "That much is as true as anything I would otherwise swear by the Holy River Styx."

"I know you too well to take you at your word, Eris," Hermes said. "And as Zeus tasked me with keeping Junia safe on Olympus, then I must insist that you keep this journey short and abstain from your games while we are in Hades' Kingdom."

"Then let me promise you this," Eris replied. "Should you lose sight of either of us for some reason or another, then know that I will keep Junia safe and return her to Olympus before sunrise."

"I can hear you, you know," Junia whined. "I'm fourteen, not deaf."

Nepheleid

"You are thirteen years, eleven months and one week old, Moppet," a voice boomed from somewhere beyond a row of white poplar trees as pale as the bones of sun-bleached skeletons.

"Eight days, Grandpa," Junia yelled out, so that the Titan-King behind the trees could hear her. "Thirteen years, eleven months and *eight days*!"

The newly crowned ruler of Elysium and his Titan brothers, and their Titan brides, along with his entire Court laughed heartily at Junia's audacity for addressing her eminent grandsire with such brazenness. These beings were all once-formerly damned and deemed as such mostly for having fought on the losing side against the gods of Olympus for supremacy over the Cosmos.

"The Nephele operates on Eastern Standard Time!" Eris shouted, to which many of the Oceanid Titan brides readily agreed.

"Those two," a familiar female voice said beyond the row of poplars. "They are just like their mother, with more courage than sense, and an overabundance of the former and a dire lack of the latter."

"Grandma Rhea?" Junia inquired as she made a beeline towards the gathering, with Eris and Hermes at her heels. "I thought I saw you in the throne room on Olympus only a few hours ago!" she added once she crossed the hedge and confirmed the source of the disparaging comment against herself, her mother, and Eris.

"Yes, child," fair-haired Rhea answered with a forbearing sigh. "I was there when you arrived. Your father asked me to fetch your mother for your return to Olympus, but since both of you made it there under your own steam, as mortals used to say, then I figured that my presence on Olympus was no longer required, so I retired for the evening. Though for the life of me, I cannot fathom why you three have decided to come here, on the night of your return among the blessed gods of starry Olympus, where you are meant to dwell until your coming-of-age!"

While Junia stared crossly at the Titan-Queen, Eris nudged her to alert her to Klymene's presence beside Iapetos, her long imprisoned husband, as the two made their way towards the gathering. For a fleeting moment, Junia thought she glimpsed Iris lurking behind the pair at the edge of the garden, then remembered that Iris had a twin sister, Arke, who fought long ago on the side of the Titans and met the same fate as her vanquished masters. If Zeus opted to release the Titans from the pit of

Tartarus out of gratitude for the part they played in finding Hera in the Garden of the Hesperides last Winter, then it made sense that their attendants would be freed as well.

"Please do not tell me that you've reconsidered leaving with the crew of the Nephele!" Rhea said before Junia could voice her purposeful and versatile, albeit salty, retort. "Would you be so foolish as to render all of your mother's work for naught!"

"What? No!" Junia stammered sharply in response. "I'm here to see – Mama!"

"Kitten!" Klymene cried out as she jogged towards Junia to embrace her. "What are you doing here? You should be on Olympus with your mother and father, at least for the next few weeks!"

Junia leaned closer to Klymene and whispered, "I told Hermes that I came here to say goodbye for the last time." She bit her lip after uttering the last few words to stop her voice from wavering, as the truth of her words struck her all at once.

"Oh, my darling," Klymene replied almost inaudibly. "We should have told you… Whatever fate you choose, this will not be the last time that you see us immortals who dwell here in Elysium. I see that Hera and Prometheus kept that from you, so that your decision would not be clouded by sentimentality."

"Wait, what?" Junia inquired, her eyes wide with surprise and confusion.

"Go to Eris," Klymene whispered as she guided Junia towards her winged minder. "Go to her and let your mother and brother, and the other adults, take care of the rest. It will be all right, I promise. Now, go on as if you did not hear this. Blink twice if you understand."

Junia did as she was told.

"You are correct," Klymene blurted in an uncharacteristically loud voice. "The shades you see all around are those of heroes and other deceased mortals of great renown!"

"And some of them were brought into my Kingdom without even tasting death," Hades said, startling everyone as he materialized in the garden at the foot of Kronos' tower, his trusty helmet tucked under his elbow.

"How long have you stood there?" Rhea shrieked, clutching her chest.

"Since Hermes and the girls arrived from Olympus," Kronos answered in their son's stead.

"Precisely," Hades agreed, nodding courteously to his mother and father, then to Hermes, Eris and Junia, and the rest of the Titan-Court. "Oh, don't mind me," he continued. "I was curious as to what you three were doing here, since the little one's presence on Olympus is clearly of the utmost importance, *Eris*?"

"Lord Hades, we are here because Junia insisted on bidding farewell to Klymene," Hermes answered before Eris could utter a single syllable. "And as Eris is Junia's guardian, she feels compelled to follow her like a shadow everywhere she goes."

The Host of Many raised an eyebrow and threw a dubious glance at Eris and Junia. "Is this true?" he asked them.

"Yes, Uncle Ninja," the sisters answered in unison.

"Very well," Hades replied coyly. "Carry on, then, as if I weren't here."

Junia bit her lip, resisting the urge to protest that the presence of an observer, even an unseen one, would invariably alter the outcome of any intended course of action already under way.

"So, you were saying something about heroes, yes?" Hades said, his gaze fixed on Klymene.

"Oh, bloody hell!" Rhea interjected, as all colour drained from her fair cheeks. "Please do not tell me that you lot came here to teach the girl about following the example of heroes to earn life everlasting! Little one," she continued, addressing Junia emphatically, "if you heed no other words of advice that I shall utter from my own lips before you decide your fate, then know this: heroes must never again be celebrated and adored as they once were in the heyday of ancient Hellas. Even your mother, who once prided herself as the crucible from whence heroes were forged, will tell you that the heroes of old were dastardly scoundrels, each and every one of them! So, you would do well to disregard whatever nonsense your Olympian brethren told you about the virtues of heroes!"

"Uh, okay?" Junia stammered with minimal coherence. *What the hell?* she mouthed at Eris, hoping for some semblance of an explanation for the Titan-Queen's unrequited tantrum.

"What your august grandmother means to say, little Moppet," Kronos answered benevolently, "is that heroes are at the root of why mortals today must seek new homes across the vast Cosmos if their fragile kind were to survive."

"The heroes of old are often praised for bringing and promoting civilization into the chaos of nature," Rhea added, her tone somewhat calmer. "However, after the followers of the Nazarene destroyed my daughter Demeter's shrine at Eleusis, and put an end to the Mysteries taught there to make mortal life tolerable, the deeds of heroes born in their wake are precisely what broke the world. As generations unfolded, mortals sought to follow the example of the ancient heroes, without understanding their place in the Cosmos, and conquered nature until Earthly Life began its inexorable decline. This is why their few descendants alive today are forced to dwell in technological enclaves, dispersed far and wide across all the nations of the broad-pathed Earth."

"Wait a minute," Junia demurred. "Didn't my Mom challenge heroes –"

"Sometimes to the point of literal psychological torture," Hermes quipped, then kept silent when he saw Hades throwing him a disapproving glance.

"As I was saying," Junia continued, glowering at Hermes, "didn't my Mom *test* heroes to bring out the best in them? So that they could help mortals' lives suck a little bit less, like what Prometheus did?"

"Prometheus was punished for his *heroism* for many centuries," Klymene said.

"Because Hera was not the one who judged him and sentenced him to be chained to his rock after he stole fire from Olympus," Junia replied. "Had it been up to my Mom, Prometheus would have been *rewarded* for what he did!"

"Be that as it may, Prometheus is not a hero in the conventional sense, not like Herakles," Hades interjected, to which all of the Titan-Court agreed. "And as a mortal Herakles was, and still remains to this day as far as I can tell, an insufferable wanker."

"Why do you say that?" Junia asked, surprised that her usually amiable uncle would utter such words. "Because he took your dog during one of his Labours? He didn't have a choice in the matter, and he returned Cerberus in the end!"

"Herakles also shot him in the shoulder to accomplish the deed," Eris reminded Junia. "And don't forget that he shot Mother in the breast with a poisoned arrow, for which she suffered terribly."

"That's awful," Junia agreed, "but Mom got better after Herakles rescued Prometheus from his rock, and she is now immune the effects of all poisons of the Earth, or something like that."

"Including the blessed wine of Dionysus," Eris muttered, "which brought joy – and sometimes death – to mortals."

"That was so much more than wine," Hades said good-naturedly, while the Titans laughed heartily at his words.

"Right," Junia agreed. "Besides, didn't Herakles take Mom's side in all things in the end, and by that, I mean when he became a god after his mortal death? And I know for a fact that he still considers himself the protector of Prometheus. I heard him say so years ago, right in front of you two," she added, gesturing at Hermes and Hades.

"And that, child, is the only reason why Hera acquiesced to Zeus' decree that she ought to accept him as one of her own children," Rhea said.

"But Zeus chooses not to see it that way," Klymene added. "Unlike Hera, Zeus considered Herakles a hero from the first simply by virtue of being born into the line he sired upon Io, which includes Perseus and others of his ilk. Zeus thought his mortal sons' deeds were meant to bring him great renown, which would serve to add to his glory everlasting. But not all heroes were intrinsically virtuous, like your brother Prometheus. Heroes were simply thought as such because they were exceptional in their own time, for reasons you and your young mortal cohort today would find terribly abhorrent. As would your mother, who of all the blessed gods who dwell on high Olympus, has evolved her way of thinking with the passage of Time more astutely than the rest of our immortal kin."

"So, my Mom hates heroes now?" Junia asked incredulously.

"No, child," Rhea answered exasperatedly. "Hera aims to foster a new *modus vivendi* among the stars that transcends heroism. One in which nature and culture will be one and the same, in much the same way that the People lived on Turtle Island before the European settlers came and broke their world."

"In much the same way as the people on the shores of Hellas once lived," Kronos said, "in those halcyon days when I was still King, and subsequently when Hera became the Queen of many a King in all the nations surrounding the ancient Inland Sea. Had I known then that Hera would have shown herself a better heir, more worthy of the Throne of Heaven, than her younger brother, I would have spared all my children the fate they met at their births and decreed that Hera ought to rule by my side for all Time!"

"What Kronos means to say," Hades interjected, partly to draw Rhea's attention away from her husband's disquieting admission, "is that Hera now understands all too well that her precious heroes of old are nothing more than renowned dunces – or worse yet, outright serial killers – with the unfair advantage of having even bigger idiots commemorate their deeds in stories and songs."

"Oh, come now," Hermes objected, having kept his peace for an amount of time quite contrary to his nature. "Not all heroes are –"

"You needn't venture far to see a fine specimen to prove my point," Hades interrupted. "Just go to my dining hall, and there you will find the still-living shell of that knave Pirithoüs, who along with Theseus thought it a good idea to come to my Kingdom to abduct my Persephone for his bride. He did not quite get his wish, although I met him halfway. He is now a permanent guest at my table, for he is forever glued to his seat!"

"I almost forgot about that wretch!" Eris giggled.

"And you know what happened to Theseus," Klymene added.

"*Everything* happened to Theseus," Junia answered, with a subdued eye roll, as the words of her kin began to take effect.

"Theseus slew the Minotaur and put an end to Minos' tyranny over the good people of Athens!" Hermes protested.

"And he deserted Minos' daughter Ariadne on the way home," Eris countered, "Even though she abandoned her father, her King and her country to help him!"

"Ariadne got the better end of the bargain," Hermes replied. "She now enjoys everlasting life on Olympus as the bride of Dionysus."

"And unlike the Queen of Olympus, she is quite receptive to the effects of her Lord's holy brew," Hades agreed.

"Theseus had his own son killed" Arke, twin sister of Iris of the rainbow wings, declared once she joined the gathering.

"That's because his wife Phaedra told him Hippolytus tried to rape her," Hermes explained, "when in fact the lad had no such appetites. The poor bastard ran afoul of Aphrodite because of his unmanly chastity, which is why she had Phaedra fall in love with the boy as a taunt."

"So, Aphrodite is worse than heroes," Junia said sardonically. "Got it."

"Oh, my dear girl," Arke said. "The gods of Olympus are so much *worse* than heroes. Even your dear mother, the Queen!"

"Especially your mother, the Queen," Hermes muttered in a stage whisper, though kept quiet after Junia answered with a murderous glower.

"It is true that, at times, your mother showed poor judgment in favouring some of the most celebrated of heroes that dwell in Elysium," Arke said. "Think of Jason of Iolcos, who sailed upon the Argo to Colchis to find the Golden Fleece. Your mother thought of leaving your father for him, you know-"

"Though at the time," Klymene explained, "Zeus had a mind to leave your mother for Thetis."

"Yes, well," Arke continued. "In the end Jason married Medea, that famous witch who murdered her own children in a fit of spite when Jason told her that he'd betray her for a younger woman. Do you know what happened to Medea after she died her mortal death? Why, she is right here, in Elysium, and is wed posthumously to mighty Achilles, son of Thetis. If you look behind that hedge, over there, you might even glimpse her!"

"That's one guy," Junia retorted. "One! And my Mom favoured Jason because he avenged a murder that was committed in her temple by Jason's uncle Pelias. So, she had her reasons to favour him above all others."

"If that were her sole reason, above all others, to favour Jason," Arke replied, "then how do you explain why Hera favoured the entire House of Atreus? They were outright twats – the whole lot of them! Do you not know how the tale began? With Atreus abducting his brother Thyestes' children, who sought refuge in Hera's temple, then cooking them and serving them up to Thyestes for supper. Did Hera punish Atreus for the impiety? No, no she did not. In fact, she remained a devoted protector of Atreus' sons, Agamemnon and Menelaus, when they led the Greeks in a ten-year war against Troy and her allies, all to bring Helen home after Paris abducted her. I'll bet you know that part of the tale."

"That's the same Helen whom Theseus abducted as a child after leaving Pirithoüs at my table," Hades added. "But go on, Arke."

"My Mom favoured Agamemnon because she wanted to see Troy burn to the ground," Junia said. "It's nothing to be proud of, but she had her reasons, and they're not what most people think."

"Be that as it may," Arke replied, "Agamemnon sacrificed his own daughter, Iphigeneia, to compel favourable winds to blow for their fleet to set sail towards Troy."

"Because he ran afoul of Artemis for not giving her due honour," Junia said. "But to get back to your point about heroes and gods being assholes, isn't Aphrodite the real villain here, for promising Paris the love of a married woman if he judged her to be the fairest? You know, after the whole kerfuffle at Thesis' wedding and whatnot?"

"What do you have to answer to that, *Eris*?" Hermes asked caustically.

"The golden apple I threw at that wedding was meant for Thetis, the bride," Eris answered. "It was a consolation gift for Zeus forcing her to marry that brute, Peleus, whom mortals also remember for some reason as a hero with glory everlasting. I cannot be blamed for the melee that ensued. And what about Athena, who along with Apollo, defended Orestes during his trial for murdering his mother Clytemnestra, who murdered Agamemnon upon his return from Troy to avenge Iphigeneia?"

"Apollo did what now?" Junia exclaimed.

"Oh yes," Eris replied. "Both Apollo and Athena defended Agamemnon and Clytemnestra's son, arguing that Orestes could not be guilty of killing a parent, as mothers are not blood kin to their children, only vessels for their father's seed!"

"Pallas would never have done such a thing, had she had ever met her true mother," Kronos chuckled, amused at Junia's genuine shock.

"Athena took the side of the murderer?" Junia asked incredulously. "She is a goddess of wisdom and justice and she took the side of a man who killed his own mother in cold blood?"

"Under the pretext that mothers are not kin to their children," Eris reiterated. "She wholeheartedly agreed with Apollo on that account, because she believes herself to be the child of Zeus alone, born fully armoured from his head!"

"Even though *mortals* know that Zeus devoured Athena's pregnant mother, my dearly missed sister Metis, shortly before she was due to give birth to the Thunderer's firstborn daughter," Klymene said.

"But she *had to* know the truth!" Junia exclaimed indignantly. "Apollo too! They are the smart ones on Olympus, after Mom and Eris!"

Hermes gave Junia a sideways glance upon hearing her words, but said nothing.

"A truth they conveniently ignored for the sake of *mercy*, or so they claimed at the time," Eris replied. "And what about you, *Hermes*? Were you not complicit in ushering the Age of Heroes when you murdered Argos, Hera's dear friend and protector, when she tasked him with guarding her hapless priestess Io, after Zeus turned the girl into a cow? Did you not aid and abet Perseus, one of Io's first notable descendants, who in the course of his heroic quest outright blinded our deathless kin, the Graeae, by throwing away their shared eye after he sought their counsel to find Medusa? And think of poor Medusa, innocent victim of Poseidon's unbridled lust, whom Athena turned into a monster for getting raped in her temple!"

"Now listen here –" Hermes griped.

"She has a point, you know," Arke said.

"You did have a role to play in ushering the Age of Wankers, Hermes," Iapetos agreed. "You are far from innocent in this matter."

"And now we have to put up with their vainglorious, self-indulgent lot here in the Isle of the Blessed until the End of all Time!" Kronos bantered as though he enjoyed the sight of Hermes losing the moral high ground against the Titan-Court.

Just as Junia prepared to add her voice to the chorus of the formerly damned, Eris pulled her aside without anyone else noticing.

"Follow me, quickly," the harbinger of Chaos said as a swirl of fractal shapes and lines blurred the very fabric of the Elysian noonday skies illuminating the abode of the mighty dead. "Don't worry about Hermes, he can hold his own against *those* wankers. Hurry!"

Nepheleid

Chapter Twelve

Long after starry Night shrouded the Heavens in her indigo mists, beckoning the gods of high Olympus to retire to their dwellings, Apollo lingered in his parlour. The god was strumming his lyre sedately as he beheld the rare spectacle of grey eyed Athena and valiant Ares studiously brawling over a game of checkers. The Lord of the golden bow was grateful for their presence, for the mortal boy Derek made for a poor companion, having fallen into a deep slumber as soon as his head hit his pillow in Apollo's guest quarters. Ares, who followed Derek and his impromptu retinue presumably on Hera's orders, asked to stay a while under the pretext that he relished pleasant company while awaiting Hermes' return from whatever errand currently drew him away from Olympus. For her part, Athena requested the same, which Apollo found rather aberrant given the Virgin Warrior's unabashed contempt for Ares, an unfortunate trait she shared with their father.

Also odd was Athena's willingness to engage the god of war in a game of checkers instead of her preferred game of chess. Perhaps this was because she believed Ares found the latter too cerebral for his brutish tastes, and the former lousy with carnage, albeit of a purely abstract nature. Apollo could not help but smile at Athena's disdain, for he knew that Ares was cleverer by far than the blessed gods of starry Olympus ever cared to admit, save perhaps for his mother and at least two of his sisters. In recent years, Apollo came to suspect that Hera's youngest son was, in fact, perhaps as clever as Junia, though the god of war did not present his genius to the world in the same disarming fashion as that of his little sister. Nor did Eris, for that matter, whose astuteness manifested in the most devastating ways imaginable. Apollo often wondered how Junia would have fared had Hera not relocated to Turtle Island all those years ago and raised her youngest child among the most learned minds of the CARINA Venture. Absent Prometheus' erudite nurturance, perhaps Junia would have ended up like Ares and Eris, expressing her unrelenting frustration at being ignored and misunderstood by her father until only battle and bloodshed, chaos and contention, relieved her of the ennui and licentious decadence of the Olympian Court.

Nepheleid

If ever Apollo questioned Hera's decision to appoint Ares and Eris as Junia's guardians and protectors, he soon came to genuinely appreciate his Queen's sagacity. Hera somehow anticipated that her youngest daughter would have a calming effect on the temperament of the bellicose twins, bringing out the best qualities in both. Truth be told, Apollo also found strange comfort in Ares' presence; though well capable of minding Derek on his own, the Archer knew that he could count on the god of war's assistance to safeguard the mortal should Dionysus decide to make good his promise to Aphrodite to turn the boy's mind and temperament to lasciviousness and indolence. As the Fates willed it, Derek remained so far blissfully ignorant of the role some immortals wished for him to play in their wicked games of one-upmanship.

As for Athena, Apollo remained at a loss in divining whether she also made her way to his parlour to safeguard the mortal, or if there was truth in her claim that she simply wished to pass the time until Hermes returned to Olympus. As if taking his cue from the Lord of the golden bow's idle thoughts, Hermes materialized on the steps of Apollo's palace, looking as though he was fighting off a swarm of angry bees he alone could see, the imaginary insects having seemingly pursued the messenger from realms unknown.

"Where is – I will *wring* her neck!" Hermes griped irately. "Eris! You impudent wench, show yourself!"

"Is something the matter, Brother?" Apollo asked casually beyond the open door of his parlour.

"Eris..." Hermes stammered. "That *bitch*! She did it again! She started another sparring match, but this time among the Titans who dwell on the White Island in Elysium. Then she spirited Junia away while I was distracted! Have you –"

"We have not seen either of them, Hermes," Athena said before the messenger could finish his sentence. "And why were you in Elysium with Junia and Eris?"

"Junia wanted to see Klymene one last time before leaving on the Nephele," Hermes answered. "Or at least, that was what she told me. Now, I am *certain* that she and Eris had other plans, and that they meant for me to lose track of them somewhere in Hades' Kingdom."

"If Eris is with Junia," Ares said calmly, "then you have nothing to fear.

She's not in danger, though the hour grows late, and Mother will eventually take heed that Junia is not sleeping soundly in her bed. If I know my twin, she will turn up soon enough with Junia and no one else will be the wiser. Your move, Pallas."

To Apollo's surprise, Ares' words had an uncharacteristically reassuring effect on Hermes' nigh apoplectic state of mind. This gave the Archer pause, after which he began to wonder whether Ares underwent a complete personality change during his sojourns on the Nephele. Otherwise, the handsome, armoured colossus seated at his table, playing a game of checkers with grey-eyed Athena was probably an impostor, and the real Ares probably lay trapped somewhere orbiting the Earth, caught inside an escape pod that prematurely ejected from the airlock, or some similarly outlandish nonsense.

"That is not what I dread the most," Hermes said after a moment.

"Oh? Do tell," Athena inquired.

"Just before Eris used her special talents on the Titan-Court," Hermes explained, "our grandsires were admonishing Junia against following in the footsteps of heroes – telling her all sorts of tales about their impiety and malfeasance despite their notable deeds, and that it would be wisest for her to leave behind the world of gods and men!"

"That is odd," Ares pondered aloud.

"Repudiate heroes and leave the Earth?" Athena asked. "That makes little sense!"

"And you think that Eris prompted the Titans to fill Junia's head with this nonsense?" Apollo inquired.

"That is the part for which I remain unsure," Hermes replied. "As far as I know, the Titans were forever Hera's staunchest allies, doing all that they could, even from their former prison in gloomy Tartarus, to help her and Prometheus bring the CARINA Venture to completion! Why would they suddenly change their minds about the righteousness and heroism of the learned mortals under our Queen's care, and still beckon Junia to leave with them on the Nephele?"

"And why would they spit on heroes," Athena agreed, "if heroism is the one virtue Hera has always extolled mortals to cultivate above all others, in whatever capacity they could?"

Nepheleid

"Is Mother not Kronos' favourite child?" Ares asked. "Did he not consistently comfort and give her solace whenever Father made her existence intolerable? It makes no sense that Kronos or his Titan brothers would ever disparage Mother's great work, or the mortals she chooses to uphold."

"Right," Athena acquiesced, as if surprised that she and Ares would ever be of the same mind.

"Well yes, it was all so very bizarre," Hermes continued, "almost as if Eris used her powers of inducing confusion to create a diversion until I was left alone with that lot, while she took Junia away –"

"Eris is capable of many things," Ares interrupted, "however sabotaging Mother's plans would never cross her twisted mind even at the worst of times. Eris fully intends to join us up there on that City-ship, and she would not even for a second have Junia consider seeding the stars with Earthly Life to be a fool's pursuit. You must be mistaken, Hermes."

"You know full well that Eris does whatever she wants whenever she pleases," Hermes protested, "filial piety be damned!"

"Eris always has a reason for doing the things she does," Ares replied. "Though it might take even the cleverest among us some time to determine what, exactly, that reason is," he added, giving Athena a sideways glance.

"Flawless logic, as always," Athena retorted sarcastically.

"Unless," Apollo interjected, "this whole business of scorning heroes was not Eris' doing at all. Perhaps the Titans themselves have another motive, of which we remain entirely ignorant. The last time we encountered the Titans on the steps of Hades' palace, I prophesied that the Titans would join Hera on the Nephele, which in hindsight explains why they were helping our Queen in all her endeavours until now. Since it is Kronos' prerogative to see all things that transpire through Time, be it in the past, present, or future, he probably foretold that helping Hera in all her undertakings would eventually win him and his Court their freedom from their prison in gloomy Tartarus. In a way, he proved correct, however I doubt he knew that he and his Titan brothers would end up ruling Elysium instead."

"You never told us that," Athena said.

"No, I did not," Apollo retorted.

"You should have said something," Athena rebuked. "The Titans were still Father's enemies until the moment they made their truce."

"There was no need," Apollo replied, "as their interests aligned with ours immediately after we found Hera bound to the tree in the Garden of the Hesperides. But Ares is right – space exploration and off-world colonization are by far the bravest, most heroic pursuits humanity is capable of undertaking, which is why it makes little sense that the Titans should be trivializing that which falls under our Queen's purview. I am eager to uncover what madness afflicts the Titans that they should make Junia question the glorious fate her mother has in store for her. Surely Hera means for Junia to achieve greatness, otherwise she would not dote on her as much as she does."

Ares furrowed his brow. "Mother told me she never plays favourites among her children, as Father does," he said. "And I believe her."

"This is not about favouritism," Apollo replied. "It's about heroism as a pathway to attain godhood. If Junia truly is somewhere between mortal and deathless, by virtue of the strange circumstances surrounding her conception and birth, then perhaps Hera will allow Junia to choose immortality by other means than remaining on Olympus to dwell among the gods. In fact, I think this is the only reason why she agreed to allow Junia to make the choice she was given in the first place, because she knows that her daughter would never choose to live forever in a realm where Zeus remains King."

"You sound fairly sure of yourself on that account," Hermes mused.

"Of all of us gathered here," Apollo replied, "I have known Hera the longest."

"You forget yourself, Phoebus," Athena retorted. "You are Zeus' eldest son, that is true, yet I am and, to this day remain his firstborn. I have known Hera since she was a Maiden Queen, then the Queen to many a King Consort in all the nations of the broad-pathed Earth, as well as Father's favourite sister, until she became *his* wife and Queen."

"So, you agree that Hera most likely intends for Junia to become immortal by other means," Apollo inquired, "once she and her crewmates on the City-ship Nephele are safely out of reach from Father's influence."

Nepheleid

"That is possible," Athena said. "However, there is more than one way for a mortal to achieve deathlessness. Perhaps the Titans were trying to spare Junia the horrible demise that Herakles endured before he wed Hebe and became a god himself."

"Junia cannot perish in the flames of any funeral pyre," Ares said flatly. "Otherwise, she would have burned up before reaching Olympus that night she jumped out of the airlock on the Nephele. Had I been mortal, I surely would have died of a heart attack myself when I saw the fireball falling to Earth. But Mother was unconcerned for her safety. Junia is more immortal than not, if there is such a thing as degrees of immortality. I'll have you know, there is *no doubt* in my mind that Mother has plans for Junia, which I trust are in the child's best interest, above even her own."

Athena gave Ares a startled look, as if the god of war unwittingly spoke some inspired words of wisdom without realizing what he had done. Apollo wondered whether in her brazenness, the Virgin Warrior forgot how close Hera had become with her older children in recent years, while repudiating the once close friendship she and Athena used to enjoy. However, Apollo sincerely held hope that Hera might forget her displeasure and honour the promise she once made to all her fellow immortals on the upper deck of the Polaris to let anyone who wanted to leave Olympus join her crew aboard the Nephele. If Hera was willing to forgo her ceaseless rancour against those who in the past transgressed against her sovereignty or the sanctity of her marriage-bed, then there might be a chance that she would forgive Athena for sabotaging her newfound freedom in favour of upholding the precarious peace of holy Olympus.

If she chose not to forgive Athena for her own sake, then perhaps Hera might soften her heart towards the Virgin Warrior out of the unfailing gratitude the Queen still held for Metis, who devised the plot Zeus enacted to free his siblings from the prison of Kronos' belly. Hera once confessed to Apollo in a shared dream that she once loved the Oceanid for her cleverness and her benevolence as well as for the part she played in her release from her father's tyranny. In the years since he became cognizant of Hera's affection for Athena's mother, who now dwelt in the prison of Zeus' mind; Apollo came to regret ever thinking that mothers were not their children's kin. Also, the realization that Hera once loved another primarily for the brilliance of their mind gladdened Apollo's heart in ways he dared not fathom, as if the very idea transgressed some imaginary boundary beyond which no god or mortal could tread.

"There is also the possibility," Ares said, rescuing Apollo from his own thoughts, "that the Titans are loath to see Hera leave the Earth on the Nephele, never to return. Perhaps that is why they tried to weaken Junia's resolve?"

"But the Titans no longer dwell in Tartarus," Athena replied. "They no longer have need of Hera's influence as Queen of Olympus to advocate on their behalf."

"And Rhea was the one who was most insistent that Junia abandon the Earth and take to the stars, without a second glance at the broad-pathed Earth," Hermes added.

"That still does not add up," Apollo said, shaking his head slightly.

"The thought occurred to me," Hermes continued, "while I was escorting Junia back to Olympus on the Hub, that she might want to return to the Underworld to retrieve Grandfather's sickle for some reason –"

"Do not let her," Ares interrupted.

"Of course not," Hermes answered. "But perhaps that is the true reason why she and Eris wanted to travel to Hades' Kingdom – to retrieve the weapon, in case Father were to overrule her decision to leave Olympus and join the crew of the Nephele."

"You mean as *insurance*?" Athena asked.

Ares shifted in his seat, as if ready to rise to his feet at a moment's notice.

"Junia is the only one among us who never swore an Oath of fealty to Father, after our insurrection failed all those centuries ago, for which Hera bore the brunt of the blame," Apollo said. "Junia could lawfully challenge Father's supremacy if he ever failed to uphold his word and let her, and Hera, join the crew of the Nephele. Hera knows this as well."

"Mother did not send Junia to fetch Kronos' sickle," Ares protested crossly.

"Perhaps not," Athena agreed, "but what if the Titans are planning to rise up against Olympus? Think about it, Father would never suspect it, not after granting them a place of privilege in Elysium among the blessed dead. Perhaps they are using Junia as a pawn, without compromising Hera or the Oath she swore to Zeus by the Holy River Styx to never again revolt against his rule. I would not be surprised if Hera knows nothing of this, caring only to leave Olympus once Junia comes of age!"

Apollo nodded, lowering his head to hide his creeping smile. He could not help but admire the astuteness of his elder sister, even if his virile pride inhibited him from voicing such thoughts in the presence of Hermes and Ares.

"We need to find Eris and Junia at once," Athena continued, while Ares rose to his feet.

"Eris is *not* on a quest to retrieve the sickle!" the god of war bellowed. "Have you forgotten that she is also bound to the same Oath of fealty we all swore when Zeus hanged Mother from the Sky? As for Junia, I stopped her myself the last time she had the weapon in hand. I'll be damned if I ever catch either of them waggling that blade anywhere near Father's balls, for their sake rather than his!"

"No one is getting anywhere near Father's balls tonight," Hermes interjected. "With or without sharp objects. It might well be a mercy that Zeus loses his appetite for carnal pleasures whenever Hera spurns him for too long. I will go find the girls, though by now I'm fairly certain that neither Eris nor Junia are anywhere near the Underworld at this point."

"I'm going with you," Ares declared, almost thumping his chest for emphasis.

Athena threw Apollo a questioning glance, to which the Archer replied, "there is no need for you to go, Ares. I will go in your stead. You can remain here and make yourself at home. There is a greater chance that I will find Junia by tracking her mind across the broad-pathed Earth, as I once did as a matter of course when she was a small child."

"You can do as you like, Phoebus," Ares said. "But I'll not sit here and remain idle while Junia is out there, being used as a puppet by the Titans. Besides, you have a mortal guest to mind."

"Right," Apollo replied, having all but forgotten about the slumbering Derek.

"Derek is fast asleep, is he not?" Athena asked.

"Hypnos and Morpheus saw to it themselves," Apollo answered. "The lad is not likely to awaken until well past sunrise. He will be safe with Ares."

"You are not leaving without me," Ares griped. "Not if you're going after Eris and Junia."

"Well, we can't leave the mortal here alone!" Hermes protested. "That would be bloody rude!"

Apollo raised an eyebrow. "All right then," he said. "I will try to find them through other means. If we are lucky, they will follow my call to my doorstep, and we can all sort this out and then get some sleep."

Placing his lyre on the polished marble floor, the Archer sat back in his chair and closed his eyes. He took a deep breath, willing the stars to shine like beacons in the darkening Night to beckon Eris and Junia to return to Olympus.

Please do not leap out of the Sky this time, his mind pleaded facetiously to the young Junia, *otherwise the King and Queen will know that something is terribly amiss, and we will never hear the end of it!*

Nepheleid

Chapter Thirteen

"So, are you going to tell me what the hell that was all about back there?" Junia griped indignantly once she stepped on the other side of the portal, following Eris to parts unknown in the vast Cosmos.

"Did your mortal *sensei* never teach you and the other children at the CARINA school about the usefulness of distraction while evading potential conflict?" Eris answered coyly, closing the portal behind Junia with a counterclockwise motion of her hand. In the span of a mortal heartbeat, the swirl of spinning stars collapsed into a central point, leaving no trace in the misty, colourless realm where the sisters now found themselves.

"I absolutely understand the usefulness of distraction as a means to protect life and limb," Junia replied, looking over her shoulder to see for herself that nothing remained of the opening between the worlds. "But that doesn't explain what the hell happened back there. I mean, with the Titans, calling heroes wankers and whatnot. And speaking of Titans, we forgot to get my sickle back from the Underworld! What the hell, Eris?"

"Again, with the sickle!" Eris sighed. "Really Junia, you truly are of a single mind. Sometimes I wonder whether you are beginning to take more after Father than Mother as your flower comes to bloom."

"I know you're only trying to get a rise out of me," Junia retorted, "so I'll pretend you didn't say that. But seriously, where is my sickle?"

"Perhaps I ought to start calling you Zoe, as Father does."

"That's not funny, Eris!"

"Oh, but it is."

"What about my *sickle*!" Junia griped, almost tapping her foot with her growing pique, then realizing that the ground upon which her feet treaded was soft and yielding. This gave Junia a most uneasy feeling with each step she took in this strange realm.

"What about it?" Eris repeated farcically.

"Isn't it the entire reason why we came all the way down here and ditched Hermes for? To get the sickle back from the Titans so that when Eros shows up on Olympus to confront Mom about filing for divorce or whatever, I can face him and, if I really have to, then cut a bitch? By the way, where *are* we? This does not look like anywhere I've ever seen in the Underworld-"

Indeed, the soft, spongy floor could not account for the dizzying fractal swirls of light that spun around Junia without rhyme or reason, in shapes and patterns that do, in fact, occur in the natural world, but not in so many hues imperceptible to the human eye. Though accustomed to perceiving the world through the lenses with which the learned mortals taught her since earliest childhood, Junia now saw her surroundings in unfamiliar gradients of blue, red, and violet, shifting and flitting in unexpected directions every time she shifted her gaze away from Eris.

"First of all," the goddess of discord pontificated patiently, "I already told you that we are not here to retrieve the sickle. If Kronos' mighty weapon were to appear on Olympus, then it would have to do so by other means. Second, the Titans are no longer in possession of the sickle. Hades alone knows where it is hidden, for he was last to leave the Garden of the Hesperides on the day you wielded it for the last time, and it was no longer there when Mother and I returned shortly thereafter."

"Then we must go back and ask him-"

"No!" Eris said sharply in a most uncharacteristic manner. "We will do no such thing. I told you we came here to seek out Elder Gods on our own behalf, and that is precisely what we will do. Now stop sulking and come meet the *Protogenoi*. And mind your tongue, for even mighty Zeus does not dare to cross the indomitable Primordial Powers of the Cosmos..."

"Or else?"

"Precisely."

"Wow – okay, fine!" Junia conceded at last. "Jesus!"

"... will not be found among those we seek, at least not today," Eris replied sardonically, while Junia contorted her lips into a rictus to hide her smile from her winged chaos-mongering sibling.

"Okay," Junia said after some time. "I get that we're here to meet some powerful gods, but *where* are we even? I get the feeling that we're not in Hades' Kingdom anymore..."

"Astute as ever," Eris replied without irony.

"I mean, the ground feels like I'm walking on a lichen field in Spring, but we're nowhere near the Arctic tundra, that much I know, and also it's Autumn, so... *where* are we?"

"Wrong question, little one," Eris answered without answering.

"Okay," Junia said, knowing the familiar game Eris was now playing. "Who are we?"

"No," Eris replied.

"What are we?" Junia tried again.

"Nope."

"When are we, why are we, why, why, *why*?" Junia continued, resisting the urge to break into song for emphasis.

"*When* is correct,' Eris answered at last. "We are nowhere bound by Time; we are at the point where Chaos begat Earth, Tartarus, and Eros, the most powerful being in the Universe."

"Eros again," Junia sulked.

"Yes... Eros," Eris answered. "A true Child of Chaos, the bringer of Life and the force that binds the Cosmos together."

"I thought that was gravity," Junia retorted.

"When you're right..." Eris said, her voice lilting into nothingness as she and her young charge drew near a luminous oblong form floating above them, if such naïve concepts as "above" or "below" even applied in this cosmic realm. This plane was unbound by the laws of Newtonian physics as the most learned mortals of the broad-pathed Earth understood their world to be.

Nepheleid

"Let me guess," Junia said snidely. "The Cosmic Egg?"

"Why yes, it is!" Eris answered in the manner of a game show host from Turtle Island in the late twentieth century.

"About to hatch and burst forth into an infinite number of universes, where an infinite number of potentialities will realize themselves into an infinite number of outcomes?"

Eris nodded.

"Meaning that it really doesn't matter *what* we're doing here," Junia continued, "since the outcome in *our* universe is already decided?"

Eris answered with a wink but said nothing.

"So, you took me all this way to the realm of Chaos at the beginning of Time," Junia said, "just to sit back and hang out and eat popcorn with the Primordial Gods of the Cosmos while watch it all go to Hades in a handbasket?"

"Something like that, but without the popcorn," Eris said. "And without Hades. This does not concern him."

"Okay," Junia replied. "Bun-less hotdogs then?"

"No," Eris answered. "You've had quite a few at supper with Mother and Derek. I would be loath if it caused you to suffer from indigestion, as unfortunately happened with the wisest and most learned philosophers of old Hellas –"

"ENOUGH!" boomed a voice from above – or yonder, depending on one's perspective in this unfathomable place.

Junia reflexively took a step backwards, then froze in place.

"They can see you, all of them, in their singularity," Eris tittered.

"You're using the word wrong," Junia half-whispered, still in shock.

"Junia Argosi," Eris said in a mock formal manner, "meet Eros the Elder, also called Phanes among the gods – the source of all that lives and all that will ever be. Even the King and Queen of Olympus bend to his inexorable will, though not always with each other... Mighty Lord, this is Junia, daughter of Hera, whom you summoned from fields of starlight across the farthest recesses of the Cosmos to see the work of our Mother, the Queen, come to completion."

"Wait, what?" Junia stammered in a low voice. "Eris, are you talking to the Egg?"

"Squint harder, little one," Eris answered. "And you will gaze upon winged Eros, after whom golden Aphrodite named her own bow-wielding little shit of a son. A fair warning, though. Once you've gazed upon the oldest and most powerful immortal in all the Cosmos, you will find Apollo's comeliness somewhat disappointing once we return to Olympus. Ah well. I suppose his light has already begun to dim in your eyes after that little revelation courtesy of the Titans –"

"Zoe," the voice said amiably, in a volume more befitting for human ears, or the ears of one who always strove to pass for mortal even among her exiled, deathless kin.

Junia blinked, as both her mothers, Prometheus, Asia, and Mnemosyne among many others, instructed her to do countless times to appear more human when in the company of strangers. As she opened her eyes, Junia beheld a winged being whose pure, golden light did not sting her eyes, and whose ineffable beauty rivalled that of white-armed Hera. Unlike the Queen of Olympus though, Eros appeared neither distinctly male nor female, but a combination of both. Junia took a breath, her mind awash in consternation and a mild, creeping sense of confusion as the very centre of her being began to tingle with a sensation she had so far only felt when dreaming of Apollo, and more recently when consciously thinking of Derek as the Archer's more attainable substitute.

"One cannot *will* away what is fated, young one, no matter how hard one tries," Eros the Elder said is a soft, calming voice. "Nor can one *will* love into being, or *will* it away for that matter. The latter is a lesson your exalted mother refuses to learn, but that is no concern of yours. She must face my trials, as mortal heroes face hers, to prove herself worthy of the throne of Heaven, which her father would have bestowed upon her alone if his will had been obeyed in the first place. But even the mighty Titan-King Kronos must bend to Fate."

"Right," Junia replied weakly, failing at mimicking bravery before a being possessing more ineffable power than her mother and father combined. She felt rather foolish at that moment for ever thinking that she could cut him with her grandfather's sickle, or mar his perfect, deathless form in any way and live to tell the tale.

Eros gave Junia a smile, causing her belly to flutter in a most surprising yet not altogether unpleasant way. "As for the boy, Derek," the Lord Eros said, "it would be best for you to put all thoughts of pursuing him out of your mind, as he loves another. So does Apollo, for that matter, but this infatuation will abate in all due time. Do not abandon all hope on that front, young one."

"Yeah," Junia said more confidently, having at last found her voice. "Thanks, but no. Hard pass."

"You appear determined to repeat your mother's mistakes," Eros chided gently, as if to a slow-witted child.

"My mother's only mistake was to let you drive her chariot to deliver her to Zeus at her wedding," Junia retorted defensively.

"Junia," Eris said with alarm, deploying her wings protectively around her young sister as if to safeguard her from the wrath of Eros.

"I have no mind to harm the Princess of Olympus," Eros told Eris, raising his hand in an appeasing gesture. To Junia he said, "Your tongue is sharp as your grandfather's sickle, young Zoe, and you wield it in much the same way as your mother uses her considerable cleverness as a sword against her foes. But your father is not among them. This is a lesson your mother needs to learn as well, and for which your father needs to be reminded. I have blessed your parents' union from the first, and I do not make mistakes, unlike the Titans born of Earth and Heaven, the gods born of the Titans, and the mortals born of the gods in all the nations of the world."

"Okay, I... I believe I said it was *her* mistake, not yours," Junia stammered.

"How can you stand here before me," Eros said, "with your sister by your side, and tell me that you are of the mind that your mother and father's union was a mistake? You are far too young to envy the dead, even so as the name your radiant mother the Queen chose to bestow upon you, your true secret name that she hid even from your father, signifies "Life"."

"Hey, I'm not jumping off bridges here –"

"You jumped out of the airlock, remember?" Eris said in a stage whisper, half-covering her mouth for effect.

"That's because I needed to talk to Phoebus or someone to get clarity," Junia protested. "And I don't regret it one bit! That was the night I found out just how awful Zeus is, and my Earth-dive removed all doubt from my mind about why I will never, *ever* live on Olympus if I can help it. It also helped Mom out of her funk and decide once and for all that she was done with Zeus."

"Would you care to elaborate on why you slander your father so?" Eros demanded.

"You've got to be kidding me," Junia sneered. "Really? I mean, you're basically Almighty-God-Squared. Do I really have to spell it out for you?"

"Humour me," Eros replied.

"For one, he's a controlling jerk," Junia said. "He actually thinks that he can bring order to the random vicissitudes of the Cosmos, and throws tantrum when anyone demonstrates that no, he cannot do such a thing, that even he is subject to the random whims of –"

"The fecund chaos that is an essential condition to all Life and Creation," Eris agreed.

"Right," Junia continued. "And he's a total hypocrite! He sleeps with everyone and *everything* and still expects Mom to be faithful to him and play the dutiful wife when she's clearly fed up with his crap! Everyone knows this! And still, he insists that others embody abstract notions of virtue and excellence, while he acts as though his own rules, the ones he made up to bring order to Chaos and whatnot, do not apply to him! Have you even met any of the bimbos at his Court on high Olympus? The ones he keeps to amuse himself when Mom wants nothing to do with him? I mean, take Dionysus' mother, Semele. She died fair and square, in a manner deserving of a Darwin award, if those things existed back then. This mortal *spontaneously combusted* when she asked Zeus to show himself to her in his true godly form! This is a woman who by all rights should be dead and dwelling in Elysium with all the other vapid lickspittles. However, she now lives – that's right – *lives* on Olympus under a different name. And Zeus expects Mom to just accept it and get on with it, when *he* will fly in a rage at the very thought of Mom dwelling among learned mortals, many of whom are *men* who genuinely and innocently admire her for her intelligence and her talents. Oh – that reminds me, we need to go back soon to check on Derek."

Nepheleid

"He'll be fine," Eris reassured her. "Right now, he's sleeping like a baby in Apollo's guest quarters. No harm will come to him as long as he remains in the arms of Morpheus... not literally though!"

"So, you think your father unworthy of Kingship?" Eros asked, bringing back Junia's attention to the matter at hand.

"That's putting it politely," Junia replied. "And why is *he* even King anyway? I'm sure he was good at fighting Titans and Giants and monsters back in the day, but now, well... It's not as if he even cares about humans or what they do. Except, of course, to have sex with some of them or complain that they've gotten smarter and more upwardly mobile that he has in the last thousand years. Yeah, that. And let's not forget what he did to Prometheus, not just stealing him away from Mom at his birth, but also torturing him for his act of kindness towards humans that led them to *become* smarter than even the gods of Olympus."

"And what of your divine mother, the Queen?" Eros asked. "Have you no misgivings about her ruling over the mortals under her care as their Goddess-Queen?"

"No, I don't, I really don't," Junia replied warily. "That's because, unlike Zeus, she actually cares about what happens to mortals, especially the ones setting out to colonize other planets. She *chose* to accompany them in their long voyage because she wants to make sure they don't all die in the vacuum of space mid-trip. And she has higher standards when it comes to choosing mortals and preparing them for greatness, no matter what the Titans said."

"Ah yes," Eros said. "You mentioned the vapid sycophants in Elysium. I see the Titans already had that discussion with you. And yet, you insist that your mother's chosen are different?"

"Mom chooses heroes among mortals by their qualities, not because they were born of Zeus or Poseidon's seed," Junia answered. "If anything, I'm growing increasingly convinced that most of the heroes who dwell in Elysium turned into dicks *because* they were descended from Zeus. I don't know, maybe knowing that his seed watered their family trees went straight to their heads? Meanwhile, my Mom laboured endlessly to challenge worthy mortals into greatness and got nothing but slander and hate for her efforts. I mean, she's not perfect and makes mistakes like everyone else but, unlike Zeus, she is capable of learning from her errors and making amends. You know... to evolve and grow as a person.

Mom understands that Life is Chaos, yet she can and will adapt to changing circumstances and become all the better for it, while Zeus would rather have the entire waking world stagnate into oblivion so as not to upset his limited view of how things ought to be. So no, I don't think he's worthy of being King, if he ever was, and I also know that my Mom deserves better than having him as a husband!"

"Now, Junia," Eris muttered. "Tell us how you really feel."

"I hear your words," Eros said after a long pause. "You have given me much to ponder. But for now, know that I have not yet absolved loud-thundering Zeus of his sins begotten by his hubris. Know that he, too, must face my trials and continue to prove himself worthy of remaining Consort to the Queen of Heaven. But make no mistake, the Queen shall not rule the Heavens beyond the firmament of broad-pathed Earth alone, even if you will it so."

"I'm afraid you're mistaken, Lord Eros," Junia replied tremulously, still reeling from her rant. "My mother left it up to me to decide whether or not I will leave with the crew of the Nephele, and I've already long decided that I will go. And if I go, that means she is free to go with me, and she will, obviously. There's nothing that Zeus or Aphrodite, or any of the other gods of Olympus can do about it."

"Are your grievances against your royal father truly your own, young Zoe?" Eros asked. "And by that, I mean, have you chosen your fate for your own sake, or for that of your mother?"

"Both," Junia answered after a moment. "My Mom doesn't want to stay on Olympus, and neither do I. Neither do many of my siblings and some of my cousins. My choosing the Nephele opens a lot of possibilities, for myself and everyone else, which completely cease to exist if Zeus has his way and I stay."

"You would tear Olympus asunder by choosing this fate?" Eros inquired.

"I would choose the fate I find most suited for myself and my family," Junia replied. "If Zeus chooses to tear Olympus asunder because he can't deal with the consequences of the wager he made with my Mom when he pretty much blackmailed her into returning to Olympus with me when I was little, then that's on him. I have no *mind* to harm Olympus, and I can't be blamed if Zeus throws a tantrum because he's not getting his way."

Nepheleid

Eris clasped her hands in a dramatic gesture. "Our little girl is growing up," she said facetiously, cocking her head to the side.

"Your sister is correct," Eros told Junia. "It takes a lot of maturity to realize that you ought not to bear the responsibility for choices that others have made on your behalf through no fault of your own, even if you stand to suffer the consequences. However, you must know that any choice you make will have far-reaching consequences, beyond anything you might ever have intended."

"And you're going to show me what will happen if I do either?"

"No, I will not," Eros answered. "I am certain that Eris has told you about the ways in which all potential outcomes exist simultaneously until –"

"I make a choice and collapse the wave function?" Junia interrupted.

"If that is how you choose to understand it," Eros said with a smile, "then yes."

"So... is that why I'm here?" Junia asked. "I already knew that the messed-up situation on Olympus is not my fault, not really, and that I'm only responsible for my own actions. Okay, maybe also for Derek's safety."

Eros smiled at the sisters. "Go home, then," he said benevolently, as Eris bowed deferentially then wrapped Junia protectively in her wings for the journey back to Olympus. "Mind only the things that are in your power to wield, young one," Lord Eros continued, "and do tend to your mortal friend. He will have many questions when he regains consciousness."

"Wait... what?"

"He'll be *fine*! Really!" Eris insisted as she jumped in the eye of the portal with Junia in tow. Then in a softer voice, she whispered, "Eventually."

Chapter Fourteen

Roused by a full bladder from the deepest, most peaceful sleep he ever experienced in his short life, Derek awoke to the sound of four distinct voices arguing somewhere in the front room of Dr. Archer's luxurious vacation home. Momentarily alarmed by his complete ignorance of the location of the bathroom, Derek staggered towards the door and quietly exited the guest bedchamber. Tiptoeing around the vast hallway in search of the Holy of Holies, he tried to remain unseen as he walked by the parlour, lest his host, who was currently entertaining Dr. Weiss, as well as Ares and Zippy, think him an ungrateful eavesdropper out to spy on his school friend's strange relatives in their unnatural habitat. At least he *hoped* that they were all members of Junia's extended family, otherwise he shuddered to think of a reason why more than half of the bedsheet-clad vacationers he had met so far referred to Mr. Diaz as "Father".

As far as Derek knew, Junia's progenitor was no priest, at least not one who belonged to any Christian denomination known to man or beast. And yet, Mr. Diaz seemed oddly familiar to him, well beyond the expected, albeit imperceptible resemblance that little Junebug bore to her father. Despite Dr. Argosi's insistence earlier that day, Derek was almost certain that he had never met the man before while dwelling at Borealis. And yet, the big guy reminded Derek of a weird dream he once had as a boy, in which Junia's mother threw a man out the highest window of her office at the CARINA-ALSESTIS Headquarters' sole high-rise building. Strangely enough, in Derek's dream the man, who should have rightfully been partially liquefied by his fall, rose from where he landed – on his feet, no less – and began to speak to Junia, Eris, and Ares as a father telling his children not to be home too late for supper. On second thought, perhaps Derek's mind somehow, for reasons yet unknown, conflated an absent paternal figure from Junia's early childhood with the very real and very intense Mr. Diaz.

That must be it. He's just a man who's in charge of this naturalist commune-resort-cult homestead place, whatever this place actually is, and he happens to be Junia's biological father. And Dr. Argosi's ex-husband.

Derek bit his lip, gladdened by the thought that the uncommonly beautiful Dr. Argosi was once attracted to males at another time in her life. However, having met her former spouse, Derek understood why Junia's mother could have felt compelled to change teams and raise her child with another woman in a domestic partnership arrangement.

Still, there is no way that Dr. Argosi could have catapulted Mr. Diaz from her office window with enough force to have him land across the plaza, no matter how toned and healthy she has kept herself for as long as I've known her. And there is no way Mr. Diaz could have survived the fall, no matter how much air drag his massive body could generate in freefall. Now, where the hell is the bathroom? A pretty man like Dr. Archer surely has a full spa somewhere in his home...

Unable to locate the lavatory without risking detection, Derek made his way towards the garden through an open window, then climbed down an elaborately ornate column, landing feet first on a row of blooming larkspurs.

"Aw, sh–" he muttered under his breath, then held his tongue for fear of being caught in the act of fleeing the mansion occupied by the Nephele's future head physician to piddle in the latter's flower beds. Once he felt secure in the knowledge that he was well and truly alone, he watered the garden, until he regained the state of unmitigated joy that only an empty bladder can provide. Unsure whether he could make the climb back up the column through the open window above him, Derek reconnoitred the grounds for another point of entry into Dr. Archer's palace. Finding none, he resolved to enter through the open front doors, making his peace with the potential embarrassment of having to explain to Dr. Archer why he ended up befouling his lovely garden after failing to find a bathroom in his home without sneaking into the master bedroom.

Derek's trepidation proved inconsequential, however, for he soon saw Ares, Zippy, and Dr. Weiss vanish into thin air, while Dr. Archer slumped motionless in his seat, his eyes shut, his chest neither rising nor falling, as if he had been struck dead.

"What the – Dr. Archer! Are you OK? Can you hear me? Oh crap... Crap, crap, crap. Stay here, I'll call for help!"

"There is no need, young one," said a bearded, long-haired local with an affectation for draping himself in vine leaves and a very realistic looking faux leopard pelt. "Your gracious host will not come to harm."

"JESUS!" Derek exclaimed in surprise. "How long have you been here? Don't just stand there, help me give him CPR!"

"I assure you, our dear friend is quite all right," said the apparent counter culturist. "Dr. Archer," he added with a knowing grin, "is not dead – he is meditating."

"Uh, what?" Derek asked, feeling foolish and confused.

"Do you not see that the colour has not drained from his cheeks?" the interloper continued. "Does he not look completely at peace? I assure you, he will awaken when he is done his repose, and then you will find him as hale as anyone you've ever seen in your entire mortal life."

"Wh–" Derek uttered as he tried to conjure up a coherent reply to the mysterious stranger.

"Oh my… you look troubled," said the eccentric draped in furs and vegetation. "Please, do come with me, so that Lord Apollo may enjoy some peace and quiet as he ponders the Mysteries of the Cosmos."

"You want me to come with you?" Derek retorted incredulously.

The annoyingly placid man nodded. "Also," he said, "my name is not Jesus, it's Dionysus."

Derek stared at the man, his eyes wide with bewilderment. "Dio… Dennis?" he tried to repeat the name he had just heard a second ago.

"Dennis is close enough, young one," replied not-Jesus. "Now come, back to the banquet hall with you, you look troubled."

"But I'm not wearing… pants," Derek said, as if suddenly realizing that he wore only a flimsy undershirt and boxer shorts.

"I assure you, young one, this will bother absolutely no one."

"Uh, Dennis," Derek stammered as his cheeks flushed an embarrassingly bright shade of crimson. "Could we not? I mean, Dr. Argosi told me to get up early to meet her at her place for breakfast… and…"

Nepheleid

"The Great Lady must not be denied," the man replied. "I understand completely, even more than you can possibly know. But first, since you are wide awake and your nervous system appears on the verge of fibrillating, why not come join me for a tipple at my dwelling? I assure you it will at the very least calm your nerves."

"Uh, okay," Derek conceded. "But... Dennis? Where did the others go? Dr. Weiss and Ares and –"

"They left," the dishevelled crank answered. "And they will return before anyone's the wiser. Now come... this way."

Derek followed the leopard-pelt-clad wonder along an unkempt pathway between the far end of Dr. Archer's home and a neighbouring woodland that looked wild and overgrown in comparison to his host's manicured garden.

"Those are the grounds belonging to Artemis," the oddball told Derek. "She is Apollo's twin sister. I do not believe you've met her yet. She delights in spending her days and nights frolicking in the newly rewilded places of the Earth, in the company of women unburdened by the duties of marriage and children."

Derek looked at his strange companion and slowed his pace for a fraction of a second. He thought he heard him call Dr. Archer 'Apollo' earlier, but surely, he must have meant 'Paul', like the friend he was sent to accompany back to the Nephele a lifetime ago. Was that even Dr. Archer's first name, Derek wondered, as it dawned upon him that he never once heard anyone refer to Dr. Archer by his first name until this evening. Also, Derek somehow failed to fully register the name of Dr. Archer's sister. What did the man whose name was not Jesus call her again? Diane, or something? Derek resolved to start getting better at remembering names if he ever hoped to excel in his future career as a psychologist to a crew of thousands.

"Her yard looks like the complete polar opposite of Dr. Archer's garden," Derek remarked to fill the awkward silence caused by his stupor and his nagging feeling of having fallen through a rabbit hole since Junia invited him to this surreal place. "An interesting contrast in personalities, I suspect..."

And perhaps also the complete opposite of Dr. Argosi, even though both she and Diane prefer the company of women. At least Dr. Argosi bore the responsibilities of child-rearing, domestic partnership, and ruling the entire department dedicated to keeping everyone alive on the Nephele with utmost competence and with serene grace, all the while looking flawless and poised at all times. Now that's a woman!

"In many ways you are correct, young one," the long-haired wild man answered. "Leto's children are like two sides of a coin, yet one cannot exist without the other."

"Is Diane also joining CARINA?" Derek asked.

"Well, that all depends on the Great Lady, does it not?"

"Dr. Argosi?"

"She whose hands hold the reigns," the rare bird answered. "Who else could I possibly mean?"

"Yeah, okay," Derek conceded. "I know she has the final word on vetting the crew, but the Nephele will unmoor and launch pretty soon –"

"Yes," the weirdo interrupted. "But my understanding is that there remain some kinks to iron out in the final selection process, as you mortals are fond of saying, as many positions in the upper management echelons are left unfilled. Meanwhile, some of us who would like to join the crew find ourselves less than welcome in the Lady's embrace."

"It can't be easy to be the one cherry-picking candidates for those upper management positions at the ALSESTIS division," Derek replied diplomatically. "I mean, Dr. Argosi already has a pretty tough job running the life support systems that ensure that we don't all die up there in space. Imagine having to also select the people to rely upon to make decisions on her behalf when her turn comes to sleep in cryostasis. I get it. It can't be easy, and no one at CARINA faults her for taking a long break to review the candidate files and mull this over. This is literally a matter of life and death! And if I were to put my life in anyone's hands, it would be hers. Absolutely."

"Your faith in the Great Lady is admirable. But is that the reason the learned mortals were given to explain her absence from your City-ship since last Spring? Mundane staffing concerns?"

"Well... yeah?" Derek stammered. "Isn't that why she's still here?"

The man nodded in a way that did not answer Derek's question in a satisfactory fashion. Before Derek could probe the matter any further, they arrived before a portico with columns overgrown with vines, and heavy with intertwined strands of ripe, green and purple-coloured grapes. The cultist walked up the stairs, pulled a thick velvet curtain at the entrance of the dwelling and bade Derek to enter. Remembering his mother's long-ago admonitions against walking off into strange houses with strange men, Derek hesitated, unsure whether to follow the eccentric into the great unknown. He also wondered whether it would be rude to decline the invite and make his way back to Dr. Archer's place, until he realized with a mild but rising panic that he failed to pay any attention to the way from here to there.

"Your gracious host will not mind, I assure you," the man whose name was not Dennis told him. "Leave him to his precious few moments of solitude, lest he become burdened by the thought that he cannot ever meditate lest some ninny think him dead!"

Derek bit his lip, momentarily embarrassed by his apparent overreaction at seeing Dr. Archer relaxing on his comfy chair. "Okay," he said at last. "But just one drink."

"How very sensible of you," not-Jesus replied with a wink, then led him inside his parlour, where a gaggle of beautiful women gathered around a large, circular cauldron, awaited.

Derek froze when he saw the women and their strange accoutrements; many of them wore the skins of fauns and other wild beasts loosely upon their bodies, in much the same way that the strange man who brought him to this dwelling draped himself in a leopard pelt, leaving little to the imagination. Stranger still, most of the women were armed with a veritable arsenal of long staves of what looked like stalks of stiff fennel or some other plant that belonged in a salad, each topped with a pinecone. Their hair was long and dishevelled, yet their crowns of leaves and ivy somehow held fast to their tresses by means unexplainable by conventional physics. At the centre of the gathering a woman stood, clad in the same strange manner as her companions, except for her crown consisting of a pair of bull horns that reminded Derek of a Viking helmet.

"Young one," not-Jesus told Derek. "Please allow me to introduce to you the lovely Ariadne... my wife, Daughter of Minos, of the royal house of Crete. She was born mortal, just as you were."

"Wait, what?" Derek stammered.

"Does the lad have a name?" Ariadne inquired, while the other women added handfuls of crushed herbs and other ingredients to the plum-coloured brew bubbling in the cauldron.

"Oh dear, where are my manners," the man answered. "The lad is called Derek. He is a friend to our Princess, on whose little shoulders the very fate of the gods rests."

"Aww," the women lamented in unison, as if disappointed that they would be required to abstain from tearing the newcomer limb from limb while in a frenzy later that evening.

"Hi... good evening," Derek mumbled artlessly to the women, who answered with muted albeit disappointed nods of greeting.

"Derek, my boy," said not-Dennis. "These fine lasses are called the Maenads. They bring joy and comfort to the weary and forlorn, much as you will once you become a Master of your chosen craft. Ladies," he now addressed the women, "our young friend has decided to join us tonight for only one drink. Now, how about we make it count?"

"As you will it, My Lord," Ariadne replied, as the women threw coy, knowing glances at Derek, making him feel exhilarated and ill at ease in equal measure. "Please... take a seat," she told Derek, nudging him towards the centre of the parlour. "Though the wine will take away all your cares, it is better not to remain standing when you partake of the blessing."

As Derek obediently followed Ariadne' lead, he glanced at the brew inside the cauldron. "Is this really wine?" he asked almost absentmindedly.

"I assure you, young one," Ariadne answered. "No mortal has tasted such wine in two thousand years!"

"Now drink up," Ariadne's mysterious husband said, handing him an overflowing cup. "And touch the Infinite long before you taste death!"

"Cheers," Derek replied sheepishly, knowing not what he was about to do.

Nepheleid

Chapter Fifteen

"This isn't funny, Eris," Junia whinged as her sister pulled her once again across the limitless expanse between the realms. This time, as they left behind the soft, womb-like world where Eros the Elder dwells, the path before them shone in brilliant flashes of light branching out in all directions in endless fractal swirls of every conceivable pattern.

"Okay, you made your point!" Junia cried out, tugging at the sleeve of Eris' dress. "Can you give it a rest for a minute? My eyes are starting to sting."

"Suit yourself," Eris said softly as their kaleidoscopic surroundings took on the more muted, albeit not unpleasant hues permeating the vastest region in the Kingdom of Hades, where deathless gods and still-living mortals seldom tread.

"Is this better?" Eris asked Junia teasingly as the young one took a few moments to rub her eyes and blink comically.

"Ow, my eyeballs," Junia complained. Once her eyes were well and fully recovered, she gazed upon her new surroundings, and quickly recognized the placid gloom of the Asphodel Meadows, where the shades of mortals who in life were neither especially blessed or damned come to rest between their endless cycles of death and birth.

"Well?" Eris insisted.

"Yeah, better," Junia conceded.

"You know, you used to fare much better during our travels between the realms when you were little," Eris teased.

"I used to close my eyes when you took me on your magical mystery tours back then."

"Oh?" Eris retorted with a raised eyebrow. "Did you never marvel at the eddies left in the wake of our journeys, thinking them particularly beautiful because they had the potential of harbouring enclaves in which Life can flourish?"

"I did," Junia answered. "Inside my head. Chaos is a wonder to behold at a conceptual level. To mere mortals, though, gazing upon the primordial eddies and all that dwells therein can lead to insanity."

"Have you been reading Lovecraft before bedtime?" Eris chided her younger sister. "I told you this was the stuff of nightmares!"

"I'm a big girl, Eris!"

"Who is getting cranky for being up past her bedtime!"

Junia pulled out her tongue, thinking her wordless reply far more eloquent than any verbal response her sleep-deprived adolescent mind could muster. "So," she said after a moment. "*What the hell was that all about?*"

"Which part, exactly, do you need me to explain?" Eris asked sardonically.

"You can start at *all of it*, thanks,"

Eris grinned.

"Okay," Junia continued. "You can start at why you're taking me on this trip as if you're trying to distract me from my purpose –"

"Your purpose, at the moment, is to keep out of trouble until your fourteenth birthday," Eris interrupted.

"Until Zeus judges me old enough to tell him off, right?" Junia retorted. "Even though we both know that he will never take 'no' for an answer, despite the fact that I've made up my mind, before witnesses, since last Winter?"

"Well, yes. That remains somewhat problematic," Eris agreed.

"And of course, he's working hard at getting everyone *up there* in on the plot to change my mind?"

"That is highly probable," Eris said.

"Meanwhile you're taking me to pay a visit to all the gods below and, I guess, *sideways* or wherever it is that Eros-Phanes lives, to show me the futility of staying here on Earth or on Olympus?"

"I do love it when you find a way to answer your own questions," Eris mused.

"Okay, fine, but can you tell me for starters why *the hell* the Titans were making such a big deal about the heroes of old being knobheads and whatnot?" Junia inquired. "I mean, wasn't Mom all about turning ordinary mortals into heroes, testing them until their breaking point so they could prove themselves worthy of godhood by doing great deeds?"

"Mother and quite a few other deathless gods, yes," Eris answered.

"Like Athena and Hermes?"

Eris nodded. "Athena and Hermes, and many others, although those two had their own reasons for helping the mortals along in their quests."

"So," Junia continued, "if, as Mom said, the people of the CARINA Venture are like the heroes of old, about to set out on the greatest adventure humanity has ever undertaken, why are the Titans trying to sow doubt in my mind about the Nephele's mission? Aren't the Titans always on Mom's side?"

"They are, albeit only when their interests are aligned with Mother's," Eris answered.

"So *why* were they harping on heroes?" Junia asked with diminishing patience.

"I can answer that, though I fear you might not like what follows," Eris replied, clearing her throat in the fashion of mortals as she curled her wings behind her shoulders.

Junia threw Eris a sideways glance, for she knew that her deathless sister could not, in fact, produce phlegm that would require her to clear her throat. "Okay," she said. "Let's hear it."

"I will tell you all, but first you must answer me this: what purpose do heroes serve?"

Junia gave Eris an incredulous stare, then pinched the bridge of her nose as if to convey that she was too tired for such inane questions.

Nepheleid

"Heroes bring Order to Chaos," Junia said at last. "They bring civilization and knowledge where there is none, and so on and so forth."

"And having grown up in Turtle Island, can you see how some may think this notion problematic?" Eris asked.

"Yeah, I guess one person's hero is another person's villain," Junia agreed. "But that's not exactly news to anyone."

"Now tell me," Eris continued. "What are Titans? Or perhaps, what were the Titans before they were supplanted by their own children?"

"They were the rulers of the Earth," Junia answered by rote.

"They were so much more that that, young one," Eris chided.

"They were – *they are* – the Pillars of the Cosmos," Junia retorted. "Grandpa Kronos told me that the first time I met him, back when they were still imprisoned in Tartarus."

"And how did Life fare on Earth fare when Kronos ruled as King?"

"He ruled as far back as the Holocene, until Zeus took his throne," Junia answered. "So, when he was King, Life was ascendant. Life had been ascendant pretty much since the end of the Ice Age."

"And what happened on Earth after the Titans were defeated by their children in their War for supremacy over the Cosmos?"

"Human beings began to proliferate like rabbits," Junia replied. "And Zeus helped."

"And what of other living creatures, both mighty and lowly?"

"They began to decline."

"And what accelerated their decline?" Eris asked finally.

"Unfettered capitalism and technological expansion?" Junia asked, knowing full well that her assumption was correct. "Okay, I see where you're getting at, but there's a difference between the normal propagation of civilization, as in culture and ideas, through commerce and whatnot, and outright conquest and its unholy spawns, capitalism and ecocide. And Mom was *never* in favour of the genocide of the people of Turtle Island when the Europeans set out across the world and claimed the lands previously unknown to them in the name of Christ under the pretext of the Doctrine of Discovery!"

"None of the blessed gods who dwell on high Olympus favoured such an outcome," Eris said. "For even the most bellicose among us understand that unrestrained War, and Conquest for its own sake, eventually become anathema to Life. That is in part why Zeus claims to take a dim view of Prometheus' efforts to spread the light of human genius to the stars through the CARINA Venture."

Junia rolled her eyes. "Yeah, he has other reasons," she griped.

"Of course, he has other reasons," Eris agreed. "And he knows exactly why Prometheus chose Mother to rule his new star-bound Kingdom, even if she consented to reign over the learned mortals as somewhat of a Dowager Queen. Unlike Zeus, Mother does not seek to tame Chaos and to remake all that lives and all that exists into a semblance of Order. Unlike Zeus, Mother understands and appreciates that Chaos is and always was an essential condition for Life. She also knows when true heroism – mortals' propensity to bring creative order to Chaos – is needed to ward off the deadlier side of destructive Chaos, and the point at which Order itself becomes destructive, leading to stagnation and entropy on a massive scale, from which Life seldom recovers. In other words, wise Prometheus always knew that Mother is, and has always been a ward against entropy, setting through her deeds the course of Fate in constant motion, whether or not she is aware of this."

"So, the Titans are wrong, and the heroes Mom favoured in the past *weren't* all useless tossers?" Junia asked hopefully.

"Well, yes, they were, all of them to a man," Eris answered bluntly.

"Oh, come on!" Junia cried out.

"The Titans were not wrong on that account," Eris explained, "although it is not fair to deem the heroes as *completely* ineffectual. They certainly had their uses. Remember, Mother favoured the dastardly House of Atreus for purely utilitarian reasons. Their sons played their part in bringing her satisfaction by sacking Troy, then Zeus' favoured city, but you already know the tale, do you not? That is also why she loved Achilles, Thetis' illustrious son by the mortal Peleus, even if he often found himself at odds with the sons of Atreus despite fighting on the same side. Mother also loved the hero Jason, for he appeared to her as the instrument of her revenge against Jason's uncle, the mortal King Pelias, who desecrated her temple by murdering his step-grandmother Sidero in front of her altar."

"What about girl heroes?" Junia asked. "Were they also wankers? Or were they just means to an end, pawns for the gods to play chess with?"

"No, young one... it was far worse than that," Eris replied. "Tales were told of the fates of heroines to epitomize what befalls young maidens who refuse the civilizing guidance of marriage and men."

"You don't say," Junia retorted sullenly.

"I know you have heard told the tale of the Danaids, but did you know about Atalanta –"

"Yeah," Junia interrupted, "that aggressively chaste huntress who thwarted her suitors by challenging them to a footrace to win her hand in marriage, on pain of literally losing their heads if they lost. Of course, she was the fastest runner, so all the poor bastards who wanted to marry her ended up with their heads on a pike. Then one day a love-struck young man named Hippomenes prayed for Aphrodite's aid in winning Atalanta, so Aphrodite went ahead and picked some of Mom's golden apples and gave them to Hippomenes to throw at Atalanta during the footrace to distract her, and it worked. I'll bet that Aphrodite wishes this trick could work on Mom! Still, this goes to show that Aphrodite is almost never on the woman's side and will act without considering the consequences of her actions. In Atalanta's case, she and her husband were turned into lions after they found themselves alone in Zeus' temple and decided to have a quickie. Zeus turned them into lions because he thought lions did not mate with their own species. I mean, seriously. They do mate with one another, like, a lot! Like for three days in a row until the lioness is no longer in heat. How could he not know that? Doesn't Grandma Rhea keep lions as pets?"

"She does, but that was not the point," Eris replied. "Atalanta's tale was told to warn young girls against the dangers of remaining virginal and untamed like wild Nature."

"Like Artemis?"

"Exactly like Artemis," Eris said.

"But isn't Artemis one of Zeus' favourite daughters," Junia asked, "precisely because she *is* wild and untamed and virginal? By that logic, Artemis is Nature and Disorder incarnate. And yet she's one of Zeus' favourite daughters, and you're not? What is that all about?"

"I am fairly certain that he bestows more affection on Artemis than upon his legitimate offspring to spite Mother," Eris answered.

"That thing he said about for as long as goddesses bore him children such as these, he could not care less about Hera's jealousy?"

"Precisely," Eris said. "The Huntress stands as a reminder for Mother of everything she never was – a perennial maiden free from the yoke of marriage and children. Zeus cares not for Ares or myself, nor Hephaestus or our sisters for that matter, because our strengths represent a threat to his rule. Ares' brute force and courage, Hephaestus' genius, not unlike that of our elder Prometheus, and my proclivity to incite Chaos to break stalemates are all things he believes will cause the downfall of his rule. And yet, Zeus runs the risk of causing his own undoing by insisting on imposing destructive Order upon the Cosmos, to the point where entropy and death will become his ultimate legacy unless a *force majeure* compels him to change course –"

"So, Artemis is a threat to no one," Junia added.

"Well, I would not quite put it like that," Eris replied, "though she is not a threat to Mother, if that's what you are wondering. Mother has little use for Artemis, and is of the opinion that Artemis would have a difficult time finding her place in the new world she, Prometheus, and their learned mortals are creating. Mother and Prometheus have fashioned their City-ships in the image of the many nations of Turtle Island, where the human world and the wilderness coexist without distinction. In such a world, there would be no need for anyone to be set themselves apart from the civilized world of adulthood and marriage through perennial childhood and wildness, as the children of the CARINA Venture are taught from a very early age. They have a cherished and important role to play in upholding and making anew the world created by their elders."

"But Aphrodite is definitely a threat to Mom," Junia added.

"Only to the extent that Aphrodite favours Zeus and has always been his ally in all things, including his misdeeds against his marriage-bed."

"So, Aphrodite is *definitely* not a friend to women," Junia continued. "Like Athena, if the Titans are to be believed."

"The Titans know many things," Eris replied, "despite having spent many long centuries imprisoned in Tartarus. But you need not protect Mother against any deathless god, as she has planned for contingencies against the inevitable resistance of even the most powerful beings of the Cosmos against her designs."

Junia bit her lip and pondered Eris' words for a moment. "Okay," she said at last. "Say that I promise not to cut any Elder Gods in half with Grandpa Kronos' sickle. Can we go back to Olympus and check on Derek? I have the sneaking suspicion that he might be getting molested as we speak. That's kind of what Eros-Phanes hinted at before."

"No harm will come to your mortal friend, child," Eris replied casually. "Well, none that he will remember. Mother will see to that. And Apollo will have much to answer for."

"Wait… what?" Junia stammered.

"Well, he *is* supposed to see to his well-being, as his host, which means he ought not leave a guest alone in his palace, with the likes of Aphrodite and Dionysus lurking about," Eris continued, in a tone that was more soliloquy than retort. "This is simply bad manners. No, Mother will be most displeased. Perhaps Mother's displeasure will persuade Lord Phoebus to stifle his unholy infatuation with –"

"I have not left my home, Eris," Apollo said, materializing before Junia and her winged Chaos mongering sibling.

Junia squeaked in surprise, clenching her chest as she leapt backwards, then landed inelegantly among a gaggle of shades at a terrific distance away from her deathless kin.

Eris grinned, deploying her wings to fetch her charge, all the while feeling a pang of regret for not having put Junia to bed hours ago, as Hera would have done.

But what will be the fun in that? Things are just about to get interesting.

Chapter Sixteen

At the exact moment the amaranthine brew touched his lips, Derek knew that the bitter, sharp-smelling drink prepared by the Maenads in Dennis' parlour was no ordinary wine. He should have known better, truly he should have, when he spied the scantily and strangely clad ladies adding *ingredients* to his drink. Alas, his lack of sleep, coupled with his seventeen years of Canadian-bred politeness and a strange brain fog that afflicted him since arriving to this place, overpowered his natural survival instincts. He drank the first draught of the "wine" without much care or thought for what may come. Ignoring further warnings issued by his now screaming pineal gland, Derek took another swallow for good measure, not knowing at the time whether he did so out of youthful bravado, or simply to not disappoint his eccentric host and hostesses.

As Derek's tummy began to tingle with an unfamiliar warmth, the walls of Dennis' darkened, fragrant parlour began to spin, causing the already seated lad to slump deeper into his cushion. What little light permeated the room began to pulsate with an eerie, yet not unpleasant glow, while the gaggle of lovely maidens gathered around him appeared to melt into one another until they all became fused with Ariadne, whose long, gossamer robes seemed to float above the floor. Turning his gaze towards Dennis, Derek noticed that his host's feet also curiously failed to touch the ground. Looking up at the oddball's countenance, Derek observed that Dennis' brow sprouted bull's horns since he last set his gaze upon him, only a few seconds ago. Or was it hours ago? How long had Derek been here, in this stranger's living room, with its peculiar denizens in the initial stages of making merry at some sort of drug-fuelled orgy?

"Um," Derek stammered as he rubbed his eyes with the back of his hand. "I think I should go… in case Dr. Archer is looking for me."

"Our dear Lord Archer will not mind your absence, young one," Dennis replied in a soft voice. "He is deep in thought, and will remain exactly as we left him, until he is ready to return."

"Right," Derek said. "But... I'm feeling a little strange."

"Oh?" Ariadne inquired unironically, without visibly moving her lips.

"I, uh, I think I'm seeing things," Derek answered sheepishly. "Like, you and..." he added, gesturing vaguely at her and Dennis, not knowing for certain where the other women had gone.

"You are seeing things as they *are*, mortal," one of the many voices of Ariadne declared. "By drinking the wine of our Lord Dionysus, your mind has triumphed over the evil spell Eris cast upon your mind. Your vision is now unclouded and true."

"Well, okay then," Derek replied, unsure what else to say, and to whom. He closed his eyes as he rose slowly to his feet, now fully aware that he had ingested some sort of hallucinogenic drug, then took a few unsteady steps towards the door.

"Where are you going?" said one of the Maenads as she visibly split from Ariadne's form. "You only just got here!"

"I know," Derek said to no one in particular, "but I've really got to go. This has been great, but I have to get up early tomorrow..." Presumably to nurse one bitch of a hangover, he sagaciously left unsaid.

"Very well," Dennis replied, while the chorus of Maenads sang that soft, plaintive tune that women often intone when a particularly endearing puppy leaves their presence. "Go if you must, but remember that you ought to trust absolutely everything you see on this night, even long after you've awakened tomorrow."

"Um, okay... thanks," Derek answered, doubting even in his drug-addled state that he would be able to remember anything the following morning.

Stepping outside the front door of Dennis' abode, Derek struggled to remember the way back to Dr. Archer's sumptuous palace with its tidy, albeit urine soaked, gardens. Feeling a pang of guilt for the role he played in defiling the otherwise perfect flower beds surrounding Dr. Archer's home, Derek looked up at the starry night sky, hoping to catch a glimpse of the Nephele, his true North Star, high above the Earth. Would the space station be visible from this latitude? Where was this place anyway? Had Dr. Argosi not mentioned that this resort-cult-honeypot was, in fact, located in a small principality that he likely never knew existed? Was it somewhere in Europe? Of course, it was in Europe.

Where else in the world were there any principalities?

Derek heaved a weary sigh. So he was in Europe. Great. Now where the heck was Dr. Archer's gilded bachelor pad?

"This way, young one," said a female voice from high above.

Derek blinked and looked up at the sky once again. He nearly jumped out of his skivvies when he saw a beautiful young woman looking down upon him from between the horns of the crescent moon. She wore a pale, almost translucent shift that came right to the middle of her shapely calves, and for some reason she wielded an exquisite silver bow. She looked somewhat familiar, like one of the staff that took residence at Borealis shortly after Drs. Archer and Weiss joined Dr. Argosi's employ a few years ago, before everyone – well, almost everyone – migrated to the Nephele. Now that he thought about it, the girl on the moon did look a lot look like Dr. Archer's sister, Diane. Was that her name? Did he not have a conversation with Dennis about this very person shortly before he caved to peer pressure and consumed a concoction he now suspected contained a hero's dose of tryptamine dimethyltryptamine, among other ingredients?

"Do not concern yourself with my name, mortal," said the Moon Girl he believed to be Diane. "It would be wise for you to leave these grounds at once, lest the Maenads find you once the Madness takes hold of them, and they tear you limb from limb –"

"Wait – what?" Derek mumbled, his forebrain trying its best to remember the lessons from his early teens about the effects of tryptamine dimethyltryptamine on the human mind. If memory served him right, many rather interesting things happened to those who partook of the blessed spores and other hallucinogens of their ilk. The most fascinating, in his opinion, was how such substances sidestep the default mode network of the adult human brain and allow one to literally think outside the box, as children do, or as adults when they dream.

"Uh, Diane?" Derek called out artlessly to the beauteous hallucination above him. "Can I trouble you to point me to Dr. Archer's place? I'm not feeling quite like myself..."

"Evidently," Moon Girl said with a soft chuckle as she pulled a silver arrow from her quiver and nocked it on her bow.

"Wait – watch where you're pointing that thing!" Derek shrieked, taking

Nepheleid

a step back towards the dubious safety of Dennis' den of debauchery.

"Follow the arrow," Moon Girl said with a hearty laugh, "and you will find my brother's dwelling. Stray too far, and you will find yourself in a world of trouble!"

I think we are way past that point, Derek thought while muttering a string of barely coherent words of thanks to the figment of his libido-addled imagination on the face of the moon. Of course, he did not see the arrow loosing from Diane's bow, only the trail of light streaming in the general direction from whence he and Dennis had come a lifetime ago. He took a hesitant step towards the flickering shooting stars lighting his way, surprised that he retained the ability to walk throughout this surreal escapade.

What would Mother think of me right now, Derek wondered as he made his way across this enchanted, pulsating landscape at a snail's pace. She would likely feel dreadfully disappointed; perhaps it would be best if she never learned of this misadventure, if Derek could help it at all. But it would far more difficult to hide this gaffe from the exquisite Dr. Argosi, who expected Derek at her breakfast table at the crack of dawn. Though immeasurably kind and magnanimous to her staff, *La belle Ella* also had a reputation for not suffering fools lightly and, if Zippy could be believed, for also holding grudges against those who proved untrustworthy, or who made egregious blunders on her watch.

What then, would the otherwise irreproachable Dr. Argosi think of him, if she caught him as he was now, addle-minded and without pants, having just left the company of Dennis' retinue of wanton cultists? Would she revoke his place on the Nephele because of behaviour unbecoming a member of her crew? If so, what would become of him? Would he never see his family again? Would he ever see Paul again, now that his best friend finally decided to leave his ancestral home to join the very first generation of brave pioneers of interstellar space? Was Paul waiting for him on the Polaris at that very moment, wondering why he was not there to guide him in his new home high above the Earth?

If Paul only knew the rabbit hole in which Derek had fallen just now, he would surely laugh his head off and call him a lightweight. Paul would also remind Derek that the descendants of European settlers never quite could handle the visions gifted to those who ingest the substances that grow in the special recesses of the Earth, as they often misused such boons for recreational or other trivial pursuits. The Indigenous peoples of Turtle Island, on the other hand, had used all sorts of psychoactive substances as ceremonial technologies since time immemorial to communicate with All My Relations.

Paul's ancestors, at least the ones who could be traced back to the time after the great disruption caused by the Indian Residential School system in the nineteenth and twentieth centuries, hailed from all corners of the continent. They came together under the tent of the heavily Plains influenced Native American Church some two-hundred-odd years ago, until their children deliberately left the Church due to its Christian and therefore colonialist associations. Was that the reason why Paul, whose family identified as Anishinaabe, had a Lakota-sounding surname? Did the Anishinaabe ever hunt the Buffalo in their once abundant hunting grounds around the Great Lakes? Derek wished he had paid more attention during his history lessons of late. Had he known more about how Paul's forebears used Peyote to gain clarity during their sacred ceremonies, perhaps he would have figured out how to keep his train of thought from derailing at the slightest distraction while under the influence. If Paul could see him now, he would also say something droll about the descendants of Vikings, specifically, being unable to properly use mind-expanding substances as penance for their ancestors' propensity at going berserk in the heat of battle.

The thought of Paul's good-natured ribbing brought a smile to Derek's face, until he glimpsed a horde of nude, leaping huntresses following Diane across the sky.

Yep, I'm screwed, Derek thought, vowing to never touch any substance stronger than herbal tea if he ever made it through the night without losing his mind or his place on the Nephele. He also swore to himself to never follow strangers into darkened parlours and partake of their strange Eucharist without proper adult accompaniment and supervision. Derek giggled, for the first time in years, or at least this evening, at his absurd conflation between Dennis and Jesus. Oddly enough, Dennis did not seem to mind at the time, nor did he scorn Derek for the mild blasphemy. In fact, the soft-spoken, long-haired Wild Man who kept the company of women appeared to accept the comparison with gentle good humour, even as he praised Derek for his loyalty towards Dr. Argosi. Had Dennis not mentioned earlier that he would have liked to join the crew of the Nephele, were it not for Dr. Argosi's evident antipathy towards him and his cortege of cultists? Was Dennis asking Derek to advocate to Dr. Argosi on his behalf to join the crew of the Nephele?

Nepheleid

Derek scoffed at the absurd notion that an adult man would ask him, a barely shaving lad of seventeen, to exert any influence on the Director of Operations of the Nephele's life support systems. It was a role akin to that of God Herself on a life raft of nanocarbon, steel, and polymer meandering through the hostile void of space. Perhaps Dr. Argosi's wisdom exceeded her uncommon beauty by leaps and bounds, for Derek could not fathom what role Dennis and his flunkies could play among her crew. Surely this merry band of mavericks would prove more than merely troublesome in the off-planet habitats where the slightest mishap or mischief could cause death on a massive scale among the denizens of the Nephele and other vessels yet to be built. As Derek's prefrontal cortex lingered on such thoughts, an avalanche of memories of long-forgotten history lessons taught by Miss Mnem, from the halcyon days of his childhood on Borealis, flooded his mind. Miss Mnem, the headmistress at the school at the CARINA Venture, and now on the Nephele, once told Derek and the other pupils that countless cultures throughout human history possessed divine or semi-divine heroic figures that celebrated the inversion of the social order, which when controlled by the State paradoxically reinforced said order.

Perhaps Dennis, with his counter-cultural aesthetic and his questionable feats of liquid magic, could play such a role in the tightly controlled and highly regimented world above the Earth. Perhaps in his own way, Dennis could pacify the crew of the Nephele and its sister-ships by distracting them from their existential dread of the void and darkness of space. Perhaps, with a little guidance from Derek, Dennis could become a force for good aboard the Nephele and be counselled to sidestep the seemingly unavoidable tendency of such charismatic leaders to eventually overthrow the established social order through murder and bloodshed, only to become the very order against which other factions will inevitably rebel.

Derek paused his dawdling meandering and sat upon the dewy ground. Who knew that his weekend getaway to Junia's strange ancestral home would yield such profound implications for his future career as psychologist to the ancestors of humanity's future? Where was Junia anyway? Why did she leave him alone with all these weirdos? No, little Junia had nothing to do with any of this, Derek admitted. It was he who followed Dennis out of the safety of Dr. Archer's home. No one forced him to do anything. It was he who took the poisoned wine of his own free will, and now, as he lay upon the soft, fragrant Earth, he knew that he bore the sole responsibility of the consequences of following a stranger into a drug den. Now that he thought about it, Derek concluded that maybe he was not cut out to counsel anyone about anything at all, at least not yet. At least not until he regained full control of his senses and faculties, and stopped hallucinating that pretty, shiny, golden mannequin that now seemed to follow him from behind that hedge by the main building where he and Junia and Zippy and the others arrived that very afternoon.

Great... now I'm seeing robots, Derek thought as he closed his eyes. I must really be out of my mind. Resolving to lay down for a spell, Derek concluded that the wisest course of action to take was to follow Dr. Argosi's lead in barring entry to Dennis and his cultists from the Nephele altogether. Far be it for him to inadvertently add more worries to his beautiful boss' already saturated state of mind-

"You! Boy!" said a sharp female voice. "On your feet at once!"

Derek opened his eyes, half-expecting to see the golden robot hovering above him. Instead, there stood one of Junia's older sisters, who greatly resembled Dr. Argosi, but somewhat lacked her mother's sumptuous grace. This one was the older sister Junia claimed to be either an obstetrician or a gynaecologist. Or was she both? Regardless of this one's profession, Derek was relieved that she was not Eris, whose flaming red hair and permanent roguish leer made her stand out unmistakably from her siblings. Still, Derek struggled to remember this one's name. It was a long, complicated name, albeit a pretty one. It sounded like... Elly-something. Allie-tata? Allythia? Lithium?

"Lalita?" Derek muttered to the comely, albeit annoyed-looking woman above him.

"No, not Lalita," the woman said. "Not unless one undertakes some spectacular mental gymnastics, but you are in no state to even attempt this feat. Now get up, on your feet, before the Maenads find you!"

"Can you take me to Dr. Archer's place, please? Miss?" Derek asked feebly, still deciding whether not-Lalita was another hallucination, one especially manifesting his sense of guilt at his foolish youthful experimentation with drugs.

"Dr. Archer," not-Lalita replied with a hint of mirth, "cannot help you right at the moment. We are going to Mother's dwelling. Quickly now, before Father sees you, otherwise we will never hear the end of it!"

Nepheleid

"Will Dr. Argosi be angry with me?" Derek inquired meekly, his voice trembling at the thought of disappointing his Goddess.

"Oh, bloody hell, Derek. Mother has more pressing worries than your little escapade! Now come with me at once, I will not ask again!"

Derek rose to his feet and began to follow his guide reluctantly. He noticed that his anaesthetized flesh had remained so far completely unharmed, yet his pride felt as if cut by a giant sickle. He bent at the waist, then curled in a ball on the ground, having lost either the will to live or the ability to move. The last thing he remembered before closing his eyes for the last time that night was the sensation of being lifted by strong metallic arms, and of floating at chest level above the Earth while his helper carried him a few paces behind Junia's older sister.

At least I'm likely to remain with the crew of the Nephele, Derek thought as he fell into a deep slumber. At least I don't matter enough to the Queen that she should deign to cast me out of her Kingdom...

Chapter Seventeen

"That was impressive", Apollo said as soon as grey-eyed Athena's feet touched the unfamiliar ground in the Kingdom of Hades. To her surprise and indignation, Hermes was nowhere to be seen. Neither was Ares. However, this annoyed the Virgin Warrior far less than being dispatched and left to her own devices within the unsettling alien realm of the Underworld without a seasoned guide. Setting aside her pique, she sought and quickly found Apollo's translucent form manifesting a few paces to the right of winged Eris, who for yet unknown reasons was clasping her hand over her mouth, as if to stifle laughter. Far behind them, Athena spied the object of Apollo and Eris' amusement clumsily rising to her feet a great distance away, in a patch of the Asphodel Meadow strangely deprived of shades.

"Though not quite as impressive as your Earth-dive from the Nephele," Apollo's ghostly projection continued. "At least this time your garments did not catch fire from atmospheric friction."

"Oh, piss off," Junia grumbled with uncommon rancour as she began walking towards her Olympian kin.

"Child!" Eris giggled. "I fear you will never live that one down, at least not for centuries yet to come!"

Bold of you to assume that Junia is fully immortal, Athena almost said aloud. The Virgin Warrior kept silent, judging it wisest not to voice such thoughts in the presence of fractious Eris, who in recent months had gained Hera's ear, as well as her unconditional amity. Apollo, unaware of Athena's arrival until that moment, turned a sympathetic glance towards her, as if divining her thoughts. Athena nodded, tacitly assuring the Archer that she would hold her tongue until they both could ascertain what nonsense filled Junia's head in all matters pertaining to the virtues of gods, Titans, and heroes.

"No need to yell," Junia whined as she closed the distance between herself and Eris. "Are you *trying* to wake the dead?"

"That almost never works," Eris retorted. "Except on the night that falls exactly between the Autumnal Equinox and the Winter Solstice."

"What the *hell* are you doing here?" Junia interrupted, addressing Apollo. "And why are you a hologram? Are you making fun of dead people in the Kingdom of Hades? That is *not okay!*"

"I thought you looked rather diaphanous," Eris told Apollo in jest. "Like one who is trying to blend in with his surroundings."

"To answer your question," Apollo answered Junia calmly, ignoring Eris' repartee, "I was looking for you. I first sought you in the fields of twilight, where we used to meet since you were barely out of swaddling clothes. Then I remembered that, with Eris as your guide, you were most probably still wide awake, and that I would have better luck finding you in the unlikeliest of places. So here we are. Though truth be told, I am not really *here*."

"I can see you," Junia said crossly.

"And I can see you both," Apollo replied. "But I am *really* in my palace at this moment, where your young friend Derek is staying as my guest."

"I admit that is clever," Eris said, "bi locating in this fashion so as not to not leave your guest unattended."

Apollo shrugged. "The hour is late. You two should return to Olympus at once."

Athena nodded in agreement.

Following Apollo's line of sight, Junia finally saw Athena, then gave her the most wrathful glower. Unaccustomed to the power of the disapproving glares of adolescent girls, the Virgin Warrior's breath halted in her immortal throat, causing Apollo's gaze to linger upon her for an uncomfortable length of time.

"But do tell," Eris continued, paying no attention to the tense, wordless tiff of sullen looks around her. "If you are here in spirit, as mortals say, then how do you know that our fellow blessed gods are not having their way with young Derek as we speak? Or did you leave your *soma* on a comfy chair in your foyer to dissuade them from setting foot in your home, to lie there like a handsome scarecrow against the more depraved among our kind?"

Apollo opened his mouth to reply but was interrupted by a familiar voice bellowing in the vast emptiness above the throngs of shades of the unremarkable dead.

"ERIS!!! YOU IMPUDENT WENCH!!!!"

"Hermes, always a pleasure," Eris told the irate-looking figure fluttering above and around her all at once.

"YOU LISTEN HERE!" said the Messenger shod in winged sandals, pointing his caduceus menacingly at the goddess of discord, until Ares appeared from thin air and swatted Hermes' hand away from the general vicinity of his twin.

"OW! Fuck!" Junia griped, rubbing the space between her temples and her ears, all the while opening and closing her jaw to massage her battered eardrums from within. "*Will! You! All! Just! Quit! It! With! The yelling!*"

"There, there," Apollo said softly as his ethereal form bent before Junia to cup his hands on either side of her face.

Junia blinked incredulously at the Archer. "Don't touch me," she hissed, taking a step towards Eris to get away from the Lord of the golden bow.

"You are welcome," Apollo retorted, intrigued at Junia's ingratitude for the rapid healing of her maltreated sensory organs.

"Yeah, well, bite me," Junia snapped.

"What in Hades has gotten into you?" Athena asked, no longer able to keep silent.

"Oh, never mind. It's not like *you* would understand either!" Junia retorted, rushing to Ares' side and wrapping her slender arms around her brother and protector. "Please tell me you're not like them," she half-sobbed. "Because you're not, right?"

Apollo raised an eyebrow and gave Athena a knowing look, tacitly beckoning the Virgin Warrior not to engage the child further.

"Eris," Hermes said through clenched teeth while striving to regain a semblance of his usual composure. "Would you care to explain *where* you took Junia after you absconded with her from Elysium and left me alone with the Titan-Court? What sort of nonsense, exactly, are you trying to impart to our very young Princess, as she prepares to decide all our fates?"

"You leave her alone, you... big bully!" Junia cried out.

"Bully?" Hermes scoffed, raising an eyebrow. "Ah well, I suppose I ought to rejoice that you have not inherited our Queen's eloquence for insults. Still, that word is rather pedestrian – even for you, don't you think?"

Junia said nothing, opting instead to raise her middle finger towards Hermes, Athena, and Apollo to effectively articulate her innermost thoughts.

"What's wrong, Stargazer?" Ares said softly as he stroked Junia's hair.

Junia took five long, deep breaths to calm herself, in the fashion taught to her by her many mortal teachers of martial arts since her most tender age. "They are not our friends," she said in a low voice, though all the immortals gathered in the Asphodel Meadow heard her words. "They are not on our side, and they will try to keep us grounded on Olympus! They –"

"Hush, little one," Ares said softly. "You are being silly, for you have stayed awake far too long. You have not slept since landing at Polaris!"

"I slept on the way down!" Junia protested.

"She did," Hermes agreed, with an edge to his voice.

"Off to bed with you, then!" Ares persisted. "Mother will be very displeased if you are not in your room when she rises at the crack of Dawn!"

"You are missing the point, Brother!" Eris chimed in.

"Why would you think that we are not on your side?" Apollo asked earnestly.

"Because I'm almost fourteen and I *still* have to go to Olympus every now and then to tell Zeus to fuck off and let me and my Mom and whoever else leave on the Nephele," Junia replied. "Because all I want to do is go to space and be with Prometheus and our Moms and Hephaestus and Asia and everyone on the Nephele to seed life and terraform planets wherever we can! Because my Mom told Zeus *the exact same thing* years ago and he wouldn't let her leave, and for *some reason* we're still at it and the Nephele is still docked to the Hub when she should have unmoored months ago! Because Zeus is keeping me and my Mom here out of spite, and *you three and a whole lot more of you are totally enabling him*! Because of course you are! But not you, Ares, right? RIGHT?"

"Of course not," Ares answered with uncharacteristic tenderness. "I am and ever have been loyal to Mother, for she has always seen my worth, even when Father refused to do so."

"I knew it!" Junia said, fighting the urge to start sobbing in her brother's arms.

"Why do you not ask Eris the same question?" Hermes sneered. "Of all the blessed gods who dwell on starry Olympus, she is the one whose loyalty is most... questionable."

Eris said nothing but chose instead to throw Hermes a look of mock indignation.

"Oh yeah? Since when?" Junia replied, as Hermes and Athena scoffed in unison.

Even stalwart Ares, defender of Olympus, bit his lip in amusement, his eyes cast downward to avoid meeting his twin's gaze. Only Apollo kept his comportment pleasantly impassable, but for all anyone knew, this could have been on account of his discarnate aspect manifesting among his kin in the depths of the Kingdom of Hades.

"Have you never heard of, oh I don't know, the Trojan War?" Hermes asked Junia. "Or did your mother the Queen forget to tell you about the part Eris played in instigating this whole sordid affair?"

"Yeah, I did, *actually*," Junia answered. "And I know that it was Zeus' idea not to invite Eris to Thetis' wedding. Just like it was Zeus' idea to have a *mortal Prince of Troy* be the judge in a beauty contest that could have been settled had Zeus just given my Mom *the golden apple that belonged to her in the first place* since it was pilfered from her Garden! But no, he took the coward's way out and outsourced his duty to a poor hapless mortal. Then he pretended to remain neutral while *obviously* favouring the Trojans all the while bitching incessantly that everyone else was taking sides! Yeah. I'm familiar with the story. And Eris was not the bad guy. She was on Mom's side all along. What she did resulted in Zeus becoming so afraid of Mom that he stopped abusing her sexually whenever the hell he felt like it!"

Athena gasped at Junia's bluntness. When her gaze lingered upon Apollo's spectral form, the Virgin Warrior noticed the Archer wincing as if he remembered something he had witnessed long ago and dearly wished to forget.

"Oh, don't act like any of you didn't know!" Junia continued. "You all knew, and you did nothing! And don't give me that crap about swearing an Oath of fealty to Zeus after failing to overthrow him. I know all about that too, and I know that *some of you* got off a lot easier than you deserved! And that *some of you* went behind Zeus' back and antagonized him for *years* but were never threatened with bodily harm the way he repeatedly threatened my Mom!"

Apollo threw a wordless, ghostly glance at Athena, who chose to swallow Junia's remark without further angering the irate and clearly overtired child.

"I was talking about you, by the way" Junia now told Athena. "Do you have anything to say for yourself about that? Or, more recently, for throwing my Mom under the bus when I was little, when you told Zeus just exactly how to blackmail her into returning to Olympus, just so you could have peace in your time?"

"All I've done," Athena replied, "including my actions pertaining to the Nephele, was in the interest of order and to preserve the lives of the learned and the just. That includes your crewmates on the Nephele, you impudent little ingrate!"

"Ingrate!" Junia scoffed. "Oh, that's rich! What exactly do I have to be grateful to you for? You are the worst hypocrite of them all – even worse than Zeus! You pretend to be all rational and wise and all for justice and peace, but you pander to Zeus all the time, just like Aphrodite does, by throwing *all women* under the bus *all the time*. Okay, I'll give you this much, at least you admitted your bias that one time you when you declared, at a trial and before witnesses, no less, that you would *always* side with males in matters pertaining to law and order because you were born from your father's head! As if this were a real thing! Do you have anything to say about that? No? I didn't think so. Goddess of Wisdom and Justice, my ass! Your mother would be *so ashamed* of you if she were alive today!"

Dumbfounded at Junia's words, Athena simply stared the child, her brow furrowed in anger. The Virgin Warrior wisely held her peace, for she knew that swift Hermes would quickly give voice to her innermost thoughts, for they were often of the same mind.

"What in the name of Tartarus are you going on about?" Hermes said, thoroughly fulfilling Athena's expectations. "Athena has no mother –"

"Oh, you didn't know?" Eris interrupted snidely, throwing Ares a knowing glance.

Ares said nothing, though his poorly concealed grin told Hermes and Athena that this was one of the few subjects for which he knew more than they.

"Phoebus," Athena protested to Apollo. "Do you know anything about this?"

Apollo's apparition heaved a weary sigh. "I've heard something of the sort, yes… years ago, before Junia was –" The Archer suddenly held his ghostly breath. His gaze turned heavenward.

"Before Junia was what?" Athena snapped, expecting a satisfactory explanation from her other long-time ally and intellectual equal. When Apollo failed to answer, Athena followed his line of sight and saw a very faint silver arrow arcing across the firmament of the Underworld, itself a pale reflection of the movement of the Heavenly bodies above the Kingdom of Hades.

"I must apologize," the Archer said. "But I must take my leave at once. This is an omen from my sister to return to Olympus without delay. Perhaps we can discuss this in the morning over brunch?"

"Oh no you don't!" Junia protested. "I'm not even close to done, and *you* have a lot to answer for too!"

"Mistakes were made, young one," Apollo replied as his form grew fainter. "This is something all children must learn sooner or later. Even the gods are not impervious to error. But now that we have found your whereabouts, I trust that Hermes will deliver you all back to Olympus rather expediently. Farewell for now."

Nepheleid

"Hey! Get back here you blond bastard!" Junia yelled at the empty space where Apollo's form stood. "What are you laughing at?"

Ares no longer made any effort to conceal his mirth.

"Now Junia," Eris said softly. "You've done what no one else ever has! You've frightened the Archer awake!"

"And now you need to go to bed," Ares added, "or Mother will hang me by the balls."

"In her parlour next to her chandelier," Hermes said. "Well then, shall we return and continue this most fascinating debate on high Olympus?"

"I'm not going anywhere with you," Junia declared. "And you can't make me, remember?"

"You try my patience, Princess," Hermes replied while rubbing the bridge of his nose with his thumb and index finger. "I did you a kindness by bringing you to Elysium to visit your Nurse, Klymene –"

"My Mama, not my Nurse!" Junia interrupted.

"Yes, yes, your *Mama*," Hermes continued, nearing his wits' end. "And I've been a terribly good sport about Eris spiriting you away to Titans-know-where, but now it is time for you, *all of you*, to return to Olympus. Now will you be so kind and abide, PLEASE?"

Before Junia could respond, Ares raised his hand to summon the Messenger's attention.

"Hermes, if I may," Ares said. "As our Queen tasked Eris and I with Junia's protection and well being, I will see to it that she returns to her bedchamber on high Olympus before anyone else is the wiser. Eris is more than capable of opening the Gates through the realms to make it so. Are you not, Sister?"

"Of course," Eris replied, casting a sideways glance at Athena and Hermes. Her crooked smile was as inscrutable as ever, as if her designs never failed to sow discord and foment Chaos for its own sake wherever she roamed.

"Very well," Hermes conceded. "But only because I trust that you, Ares, will keep your word and see our Princess safely back to Hera's abode before Zeus hears about any of this."

Ares nodded courteously, then gently prodded Junia towards Eris, who began unfurling her wings to enfold her twin and their young charge. As Eris conjured up her needlessly garish kaleidoscopic spectacle of colours and ever evolving symmetric patterns, Athena saw Eris staring straight at her. The Virgin Warrior could have sworn that Eris winked at her as she and her siblings took their leave, but the three were gone in the span of a mortal heartbeat, leaving Athena and Hermes alone among the shades of the dead.

Once the usual gloom returned to the Asphodel Meadow in the Kingdom of Hades, Hermes turned his gaze towards Athena and said, "Well then, at least the big brute can be trusted, most of the time. Shall we go?"

"Not yet," Athena answered, her usually serene countenance betraying her displeasure.

"And why not?" Hermes asked, raising an eyebrow as if sensing that trouble was afoot.

"I have some questions of my own," Athena replied. "And they cannot be answered freely by the blessed gods who dwell on starry Olympus. At least not while Father is there."

Hermes heaved a weary sigh, eliciting from Athena a momentary softening of her features.

"I apologize in advance," she said. "But I will need you to guide me to one final destination in the Underworld before we return to high Olympus."

"To Elysium, then?" Hermes asked, though he already knew the answer.

Athena nodded, then took Hermes' outstretched hand into her own as they both faded from the realm of the unmemorable dead.

Nepheleid

Chapter Eighteen

Buttressed under a pile of blankets and cushions like a newly adopted pet spending his first night in his masters' dwelling, Derek stirred lightly, luxuriating in the warmth and softness of his bed. He knew he was likely no longer in Dr. Archer's guest bedroom, for he heard several distinct female voices arguing beyond the walls of this strange but elegant chamber. Derek stretched, feeling as a swaddled infant would in days of old when children were brought up almost exclusively by women. This, he had learned in his younger years, gave rise to the ancient belief that Consciousness itself was feminine in nature, enduring and immortal as Time itself, so long as humans kept their thoughts alive through Memory.

Speaking of Memory, what in the name of Odin's eyepatch happened last night?

Despite his best efforts, Derek could not remember how he found himself nestled in this cocoon, nor did he know the identity of his current host, for the furnishings in this room appeared far too feminine to belong to Dr. Archer's abode. No, this was somewhere else entirely, he concluded as he tried to recall what transpired after breaking free from Dennis' Emporium of etheromaniacs. Hallucinations notwithstanding, he did remember crossing paths with Junia's helpful, albeit aggrieved-looking older sister. Did Alita, or whatever her name was, take him home? Had he even remained capable of normal human locomotion in his altered state? Probably not. Big Sis presumably dragged him here, wherever *here* happened to be, after he lost consciousness, and then his reptilian brain likely overrode his drug-induced stupor and took control of his motor functions to build this pillow fort. That was the only explanation that made sense. Wait, was there a shiny golden robot maiden following them both? No, that must have been another hallucination.

Damn. I'm in so much trouble!

Derek closed his eyes and let the pangs of shame pass through him like a spell of nausea, then willed himself to regain his composure lest Dr.

Nepheleid

Argosi find him in this pitiful state and expel him from the Nephele's roster in disgust. Pressing his eyelids shut, Derek counted to ten, until he began to see stars behind his eyelids.

Breathe, dumbass! he heard his cerebellum holler from the most primitive parts of his psyche. *You can't be part of the crew up there if you're dead or in a coma!*

Right. Maybe the beautiful boss lady did not yet know that he was here, sleeping off the lingering effects of last night's terrible decisions. Derek took a calming breath, hoping that Alita-Lalita-Yaya somehow found the goodness in her heart not to inform her mother of his predicament. For all he knew, this room was one of many in an infirmary, where resort guests came to sober up after encountering Dennis in the most imprudent way. Derek smiled at the absurdity of this notion, as if any holiday centre would allocate a room specifically for those poor souls woefully unprepared to meet one of its most colourful denizens. As the levity of his thoughts unburdened his heavy heart, Derek found himself drifting off to sleep once again in his soft, cozy nest.

He dreamt of primal ancestral mothers, aunts, grandmothers, and older sisters speaking of matters of life and death, of keeping watch over their mortal descendants yet to be born, especially during their long voyage across the stars. One of these voices rose above all others; it was a familiar voice, one that never failed to bring Derek comfort and joy, and in recent years, to stir his rapidly maturing loins. This feminine power, this goddess of might and right, now proclaimed her ire in galvanized tones at one who failed to watch over one such precious mortal, and bemoaned how this slight would surely vindicate the smug ramblings of the Cloud-gatherer.

I must be dreaming, Derek pondered, his unfettered mind now imagining such an entity as a Cloud-gatherer, a transcendent being capable of amassing water vapour from the skies… the same way gravity gathers clouds of gases and dust in outer space, to create order from the chaos from whence stars and planets are born, and from which all life springs forth. Derek smiled at the fruit of his drug-fuelled fever dream, pleased at the high-mindedness of his musings, until he heard Dr. Archer's distinctive masculine voice joining the female chorus in the other room.

Derek rose to his feet, his blood pressure catching up a split second after his limbs achieved verticality. Dizzy and disoriented, he tiptoed towards

166

the door, only now noticing that someone had mercifully dressed him in a CARINA-logoed sweatshirt sometime between losing consciousness in the wee hours and this very instant. Grateful to be clad in more than his tighty-whities, Derek opened the door the width of a human hair, then instantly questioned whether he had, in fact, sobered up sufficiently to be witnessing the spectacle before him. He instantly recognized the room beyond as Dr. Argosi's parlour, and the women therein as Dr. Argosi herself surrounded by some of her older daughters, including the one who presumably brought him here last night. There were other women too, some he saw at the banquet the previous evening and others he had met at the CARINA campuses in Turtle Island. What troubled Derek the most was not the identity of Dr. Argosi's retinue, but rather how ethereally luminous they all seemed, as though blessed with an otherworldly comeliness he had not thought possible for mere human beings.

Dr. Argosi, in particular, radiated an aura of elemental power and a species of terrible beauty that both frightened Derek and titillated him in equal measure. Derek bit his lip, forcing his forebrain to concoct some semi-rational explanation for his reaction involving his latent Oedipal urges and his lack of experience in matters of physical intercourse with the fairer sex, of which Dr. Argosi represented the most perfect living specimen under the sun and among the stars. Derek blinked, then glimpsed Dr. Archer among the women. His senses had been correct even in his adulterated state, Derek remarked to himself as he began to notice that Dr. Archer, like the ladies, also appeared endowed with a preternatural and seductive allure. For the first time in his life, Derek questioned whether he was as set in his ways in matters pertaining to his unabashed attraction towards the opposite sex.

"You had but one task!" Dr. Argosi shrieked at Dr. Archer, the ferocity of her words breaking the spell of awe for Derek.

"To be fair, I never left the grounds of my palace," Dr. Archer replied, looking uncharacteristically contrite despite his augmented handsomeness.

"Well, you left him alone, *in spirit*", the lovely Dr. Argosi retorted with a hiss, "and Eileithya had to find him wandering about all of Olympus doing Titans-know-what, obviously in the throes of some wine-induced madness!"

Eileithya. Ei-lei-thya. Ei-lay-thaaaa-ya

Nepheleid

"My Lady –"

"Don't you dare '*My Lady*' me, young one!" Dr. Argosi said with the fury of a thousand neutron stars collapsing into a supermassive black hole of maternal wrath. "What would have happened had the Maenads gotten hold of him? We would be picking up his pieces scattered here and there until Dusk! What in the world were you thinking, leaving him unattended, when you know that there are those among our kind with evil intent towards the crew of the Nephele and its righteous mission?"

"Artemis kept watch over him from high above," Dr. Archer replied calmly.

Wait, what?

"She sent me a silver arrow as a warning that the lad was out and about," he continued. "He was never in any real danger-"

"That is not the point! He was *your* responsibility, not your sister's! And where, pray tell, did you drift off to while your charge got spirited away by that fiend Dionysus? The poor child, he must have been so frightened. Nothing in his sheltered existence could have prepared him for the unmitigated horrors he must have seen!"

Sheltered? Dr. Argosi thinks I am sheltered? And a child?

"Derek is quite all right, Mother," Eileithya interjected. "I put him to bed myself. There is not a scratch on him, and nary a hair out of place."

Aw, thank you, Ei-lay-thaaaa-ya.

"And the lad appears to have recovered his wits," Dr. Archer added, turning his gaze towards the door behind which Derek hid.

Dr. Argosi followed Dr. Archer's line of sight. When her intense glower met his eyes, Derek winced, causing Dr. Argosi to soften her gaze.

"Derek," she said in her usual caring, maternal tone, "why don't you come here, and let us make sure you're all right?"

"He is hiding his shame," Eileithya answered.

What the hell, Eileithya? Hey, I got it right!

"He fears you mean to expel him from the Nephele for his misadventure last night," Dr. Archer elaborated.

"And he's not wearing trousers," Hebe, Junia's other sister, the one that used to run the diner at Borealis on Turtle Island, explained while pantomiming Derek's predicament with an upraised finger. Barely concealing her grin, Hebe turned towards another stunning maiden standing by her side and said, "Thetis, be a dear and fetch the boy some pants from his luggage in Phoebus' palace. I would go myself, but Mother has tasked both Herakles and I with bodyguard duty."

The woman named Thetis at first appeared to balk at the request but complied and promptly left to relieve Derek of his plight.

"It's quite all right, Derek," Dr. Argosi said. "You can come out now. No one is cross with you."

Derek poked his head out from behind the door.

"Uh," Derek stammered. "Are you sure?" he continued, regretting his words immediately.

"Of course!" Dr. Argosi replied benevolently. "What happened last night was not your fault. Dionysus can be very persuasive. You should have been better warded against him," she added, throwing Dr. Archer a disappointed look.

"Um," Derek said. "I'd rather wait until…"

"Thetis," Hebe said helpfully.

"Thetis," Derek continued. "Until Thetis returns with… my pants."

"Oh, don't be ludicrous," Dr. Argosi scoffed. "I've raised many children before I jointed the CARINA Venture, I'll have you know. Boys and girls, some of them my own, others… not so much."

"Like Thetis?" Derek asked absentmindedly, his gaze darting in the general direction where Thetis had gone.

"Why yes," Dr. Argosi answered. "That is very perceptive of you. Yes, Thetis is one of my adopted children."

"There are more?" Derek continued, feeling more like an idiot with every passing moment.

Nepheleid

What is wrong with you? Keep it together!

"Yes, like my husband," Hebe answered in her mother's stead. "And no, we do not find this strange," she added almost as a warning to Derek to not press the matter any further.

"Uh, okay," Derek replied, his hands holding the door before him as if to safeguard his life. At that moment, a rather large gentleman stood up behind Hebe. Derek recognized him as the cook from the diner that Hebe used to run at Borealis. Somehow, the man looked even more imposing than Derek remembered, standing at approximately seven feet tall, and almost as wide from shoulder to shoulder. However, Derek knew that his senses could not be trusted at the moment, for everyone looked exaggeratedly enhanced in every imaginable way.

So Miss Hebe is married to the panini guy, and the panini guy is Dr. Argosi's adopted son. I guess that's cool, so long as Dr. Argosi and the panini guy are not related by blood. Wow, it must have been nice to have Dr. Argosi as a mom!

Dr. Archer bit his lip to stifle his laughter, as if he had heard Derek's silent musings. Now that he thought about it, it did seem to Derek that Dr. Archer usually went about his business as though he could hear everyone's innermost thoughts, and that these constituted a source of endless amusement for him. At that instant, Derek felt the tightness in his skivvies slacken, and the colour return to his face.

"I see that Derek is back to his old self," Dr. Archer said stoically, though Derek could tell from his voice that there was so much more he wished to say. "And here is Thetis with his garments. I hope that was not too much trouble, my dear?"

"None at all," Thetis replied flatly, handing Derek's folded pants to Dr. Archer. "Here, you can do the rest, lest I frighten the poor lamb."

"Thank you, darling," Dr. Argosi said. "You may take your leave, the lot of you, I can take it from here. Poor Derek has had quite the eventful night and likely hungers for breakfast. No, not you –" she directed at Dr. Archer. "You have much to answer for."

"Very well," Dr. Archer replied demurely, taking a seat on a divan in the sumptuous parlour. "But perhaps later might be more prudent."

"Mother, may I go?" Eileithya asked. "I am needed elsewhere."

"Of course," Dr. Argosi answered. "You have done well. Hebe and Herakles will safeguard the boy until he returns to the Nephele with his young friend, Paul Red Buffalo."

Paul. Oh god, Paul! Wait until I tell you all about these people! You have no idea!

Once Eileithyia and the host of preternaturally lovely ladies left the parlour, Hebe and her husband disappeared through a door at the far wall, then swiftly returned with trays of sandwiches and other hearty breakfast fare. They placed the food at a low table in the middle of the room and bade Derek to take a seat on one of the divans. Derek sat opposite Dr. Archer, who looked at the food impassively, while Hebe and the panini guy flanked Derek to his left and his right.

"So, Derek," Dr. Argosi said kindly as she took a seat next to Dr. Archer. "How are you feeling this morning, other than slightly embarrassed?"

"Uh, I'm fine, I guess," Derek answered.

"And you need not worry about your place on the Nephele," Dr. Argosi continued. "As I've told you, none of this was your fault."

"Thanks," Derek replied sheepishly before taking a bite of his breakfast club sandwich.

"Coffee?" Hebe asked him, pot in hand.

"Yes, thanks," Derek answered.

"You must think we are a bunch of degenerates," Dr. Argosi added contritely to Derek's surprise. "I assure you, none of this will happen again when we are high above the Earth and bound for the stars. I hope this experience did not sour you from remaining part of our crew."

"Oh, not at all," Derek replied truthfully.

"If there is anything I can do to make this up to you, please, do say so."

"Uh, well..."

"Yes?" Dr. Argosi asked. "Speak freely. There ought not to be any hard feelings between us."

"There is this one thing I was thinking about last night," Derek said.

Nepheleid

"When I was... you know."

"High as Icarus before he fell to Earth?" Hebe interjected, eliciting a snicker from Dr. Archer.

"Pretty much," Derek agreed. "Okay, so here's the thing: is Dennis joining the crew of the Nephele? I mean, I noticed that a lot of people who are on the CARINA roster actually come here to this resort, and I was wondering if Dennis was one of them."

"Why in the world would you ever think such a thing, Derek?" Dr. Argosi asked. "Dionysus almost got you torn limb from limb to quell the madness of his followers. I assure you that he and his retinue are very much personae non grata at the CARINA Venture, whether on the ground or high above the Earth."

"But I think that's a mistake," Derek retorted, causing the panini guy to spit his coffee all over his overly tight apron.

Dr. Archer raised an eyebrow but kept silent.

"How so?" Dr. Argosi asked in a neutral tone.

"Well, when I was under the influence," Derek explained, "I was feeling a lot of things... but I was not afraid anymore. I wasn't afraid of anything, except, you know, getting kicked out and all –"

"Right," Dr. Argosi said. "Do go on."

Derek paused, trying to find the words to explain how Dennis had appeared to him the previous night... as a being far older than he seemed, with a wisdom conjured up from the depths of Time, a Companion of Death, and one who removes all fear from human beings in times of imminent obliteration or dire desperation.

"Okay, maybe it was whatever he put into my wine," Derek said at last, "but Dennis seemed to know exactly what he was doing. He knew that I was feeling a bit out of sorts, full of doubts even, and he made that go away."

"Well, yes," Dr. Argosi agreed. "He drugged you into a stupor. That is what his kind does. I should not be surprised, really. He reminds me too much of El, one of my former Consorts. He was another twice-born, thrice-be damned God of wine I did well to be rid of... until my current ex-husband brought him back from the dead through the loins of his undead hussy! But I will not be burdened with the likes of either of them any longer. The Nephele and City-ships of its ilk are vessels of Life that will shine a light upon the darkness of the vast Cosmos, not instruments of mental oblivion!"

Derek looked upon Dr. Argosi as is for the first time, disbelieving the amount of resistance he encountered from one he thought as immeasurably wise.

"But I think that's wrong," Derek said boldly, his voice barely above a squeaky whisper. "I think Dennis has something to bring to the crew of the Nephele. Especially when we'll all be waiting to launch the CARINA fleet into interstellar space in a few decades, when some people will start to feel the effects of cabin fever on a massive scale and be too afraid to go into prolonged hibernation for fear they'll die along the way!"

Dr. Archer stirred in his seat, obviously captivated by what Derek had to say.

"I think," Derek said finally, "that Dennis could contribute greatly to the CARINA mission by removing people's fears. The fear of death, fear of the dark, fear of oblivion... by synthesizing his party favours and using it as medicine –"

"The mortal whelp makes a good point!" a familiar voice interrupted from beyond the front doors of Dr. Argosi's home.

Before Derek could continue his plea, he saw Hebe and the panini guy rising to their feet as Mr. Diaz strode through the front door of the parlour.

Dr. Archer turned around and slowly did the same, then closed the distance between himself and Derek to lay his hand upon his head.

"You have seen much, young one," Dr. Archer told Derek as Dr. Argosi and Mr. Diaz began arguing fiercely. "But now you must sleep. This is for your own good."

No, not again!

As Derek's lids grew heavy, he struggled against the enchantment Dr. Archer cast upon him with all his mortal might. Before his mental exhaustion finally overcame his resistance, his gaze turned towards his hostess and her unwelcome visitor. The intensity of their quarrel looked to Derek as though he was witnessing the proverbial irresistible force encountering the immovable object, like two diametrically opposed forces of nature whose clash lay at the heart of all Creation.

But this time, Heaven and Earth were in disarray, and Derek slumbered like a powerless child while the fate of the Universe was decided by the powers that be in Dr. Argosi's parlour.

Chapter Nineteen

Harried by the grievous turn of events unfolding in Elysium, rainbow-clad Iris emerged from the depths of the Underworld, her thousand-hued wings deployed with a vigour matched only by her unfailing resolve to complete her mission. Speeding towards the Nephele high above the Earth, Iris felt great relief that starry-robed Nyx had yet to return to her subterranean abode and yield the Heavens to Eos, goddess of the Dawn. Calmed by the certainty that her flight would at least elude slumbering mortals and unvigilant gods, the messenger goddess cast her gaze skyward, thinking only of reaching her kin awaiting her return in Hephaestus' quarters. Perhaps, Iris hoped, the smith god and his brother Prometheus would have grown weary of watching the endemic tomfoolery that besets Olympus after nightfall and set their minds instead to the finer workings of provisioning the golden apples from their mother's nuptial Garden with the building blocks of Life. Perhaps such an endeavour would find them both pleasantly gratified and more pliant to receiving alarming tidings about the whereabouts of grey-eyed Athena and swift Hermes who, for reasons known only to themselves, were presently paying an unforeseen visit to the Titans in Elysium.

Landing outside the bottom level of the freight compartment of the Hub, at a designated blind spot where immortals could surreptitiously board the nadir of the Nephele, Iris opened an outer service door and quickly slid through the airlock. Shaking loose the rapidly melting ice crystals enveloping her rainbow wings, the messenger goddess waited until the ichor returned to the surface of her flawless skin. She then put on a glamour to temper her considerable beauty, lest the few mortals she might encounter in this deserted area discern her deathless nature. Iris stepped into the cavernous chamber where the Henokhie lay motionless in the penumbra of the cargo bay, somewhat amused at how lifeless this place seemed when compared to the vibrant and industrious metropolis of learned mortals a few levels above.

Forsooth, Iris preferred the lofty liveliness of the Nephele and her highbrowed mortal crew to even the wistful bliss of Elysium where the shades of the Mighty Dead endure in perpetual nostalgia of their halcyon days of past glories. Iris never spent much time in the Kingdom of Hades, except when loud-thundering Zeus sent her to the shores of the Holy River Styx to fetch the sacred waters upon which the blessed gods swear oaths whenever the King of Olympus suspected his fellow immortals of deceiving him. Truth be told, Iris dreaded visiting the Underworld, for it also contained gloomy Tartarus, the Pit of the Damned where her twin sister Arke lay imprisoned with her Titan masters until Zeus declared a truce with his former foes. Iris had never known of any deathless god or Titan that fell into the dark abyss that lay at the very bottom of Tartarus – except perhaps for Eurymedon. That was Hera's first husband, and the true father of Prometheus whom Junia attempted to find when she first came to the Kingdom of Hades as a small child. If Junia told it true, Eurymedon's shade had crossed over into whatever lay at the other end of the abyss that frightened even the Titans, for it was said to swallow light in a swirl of vertiginous speed from which nothing escaped.

Until a few moments before Iris' abrupt departure from Elysium, everything had gone exactly according to plan; the messenger goddess arrived in Elysium in the nick of time before Eris, Junia, and Hermes emerged there from the living world above. Arke gladly let her twin take her place so that Iris could deliver her message to the sires of the gods, warning them that her Queen was in danger of forsaking their long-standing alliance. Iris told the Titans that Hera, through her singular ability to foster among mortals a sense of unabashed heroism in the service of their Queen, aimed to render the crew of the Nephele and the City-ships yet to come more exalted than the blessed gods who dwell on holy Olympus and their mortal hero offspring of old. When Iris' admonition failed to vex the Titans, the messenger goddess told them that Hera meant to inspire the mortal crew of the Nephele under her care to achieve deeds that would render the exploits of the Titans obsolete. Iris told them that Hera deemed the colonization of worlds warmed by distant stars far more illustrious than the Titans' feat of sundering their father Ouranos, the very first Sky-King, from their mother Gaia in the act of procreation, and becoming the Pillars of the Cosmos and the architects of the world of matter and flesh in the aeons that followed.

When King Kronos, the Master of Time and Infinity who sees all that has come to pass and all that has yet to be, asked Iris how this eventuality could prevail when he had not foreseen it himself, Iris answered that

Hera had grown resentful against the Titans for remaining silent about Zeus' murder of Eurymedon. Hera no longer saw her friendship with the Titans as a boon, for the Titans never had cause to keep Zeus' most egregious trespass against her a secret. Suspicious that Iris' words were meant to deceive him, Kronos countered that his favourite daughter ought to have more compassion towards her elders, for he and his brothers had told her everything they knew about Zeus' dalliances and other dastardly acts throughout the millennia. Everything, except for the murder of Eurymedon, for at the time Zeus required all the gods of the Earth, Sea, and Sky, as well as those imprisoned in gloomy Tartarus to swear an Oath of secrecy by the Holy River Styx. Satisfied that she had at long last roused the ire of the Titans, Iris retorted that Hera may yet forgive her father and his formerly imprisoned brothers if they somehow convinced the young Junia that the world of mortals, fashioned over aeons upon the broad-pathed Earth by the hands of Olympian-born heroes and countless others of dubious moral character, held nothing for her.

Complicit in Iris' deception, Klymene voiced her agreement, reminding King Kronos and her Titan husband Iapetos that even they could not afford to stir Hera's enmity. It remained the Queen's prerogative to ban the Titans from boarding the Nephele and the future City-ships of its ilk, thus denying the sires of the gods a hand in fashioning the world of mortals yet to come. When the Titans scoffed at this eventuality, Iris reminded them that they ought to have known that Hera would one day learn of their unwitting complicity in keeping Zeus' heinous deed a secret and that they should never doubt the degree of spite that would surely surface from the deep well of anger from which Hera drew much of her strength of will. It was only a matter of time before Hera's wrath fell upon the Titans, Klymene added, to which Iris nodded in assent. Iris remembered trying to hide her mirth at the Titans' reaction, for she believed they truly deserved some of the disquiet her words had brought until Hermes and Athena appeared in Elysium with inquiries of their own. And now, Iris feared that the blessed gods who dwell on starry Olympus would soon face an entirely different species of formidable peril: the wrath of the Virgin Warrior once the Titans, unnerved by Iris and Klymene's goading, revealed to her the fate that befell her mother after Zeus swallowed her whole!

Even in peaceful times, Iris sometimes fantasized about what it would be like to abandon her station as messenger of the gods – and of Hera in particular – as her duties often took her away from the loving arms of her husband, Zephyrus, god of the west wind and long a rival to Apollo. Iris' duties also took her away from her son Pothos, a loyal servant of golden Aphrodite. Pothos reminded his parents, time and again, how much he dreaded the prospect of leaving Olympus to dwell on the Nephele absent his mistress, for Hera continued to ban Aphrodite from joining her crew on their voyage across the vast expanse beyond the stars. In days of old, long before mortals abandoned the piety of their forefathers and replaced their gods with the Nazarene, Iris spent her days and nights running interference and relaying messages between the gods. During the Trojan War in particular, she did her best to prevent her kin from annihilating one another in the throes of rage. At one time, she even had to foil Hera and Athena from joining the fray among the Argives, warning them of Zeus' wrath if they disobeyed his decree against the blessed gods meddling in the affairs of mortals during that sordid war. But the aftermath of Athena visiting the Titans in Elysium, a first since the very Cosmos began, would likely render the world-shattering Trojan War into an inconsequential tiff by comparison. Iris now wondered how she would ever give such dire tidings to Prometheus and Hephaestus and the others, without the smith god leaping to Olympus in free-fall, possibly without his parachute-equipped tool belt, to evacuate his mother, his sisters, and perhaps, should he feel particularly generous today, his brother Ares, and Aphrodite.

Steeling herself for the bedlam to follow, Iris raced through deserted cargo bays and into scantily staffed service corridors to the main habitat tier housing the living quarters of the Nephele. Once outside Hephaestus' dwelling, she paused before the closed door to gather her thoughts. To her surprise, the door opened unbidden. In the room beyond, Hephaestus, Prometheus, Asia, Mnemosyne, and Hephaestus' golden handmaiden Aglaea sat in a semi-circle, waiting for the messenger goddess to enter.

"My Lords and Ladies," Iris began mechanically, momentarily forgetting the lack of formality common among immortals aboard the Nephele. "I have some strange news from the world below-"

"You need not fret, my dear," Mnemosyne replied warmly. "Prometheus has already foretold that which you mean to tell us."

"Oh?" Iris retorted, caught unawares. "When did you –"

"I knew what had come to pass as soon as Galatea told us that Ares and Apollo returned to Olympus with Eris and Junia, but without Hermes and Athena," Prometheus replied calmly.

"Ares and Apollo?" Iris inquired, fleetingly confused. "Wait, what did they have to do with this? Did I miss something?"

Asia and Hephaestus exchanged a knowing look, then chortled, to Iris' growing annoyance.

"When Hermes returned from Elysium without Eris and Junia," Aglaea answered, "he told Athena, Apollo, and Ares that the Titans turned the child against the heroes of old, as well as her Olympian brethren. They all went looking for them, although Apollo never really left."

Iris' lovely countenance affected a most perplexed expression, prompting Asia and Hephaestus' laughter to grow into a rapid crescendo.

"I think you two need a nap," Iris retorted in exasperation. "Because what I have to tell you is no laughing matter!"

"To be fair, my dear," Mnemosyne said, "if you saw what Galatea has been showing us all night, you would also be in stitches."

"Of that I have no doubt," Iris replied neutrally. "But Athena and Hermes... they detoured to Elysium and then Athena started to ask the Titans some questions."

"They did not see you, I hope," Hephaestus inquired once he regained his composure.

"I think not, but if they did, they might have mistaken me for my sister."

"You ought not to worry about that," Prometheus said. "I saw Athena in my mind's eye just now. She is most preoccupied with another matter entirely."

Iris nodded, glad in knowing that Prometheus understood the severity of their plight.

"So, what shall we do now?" Iris asked Prometheus. "When I left Elysium, Athena came upon the Titans looking as flustered as I had ever seen her. As for the Titans, they might be of the mind that it is now in their best interest to always tell the truth to any Olympian that crosses their path in the Kingdom of Hades."

Nepheleid

"You think they will tell Athena the truth about her mother? Their truce with Zeus be damned?" Asia asked, all mirth gone from her voice.

"They might," Iris confessed.

"And they will," Prometheus agreed, giving Hephaestus a most solemn look.

Hephaestus turned to the viewing screen behind him, then whispered something to Galatea who stood by on Olympus below them.

"So, now what?", Iris asked again.

"Now you will find the mortal, Paul Red Buffalo, and send him to starry Olympus much sooner than anticipated," Hephaestus answered, his gaze fixed on the viewing screen.

"Oh, young Derek will like that very much," Asia retorted.

"And Heaven knows," Mnemosyne said, "his presence will provide some much-needed distraction and defuse tensions until –"

"Until we can be certain of Athena's plan of action after she learns the truth about what became of her mother," Prometheus added. "This will also buy us some time to muster whatever forces we may need to intervene, should the need arise. Until then, we will remain on standby and keep watch through the eyes of Galatea on Olympus."

"Very well," Iris said, as she began to unfold her rainbow wings and prepare to take flight.

"Iris, wait!" Asia interjected before the messenger goddess took her leave. "Take the Henokhie this time. You are in danger of giving the Red Buffalo lad quite a fright!"

"Right," Iris agreed as she turned to walk towards the exit to Hephaestus' quarters.

Though I doubt even I could frighten Paul Red Buffalo. He is of the Anishinaabe people; he does not frighten easily, and I suspect he knows more about us than even Prometheus can divine.

Chapter Twenty

In a prismatic din of many-hued entropic forms, stalwart Ares followed fractious Eris out of the expanse between the worlds, holding fast to young Junia's hand as the three siblings landed upon their mother's Garden behind the Queen's palace. Blinking quickly to cast aside the strange geometric shapes crowding his field of vision, the god of war bade his sisters to crouch beside him for a moment, if only to give him enough time to get his bearings upon this hallowed and welcoming ground. He recognized the tree under which his mother slept for many days upon her eventful return from the Garden of the Hesperides when Winter last turned to Spring, after her battle with Gaia over the fate of humanity's future ended in a most confounding stalemate to all those present.

Ares and his siblings took turns keeping watch over their mother during her long slumber, enjoying the peace of her Garden, where the stars and the wanderers appeared so much closer than anywhere else upon the broad-pathed Earth. On this morn, however, as the starry firmament paled with the emerging Dawn, the quietude of Hera's Olympian refuge was broken by the familiar din of the King and Queen arguing loudly in the front parlour of her majestic palace.

"Odd," Eris quipped. "They have not had a spat of this decibel level in ages!"

"This bodes ill," Ares replied.

"Why?" Junia inquired.

"Because the greater the quarrel," Eris answered, "the longer they linger in their marriage-bed upon reconciliation!"

"That's ridiculous!" Junia protested incredulously.

Ares chuckled. "Oh, we are well aware, Stargazer," he said. "And yet it was always so."

Nepheleid

"How do you think the lot of us were conceived?" Eris japed when Junia threw her a dubious glare.

"Never mind that," Ares said as he rose to his feet. "We may as well use the distraction to sneak this one back into her bedchamber. You two, after me!"

Lifting his shield, Ares led the way into the rear entrance of their mother's palace, where in a mortal dwelling one could have expected to find a scullery. Eris followed at his heel, hiding behind her twin's massive form, and deploying her wings to hide Junia from view despite the child's muffled protests. Once inside, the god of war took a step towards the main corridor leading towards the cloister housing the countless bedchambers in which Hera had housed her children and other wards over the course of centuries. Satisfied that no one noticed or cared about their arrival, Ares stood guard as Eris spirited Junia into the child's bedchamber. He kept a watchful eye on the passage towards the parlour while Junia hopefully changed into her sleeping apparel, all the while straining to discern the cause of his parents' latest squabble.

The god of war did not relish having to intervene in yet another conflict between the King and Queen of Olympus, even if he, whether for good or ill, unfailingly elected to take his mother's side in her unceasing clash against the Cloud-gatherer. Ares often justified lending his boundless might towards enforcing Hera's interests to avenge himself and his mother against Zeus' inexplicable habit of favouring his bastards over his legitimate children, though at times his conscience struggled with the outcome of his partisanship. It was Ares who forbade the lands of ancient Hellas from giving refuge to dark-robed Leto while she laboured to give birth to her twins, bright Apollo and fleet-footed Artemis, with whom the god of war had no further quarrel. Ares also found himself on many occasions at odds with Herakles when he was still mortal, for the demigod often slew his mortal-born children during his many adventures.

Nevertheless, Ares possessed few qualms about charging to Hera's rescue whenever his father's ill-conceived machinations threatened his mother's virtue and integrity. It was he, not Hermes, who arrested Ixion when the scoundrel was caught fornicating with the cloud-nymph Nephele, fashioned by Zeus in Hera's image to entrap the villain who attempted to rape the Queen of Olympus after she refused his advances. Had Hermes not stayed his hand, Ares would have torn the mortal to pieces before the innocent cloud-nymph bore the fruit of the miscreant's impious lust. Putting this vile recollection out of his mind, Ares focused instead on the exact words being shouted at the front of the palace. Of course, the only voices he could hear were those of his mother and father, for no one ever dared to interject in the quarrels between Zeus and Hera – not since Hephaestus found himself flung from the abode of the gods when he came to the Queen's aid on the night the blessed gods rebelled against their King.

This time, the apple of discord consisted of Zeus decrying Hera's prohibition against Dionysus joining the crew of the Nephele, among many others. Ares frowned upon hearing Zeus utter the name of his favourite bastard, the one Hera tried to annihilate more often than Herakles for his affront to the natural order by having been conceived through so many avenues of unholy incest, including Ares' own lineage. The god of war then smiled as he recalled how grateful his mother had been when he opposed Dionysus and Herakles in their campaign against the people of India.

Ah yes, that whole sorry business. And to think, after all these years, Father persists in accusing me of possessing ceaseless bloodthirst, after he summoned his own mother, rich-haired Rhea, to goad Dionysus into conquering the Brahmans by storming the Hill of Sages! At least Eris made short work of that twice-born whelp in this whole sordid affair, albeit by the lights of her very own genius.

Ares turned around to glimpse at the closed door of Junia's bedchamber, while Zeus now griped about how Hera had lost her way ever since the Hydra's venom rendered her immune to all the poisons of the broad-pathed Earth, even the ones with pleasant effects.

"Well then," Ares heard Hera retort. "I should be so lucky to have lost my way, for I know above all other blessed gods and mortals how to peer through the veil that blinds most from seeing the Cosmos in its true guise, without addling my senses or compromising my sanity! I, know all too well that if one develops the discipline one can only acquire through heroism and hardship, one could learn to see through the Mysteries of Chaos and Time the way I did when trapped in the belly of Kronos."

"Are you two ready to come out?" Ares asked his sisters through the closed door. *Please be ready, this argument is getting more absurd by the minute!*

"I knew plenty of hardship in my day, I'll have you know!" Zeus shrieked in reply.

"Oh really?" Hera inquired sardonically. "When pray tell, have you, who were favoured above all others by our mother and spared the dreadful fate that befell the eldest daughters and sons of Kronos, ever experienced hardships that were not of your own design!"

"Mother spared me from Kronos, that is true," Zeus conceded. "But she did not bring me up in the lap of luxury in the same manner that Okeanos and Tethys raised you! Oh, no, she left me on the Isle of Crete, far from starry Olympus, in the care of the Curetes who made a dreadful racket with their drums and cymbals every time I cried or made a noise!"

"They did that so Father could not hear you or find you!" Hera objected.

"Still," Zeus continued. "I had to put up with that bedlam until I grew to manhood and was old enough to rescue the lot of you! And *you're welcome*, by the way!"

"And still, for all your might," Hera countered, "you still need to partake of the rot that binds the fertile soil of the Earth to the Web of Life to have even a glimpse of the Mysteries that even the gods cannot easily perceive; the same that Dionysus gave to that poor mortal boy Derek!"

As if prompted by the sound of her classmate's name uttered in such an unexpected manner, Junia, now clad in soft-hued pyjamas adorned with endearing albeit jejune figures, opened the door of her bedchamber and gave Ares a sharp look.

"What the hell did Mom say they did to Derek?" Junia inquired bluntly.

Ares held his tongue, knowing full well that the truth would arouse the child's displeasure to an unfathomable degree.

"He was drugged, obviously," Eris answered bluntly from inside the bedchamber, "we told you as much while we were in the Underworld, albeit not in quite so many words."

"No, you didn't!" Junia protested. "And one more thing –"

Interrupting herself to distract her siblings, Junia sprinted towards the front parlour before Ares could catch her by the scruff of her suspiciously unwrinkled nightshirt. Eris took flight to follow Junia, though without attempting to stop her from reaching her destination. Ares sighed, then brought up the rear at a rapid yet measured pace, well aware that Junia would not take the news of how exactly Derek's mind became addled in their absence with the gentle good humour one could expect from a more seasoned immortal.

Ares, Eris, and Junia predictably found Zeus and Hera verbally sparring at the centre of the sumptuous sitting room, while Apollo stood placidly between the quarrelling pair, and Hebe and Herakles flanked a very unconscious Derek. The boy somehow managed to slumber peacefully while the King and Queen of Olympus argued with the fury of a thousand simultaneous supernovae. While their parents were distracted with one another's vexing presence, Herakles proceeded to gently pry Derek off the couch, as Hebe took great care to pull the sleeping lad's pants back up around his waist. As Ares feared, the sight of Derek's garments left untied around his waist visibly infuriated Junia, as evidenced by the child clenching her fists and her jaw with terrifying force.

Momentarily ignoring all others – even their mother, which Ares found rather strange – Junia turned her gaze towards Zeus and glowered at him ferociously.

"What. Happened. To. Derek," she asked with an emphatic staccato.

"Well, good morning, Zoe," the Cloud-gatherer replied with exaggerated cheerfulness. "Did you sleep well?"

As Hera conspicuously rolled her eyes, Ares suppressed a chuckle. Very few blessed gods or mortals could convey their contempt with such artful flair, he thought, while Zeus ignored his wife's tacit commentary on his perfunctory parenting.

"What in THE ACTUAL HELL did Dionysus do to DEREK!" Junia continued, undaunted by her parents' theatrics.

"He is quite all right, really," Apollo answered in the Thunderer's stead. "At least he will be when he awakens."

"It's a little late for that, he's already had quite the awakening of his own!" Hebe said with an earnest giggle, echoed by Herakles and Apollo despite the latter's efforts to keep his composure.

"Come, children," Hera told Junia, Eris, and Ares with a soft, inviting tone, as if she had not tried to verbally obliterate the King of Olympus a mere few moments ago. "Come join us for some breakfast."

Eris said nothing, letting her usual sly smile convey her amusement. Though no longer concerned with Zeus and Hera's quarrel escalating into a cataclysm of cosmic proportions, Ares kept his shield raised and took a stance to remove all doubt that he was at the ready, as if expecting battle.

"And pay no mind to the mortal fare," Hebe said. "That was for Derek's benefit."

"What did Dionysus do to Derek!!!!" Junia asked Zeus, unmoved by her mother's words of welcome.

"You truly are of a singular mind!" Zeus retorted snidely. "She takes after you on that account!" he then told Hera.

"Derek was left alone all night," Hera answered Junia while throwing a baleful glower at Apollo. "He woke up sometime during the night and imprudently joined Dionysus for a drink."

"Your friend is quite the lightweight, little one," Herakles said while effortlessly carrying Derek across the room and towards the corridor leading to the cloister of bedchambers. "When I was his age, I could drink an entire symposium under the table!"

Hebe let out another giggle as she caught up with her husband. "Don't you worry about him," she said as she tied the drawstring of Derek's pants more securely around his waist. "He will sleep off the ill effects of the wine and be none the wiser in a few hours."

"I'm afraid you are dreadfully incorrect, my darling," Hera told Hebe. "But it is of no consequence. You can all thank Eileithya for finding him when she did, otherwise, Eris would have had to confound the poor lamb once again while dead Maenads fell from the Sky with the rising of the Sun!"

"Now you are being dramatic," Zeus retorted, shaking his head. "The Maenads would not have murdered the boy, he is our guest!"

"Shut up! Shut up! Shut up SHUT UP!!!" Junia shrieked, to the alarm of everyone present, save for Eris and Hera. Eris persisted in her state of constant bemusement while white-armed Hera affected her characteristic inscrutable demeanour, as she often does, whenever events took an unexpected turn.

"Mom," Junia said at last after taking a few frantic breaths, "I want out! Right now! I want to go home! I've made my decision, and I want to go back to the Nephele!"

"Not before you take a nap, you little brat!" Zeus replied. "You look as though you've been up all night!" Turning his gaze towards Eris, the Father of gods and men added, "You wouldn't happen to know anything about that, would you?"

Eris wisely opted not to answer, as Ares' fingers found their way around the hilt of his sword. Before the threat implied in his conditioned reflex could materialize, his nephews Anicetos and Alexiares, the strong and stalwart sons of Hebe and Herakles who forever guard the ramparts of starry Olympus, ran into the room looking rather agitated and excited in equal measure.

"Grandfather, Grandmother," Alexiares said when he finally found his voice. "A young man – a mortal – just arrived beyond the citadel walls... He was inside a ..."

"A flying watercraft of some sort," Anicetos continued as his brother caught his breath.

"A flying *canoe*?" Hera inquired. "Like the one Zeus rode into the Kingdom of Hades when Winter last turned to Spring?"

"The boys weren't there when that happened," Ares said to everyone's surprise, for he had not uttered a single word after entering Hera's parlour with his sisters.

"Right," Zeus agreed, begrudgingly acknowledging the god of war's observation. "Now, who is this mortal, and why the bloody hell is Hermes not the one telling me this?"

"Here I am, Father," Hermes said as he entered, with bright-eyed Athena a few paces behind him. The Virgin Warrior looked uncharacteristically irate, which Eris must have thought rather intriguing, for her demeanour changed when she saw the pair materialize out of thin air just outside the open doors of Hera's palace. All the others stared at Hermes and Athena in silence, as if they all needed a moment to fully comprehend the strangeness of the morning's events.

"Uh, guys?" said a familiar voice from beyond the palace doors. "Hello?"

Nepheleid

In the span of a mortal heartbeat, Hera walked briskly out onto the landing, followed by Anicetos and Alexiares, then Hermes, Athena, Apollo, Zeus, Junia and Eris, with Ares bringing up the rear for a second time. Hebe and Herakles remained within the confines of the palace, keeping a watchful eye over the slumbering Derek lest another immortal spirit the lad away for more consciousness-expanding escapades.

Hera gasped when she saw the newcomer, whom Ares recognized as Derek's close friend and classmate. Before the Queen could utter words of welcome, Apollo walked ahead of the gathering of blessed gods to greet the young man, who stood beside his hovering conveyance a few paces from the steps to the palace.

"Paul Red Buffalo," the Archer said in a blithesome tone. "It looks as though you've arrived among us in the nick of time!"

Chapter Twenty-One

Like all the gods and goddesses who make their home in the depths of the wine-dark Sea, silver-footed Thetis possessed the gift of prophecy. Sometimes – usually ineffectually – she used it to conspire against the decrees of the Fates to protect those dearest to her heart. That is how Thetis knew the moment she laid eyes upon the mortal boy Derek that trouble was afoot, regardless of whether the innocent lad fully understood where he was and in whose company he would spend what would prove to be, in all probability, the last days of his mortal existence. The dread for the boy's longevity abated somewhat when Eileithya and the golden maiden Galatea brought the half-conscious youth to the Queen's palace. However, it rekindled the moment Thetis' foster-sister Hebe, the long-reigning former Princess of Olympus before her marriage to stalwart Herakles, tasked her with retrieving Derek's garments in Apollo's abode.

A sovereign's daughter in her own right, brine-born Thetis should have scoffed at the assignment, for she had not come to starry Olympus the previous year to play handmaiden to mortal fools trespassing upon the Citadel of Heaven. She came instead to petition Hera to use her lingering queenly influence to help restore the health of the ailing Seas and Oceans. Much to Thetis' dismay, she found her foster-mother inordinately more preoccupied with leaving her King, and the world behind, with a crew of learned mortals aboard a City-ship than helping what remained of the mortal and deathless inhabitants of the Earth thrive in a languishing biosphere. Hera did eventually rescue all Life upon the imperilled Earth, albeit in a most circuitous manner, on the day she siphoned into herself all the toxic poisons out of the air, the lands and the waters. Hera's intent was not to cure the world of its many ills, but rather to forge a mighty weapon against Gaia, should the Earth-Mother persist in resisting Hera's plans to abandon her post as Queen of Olympus and fly away to parts unknown aboard the Nephele.

The Queen's gambit succeeded. Gaia relented, giving Zeus the opportunity to retrieve his errant bride and return her to Olympus.

Nepheleid

There Hera cleansed herself of the miasma in a bathing pool inside the Thunderer's palace, now sealed with an enclosure of iron and star-metal. Then Hera fell into a long slumber, leaving her bridegroom in a state of abject frustration. Still, the Queen's act of brazen gumption earned her renewed respect and gratitude from the Sea-Court. For this reason alone, Thetis swallowed her pride and complied with Hebe's command that she retrieve the pants of the mortal boy Derek, intending to quietly abscond from Olympus even before Hera dismissed her entourage the moment Derek regained a semblance of consciousness.

As Thetis made her way beyond the ramparts of starry Olympus, she could hear the Queen having a row with Zeus. Before Hera left Olympus to dwell on Turtle Island among mortals, these frequent disturbances to the tenuous peace in the abode of the gods would end with the King and Queen reconciling in their marriage-bed. Now, they seemed to never resolve their unceasing quarrels leaving it to linger in a constant stalemate that threatened to seal the very fate of Olympus. Junia would soon come of age and make her choice known of whether to stay among her kin in the Olympian court or to leave aboard the Nephele with its crew of learned mortals, never to return. Knowing full well that Junia would choose the latter, and that Zeus would find cause to disregard her choice if it did not align with his designs, Thetis feared that another potential war among the gods of holy Olympus was soon to unfold. For this reason, she intended to seek the counsel of immortals far older and wiser than herself, as her last attempt to thwart a war among the blessed gods who dwell on starry Olympus ended in Zeus chaining Hera to the Sky for a night, and Thetis becoming unwittingly betrothed to the King of Olympus.

At times, Thetis almost felt sympathy for the Cloud-gatherer's current plight of being slowly and elaborately abandoned by his beloved wife of more than three millennia. Then she came to her senses. Thetis remembered that Zeus very much deserved all the spite Hera could throw at him, not only for being the worst of husbands but also for standing idle as the world ran amok when mortals abandoned the faith of their ancestors and turned to the worship of the Nazarene. This was a turn of events Zeus should have foreseen when he favoured his son Dionysus above all others, long before the rise of old Rome. Forsooth, there were times when Thetis thought Zeus to be an absolute idiot, an opinion often shared by Hera and other blessed gods. Though brilliant at leading his siblings and allies in their struggle to wrest the throne of Heaven from their father Kronos – in much the same way that Kronos and rich-haired Rhea robbed their siblings Okeanos and Tethys from the same throne – Zeus' reigning style left a lot to be desired.

The Thunderer seemed to forget that he did not become the current ruling Sky-King on his own, nor could he have liberated his siblings without the help of the ill-fated Oceanid Metis. Zeus also often, and conveniently, overlooked the role his allies – especially Hera – played in achieving victory over the Giants in their war against the children Gaia who sought to avenge the death of of the gentle and innocuous Eurymedon. Hera had prophesied that the Gods of Olympus could only attain victory over the Giants with the help of a mortal hero born under the sign of the Lion. Zeus repaid her by scorning and humiliating his Queen through countless infidelities and favouring his ill-begotten bastards over their own legitimate progeny his wife dutifully bore him. It was little wonder, Thetis surmised, that Hera soured on her union with Zeus to the point of disavowing her pledge to Phanes, whom mortals call Eros the Elder.

In a perfunctory show of paternal remorse, Zeus attempted to reverse course by lavishing undue interest upon young Junia. However, his decision to leave the fate of Olympus to the whims of a child also proved a reckless gamble that even he would have scorned had it come from any other immortal. For this reason alone, Thetis could not help but feel as though Zeus deserved the humiliation that would doubtlessly ensue. Despite that, she could not in all good conscience allow the fragile peace of starry Olympus to evanesce on account of the foolhardiness of its King. This was why she dove to the depths of the Sea to a cave she knew well to elude at the best of times, for in the darkness beyond lay a passage to the Kingdom of Hades, known only to herself and the brine-born daughters of Nereus, but undetectable by the learned mortals and their sophisticated instruments.

The first time silver-footed Thetis visited the Kingdom of the dead, she sought to fetch the Hecatonshire Briareus. This was the hundred-armed son of Gaia, and a guard of the gate of gloomy Tartarus. He helped free Zeus from his bonds on the night the blessed gods rebelled against their King. Back then, Thetis had also only meant to prevent a war among the gods, but her intervention proved disastrous for her beloved foster-mother, who almost lost her throne as Queen of Heaven when Zeus sought to repudiate Hera and replace her with his saviour. Truth be told, Thetis owed a debt of gratitude to Prometheus, then newly freed by Herakles, for telling Zeus the prophecy about Thetis bearing a son who would exceed the might of his father. This spared the Nereid from becoming Zeus' Queen, a fate for which she did not possess the forbearance. Still, this whole sordid affair left Thetis unwittingly betrothed to the mortal Peleus, a crew member of the famous ship Argo, and her wedding subsequently became the underlying cause of the Trojan War.

The last time Thetis came to the Underworld, she elected to remain in the shallows of the Holy River Styx and dunk her infant son Achilles in its waters to render him invulnerable to death. In hindsight, Thetis should not have held the boy by his heel, but instead submerged him in a porous reed basket so that every surface of his little body could have been bathed in the Holy River's beneficial waters. But such was no longer her concern, for the divine Achilles was long dead and enjoying a blissful afterlife in Elysium with that battleaxe Medea, the former bride of Jason, captain of the glorious Argo. It was a strange thing that Medea should have wed Achilles after their mortal deaths. When Medea was newly wed to Jason, Thetis has been long estranged from her husband Peleus due to the mortal's interference in the goddess' attempts to render their children immortal by immolating them in fire late one night while Peleus slept. The pair were reconciled when Thetis, under Hera's coaxing, came to the aid of the Argonauts along with her Sea-nymph sisters. They had helped the Argonauts to cross the deadly straight between Charybdis and Scylla, where mortal sailors invariably met their doom.

At times she longed for the days when she dwelt with Peleus in Iolcus along with Jason and Medea. However, brine-born Thetis thought it wisest to keep her presence in Elysium discreet to avoid crossing paths with the shades of her mortal husband, son, her former friend, and Jason – she had a task to bring to completion. Steeling her resolve, Thetis sidestepped Charon's barge ferrying the shades of the newly departed and crossed the Holy River Styx on foot, as befits a Sea-nymph. Once her feet touched the other shore, she made her way towards Elysium to seek an audience with the Titan-King Kronos who, despite his considerable failings as a father, once ruled as a just and wise King over mortals during the Golden Age of Man. During Kronos' reign, human beings abandoned their rude and wretched way of life, hidden in the deep and dark caverns of the world, and embraced a more refined existence when the cold mantle of Ice that covered the whole of the broad-pathed Earth melted and gave way to gentler, greener pastures.

Keeping such thoughts at the forefront of her mind, silver-footed Thetis crossed over to the Isle of the Blessed, hoping to be greeted by an emissary of the Titan-King such as Arke, twin sister to Iris of the rainbow wings. She was met instead by rich-haired Rhea, Kronos' Queen and mother of the King and Queen of Olympus. As a foster-child of Hera, Thetis learned long ago to be wary of the Titan-Queen's counsel. While Rhea eventually arranged for her imprisoned children to be released through the intervention of her youngest son and Metis, his Oceanid paramour, her child-rearing methods also left a lot to be desired, much like those of her son her son Zeus. Indeed, the only child Rhea ever did raise from an infant was her grandson Dionysus, rescued from Hera's wrath by swift Hermes, a fact that failed to endear the Titan-Queen to the reigning Queen of Olympus. To make matters worse, for centuries Hera believed that her mother had forsaken her, leaving her in the care of Okeanos and Tethys when she was a young maiden for reasons she never fully understood, until she learned the truth about her doomed first husband Eurymedon and what became of the son she bore him.

Of course, Thetis could never begrudge Rhea for taking her grandson Dionysus under her care. The Nereid had granted the young god shelter in the depths in his flight from King Lykourgos, an ally of Hera and Ares opposing Dionysus in his campaign against the people of Asia Minor, India, and beyond. There, Thetis encouraged Dionysus not to abandon the fight against his foes, for though even Zeus himself at times surrendered to Hera's fury, Dionysus' triumph over the Queen's forces would give him far more to boast about – and maybe earn him Hera's respect once he took his rightful place among the gods. To this day, Thetis thanked the Fates that Hera never knew about the kindness she had shown Dionysus, who proved a far worthier and longer-lived scion of Olympus than Zagreus, his previous incarnation born of Zeus' incestuous lust for rosy-cheeked Persephone.

Still, having been raised at Hera's breast and in the Queen's palace until she came of age and made her home in the Sea, Thetis knew all too well that Rhea invariably favoured Zeus in her dealings with her royal children, even when Hera proved right in challenging Zeus' decrees. Perhaps Rhea possessed her own strategy for keeping Hera on her golden throne on starry Olympus, despite knowing full well that the Queen would follow Junia to the Nephele should the child choose this fate for herself. Mindful that her dealings with Rhea might involve some degree of subterfuge, Thetis thought it best to quickly devise a clever excuse for her presence in the Kingdom of Hades, a place most unsuited for Sea-dwellers like herself.

Nepheleid

"My dear child," rich-haired Rhea told Thetis as she walked to the shore to greet her. "What a wonderful surprise! May I ask what you are doing here? Is trouble afoot on holy Olympus?"

"I, I –" Thetis stammered, her clever excuse still eluding her. "I... am here to see my son, Achilles. And his father, Peleus, and –"

Rhea frowned. "You are a terrible liar, Brine-born," she scolded Thetis. "I would have thought you far craftier for having been raised by my daughter. I suppose such things happen when the apple and the tree are not of the same root!"

"Right," Thetis replied, careful not to show anger at the insult. "And, oh look, King Kronos. I came to have an audience with the Titan-King, Queen Mother."

"Does Zeus know you are here?" Rhea asked Thetis skeptically.

"No, Queen Mother," Thetis answered truthfully. "No one knows I am here, not even Hera."

"And Hera knows just about everything, does she not?" wily Kronos answered in his wife's stead, as Rhea stepped aside to sit on her couch. "Things above must be dire indeed, for until earlier today, the only denizen of Olympus that ever came to visit us Titans, other than our wives, was Hera."

"My Lord Titan?" Thetis said, unsure how to reply.

"Strangely enough," Kronos continued, "we've not seen hide nor hair of our daughter today, but we saw almost everyone else here in Elysium in the span of one Autumn Night upon the broad-pathed Earth. Do you not also find this strange, young one?"

"I suppose this is quite unusual," Thetis agreed.

"And now here you are," Kronos said. "Have you had enough of the tomfoolery high above the clouds on starry Olympus?"

"No, that's not why I'm here," Thetis said weakly. "I'm –"

"Tired of feeling like a pawn of the Fates?" Kronos interrupted.

Thetis paused, letting the truth of Kronos' words penetrate her mind.

"Why, yes," the Nereid agreed after a moment. "Although I feel more often like a pawn in Eris' game to sow Chaos among the gods whenever they displease her."

"Oh?" Kronos replied, raising an eyebrow. "Do go on."

"I know it must not be easy being an unloved child," Thetis continued, "but I feel as though the latest events on high Olympus are part of a game she is covertly playing, to sway Junia's mind on the matter of leaving the Earth with the learned mortals aboard the Nephele."

"The child would not need much convincing," Rhea interjected. "Unless memory fails me, just this past afternoon her mind was all but made up. She essentially announced as much when she brought a mortal guest with her on Olympus to drive the point!"

"But that is not what troubles your mind," Kronos observed. "You fear what another will do if the little moppet confirms before all the blessed gods who dwell on starry Olympus a choice he does not approve?"

"Yes, Lord Titan," Thetis conceded.

"You needn't worry too much about that, young one," Kronos replied. "Whatever Junia decides, we Titans will depart this place with the cleverest of mortals aboard their City-ship, Zeus' decree be damned."

"But, how ... what?" Thetis sputtered, her confusion growing with every passing moment at the strange revelations coming from her elders.

"Never you mind," Kronos retorted. "Your King will be far too distracted with keeping his own house in order to even notice we will have left Elysium when the dust settles on Olympus."

"I was hoping to avoid the conflict from escalating, if at all possible," Thetis confessed. "That is why I came all this way, to seek your counsel on the matter."

"This one still thinks she can prevent the gods from fighting themselves into oblivion!" Rhea spat out. "Really, Thetis, you ought to have learnt the lesson by now! You must not interfere in the affairs of your King and Queen! When you do, things only get worse!"

"Your fears about how Zeus will respond to Junia's choice no longer matter," Kronos said. "He will have a far greater threat to contend with when Pallas inevitably confronts him about the fate that befell her mother."

Thetis gasped. "How would Athena even know about this, unless you told her yourselves?" she inquired, her voice trembling with outrage and apprehension.

"She asked us herself," Kronos answered. "She and Hermes left just now, right before you arrived. I was beginning to wonder when the parade of young ones would stop until you arrived. Were you followed, perchance? Are we to expect any others among your fellow Olympians?"

"I have no knowledge of such, my Lord Titan," Thetis replied. "I only hoped to seek your counsel in preventing further animosity between our King and Queen, which will involve all the blessed gods who dwell on high Olympus."

"The gods above will need to choose sides in creating the world anew on the surface of the broad-pathed Earth," Kronos said. "Meanwhile, we Titans will once again rule over mortals as we once did. They say my reign was the Golden Age of Man, long before Zeus and my other children robbed me of my throne, and by Tartarus, this Aeon shall come again!"

"Husband!" Rhea cried out. "Hold your tongue before the adoptive daughter of Hera!"

"No, let her hear of the things that are to come, before her prophetic gift reveals them!" Kronos declared. "Let her tell the gods above, our glorious daughter included, that the future no longer belongs to them, for they have made a mess of things for far too long! Let her tell them that we Titans will leave our gilded prison with the cleverest of mortals, who will thrive under our care for as long as needed as we journey across the stars to find new worlds where to make our homes. Then we will see to it that the descendants of the Nepheleids become as docile and compliant as their forebears were millennia ago, when I sat on the throne of Heaven on high Olympus!

"Under my rule, mortals will once again treat one another with justice and kind-heartedness, for their guilelessness will render them harmless! They will never know want or hardship and will therefore have no need to grow clever to supplant cruel masters or make their newly found Earths compliant to their needs! If the last few hours here in Elysium have taught us anything, it's that your King no longer holds the reins on starry Olympus, nor was he ever willing to rule for long, as he once sat his ill-begotten whelp on the throne of Heaven before my brothers and I made short work of him at Hera's behest!"

Thetis bit her lip. Her gaze lingered upon rich-haired Rhea, whose fair features were reddening with every word the Titan-King uttered. This left Thetis unsure of whether Kronos knew that Rhea raised the very same ill-begotten son of Zeus in his subsequent incarnation as Dionysus, who now dwelt happily among the gods of holy Olympus.

"But now," Kronos raved, "this unworthy King of yours fails to keep his own diminished Kingdom intact, leaving once again the fate of Olympus in the hands of a child! Clever though Junia may be – and I assure you, she inherited that from me, just like her mother did – a child of fourteen should never be put in a position to rule over the Cosmos because her father is too craven to assert his authority over his dominion! When I am King once more, I will put an end to such foolishness! Now go, Thetis, daughter of Nereus, and tell you masters above what I just told you!"

In a stupor, Thetis bowed and withdrew from Kronos and Rhea's presence on the Isle of the Blessed, frightened and confused in equal measure. As she made her way to Elysium's shore to cross the Holy River Styx on foot, she felt a hand tapping her shoulder. Thinking it strange that a shade should have the substance to touch her flesh in the Kingdom of Hades, she spun on her heels and saw the Oceanid Klymene standing before her, her demeanour as alarmed as Thetis had ever seen.

"Thetis," Klymene said. "For the love of Olympus, do not tell anyone there what you saw and heard today! Not even Hera. Especially not Hera!"

"How long have you known about Kronos' designs?" Thetis asked.

"As long as you have," Klymene answered. "I assure you, he had no such things in mind this morning. It must have been all those young ones making their way here almost all at once that broke something in his venerable mind!"

"Well, I cannot let this be!" Thetis exclaimed. "Even if I somehow end up making things worse, I cannot have whatever it is Kronos means to do on my conscience!"

Nepheleid

"You are right," Klymene agreed. "We need to thwart whatever unpleasantness is sure to come to pass on Olympus. But in order to do so, you must supplicate a being far more powerful than the Titans ever were, long before Zeus and Metis and Zeus' imprisoned siblings supplanted Kronos and his brothers. You must seek the aid of one who is far older than the Titans. One who dwells at the very heart of the Cosmos, one who is –"

"One who is alone but has the power to create multitudes," Thetis said. "One who is the most powerful being in the Cosmos, but who has eschewed involvement in the affairs of gods and men since he drove Hera's bridal chariot on the day of her wedding to loud-thundering Zeus..."

Klymene nodded. "Have you the means to reach Phanes?" she asked.

"I will find a way," Thetis answered, her gaze fixed upon the vast crossing ahead of her.

"It will be difficult to travel between the realms, unless you have a guide such as Hermes," Klymene said. "And as Hermes is sworn to serve Zeus with the utmost fealty, he might challenge you on your cause to visit Phanes."

"I will not seek Hermes' help, obviously," Thetis replied. "I know of others who can travel with ease between the realms. Besides, Eris owes me a favour for turning my wedding into a world-changing conflict!"

Klymene chuckled. "Do be careful," she said at last. "Tartarus is empty of immortals now, and we would like to keep it that way."

"As would we all," Thetis said with a wan smile, then spun around and walked onto the waters of the Holy River Styx towards the still-living world.

Chapter Twenty-Two

As soon as fair Hebe and stalwart Herakles put Derek back into his bedchamber and lay him on his soft nest of pillows, a loud commotion in the front of Hera's palace echoed through the corridors. Concerned that the noise might rouse the anaesthetized mortal lad, Hebe threw an inquisitive glance towards her Consort.

"It's all right, my love," stalwart Herakles told his bride. "I will keep watch on the lightweight, though I am certain that Dionysus and his Maenads have the good sense not to try to abduct him here in Mother's dwelling, lest they forfeit their blessed existence on holy Olympus."

Hebe replied with a wordless chuckle, then quickly made her way towards the open front doors to investigate the source of the disturbance. There she found Eris blocking the entry, her left shoulder leaning against the frame of the heavy doors and her bearing suggesting a certain species of unconcerned bemusement that only she possessed. Behind Eris stood Junia, whose futile attempts at crossing the threshold were thwarted each time by Eris' shifting from one side of the doorframe to the other.

"I can do this all day, Child," Eris told Junia teasingly. "Mother said that you ought to go to bed. She did not say as much, but she knows you were up all night."

"Come on!" Junia protested. "Besides, since when do you follow the rules?" Junia asked.

"Who said this was about following rules?" Eris replied, glancing over her shoulder at her young charge.

"I'm not in any danger!" Junia said.

"Who said this was about you being in danger?" Eris retorted.

"Ugh!" Junia grunted in frustration, though she fell silent when she saw

Nepheleid

Hebe approaching.

Hebe smiled at Junia, then tapped Eris on the shoulder to be let through. To Hebe's surprise, Eris stretched out her right arm to block Hebe's exit.

"Let me through, Eris," Hebe said. "I must attend to Mother!"

"Not unless the little one stays inside. Mother's orders."

Hebe tried to duck under Eris' outstretched arm, but the Harbinger of Chaos was too quick and caught Hebe by the shoulder, then pushed her down on her knees beside her. Eris then put her leg in front of her crouching sister to fully block her exit.

"What are you doing?" Hebe heard Hermes say from somewhere outside the doors of Hera's palace. Beyond the outline of Eris' shapely thigh, Hebe saw Hermes and Athena standing a few paces away from the top of the stairway, while a small crowd of immortals had gathered at the bottom around an unseen visitor.

"So where have you two been?" Eris asked Hermes and Athena, blatantly ignoring Hebe and Junia's comic predicament. "You were uncommonly slow in returning to Olympus! Did you get lost on your way back from the Underworld?"

"Never you mind," Hermes replied curtly, while grey-eyed Athena answered with a glower.

"Well, something ruffled your feathers," Eris continued, her gaze fixed on the Virgin Warrior. "And for once, it was not I. Wonders never cease!"

"We encountered some turbulence on our way back," Hermes replied casually, eliciting a derisive snort from Eris, while Junia sighed loudly, and Hebe giggled at the obvious lie.

Even wise Athena, who had remained unusually indignant since her return to starry Olympus, raised a sceptical eyebrow.

"Through the realms?" Eris inquired mockingly. "Now that is a first, even for you!"

"Yes, well," Hermes dithered.

"Is that... young Paul Red Buffalo?" Hebe asked, pointing a slender finger at the gathering at the bottom of the stairway. "Here on Olympus?"

"Why, yes," Eris answered with a flourish. "He made quite an entrance, coming here aboard a flying watercraft. Not unlike Father in the Kingdom of Hades when Winter last turned to Spring –"

"HERMES!" Hebe heard loud-thundering Zeus bellow from the centre of the gathering. "What the hell are you doing over there? And *where were you* when this one found his way to Olympus on his own?"

Eris raised her head as if preparing to give a pithy answer but was thwarted when grey-eyed Athena put her strong hand over the minx's mouth.

"Don't you *dare!*" the Virgin Warrior said wrathfully, to which Eris sagely acquiesced with a nod.

Once Athena released Eris, Hebe poked her fractious sister in her ribcage, right between the bodice of her chest armor and exposed abdomen. Surprised by the stealth assault on her tender flesh, Eris withdrew her right arm from the doorframe, allowing Hebe and Junia to escape. The three sisters then followed Hermes and Athena towards the rest of their assembled kin, where they found their mother and father, as well as Apollo, Ares, and other Olympians gathered around Paul Red Buffalo, who was presently flanked by Hebe's own sons Anicetos and Alexiares.

The mortal lad stood beside his strange-looking conveyance. It was indeed a flying canoe of some kind, but much larger than the one upon which Zeus had ridden his chariot into the Kingdom of Hades, to everyone's bewilderment. Paul Red Buffalo had brought some complex machinery in his vehicle, which consisted of large hoses, heavy industrial filters, and some sort of reservoir or tank. He had come unaccompanied, which Hebe thought rather strange, as no mortal had ever made his way to starry Olympus without the guidance of one of its deathless denizens. Even the hero Bellerophon, who believed himself worthy enough to join the gods on their holy mountain on the back of the winged horse Pegasus, met his end when Zeus struck him with his thunderbolt for his brazen hubris.

"Paul!" Hebe heard Hera say with the buoyant enthusiasm she usually affected when addressing the learned mortals under her care. "Please, do come in. We've only just now served breakfast. Your friend Derek is currently indisposed – he stayed up a little too late last night, but he should be right as rain by midday!"

"Thank you, Dr. Argosi," the young mortal replied. "But I won't be staying here long. I was sent here by Nephele High Command to see about evacuating a highly toxic containment unit within a private residence and then bringing Derek back to Polaris to return *up there*."

"Ah, yes," Hera replied, ignoring the disconcerted glances amongst her fellow gods at the casual way in which Paul had just described the new, mortal-made world above the Earth and lofty Olympus itself. "I was warned to expect a parting gift from the people of Turtle Island before my own return... up there. Very well, then. Hebe! Paul, do you remember my eldest daughter? She was there briefly at Borealis before all of CARINA migrated to the Nephele. Hebe, take young Paul to your father's baths. Get Ganymede to help you if you must, or better yet, get Herakles to come along, you might need his help to unseal the heavy cover. I will keep watch over Derek in the meantime. Anicetos and Alexiares, you may return to your posts at the ramparts –"

"What in Tartarus is going on?" Zeus asked, his growing annoyance manifesting through darkening skies.

"You've been griping about the foul stench emanating from my virginity bath ever since the waters of the sacred spring cleansed me of the miasma that I took into myself during my battle with Gaia," Hera answered curtly.

The Cloud-gatherer opened his mouth to reply, but words failed him as he furrowed his brow in consternation.

"And as it is no longer for me to bear the burden of purity," Hera continued, "our young friend here has come to rid your abode of the effluvium in the dunking pool."

Zeus said nothing as Hera's gaze fixed upon Hebe, in the usual matter by which the Queen gave her daughter unspoken orders to do her bidding.

"Right this way, please," Hebe told Paul, who swiftly climbed aboard his conveyance and took hold of the navigation console. The hovering contraption made an almost imperceptible whirring noise as the devices within activated simultaneously.

"And Paul... one last thing," Hera said.

"Ma'am?" Paul inquired as he jumped out of the vehicle, console in hand.

"Chi-miigwech," the Queen replied in thanks.

The mortal lad answered with a polite nod, then punched a few keys on the console to direct the vehicle in whichever direction Hebe might lead him.

Before she could take a single step to escort Paul towards her father's royal abode, fair Hebe caught a glimpse of Derek running down the stairway from Hera's palace.

"PAUL!" Derek shrieked as he skipped the last few steps and landed, rather improbably, right beside Eris, who had kept her wings half-deployed as if to conceal something – or someone – behind her.

Taken by surprise, Eris quickly folded her wings at her back, causing Junia to utter a muffled shriek in protest. Eris diverted Derek's attention by staring straight at a rather startled-looking Herakles, who valiantly followed his runaway charge down the stairway.

"The lightweight woke up when he heard this one's voice," Herakles explained. "He's quicker than a lion pouncing on his prey!"

"We should have warned you," Ares told Herakles. "Derek has ears like sonar."

"That's why he is to become our future collective psychotherapist," Eris interjected. "He might eventually overhear all our secrets, but when that day comes, he will be held to doctor-patient confidentiality standards."

"Not *all* of your secrets, Big Sister," Hebe heard Paul mutter under his breath with some measure of humour. When Hebe threw him a quizzical glance, Paul replied with a sly smile, and nothing more.

"Let me go!" Junia squealed as she broke free from the confinement of Eris' folded wings.

"Junebug!" Derek exclaimed cheerfully when he saw his diminutive friend and hostess.

"Oh, hi Derek," Junia replied sheepishly.

Nepheleid

"Hi Junia," Paul said emphatically, as if amused at Junia's entrance.

"Hey," Junia mumbled in Paul's general direction.

"Dude, what are you doing here?" Derek asked, his dilated pupils all but swallowing the blue irises of his eyes.

"It's a long story," Paul answered with a hint of a smile. "I'll tell you all about it when we're on our way up on the Hub when we'll have nothing else to do... and when you're *better rested.*"

"And with your faculties restored to innocence," Eris said in a low voice, eliciting an inadvertent chortle from both Ares and Apollo while loud-thundering Zeus remained unamused.

"Right," Hebe said. "Shall we to Father's palace, then? You know, so as not to waste young Paul's valuable time?"

"Yes Ma'am," Paul agreed.

Derek gave Hera a pleading look.

"Go with your friend, young one," the Queen told him. "My daughter and son-in-law will ensure that the bad man and his gaggle of murderous tarts stay well clear of your tender adolescent flesh."

"I promise we will return the runt in one piece, Mother," Herakles assured her. "And his friend as well."

"Paul can take care of himself," Hera replied with a chuckle, to which Paul nodded in agreement.

As Derek took a step towards Hebe, Herakles, Paul and his strange conveyance, Junia tiptoed around Eris to follow them.

"Not so fast, Zoe!" Zeus called out. "You are not going anywhere with these boys without a chaperone!"

At a loss for words, Junia gestured at Hebe and Herakles to impart to her sire the absurdity of his objection.

"Well," the Father of gods and men continued, "you need not be there when your mortal friend performs a thankless task worthy of the Danaids, who forever dwell in Tartarus for having murdered their husbands on their wedding night – all save for one."

"Right," Junia retorted. "You don't want me getting any ideas."

Zeus raised an eyebrow. "What do you mean exactly, little one?"

"Well, for one," Junia answered, her gaze deliberately fixed on Apollo. "You don't want me to realize that when you force someone to marry against their will, someone might end up getting stabbed!"

Hebe gasped at Junia's unexpected rudeness, though Apollo made great efforts to remain impassive at the implied threat.

"And where did that come from?" the Thunderer asked Junia vexedly. Turning his gaze towards Eris, he asked, "And what in Tartarus have you two been up to all night?"

"Kitten," Hera interjected. "I think it would be best if you stayed here a while. Besides, young Paul knows what he's come to do. You can catch up with your friends later, after you've had some rest." Turning towards Ares and Eris, she said, "You two, with me!"

Ares nodded and took his place at Junia's right, while Eris remained at the child's left.

"Yes, Mother," the Harbinger of Chaos acquiesced.

"Ugh, fine!" Junia conceded, clearly unwilling to engage the Queen of Olympus in a battle of wills.

"Everyone else," Hera continued, "you may return to your homes, or stay, as you wish. I have some CARINA business to attend at the moment, but whoever wants to help me plan Junia's birthday celebration later will have my eternal gratitude. But not you," she added, staring emphatically at Zeus.

Taking their cue to return to their place at the ramparts of holy Olympus, Anicetos and Alexiares took their leave from the company of their kin, as did Apollo, Hermes, and bright-eyed Athena, while Ares and Eris took Junia back into their mother's palace. Only Zeus remained at the landing, his countenance as aggrieved as when he entered Hera's palace that very morning, as low rolls of thunder reverberated beyond the ramparts of high Olympus.

"Oh, dear," Hebe said as she led Paul, Derek, and Herakles to Zeus' palace.

Nepheleid

"What's the deal with those two?" Derek asked no one in particular.

"I'll tell you later," Paul answered. "But not here."

Chapter Twenty-Three

At least the Child is immune to indigestion, unlike the learned, grey-bearded mortal men of old Hellas, Eris mused in the confines of her own mind as white-armed Hera prompted young Junia into feeding herself to calm her nerves before heading to bed. As her younger sister accepted the offering of cold mortal food left over from that morning, Eris bit her lip feeling a pang of pity for Derek who was soon to be exposed to the noxious fumes in the bath chamber of Zeus' neighbouring palace.

"Ah well," Hera said, unsubtly displaying her ability to read others' thoughts. "Ganymede will take care of cleaning up the mess. That is the price he must pay for his charmed life amongst the gods of holy Olympus."

Ares, who had taken his seat by Eris' side on a divan, chortled at the image conjured up by Hera's reply.

"But Mother," Eris retorted. "Favoured as he is by Father, Ganymede is no more than a pampered prisoner in a gilded cage. He has never been free to choose his fate ever since Father abducted him from the ramparts of Troy before the city fell,!"

"Few of us are, young one," Hera said. "That is why we will see to it that *this one*," she continued, throwing a glance at the scowling adolescent girl grazing on a breakfast sandwich, "becomes the first among us to choose her fate of her own free will."

Junia finished her bite and gave Hera a blank, exhausted stare.

"Off to bed with you!" Hera declared, to which Junia offered no protest. Still, the Queen of Olympus took her youngest child by the elbow and led her towards her dwelling's long, cloistered corridor of guest bedchambers, presumably to ensure that Junia would well and truly go to bed.

"So much for free will," Ares told Eris once their mother was reasonably, albeit never fully, out of earshot.

Eris nodded slightly, then turned her gaze towards the golden maiden Galatea, who stood sentinel somewhere between the parlour and the still-open door to Hera's palace.

"Are you not entertained?" Eris asked the automaton, knowing full well that Hephaestus had long ago retrofitted his mechanical handmaiden with sensory devices that could broadcast whatever she heard or saw on Olympus to the Nephele high above the vault of Heaven.

"Sister," Ares said. "Galatea cares not for our running commentary on Mother's questionable parenting skills."

"I heard that!" Hera answered from the great expanse beyond her palace's cloistered corridor.

As Ares' countenance achieved an improbable shade of crimson, Eris let out a guttural laugh that she knew would be shared among the small council of immortals watching from Hephaestus' quarters on the Nephele's upper tier.

"You can stop laughing now, Hephaestus," Ares said, though not daring to look Galatea in the eye.

"Now, now," Eris replied. "Our dear brother is far too stoic for that. Prometheus, on the other hand..."

"Is now, quite improbably, Hephaestus' best friend in the Cosmos," Ares said, trying to draw attention away from his gaucherie. "All that, despite Hephaestus being the one who chained Prometheus to his rock."

"Hephaestus was only doing Father's bidding, the poor lamb," Eris retorted.

"For which Zeus never once showed him an iota of gratitude," Ares agreed.

"When has Father ever shown any of us, his trueborn children, gratitude?" Eris asked. "Even when Eileithya disobeyed Mother's orders and tended to Leto as she birthed Artemis and then Apollo. Hebe told me that Father never thanked her once, only scolded her for not having done so sooner! Is it any wonder that us five will follow Mother and Junia to the Nephele?"

"Us seven," Ares corrected her "Herakles is bound to Hebe at the hip.

He will follow her wherever she will go. So will their sons, so that's nine."

"Someone's missing from your count," Eris said.

"Thetis," Ares answered. "Wherever Mother goes, she is never far behind. Although… I've not seen her in a little while. Where on Earth has she run off to?"

"Perhaps nowhere on Earth," Eris mused with a sly grin.

"At any rate," Ares continued, "I know through Aphrodite that Hephaestus regretted the whole business of chaining Prometheus to his rock, even if Prometheus stole the fire from his own forge!"

"Well, nothing fosters peace between foes like having a common enemy," Eris replied.

"You mean… Zeus?" Ares inquired, though he already knew the answer.

Eris tapped her forefinger to her nose, her gaze fixed on Galatea.

"In that regard, Hephaestus and I ought to be the best of friends," Ares griped. "It's true that Zeus never threw me off Olympus, but he's told me to my face that he hates me, even though I doubt he knows or cares that the feeling is mutual."

"It doesn't help that you slept with Hephaestus' wife, repeatedly – even after he caught you in the act and trapped you both in a golden net!" Eris said.

"Right," Ares conceded, "but to be fair, Aphrodite has shared her bed with many a god, and none of them suffer Hephaestus' resolute disdain."

"Why would you ever care about what anyone thinks of you?" Eris asked.

"I've always cared," Ares replied. "You're the one who could not care less about what others think."

"That is because I am free!" Eris answered.

"You think that because you fancy yourself free from consequences," Ares retorted. "Speaking of consequences, where did you go with Junia last night?"

"Oh, I took the child to meet our Elders."

"Yes, yes. I already know that part," Ares griped. "Hermes said as much when he returned after taking you both to the Titan-Court on the Isle of the Blessed. I meant after that... after you vanished from Elysium but before we found you on the Asphodels."

"As I've said, I took her to meet our Elders, and then, *their* Elder," Eris said. When the ichor began to drain from Ares' features, she continued, "Yes, *that* Elder. The self-begotten and first-born among our kind. The one after whom you and our brother's wife have named one of my nephews. He who holds the formless void and all things yet to come within Himself. He who is truly Chaos in a way that I can never aspire to become, though I do try."

"And what on Earth could have possessed you into taking Junia to meet the oldest and most powerful being in the Cosmos?" Ares asked once he regained the ability to speak.

"For the Child's own edification," Eris answered casually.

"She is far too young for such an immensity!" Ares muttered under his breath, hoping that Hera would not hear his words. "Even Mother has been known to bow before Phanes, and she otherwise bows to no one, not even to Zeus! Is that why Junia was all out of sorts when we found you both in the Underworld? What did he tell her that could have upset her so?"

"Phanes said nothing that upset the Child," Eris replied. "At least nothing that immediately comes to mind, though Junia's mind is quicker by far than even the cleverest among our kind."

"Then why was she engaging Hermes in a fruitless battle of wits, clinging to me like a stray urchin, and abusing Apollo and Athena with her words? Not that Athena didn't deserve it..."

"Mother tasked me with ensuring that the Child chooses a future to guiding the learned mortals of the Nephele and City-ships of their ilk in their voyage across interstellar space, instead of an eternity of hallowed indolence among the blessed gods of holy Olympus," Eris answered. "In other words, Mother wanted Junia to make the choice she would have made, had she ever had the opportunity to have been a child herself. And, of course, I delivered."

"And why, exactly, was Junia throwing childish tantrums in the Asphodel and flinging insults at our siblings, when she is usually far more artful with her repartee?" Ares asked, making no effort to conceal his dismay.

"It's not what Phanes said or did *per se* that got Junia's panties in a bunch," Eris said. "It's the realization that all the gods and mortals once praised for building the world as it has become have in their hubris driven Earthly Life itself to the brink of oblivion."

"Is that all?" Ares asked incredulously.

"That is quite a tall order for one so young, I know," Eris answered, "but it would be best that she learned such things now, before she can exercise the illusion of choice when it comes to her Fate. As you've probably guessed, the Child came to her own conclusions about how Father and his by-blows that long-dead mortals used to call heroes, in their attempts to impose their supremacy over the forces of Chaos that have brought the Cosmos into Being, have actually ruined this living world, all in the name of Order. When Chaos ceases to exist, all Life will have been snuffed out, even long before the heat death of the universe, as Mother's learned mortals would call it."

"You've been spending too much time with the denizens of the Underworld," Ares griped.

"Have I, now?" Eris replied, raising an eyebrow.

"You sound like a herald for Nyx, the dark-robed starry Night, and other Titan spawn who thrive when the bright Sun takes his leave of the Heavens."

"Well, you know, Mother did have her hands full raising you and Hermes and me at the same time," Eris explained, "so she entrusted me to Nyx's care, far from Olympus, when I became old enough to ask her unceasing questions about the very fabric of reality. By then Mother, poor thing, had lost all patience for all precocious infants nursing at her ample bosoms, regardless of whether or not she had borne them from her holy womb, so off I went. Though now I suspect Mother might be starting to feel some remorse for having done that..."

"She's not been herself for the last fifteen-odd years," Ares admitted. "And she's grown fond of your company, which is a first."

With her characteristic guileful smile, Eris tapped her forefinger to her nose again but said nothing.

Nepheleid

"Perhaps Mother has finally found common cause with you for having the same enemy," Ares commented. "What with this whole business of restoring Life upon the broad-pathed Earth and throughout the Cosmos, thereby taking utmost delight in vexing the very Master of destructive Order at every turn."

"Not I alone, dear brother," Eris answered, turning her gaze towards the immobile Galatea.

"I suppose we are soon to find out who else will choose to join Mother's covert Holy War, without breaking the Oath we all swore to Zeus on the night Mother, Poseidon, and Athena failed to depose him as the tyrant he's proven himself to be time and again..."

Eris raised her hand, urging her twin to keep his peace. Rising to her feet, she walked past Galatea towards the door of Hera's palace, with Ares following at her heel.

"Speak of the devil," Eris muttered with a grin, as Hermes and Athena walked towards the open door.

"No, not him, Eris, only us two," Hermes said as he entered unbidden into the Queen's dwelling, with Athena at his side.

"Have you come to help Hera plan for the Child's birthday party?" Eris asked Hermes mockingly, her gaze fixed upon Athena. "How about you?" she asked the Virgin Warrior. "Have you come to take your mind off whatever has made you utterly miserable since you returned from Titans-know-where?"

"Perhaps we have," Hermes answered, while Athena surreptitiously twitched her left eye at Eris' last comment.

Eris grinned. "This way please," she said, aping the sweet, dulcet tone Hebe affected whenever she welcomed visitors to the Queen's abode.

"Right," Hermes replied, while Athena made a concerted effort to stop scowling as she and Hermes took their seats in the parlour.

As soon as Eris motioned to follow them back inside, Galatea's mechanical pupils dilated, as if the golden maiden detected movement from somewhere beyond the open door. Eris spun on her heels, then spied another gaggle of immortals headed up the stairway to Hera's palace. This cohort, consisting of Demeter and Hestia, gave Eris a cordial and warm greeting as they entered.

"I hope we're not too late," Demeter said. "You know, for Junia's birthday."

"The actual celebration will be much later, at the evening banquet," Eris answered. "Or at least that's when I think Hera is planning to do it, to better make a scene."

"Right," Hestia said. "So, we have not missed anything."

"Regrettably, no," Eris replied.

"Not yet," Ares added.

"That's good to hear," Eris heard Eileithya say as she appeared behind Hestia and made her way inside, followed by golden Aphrodite.

"Well, then," Eris said, stifling a laugh as she gazed upon the goddess of love. "This will be a good time after all!"

"We're here for Junia, not to start a fight," Aphrodite answered curtly.

"So much for being a lover of smiles," Eris retorted. "Why don't you sit next to Athena over there, you two seem to have a lot in common lately."

"That would be a first," Eris heard Apollo jape as he followed Aphrodite a few paces away, with his twin Artemis and gentle Leto bringing up the rear.

"Really?" Eris said as she gazed upon Hera's perennial rival and the fruit of her adultery with the Cloud-gatherer.

"Yes, Eris, really," Leto answered emphatically. "If your mother meant what she said on the upper deck of the Polaris all those years ago, then she ought to have laid her quarrel with me to rest on the shores of Turtle Island."

"And I have," Hera said as she entered the room alone, having evidently succeeded in putting Junia to bed. Turning her gaze towards the assembly of immortals as they rose to their feet to greet her, she said, "Please, help yourself to some of the leftovers from breakfast. We can begin. Hebe and Herakles won't mind that we've started without them. They ought to return shortly with the mortal boys anyway. Eris, please leave the door open, in case Thetis or others care to join us."

Nepheleid

Eris acquiesced with a nod, then winked at Galatea as she passed her by on her way back to the parlour. Leaning over to the golden maiden's ear, she said in a low voice, "it looks like the gods are choosing their sides, my lovelies. Let the fun begin!"

Chapter Twenty-Four

Fair-haired Ganymede, the most beautiful youth ever born from the race of mortal men, stood incredulous as lovely Hebe, the antecedent Cupbearer of the deathless gods who dwell on Holy Olympus, appeared before him at the hallowed gates of loud-thundering Zeus' abode. The long-reigning Princess of Olympus came accompanied by her Consort, stalwart Herakles, as well as that whelp Derek and another mortal youth whom he did not know. The copper-skinned mortal stranger seemed friendly enough, however, it took Ganymede far too long to understand why the young man jested about having come all this way to empty the royal palace's septic tank, which the others thought rather amusing. Confused and annoyed for having been roused from his midday nap – having spent the better part of the night gratifying loud-thundering Zeus' exacting appetites – Ganymede thought it best not to argue and let Hebe and her escort inside, lacking the will or the daring to argue with white-armed Hera's beloved daughter.

Without prevarication, though he never fully forgave Hera for the role she played in obliterating his homeland some three millennia ago, Ganymede could not deign to begrudge Hebe for being one of the Queen's preferred children. Hebe had remained unfailingly sweet and kind to him ever since Zeus abducted him on Mount Ida in the guise of an eagle. Hera, however, so hated the inculpable prince of Troy for supplanting her daughter as Cupbearer of the gods, and for having become one of Zeus' favourites. This was at the time when the King and Queen of Olympus were most estranged, and Hera would have led the Argives into battle against the Trojans herself, had Zeus not threatened her with all manner of unpleasantness to stay her murderous rage. When the Argives did breach the gates of Troy during the ill-fated city's final days, Ganymede could no longer bear to witness the ongoing assault on his fatherland, and begged Zeus to spare him from the grisly spectacle. Taking pity on his catamite, the Thunderer covered the illustrious city's burning ruin with a vast cloud that no eye could pierce, while Hebe temporarily resumed her duties as Cupbearer of the deathless gods who dwell on high Olympus until Troy was no more.

Nepheleid

Three-and-a-half thousand years had passed since Zeus ransomed far-famed Troy's hapless mortal denizens to assuage Hera's insatiable ire against Ganymede and his land of birth. Yet even today, the Queen showed little sign of forgiving the mortal prince for having caught Zeus' roving eye while he innocently tended his flocks outside the ramparts of Troy. Verily, of all the deathless gods who make their homes on high Olympus, the Queen should have felt the utmost sympathy for Ganymede's plight, for unlike Hera, he never chose to arouse the Thunderer's passions or to share his bed. Unlike Hera, Ganymede did not of his own volition board a golden chariot driven by Eros the Elder to be brought before the Father of gods and men as his bride. Hera should have pitied Ganymede for being torn from his family, never to know a woman's tender touch or sire a bloodline of his own. For all Ganymede knew, had he failed to captivate Zeus with his uncommon beauty, perhaps his descendants would still dwell on the Troad by the banks of the river Skamadros, even if they, like the many tribes of mortals alive today, no longer worshipped the gods of their forefathers.

But such was not Ganymede's fate; as compensation for the prince's abduction, Zeus ordered Hermes to grant the boy's grieving mortal father, King Tros, a pair of horses from high Olympus, as well as assurances that Ganymede would never taste illness or death so long as he dwelt among the gods. These immortal mares remained in Troy until Tros' descendant, King Laomedon, gave them to Herakles. This was payment for rescuing his daughter Hesione from a sea-monster sent by Poseidon as punishment for the king's refusal to pay the reward promised to Poseidon and Apollo for building the ramparts of Troy. Like Ganymede and the immortal mares, Herakles now also dwelt among the gods, living a blessed and deathless existence, save for the few menial chores given to him by his venerable elders. One such task was lifting the weighty metal lid covering the small bathing pool Zeus had gifted Hera some years ago, shortly before Junia was born.

The bathing pool tapped into the Spring of Kanathos whose restorative waters allowed Hera to renew her virginity. Zeus had hoped that this device would embolden Hera to curtail her yearly excursion to the springs, at the appointed time by the Seasons. Little did Zeus know that Hera, in an otherwise uncharacteristic show of altruism according to Ganymede, would use the bathing pool instead to rid the living waters of the broad-pathed Earth of the lingering poisons left by careless greedy mortals over the course of centuries. And now, by some act of dark magic which Ganymede failed to understand on account of his sleep-deprived stupor, the mortal stranger now commanded a strange-looking barge above the palace's perennially polished floors and into the bath chamber. Meanwhile, the others carried on as if they saw nothing strange, save for Derek who appeared somewhat unnerved as if he had tasted Dionysus' brew sometime before Night last yielded to the bright Dawn.

The tawny mortal seemed to notice Derek's bewildered state and found it rather droll, as did fair Hebe and stalwart Herakles. "I'll tell you all about it, I promise," he told Derek. "Once you're able to process information again."

Hebe and Herakles chuckled at the stranger's words, yet neither paid any mind to Ganymede's own bafflement, as they quickly turned their attention to the task at hand. Herakles took the lead by removing the heavy star-metal cover over the rancid contents of the bathing pool, while the mortal stranger busied himself with fitting hoses and other apparatus onto the mechanical abomination aboard his flying contraption. Hebe drew Derek aside, presumably to protect his tender mortal senses from the foul stench under the cover. The other mortal needed no such care, as he donned a grey jumpsuit over his trousers and sweater, then covered his nose and mouth with a complex-looking mask with an elaborate breathing device, and his eyes with protective goggles. Hebe then turned her attention towards Ganymede, as if to ensure that he also remained unharmed by the effluvium emanating from the bathing pool. Ganymede gave her a courteous nod, knowing that Hebe was only showing him a kindness, for she was fully aware of Ganymede's immunity against sickness while he dwelt among the blessed gods who make their homes on starry Olympus.

After Herakles set down the heavy lid beside the pool, the mortal stranger set to work spraying a thick grey power onto the surface of the feculent sludge, until the entire surface of the pool was covered with the material. Once he was done, he stepped a few paces away from the pool and took off his goggles and mask.

"That ought to do it for the first round," the stranger said as if covering the stench of centuries of human malfeasance against the sons and daughters of Ouranos and Tethys were the most ordinary thing in the world.

"What... what was that?" Ganymede asked, affecting an air of casual indifference to the affairs of mortals even though his curiosity was well and truly aroused.

"That," the stranger answered as he removed his jumpsuit and folded the garment into a bundle, "that is a mixture of several species of fungi to help break down the toxic soup."

"Fungi?" Ganymede inquired. "You mean... rot? You add that filth on top of the festering stench to *diminish* the filth?"

"Pretty much," the stranger answered as he stuffed the bundle in a large bag. "It's a tried-and-true method for cleaning up heavy metals and other industrial waste, and it's been used for generations in some of the places most impacted by pollution since the late-stage Anthropocene."

Ganymede said nothing, his blank stare betraying his abject ignorance on such matters.

"Think of fungi as the Earth's antibodies," the stranger continued, "healing a sick patient at the site of infection."

"Yeah," Derek agreed. "We had a whole class on the role of fungi in terra-forming a few years ago in the lab at Borealis, with Doctor Summers. You know her, she is here with Doctors Argosi and Archer and the rest of them!"

Now Ganymede shifted his attention towards Derek, who had somehow found the audacity to address him in Zeus' sacred abode.

"You must choose other words, Paul," Hebe said when Ganymede failed to reply. "I'm afraid that our dear friend Ganymede was born too long ago to understand such things."

So the dusky stranger has a name, and it is Paul. And he and the whelp are friends.

"What do you mean, born too long ago?" Derek asked, his own disorientation growing by the minute. "That guy is *our* age! Well, not *your* age, because just like your mom, you're obviously older than you look... I mean, you're married, and you have kids – grown kids – and *they're* my age, but yeah, mine and Paul's age!"

"Ganymede is also far older than he looks, Hebe answered cryptically, while Paul gave Derek a knowing look, as if privy to a great secret. "He was born long before his homeland's foes, the Hellenes, invented science, reason, and civilization as you know it. I meant no offence, Paul, but there is truth in these words."

"None taken," Paul answered with a shrug.

"Huh?" Derek grunted inquisitively.

"Are we going too fast for you?" Hebe asked Derek, while kindly and deliberately drawing her entourage's attention away from Ganymede's utter bewilderment.

"I'll tell you later," Paul told Derek in a stage whisper.

"Never mind that," Hebe said. "You really ought to rest, Derek. You've had quite an eventful night. My husband will escort you back to your room. We will summon you when Junia's birthday party is about to start. Until then, you can rest easy knowing that the Earth will remain in good hands, even if some among our kind decline Mother's invitation to take flight aboard the Nephele to worlds unknown."

"You are optimistic," Ganymede mumbled under his breath, for he was certain that Hera, despite her occasional moments of magnanimity, never meant to extend the invitation to him or, for that matter, to loud-thundering Zeus.

"Optimism is the prerogative of youth," Hebe answered Ganymede as discretely as she could manage with two mortal youths and stalwart Herakles listening between the reverberating walls of the cavernous bath chamber.

Derek gave Hebe a vacant look, then turned his gaze towards Paul.

"It's okay," Paul told him reassuringly. "I'm pretty much done here for now. We must let the formula set overnight before we can begin to pump it out." Turning his attention to Ganymede, he continued, "You'll want to avoid this room if you can help it. It's going to keep smelling rough as the fungi and the accelerating agent do their job."

"Shall I put the cover back in its place?" Herakles asked.

"No," Paul answered. "It has to breathe."

Herakles nodded in assent, then walked towards Hebe and Derek and put his hand on Derek's shoulder. "Shall we, then?" he asked Derek, though even Ganymede knew this was an order and not a question.

"Uh, sure," Derek acquiesced sagely as the towering demigod led him out of the bath chamber.

"If you are hungry," Ganymede heard Herakles say once the pair had crossed into the corridor, "I can make you some paninis like I used to back in Borealis."

"Oh god, please no!" Derek pleaded feebly. "It's not your paninis – they're great – t's just that after smelling this crap, if I see any amount of food, I'll throw up!"

"As you wish," Herakles said finally, as he and Derek exited the royal palace.

"I think your friend is in for quite a rude awakening," Hebe told Paul when Herakles and Derek were well out of earshot.

"Oh, trust me," Paul replied as he began to tidy up the hoses and other equipment back inside the hovering barge. "He still has no clue what's going on. But don't worry, I'll tell him when we're back on the Hub. He'll either have to accept that he's about to be the mental health provider of ancient immortals, or he'll think this was a fever dream brought on by food poisoning or something. Either way, he'll be fine."

"You are going to join the Nephele with the others," Ganymede surmised.

"Well, I certainly hope so," Paul answered cheerfully. "I have an in with the boss lady at Life Support. You know, the one you call Queen Hera."

"You know who we are?" Ganymede asked incredulously.

"And he knows *what* we are," Hebe said.

"Then why are you so calm?" Ganymede asked Paul without irony.

"I'm Anishinaabe," Paul answered with a wink.

"Then why do you have a Christian name?" Ganymede inquired. "If I may be so bold."

Hebe threw Ganymede an uncharacteristically sharp look, however, Paul raised his hand and said, "No, it's okay. My mom did some genealogy research while she was pregnant with me and found out that she's one-sixty-fourth white people. So... Paul it is."

"None of this will matter aboard the Nephele," Hebe said when

Ganymede failed to reply.

"I would never know," Ganymede said, "for I was never invited."

"The invitation was for all the immortals of Earth, Sea, and Sky, in all the nations of the broad-pathed Earth," Hebe retorted. "That includes you. And if you do not believe me, then ask Mother yourself at Junia's birthday celebration tonight. I will be by her side, filling her cup with nectar, so that she does not feel compelled to turn her hand and her cup away from you."

"This will anger our King," Ganymede bemoaned.

"Then all the more reason for her to invite you to join the crew," Paul said, to Hebe and Ganymede's surprise. Turning his gaze towards Hebe, he said finally, "Now, I heard that there was some talk about your husband making some paninis?"

"Of course," Hebe said. "How uncouth of me to assume that you shared Derek's delicate constitution. This way please."

Paul gave Ganymede a polite farewell nod, then followed Hebe out of the royal palace, leaving Ganymede slightly less confused and dejected than he had been the night before.

Optimism is the prerogative of youth, and I will remain forever young, as long as I dwell among the deathless gods – even those who leave the hallowed halls of starry Olympus.

Nepheleid

Chapter Twenty-Five

Goddess of Wisdom and Justice, my ass! Your mother would be so ashamed of you if she were alive today!

More than three millennia had passed since Triton, son of Poseidon and the Oceanid Amphitrite, brought up bright Athena alongside his own daughter, the ill-fated Pallas. They had raised the maidens to excel in the military arts at a time when such an upbringing was not unusual for firstborn daughters of powerful Kings. Almost as many years had come and gone since Athena felt a close connection with a member of her own sex, until the rueful day when the Virgin Warrior mortally wounded Pallas as the pair practiced their martial prowess with the sword. Devastated by the outcome of this tragic accident, Athena immortalized her dear friend by taking the young girl's name before her own. Since that day, Athena resolved to keep mostly in the company of immortal gods and mortal men, whom she found sturdier and more dexterous than fragile females. She preferred instead to think of the latter as weak of mind and body, despite indisputable proof that women possessed considerable intelligence, as evidenced by how the sharpness of their words could sting far more insidiously than spears and swords wielded by virile soldiers.

Even the endless centuries of watching white-armed Hera scheming against, and outwitting Zeus at every possible turn, failed to convince Athena of the error of her reasoning pertaining to the wit and cunning of the feminine mind. Instead, she chose to perceive her stepmother and Queen as the proverbial exception to the rule, concluding that Hera had learnt her rather formidable skills of cogitation from wily Kronos after years of imprisonment in the Titan's belly, and through no fault of her own. Though Athena had always been rather fond of Hera, she never considered herself as the Queen's equal, even long before Hera wed the Cloud-gatherer – Athena knew her merely as Zeus' favourite sister and her favourite aunt. Still, despite never feeling deprived for having been brought up without a mother, Athena was grateful that Hera always treated her like a daughter, a privilege that the Queen seldom extended to others among Zeus' innumerable progeny. Oddly enough, Hera's special affection for Athena, notwithstanding the Queen's incessant aversion to loud-thundering Zeus, caused the Virgin Warrior to never once doubt her father's assurances that she was begotten from him alone. For if this were not the truth, surely Hera would have told Athena about her genuine origins, if only to stoke the fires of resentment in her heart and reinforce their reiterative alliance in most matters concerning Zeus' frequent lapses in sagacity.

Perhaps, Athena thought charitably, Hera had also not known about Metis, in the same way that the Queen remained ignorant of having borne Prometheus for untold millennia, until the events that unfolded during the Winter before Junia's birth. However, Athena knew this to be impossible, for Junia, who has dwelt upon and above the broad-pathed Earth for a mere fourteen years, undeniably knew about Metis. At first, Athena thought that Junia, who had barely begun undergoing female puberty in a manner that the Virgin Warrior herself never experienced, spontaneously invented the idea of Metis in the Asphodel to shame Athena for her lack of female solidarity and for taking pride in having emerged fully grown and in full armor from Zeus' head. However, when Athena and Hermes visited wily Kronos and rich-haired Rhea a few moments later in Elysium, the Titan-King and Queen confirmed to Athena the truth about the fate that befell her mother.

Thus, Athena learned, at the cost of her once unfailing conviction in Zeus' righteousness and in the justness of his rule, that her mother, the Oceanid Metis, was great with child when Zeus swallowed her whole to prevent her from giving birth to a son who would later supplant him as he had his own father. When Kronos added that Zeus could not have succeeded in forcing him from the throne of Heaven and releasing his other children from the prison of his belly without Metis' counsel, Athena fully felt for the first time the fiery pangs of feminine rage, of which she had long denied herself capable or otherwise sought to sublimate by identifying in all things with the male. For the first time in the long centuries of her deathless existence, Athena felt a deep sympathy for Hera, knowing at long last the full brunt of the Queen's rage, as well as some small measure of guilt for having brazenly thwarted Hera in the past from taking revenge against Zeus and his bastard children.

Of course, Zeus had his reasons for hiding the truth about Metis from his firstborn and favourite daughter, and one could certainly argue that his reasons made perfect sense. Who in their right mind would want

Athena, saviour of cities and unbending of heart, as their enemy? Though Athena now wished that Zeus suffered worse pains than women do in childbirth when Prometheus struck him with an axe to deliver him of the child growing inside his head, she still could understand his motivation for lying to her for centuries about her mother. What Athena could not fathom was why Hera never once uttered a word about Metis, nor why she first heard of her mother's existence from *Junia*, a mere child who felt as rightfully entitled to hating Zeus as Hera did.

Did Hera hold her tongue because Zeus threatened her with violence if she ever told Athena about her true genesis? Was this the reason why Hera loved Athena like a daughter, because she pitied her for being a motherless child? Then why in Tartarus did Hera ever agree to wed Zeus, knowing full well that he swallowed Metis in much the same way that her own father had swallowed her at the moment of her birth?

Athena shut her eyes as spiteful embers began to enkindle in her viscera, or where she imagined her womb would be had she ever bled in the way other goddesses and women do. Was this the fire that Hera felt igniting in her belly every time she felt cheated and disrespected by Zeus? Was this how Hera always felt when she dwelt on starry Olympus? Did the Queen endure this degree of spite every time Athena or other immortals sided with Zeus despite the righteousness of her cause? In a way, Athena began to understand why Hera had remained so insistent that Junia should choose to leave Olympus behind, even if such an outcome did not truly constitute a choice for the child. It now dawned upon Athena that Hera was never properly a child herself, nor had she ever had a proper mother, until rich-haired Rhea sent her away to dwell in the House of Okeanos and Tethys – Athena's own grandparents – at the boundaries of the broad-pathed Earth. This became quite clear to Athena earlier that day when Kronos admitted to her and Hermes that he wept upon learning of Hera's impending nuptials to Zeus, for the Titan-King then feared that his favourite daughter would meet the same fate as Metis.

"Not after I made him swear an Oath by the Holy River Styx that he would never do such a thing," Rhea had scoffed, as if such an assurance sufficed to protect her daughter from her son's arrogance and entitlement after securing the throne of Heaven at the expense of Athena's mother.

Your mother would be so ashamed of you if she were alive today!

Nepheleid

In a strange way, Athena almost admired Junia for her temerity in saying such terrible things to a formidable war-goddess without fear of consequences. Athena also knew that Junia's audacity came from knowing that her mother and older siblings would always protect her against harm, as would the entire tribe of mortals dwelling in the Nephele high above the Earth for that matter. Truly, Junia was the child Hera never was, for the Queen's life was forfeited the moment she was born. Junia was also the little girl that Athena never could have been, for even as a young godling, Athena never thought of herself as a girl. Girls were small and weak and vulnerable, and she, the Virgin Warrior, resolved to never become such. Perhaps this was the reason why she emerged in full armor from Zeus' head. Or perhaps Metis, in her last deed as an expectant mother, armed her child so that Athena could protect herself against Zeus if he ever decided to follow the example of his father pertaining to the treatment of his own offspring.

Perhaps Metis always intended for Athena to feel invulnerable before the King of Olympus. Or perhaps she meant for Athena to also become a shield against the men who threaten women, who bleed from their wombs so that Life may endure.

But perhaps Metis would be ashamed of Athena if she were alive to see what had become of her only child.

Athena took a long, deep breath, casting her eyes downward so that the other immortals gathered in Hera's parlour could not see her torment. She no longer cared about their inane prattling about the minutiae of planning an adolescent girl's birthday celebration, nor that they might think her churlish for her unhelpfulness in completing the task at hand. As the Fates willed it, no one paid any mind to Athena's inner turmoil. No one, except –

"The truth hurts, does it not?" Athena heard Eris say in a soft yet strangely impassioned voice. "This must all feel so very new to you, this seething, nigh irrational, *hysterical* rage. One never gets used to it. Just ask my mother!"

Athena lifted her gaze and was surprised to see the minx seated right across from her, while Hermes, who sat next to Athena on the divan, appeared to have heard nothing.

Eris smiled. "Look at my face," she said without moving her lips. "And now you know I've inherited more from Hera than my stunning beauty!"

Athena gasped, prompting Hermes to turn his gaze towards her. In an uncharacteristic show of solidarity, Eris drew Hermes' attention away by throwing a piece of uneaten breakfast sausage at his head. Undaunted, the messenger god retaliated by flicking the small hunk of meat right back at Eris, who caught it in her mouth triumphantly.

"Now, really, Eris," Hestia said, at which all other immortals ceased their chatter. "What are you, five years old?"

Eris replied with a wide grin, unabashedly displaying the piece of meat between her teeth, then swallowing it in a single gulp.

"We are *not* having a bun-less hotdog eating contest, Eris, even if mortals are among our guests," Hera declared. "Friday was yesterday, and the moment is now gone. Right. So, Hebe, what were you saying about –"

In her stupefaction, Athena never heard the rest of Hera's words, for Eris now commanded her undivided attention.

How did you know? the Virgin Warrior asked Eris tacitly.

"You and Hermes were a little too late in getting back to Olympus," Eris answered, while her *soma* picked the seeds out of a pomegranate left before her on the low table. "And Hermes is never late!"

"So what do you want from me?" Athena asked, her patience wearing thin.

"Who said I wanted anything from you?" Eris replied in an almost mocking tone. "Maybe I just wanted you to know that I understand *exactly* how you feel right now. And perhaps I ought to tell you that your feelings are not, nor were they ever, a weakness. However, I've always wondered how one in possession of your intellectual proficiency could ever fail to realize this?"

"Be careful, now," Athena growled in the confines of her mind.

"Just know that you are not alone, O Goddess of Wisdom and Justice –"

Athena clenched her fists and inhaled sharply. This time, Hermes took notice and asked, "Is something the matter, Pallas? Are you all right?"

"NO!" Athena yelped, as all the others gathered in Hera's parlour once again held their tongues and fixed their gazes upon the irate-looking

Nepheleid

Virgin Warrior, all save for Eris, who for reasons known only to herself now stared directly at the golden maiden Galatea.

"My Queen," Athena said as she rose to her feet. "If you will excuse me, there is a matter I must –"

"It's quite all right," Hera mercifully interrupted her. "Take all the time you need."

As Athena respectfully bowed and took her leave, Hermes rose to his feet and followed her out of the Queen's palace, closing the heavy double doors behind them.

Athena remained silent for a long time at the top of the stairway to Hera's palace, her harried thoughts visibly roiling under the surface of her usually serene mien. Hermes also held his tongue, knowing better than to fill the uncomfortable silence with flippant chatter, which under other circumstances the blessed gods who dwell on high Olympus would have found most peculiar.

At long last, the Virgin Warrior turned her gaze toward Hermes, who looked rather shocked when he noticed that Athena's once placid grey eyes were now striated with red bolts of indignant fury.

"There is something I need you to do," Athena said resolutely.

Hermes sighed deeply as if he already knew the terrible deed Athena would have him commit to ease her wrath.

"I've seen that look before, Pallas," he told her. "Whenever Hera –"

"This is different," Athena interrupted. "This is… *Justice*."

"Are you certain about this?"

"As certain as I've ever been about anything since the Age of Taurus," Athena replied.

"And what if you – if we – fail in this endeavour?" Hermes asked, the words almost halting in his deathless throat.

"Then I will lie breathless for a year in a cold sleeping chamber for mortal travellers aboard the Nephele," Athena answered, "and remain exiled nine years thence from the company of immortals who dwell on starry Olympus… as will you."

"How can you be certain that Hera will grant us both safe passage," Hermes asked, "after we've broken our Oaths of fealty to Zeus?"

"Because Hera understands, more than any other sentient being in the Cosmos ever has or ever will," Athena said determinedly. "That I promise you."

"It is unlike you to speculate an outcome on a presage," Hermes argued.

"Then I swear it by my own cunt!" Athena hissed with undue fury, causing Hermes to take a step back and almost lose his balance at the top of the stairway.

"Very well," the messenger said after regaining his composure.

Athena gave him a grateful nod, then wiped the unfamiliar tears flowing down her lovely cheeks only after Hermes had completely vanished into thin air before her eyes.

Nepheleid

Chapter Twenty-Six

The mists of Chaos rise higher today than the spray from the Rivers of the Underworld, Lord Hades pondered as he spied, for the third time in the span of a day on the broad-pathed Earth, Hermes crossing the expanse above the Holy River Styx separating his Kingdom from the world of the living.

"This bodes ill," he said aloud to his hound Cerberus, stirring the Beast to tilt one of its three heads in bewilderment. "Now, now," he told the hellhound. "Let us see what tidings the winged bastard brings us this time, from starry Olympus."

Securing the leash on Cerberus' collars, the Lord of the Underworld stepped out of his throne room, then took a stroll behind his palace towards his orchard of pomegranates, from which he picked the fruit that secured him his bride Persephone aeons ago. He and his hound paused by a grove of white poplars lining the winding River Acheron, in whose waters all mortal shades must surrender their old selves should they ever leave the Kingdom of the Dead. Hades pretended to take little notice when Hermes landed beside him, taking a pregnant pause until he felt ready to face Zeus' messenger and the turn of events that he knew would somehow become his burden.

"Uncle," Hermes said politely when Hades finally turned around to acknowledge his presence.

"Hermes," Hades said. "What fresh hell has brought you to my Kingdom this time? Surely the rest of the Olympian Court is not about to pay me a visit, what with you,Eris and Junia, and everyone else using my Kingdom as a reception venue? I may be the Host of Many, but my hospitality is for the shades of the dead, not my brother's deathless progeny!"

"Well, no, Lord Hades," Hermes replied. "I came here for a more... personal matter."

"Did you, now?" Hades said, raising an eyebrow. "Then to what do I owe the pleasure?"

"I've come to retrieve the sickle that King Kronos gifted to Junia when she was a small child," Hermes replied.

The Host of Many gave Hermes a cold, hard stare. "That bloody thing again," he grumbled. "Eris did return it to Junia last Winter and it was last seen in the Garden of the Hesperides, when Ares gallantly thwarted Junia from using it against Zeus. What makes you think it found its way back into my Kingdom?"

Hermes answered with a wordless grin and a slightly cocked head.

"Right," Hades said. "Well, do not thank me all at once for keeping you brats safe from the reckless usage of a weapon that once sundered the very Heavens from the Earth!"

"Yes, well, I mean to return it to Junia on the occasion of her birthday, which the blessed gods who dwell on holy Olympus will be celebrating later today."

"Kronos' sickle is not a gift suitable for a child," Hades admonished. "Hera entrusted it to me for safekeeping until Junia is old enough to comprehend the terrible power of that blade."

"Junia will be fourteen years old in a few days," Hermes insisted. "And loud-thundering Zeus decreed that the time has come for her to decide her fate and –"

"Were you aware that the Titans intend to pay a visit to your King and Queen on the occasion of Junia's birthday celebration?" Hades interrupted.

"Why, no, I had no idea!" Hermes answered. "Why would they do such a thing?"

"You tell me," Hades replied.

Hermes answered with a look of utmost befuddlement and innocence.

"You and Athena must have said something to them," Hades continued, "that they should try to leave the shores of the Isle of the Blessed, even if for a day. Of course, the Titans are rather fond of the girl, and as they now dwell in Elysium, where even the shades of the Mighty Dead may return to Earth if they so desire, I have no reason to deny them this request. And now, you tell me that you want the sickle reunited with its new proprietor on high Olympus, on the day that King Kronos and his Titan-Court intend to pay a visit to his favourite granddaughter? Do you not see how... ill-advised this all seems?"

"To tell the truth," Hermes said meekly, "I mean to return the sickle to Junia to petition for her favour, so that she may look kindly upon my request to join her and her mother on the Nephele. As you remember, she and I did not exactly get off on the right foot, as mortals say, when we met right here outside your palace when she was a little girl... though on that account Hera was mostly to blame –"

Hades halted Hermes' rambling by heaving a loud, theatrical sigh. "Do you see this River here, Hermes? The one with the moaning shades of confused mortals wading about every which way? Do you see it, truly, young one?"

"The River Acheron..." Hermes said, mildly confused as to Hades' intent with the sudden change of subject.

"Yes," Hades agreed. "The River Acheron, one of the Underworld's most formidable Rivers for the shades that dwell in my Kingdom, though not because of its size. The River Acheron is not even the largest River in the Cosmos. That would be Okeanos, the Father of Rivers, whose waters surround the Earth and extend even beyond the boundaries of the Helioshpere, in a cloud of ice crystals that twinkle like stars far from the Sun, as my sister your Queen's learned mortals have long known. No, the waters of the River Acheron flow in the opposite direction from mighty Okeanos, in a realm parallel to the broad-pathed Earth but very much of this world, and they end in the Acherusian Lake, right there. Many mortals and some deathless gods think that the shades of the dead are bathed and purified in the Holy River Styx, but that is a common error."

"The shades of the departed dwell in the Acherusian Lake until they are ready to be reborn among the living, in whatever form the Fates decide. Yet between the Rivers Okeanos and Acheron flows another River, the Pyriphlegethon, and this River winds and eddies through the fiery and Chaos-ridden places of the Cosmos, tempering boiling matter inside the forge of stars, before ending in the pit of Tartarus, now absent its long-reigning Titan-Court. The waters of the Holy River Styx, as you know, are serene, placid, and pure, flowing in the opposite direction from the River Acheron into the twilight, indigo-hued recesses of the Cosmos. Her waters never mingle with the Rivers Okeanos and Pyriphletethon, or any other Rivers that flow through my Kingdom, or upon the broad-pathed Earth. All these Rivers spiral around one another like galaxies beyond the boundaries of the Heavens, yet never meet. Should they do so, the Cosmos as we know it would cease to exist. But back to the Acherusian Lake."

"As you can see here with your own deathless eyes, some shades dwell in its waters for some time, yet others who are found guilty of egregious impieties are taken to Tartarus, where they dwell for a year until they are deemed cleansed of their crimes. Then the tides take them back to the Lake, where the shades of the formerly damned must beg forgiveness for their crimes to those they have wronged. If forgiven, they must leave the Lake and drink of the River Lethe to return to the world of the living. Those who remain unforgiven are sent once again to Tartarus for another year, and again it goes until they are reconciled with those they have outraged. Keep in mind that the wronged parties also must dwell in the Lake, until they truly forgive their tormentors, or grow weary of the endless cycle and grant them this grace if only to move on to the next stage in their existence."

"So, Sartre was right," Hermes quipped. "Hell truly is other people."

"Right," Hades continued. "Now, the worst offenders are the sons and daughters who commit crimes against their parents, then there are those who have committed murder, and so on. And as you also know, my father Kronos and his Titan brothers, all save for the mighty Okeanos who at the time dwelt on Olympus, were the first to commit a crime against their father, even if their cause was just. But you already know the tale. And you can now begin to understand why I have hidden the instrument by which Kronos defeated his father Ouranos in the one place in the Cosmos where no one will ever seek to retrieve it, lest another tries to commit impiety against their father or mother with the cursed object."

"You've hidden Kronos' sickle at the bottom of the Acherusian Lake?" Hermes asked incredulously, as the ichor drained from his usually ruddy countenance.

"I see that nothing gets past you, young one."

"You sank the sickle? Even though Kronos outright gifted it to Junia when she was a child?"

"Hera was right to have me safekeep it," Hades said, "for Junia was too young to shoulder the responsibility of such a terrible instrument."

"But now Junia has come of age –"

"Only because it suits Zeus to think of her as such," Hades said. "My own bride was not much older than Junia when Zeus granted me her hand in marriage, and back then Persephone was not old enough to understand what was expected of her as my new Queen. She tried to starve herself in protest for having been taken from her mother. She would have succeeded, had I not tricked her into swallowing a few seeds from a pomegranate plucked in this very orchard!"

"Yes," Hermes replied. "I remember it well. I was there, you know. But still, Junia is the one to whom Kronos gifted the sickle, and it is proper that I should reunite her with it!"

"Not if she means to commit an act of filial impiety with the sickle," Hades retorted. "I have my own duties and responsibilities as King of this realm."

"You are the Host of Many," Hermes said, "and your guests are the shades of mortal men and women and children, not the deathless sons and daughters of Zeus, as you've said yourself."

"Yes, yes," Hades agreed. "But therein lies a caveat, for you see, Junia appears to have been born as mortal as we the children of Titans once were. Should she perish on the broad-pathed Earth or in the expanse beyond the Heavens, her shade will nonetheless find its way here, into my Kingdom, and she will bathe in the waters of the Acherusian Lake until cleansed of her former life, like all mortals who were born and have died since Life began. And should she be found guilty of a crime of filial impiety, such as relieving her father from his manhood, as Kronos did to his own father, then I would have no choice but to see her confined to the waters of the Acherusian Lake and Tartarus until loud-thundering Zeus saw fit to release her from her prison. And since I also once swore to Hera that none of her children would ever be forced to dwell in any realm within my Kingdom, be it Elysium or Tartarus, well, you can see that I would be in a bit of a bind, were I to allow you to retrieve the sickle and return it to Junia."

Nepheleid

Hermes pondered these words for a moment, then said, "What if I could guarantee that Junia has no such ill intent toward Zeus – or Hera for that matter?"

"Junia is at an age where she will likely turn her thoughts to such transgressions, whether or not her cause proves just," Hades answered.

"But Junia is wise beyond her years!" Hermes countered.

"She is very clever, yes, but cleverness is not the same as wisdom," Hades replied. "In fact, cleverness without wisdom is far more dangerous than a dull mind."

"And what if I were to give you assurances that Pallas, the wisest among the blessed gods who dwell on high Olympus, would safeguard the sickle, until *she* deems Junia worthy to wield our grandfather's mighty weapon?"

"This is not Athena's burden, wise as she may be," Hades replied. "It is mine and mine alone."

"Then what if I relieved you willingly of this burden, Uncle?"

"Why would you ever bring such a thing upon yourself?" Hades inquired. "Unless... you have other designs for that sickle, of which you intend to keep me ignorant."

"What ever do you mean?" Hermes retorted, affecting an expression of mild shock.

"I've known you since you were but a small child yourself," Hades answered. "Stealing your brother's cattle and causing all sorts of mischief from the moment you were born. Do not think me a fool, only because I hardly leave the confines of my Kingdom! If you truly mean to retrieve the sickle, and I know you do, since no one in their right mind would argue with me for so long as you have just now, then I must have assurances that your words are not outright deceitful. I must know, without a doubt, that you do not seek to bring the weapon to one of your fellow immortals who dwell on holy Olympus to use for ill intent. Swear this to me by the waters of the Holy River Styx, and I will allow you to dive into the Acherusian Lake to retrieve Kronos' sickle. However, should these waters and those of the Holy River Styx find you guilty of duplicity, not only would you have to suffer the penalty of oath-breakers among our kind, but you would also have to undergo the purification befitting mortals who have committed crimes of impiety against their parents. And once you are judged cleansed of your sin, you will be allowed to return to the surface of the broad-pathed Earth after drinking the from the River Lethe, as mortal shades do when they return to the world of the living without recollection of the lives they've lived before."

"Really, Uncle? Do you know what happens to immortals when they drink of the River Lethe? Have you not *met* Hera?"

"Your father might find your facetious insults towards my sister amusing, young one, but not I," Hades answered. "And unlike Zeus, I do not possess the luxury of over-indulgence towards those who tread upon my Kingdom. It will be as I say, or you must return to starry Olympus empty-handed, and give young Junia another gift for her coming of age."

Hermes rubbed his temples wearily and remained silent for a long moment. "What other gift can I give her," he said at last, "but the instrument that would guarantee her freedom, and Hera's freedom, should Zeus decide to ignore her decision pertaining to her future? Do you not remember, Uncle, that you made me swear an Oath, by the Holy River Styx, that I would never suffer to see Hera and Junia brought to Olympus and detained there against their will? Would you see me endure the penalty of immortal oath-breakers, as well as that befitting mortal sinners, for carrying out my sworn duty? You, the Host of Many, would see me lie breathless for a full year, then wander the broad-pathed Earth alone and exiled, in the guise of a temporarily addled imbecile? All because I seek to uphold my Oath, as is just and righteous by our laws?"

"I see," Hades said gravely. "Very well," he added after a moment. "I will allow you to try to retrieve the sickle. But know that I will hold you fully responsible for the outcome, whether good or ill."

As a sense of relief visibly washed over Hermes' features, the messenger wasted no time removing his winged sandals and his loosely fitting chiton. "You will safeguard these, will you not?" he told Cerberus as he placed his apparel at the hound's feet. The Beast answered by licking him with its three tongues all at once and by wagging his scaly tail, a spectacle both endearing and terrifying for the shades bobbing nearby in the waters of the River Acheron.

Hermes then dove into the Acheron without further ceremony,

disappearing beneath the waves rife with the innumerable shades of the dead.

Once Hades was satisfied that Hermes had reached the bottom of the Acherusian Lake, he turned his gaze towards Cerberus and said, "It does appear that you will have to safeguard the Underworld for a few hours, while I attend my niece's birthday celebration."

Cerberus answered Hades' words by tilting two of his three heads in bemusement.

"I knew you would understand," the Host of Many told Cerberus, patting the remaining upright head.

Chapter Twenty-Seven

Sea-born Aphrodite, furrowed her fair brow as she left Hera's parlour after young Junia and the mortal boy Derek had risen from their midday nap. It was now the Queen's decree that neither ought to be in the presence of the blessed gods who dwell on holy Olympus without the full escort of her older children, Ares and Eris – at the moment Eris was nowhere to be found. Without anyone noticing, the Harbinger of Chaos absconded from the gathering of immortals assembled to plan Junia's birthday party shortly after Athena and Hermes left, both looking worse for wear as if knowledge of an impending calamity burdened their deathless minds.

Never mind them, the goddess of love pondered as she walked down the stairway outside Hera's palace and onto the path that led to her own dwelling. She had troubles of her own: her plan to compel Derek to become enamoured with living among the gods, and for Junia to fall in love with him as a means to persuade her and white-armed Hera to remain on starry Olympus, had come to naught. Even without the meddling of the Queen and her retinue, Aphrodite's designs were destined to failure for she never knew the extent of Derek's artless innocence and purity, and how the best-laid plans to rob him of both could never match Hera's protective instincts against those who would corrupt her young mortal charge. As for Junia, her blossoming into young womanhood proved more fraught of late than Aphrodite ever anticipated. If Apollo and Ares told it true, the maiden appeared destined to grow as irascible as her mother, her flower becoming more thorn than rose-petals with each passing minute.

What in the name of Tartarus is the matter with all these virgin goddesses? Such was Aphrodite's persistent refrain, for she often lamented to Eros the Elder, whom immortals call Phanes, of her inability to sway the hearts of Athena, Artemis, and other chaste goddesses on high Olympus. And now, it would seem, Junia might become as one of their ilk.

As would Hera, if nothing is done to restore the Queen to her rightful place in

Nepheleid

the Cloud-gatherer's bed and urge her to abandon her reckless pursuit of forsaking her marriage and leaving her King behind.

She bade the Charites, her gracious attendants, to prepare her golden chariot. It was an exquisite wedding-gift from Hephaestus at the time when the smith god still had hopes of winning the heart of the goddess of love. There were times when Aphrodite almost regretted how the whole sad business of her marriage unfolded, for absent the supernal beauty of his mother and the straight, sturdy limbs of his father, Hephaestus did make a splendid effort of trying to impress his new bride instead with his brilliant skill at metalwork, and with the unmatched kindness of his heart. This chariot, the first among many luxurious gifts he bestowed upon her, had an intricately carved frame, most notable for the amount of gold filed away to create the masterpiece.

Perhaps there is a metaphor to be gleaned from this, Aphrodite mused darkly, given how poorly her own marriage turned out, for which she believed to bear only some of the blame.

At once, the Charites released four white doves from their gilded aviary and tethered the delicate creatures to their jewelled yokes upon the golden chariot.

If only it were as simple to yoke women thus to their natural desires, Aphrodite wondered. Centuries of civilizational decline had rendered women wary of binding themselves in marriage to men and producing enough offspring to replenish the once teeming nations of mortals. And yoking a Goddess-Queen once known to mortals as the Mistress of all Life by the act of Love, the only means by which Phanes, the eldest and most powerful force in the Cosmos, meant for her to sow Life on the broad-pathed Earth, would prove nigh impossible without the aid of this very same immensity. Resolving that the King and Queen of Olympus' sexless stalemate could no longer continue, Aphrodite set forth to meet Phanes in the realm where he dwells, confident that he would not deny her request for succour, as she had long served him above all others, even Zeus.

As her chariot soared towards the Heavens, a flock of sparrows and other songbirds followed in her wake, though far fewer in number than in days of old. There was a time when their ancestors obscured the noonday Sun in their flight, a sight from which mortals gifted in the prophetic arts divined the future. Fearing that eagles or falcons would prey on her modest cortege, Aphrodite bade her father, the primordial Sky-King

Ouranos, to let her chariot cross into Phanes' realm at the very centre of the Cosmos. Ouranos heard his daughter's pleas and opened a starry aperture in the firmament, into which the goddess crossed over until lovely Hebe and stalwart Herakles' sons, Anicetos and Alexiares, could no longer see her flight from the ramparts of holy Olympus.

No sooner had golden Aphrodite stepped off from her chariot onto the soft, rosy-hued ground upon which Phanes treads did she notice that the First-begotten among the deathless gods was not alone. Before the Cosmic Egg stood Thetis, daughter of Nereus, as well as Eris. At first, neither goddess took any notice of Aphrodite's arrival, preoccupied as they were by their discussion with their eminent host. In the span of a mortal heartbeat, Phanes raised his venerable head and smiled at Aphrodite, distracting the others at once. Fractious Eris, ever the bold instigator in all manner of mischief, gave Aphrodite a wink, then vanished into a kaleidoscopic visual din from which Thetis and even Aphrodite's doves quaked in surprise and confusion. Thetis then looked at Aphrodite sheepishly, as if suddenly realizing that she was now stranded in this isolated and exalted realm, seldom visited by the blessed gods who dwell on starry Olympus.

What business could these two possibly have with Lord Phanes? What in the name of loud-thundering Zeus is going on?

"Venerable Lord," Aphrodite said as she bowed before Phanes, then acknowledged Thetis with a polite nod. "You who sows life upon the broad-pathed Earth with the seed of all Creation-"

"Mighty Aphrodite, lover of smiles," the First-begotten replied. "I always delight in your presence, but I fear that today your petition may go unanswered, for the lovely Thetis has come to me today with an equally pressing concern."

Aphrodite gasped and took a step back in her shock. "What could be more pressing," she said after a moment, "than the matter for which I beseech your benevolent aid?"

Thetis huffed nervously but said nothing.

"It is a matter of grave importance," Phanes continued, "for it threatens to rend the starry Heavens and the broad-pathed Earth asunder.

"But that has already happened!" Aphrodite cried indignantly. "That is precisely how I came to be!"

"Not all matters in the Cosmos pertain to you alone, Aphrodite!" Thetis said angrily once she found her voice.

"And what in the name of –"

"Oh, come off it!" Thetis interrupted. "Even the *birds* know that you're here to ask for Lord Phanes' support in your endless campaign against Hera's sovereignty, as you have always done, and always for the same reason – to curry Zeus' favour and keep your pride of place on starry Olympus! Have you no shame?"

"Oh, really?" Aphrodite retorted crossly. "Name *one thing* I've ever done against Hera to undermine her sovereignty before loud-thundering Zeus!"

Thetis scoffed at Aphrodite's words, while the birds shrieked incredulously, flapping their wings in protest. Even Phanes, in his terrible and beautiful aspect at the centre of the Cosmic Egg, cocked his head slightly to the side and threw Aphrodite an incredulous glance, like an amused parent catching a child in a blatant lie.

"All right," Aphrodite recanted. "Name one thing I've done *lately* to undermine Hera..."

"What about your little stunt with the golden apple from Hera's Garden, for instance?" Thetis retorted.

"I have no idea what you're going on about," Aphrodite said dismissively. "Now Thetis, be a dear and let the Elders among the gods speak."

"You stole an under-ripe golden apple from the Garden of the Hesperides," Thetis replied, "and placed it in Hera's hand as she recovered from her ordeal against Gaia last Winter. Eris saw it! And when she pried open her mother's hand to retrieve it, Hera awoke and threw the apple in the Sky –"

"And then Hera found the true purpose of these enchanted apples, did she not?" Aphrodite retorted. "Besides, I plucked that thing from my own garden on the isle of Cyprus, I'll have you know. Hera is not the only one in possession of such orchards."

"Do you think me a fool?" Thetis asked accusingly.

"Do not ask if you do not wish to know the answer," Aphrodite said. "But back to the tree – it was the very same one from which I plucked the three golden apples that I gifted the young Hippomenes so that he could prevail in his footrace against the virgin huntress Atalanta and win her for his bride! I stole nothing from our Queen!"

"Was this the same Hippomenes and Atalanta whom you transformed into the lions that now pull rich-haired Rhea's chariot?" Phanes inquired. "All because of Hippomenes' blunder of not offering you incense in thanks for answering his prayer and granting him his heart's desire?"

"The very same, my Lord," Aphrodite answered triumphantly.

"Then why did you do it?" Thetis asked.

"One cannot allow mortals to enjoy the fruits of the gods' favour without acknowledgement," Aphrodite replied with a hint of righteous indignation in her otherwise mellifluous voice.

"No, not that you git!" Thetis replied.

"Then be more specific," Aphrodite said.

"Why did you place the apple in Hera's hand as she slept?" Thetis asked with rising pique. "Was it to distract her while you *entertained* her King? In the same way that you distracted Atalanta and had her pick the golden apples up from the racetrack so that Hippomenes could prevail? Hera was right about you; you are no friend to women!"

At a loss for words, golden Aphrodite glanced at Phanes, as if expecting the First-begotten to chide Thetis on her behalf. Phanes merely nodded at Aphrodite and gave her a wan smile.

"I did it," Aphrodite said, "so that Hera could discover for herself that she can bring to completion the task of seeding the Cosmos with Earthly Life without leaving starry Olympus, and without turning all of humanity into sexless ninnies while doing so. But as always, Hera misunderstood my intent, and I have failed in my endeavour to compel her to stay by our King's side. So, I've come to supplicate the most powerful being among our deathless kind to ensure that *Hera* does not rend for a second time the starry Heavens and the fruitful Earth asunder. And what request could *you* possibly have that anyone in their right mind might consider more dire than mine?"

Now it was Thetis who glanced up at Phanes, who once again responded with a benevolent smile and a more pronounced nod.

"The Titans," Thetis said, "mean to usurp Hera's supremacy over the CARINA fleet and take upon themselves the burden of sowing Earthly Life across the starry Cosmos – "

"And how could you possibly know such a thing?" Aphrodite interrupted.

"I paid them a visit in Elysium earlier today," Thetis answered. "As did most of Olympus, if King Kronos and Queen Rhea are to be believed."

"So let them," Aphrodite retorted.

"What did you just say?" Thetis asked, visibly aghast.

"I said let them! At least the Titans have the good sense to allow mortals to multiply through the act of Love and not with ghastly machines!"

Thetis looked at Aphrodite angrily. "Machines?" she said. "What on Earth –"

"Oh, you know full well that Hera intends for her learned mortals to reproduce by using machines in the vast expanse between the Stars!" Aphrodite answered condescendingly. "Our Lord Phanes ought to be utterly outraged at this very notion!"

"Those machines are necessary for the survival of the learned mortals of the CARINA Venture!" Thetis said, glancing nervously at the First-begotten above her in his Egg. "And the Titans, they intend on taking over Hera's command of the Nephele and City-ships of its ilk to yoke the minds of the learned mortals therein and to render them as guileless as they once were when Kronos was King before Prometheus gifted them with fire from Olympus to liberate them from their wretchedness!"

Aphrodite shrugged with utmost indifference. "At least this time they will not be castrating anyone," she said after a moment. "While Hera may as well be neutering all of humanity when they leave the embrace of the broad-pathed Earth, as they set out to seed the vast Cosmos with Earthly Life! Do you not find this a bit ironic?"

"So, you care not a whit about Hera's designs to make mortals better as they explore the expanse between the stars and seed the wanderers with Life?" Thetis asked incredulously. "You only care if they honour your ways in how they increase their numbers? You truly are as selfish and shortsighted as our Queen has always judged you to be. Do you not agree, Lord Phanes... My Lord?"

To Aphrodite and Thetis' dismay, the Cosmic Egg in which Phanes dwells lay empty, its occupant nowhere in sight. The goddesses glanced at one another inelegantly, at a loss for words.

"You do not suppose he's run off on his own to Olympus, do you" Thetis asked.

"Of that, I have no doubt!" Aphrodite answered with an incredulous sneer.

"We should have gone with him," Thetis lamented.

"We should have," Aphrodite agreed.

"Could you... take me along with you back to Olympus on your chariot?" Thetis asked.

Aphrodite raised an eyebrow.

"Oh, come now!" Thetis exclaimed. "You owe me this much for playing your part in turning my wedding-feast into the cause for the longest war that mortals back then had ever known!"

Aphrodite heaved a loud, theatrical sigh. "You will never let that go, will you?" she asked, stepping onto her chariot. "Well, come on then!" she said, making a show of leaving enough room for Thetis to take her place beside her.

Once again, Aphrodite bade Ouranos to open the Heavens above to let her golden chariot pass, with its modest retinue of small, lovely birds in its wake, bound for what would surely prove a very lively and memorable birthday celebration on high Olympus.

Nepheleid

Chapter Twenty-Eight

Long after the Sun arced past its zenith, swift Hermes flew on winged sandals towards high Olympus. His flight was hindered by the burden of Kronos' sopping wet sickle dripping the waters of the Acherusian Lake over the fields and valleys surrounding the holy mountain. Still drenched himself, Hermes set his mind to meeting bright Athena in the banquet hall, and to perhaps dissuade her from her ill intent in using this weapon of legendary renown. Even after his feet touched the polished floor of starry Olympus, the messenger kept the sickle at arm's length, or as far as his godly strength allowed, for he remained wary of the blade. This was the weapon that the Titan-King Kronos made for the sole purpose of castrating and supplanting his father, the primordial Sky-King Ouranos. The sickle was also the one with which the monster Typhon, midwifed by Hera and birthed by Gaia, used to severe Zeus' sinews when he briefly prevailed against the Father of gods and men in his campaign against Olympus.

Zeus came into possession of Kronos' sickle after he and his brothers defeated the Titans and cast them into the pit of Tartarus. On the day Typhon rose up to avenge his imprisoned brothers, the gods fled to Egypt in the guise of animals, leaving Zeus alone to face the terrifying foe. The Cloud-gatherer tried to bring down Typhon with his father's sickle, but he missed his target. Typhon caught Zeus and wrestled him to the ground, then used the sickle to remove Zeus' sinews on his hands and feet. Defeated, Zeus was taken across the sea to a cave in Silicia as a prisoner. Typhon then hid Zeus' sinews in a bear pelt and bade the Drakaina Delphyne, a maiden who was half-girl, half-animal, to guard it. Hermes and his son Pan came to Zeus' rescue, first by distracting Typhon with the promise of a banquet of fish. Once the monster was sated to near incapacitation, Hermes used his great skill at thievery and robbed the bear-pelt from the Drakaina, then he and Pan snuck inside the cave where Zeus was imprisoned and reattached the sinews upon his father's hands and feet.

Now in possession of his full strength, the Thunderer pursued Typhon relentlessly, flinging thunderbolts at him, and chasing him all the way to Mount Nysa, where the three Fates tricked Typhon into partaking the intoxicating fruit on the vine, telling him it would make him strong enough to defeat Zeus once and for all. Addled from consuming vast quantities of fermented grape, Typhon drunkenly hurtled mountains at Zeus from the Earth, while Zeus threw thunderbolts at him from the Sky. In his flight, Typhon found himself once again in the southern Italian peninsula, where Zeus threw a mountain back at him, burying the fiend under what is now Mount Etna, which still belches fire from Zeus' thunderbolts from the bowels of Typhon's rocky prison.

Such were the reminiscences that burdened Hermes' mind as he crept through the hallowed halls of snowy Olympus, leaving a wet trail behind him wherever he went. He was careful to avoid the glances of his fellow immortals as he made his way to a side door to the banquet hall with his heavy and awkward burden. Though loath to see the Virgin Warrior break her Oath of fealty to Zeus and use the sickle against their father, Hermes reluctantly admitted that Athena's cause was just, for Zeus committed a grave error in deceiving her about her true parentage, and the role he played in her mother's disappearance. He also knew that Hera would be sympathetic to Athena's plight, even if the Queen was also bound by the same Oath of fealty after the insurrection she led against Zeus many centuries ago failed spectacularly. Still, the thought of him and Athena both petitioning Hera's protection and safe passage to the Nephele with the other blessed gods as a last resort sickened Hermes, as much as an immortal scion of Olympus could experience sickness in his deathless flesh. Hermes reminded himself that, though Hera hated him so very much, she was far too clever not to perceive the advantage of having him and Athena by her side as trusted members of her crew.

If only Hera could be persuaded to trust us, that is.

Hermes often found himself at odds with the Queen, but his antagonistic relationship with Hera was never truly intentional, for he angered her solely when obeying the orders of his King. Zeus, however, was always cognizant that his multiple infidelities and the ways in which he needed Hermes to intervene on his behalf would inevitably render his bride deeply embittered towards them both. If the Fates were kind, perhaps Hera would see Hermes' change of loyalties as an opportunity to give Zeus a healthy serving of his just desserts and sidestep millennia of resentment towards her King's messenger. But Hera had always felt all manner of sentiment – whether love or hate – acutely, and despite her long-abandoned habit of sampling the waters of the River Lethe whenever overwhelmed by Zeus' mockery of their union, she seldom forgot insults, having grown immune long ago to the effects of the river of oblivion.

To this very day, despite the alleged softening of her heart in recent years towards those who have displeased her over the centuries, Hera's hate ran distressingly deep. So deep, in fact, that Hermes suspected that she would find reasons to retract her generous offer to unquestioningly grant safe passage to the Nephele to any immortal, while continuing to ban Hermes, Aphrodite, Dionysus, and of course Zeus. Without uttering a single word concerning the latter, Hera made the point abundantly clear that her involvement with the CARINA endeavour was but a means to an end, that is, finding righteous purpose to leave Zeus behind forever. Hermes understood this at a visceral level, for he more than any other blessed god suffered the consequences of being Zeus' messenger and enforcer during the Queen and King's latest estrangement, being cast out of Olympus himself until Hera reluctantly returned to Olympus with the young Junia.

Hermes understood quite well Hera's antipathy towards Zeus and towards himself, and even her animosity towards Aphrodite, whose offences against the Queen were far too many to recount. However, he still considered her repudiation of Dionysus as rather jarring, especially since Hera supposedly reconciled with Zeus' twice-born, half-mortal scion upon Dionysus' apotheosis. Once Hera ceased to view Dionysus as her sworn enemy, she went so far as to offer him her daughter Hebe in marriage as a sign of goodwill, which Zeus disallowed, for he intended to have the maiden wed to Herakles – another demigod Hera despised during the span of his mortal years. Then again, after attaining his full godhood, Dionysus brought his mother Semele back from the Kingdom of Hades and bade her to dwell on starry Olympus under the name Thyone. This was something that likely failed to endear them both to Hera.

So perhaps forgiveness was not in the Queen's nature after all.

Likewise, Dionysus embodied every character flaw that Hera disliked in men. He was soft, effeminate, and hedonistic, instead of stalwart and stoic like Ares, Hephaestus, or Herakles – or even Prometheus, for that matter. Dionysus was also licentious and indulgent, qualities the Queen found loathsome in men who were overly pampered during childhood. She also likely resented Dionysus for having been brought up by her own mother, rich-haired Rhea, whereas Hera was sent away as a maiden to dwell with Okeanos and Tethys, the Father and Mother of Rivers, at the boundaries of the broad-pathed Earth. Perhaps Hera told it true when she stated her intent to create a world where Dionysus' presence would prove obsolete, a world in which no mortal would feel compelled to engage in drunken revels in the new universe that she and Prometheus and their learned mortals aimed to create. Or perhaps having Eris among her crew constituted the only species of chaos the Queen was willing to endure – something Hermes thought the most plausible. This would render Dionysus' intemperance intolerable in the stark, disciplined world of the Nephele and the City-ships of their ilk yet to come.

Even so, Hera could do far worse than to accept in this new world the presence of those immortals she most disliked – including Zeus. Hermes agreed that Zeus was a deceitful bastard and a master manipulator, however, no one could deny the Thunderer's skill at vanquishing monstrous enemies when he found himself at his full strength. And yet, after becoming King of Olympus, Zeus consistently found a way to make enemies of his former allies. Gaia, for instance, had been complicit in sparing Zeus as an infant from Kronos' tyranny by finding a cave in Crete where rich-haired Rhea could hide him until he grew to manhood. But when Zeus and his recently rescued brothers supplanted the Titans and imprisoned them in Tartarus, Gaia no longer favoured the newly crowned Sky-King and his Olympian Court. The alliance between the Earth-Mother and the Father of gods and men concluded when Zeus murdered Gaia's son Eurymedon, King of the once peaceful race of Giants, who at the time was happily wed to white-armed Hera.

This was the reason, Hermes later learned, why Hera was sent away to dwell at the boundaries of the Earth, for she lost all recollection of her marriage to the King of the Giants when Zeus threw her into the River Lethe after she birthed Eurymedon's son Prometheus in the Kingdom of Hades. Strangely enough, as a maiden dwelling in the House of Okeanos and Tethys, Hera considered Zeus her dear brother and friend, until he began to pursue her in earnest over the course of centuries, resorting to trickery to shame her into becoming his Queen. The rest Hermes knew well enough, for he was the fruit of one of Zeus' countless infidelities, and even aided and abetted his father in his endless quest to stray from his marriage-bed.

And now grey-eyed Athena, skilled in tactical warfare like no other immortal in any nation on the broad-pathed Earth, had set her mind to challenging Zeus' supremacy by using the same weapon Kronos used against his own father, for the crime of dispatching her mother and lying about it for as long as the Virgin Warrior had drawn breath. Though Athena had participated in the failed coup against Zeus led by golden-throned Hera, Apollo and Poseidon, she did not suffer the consequences of Zeus' wrath when he prevailed against the insurgents, except for having to swear the same Oath of fealty to her King as did all the blessed gods who dwell on holy Olympus. This time, Zeus would have no moral recourse against Athena's wrath, for her cause was just, as Zeus' enmity towards Kronos had been when he forced the Titan-King to surrender his older siblings trapped inside his belly.

This time, Hermes would be found complicit in the outcome, whatever it may be, for he was the one who retrieved Athena's weapon of choice from its hiding-place in the Underworld. Even if Athena prevailed in her challenge, Hermes feared that both he and his eldest sister would be found guilty of breaking their Oath. Worse yet, that they would carry the blemish of treachery for all eternity, regardless of whether he and Athena found themselves dwelling on a distant wanderer, far from the familiar embrace of the broad-pathed Earth. But it was now too late to undo what had been done, for Athena found Hermes skulking outside a back entrance to the banquet hall on starry Olympus.

The Virgin Warrior halted when she glimpsed Hermes' countenance, divining the state of mind that burdened the messenger as he bore the burden of Kronos' sickle into the hallowed abode of the gods.

Athena took a moment to compose herself. "You are soaking wet," she said causally. "How can that be?"

"The waters of the rivers in the Underworld have strange properties," Hermes replied. "It will take some time to dry off after a dive in the Acherusian Lake."

"Come," Athena said, once her initial scepticism at Hermes' words waned. "You can put the sickle here, under the table at the end of the hall. That is where all the others have begun placing their gifts for Junia, on the occasion of her birthday."

Hermes complied, making certain that none of the other blessed gods who dwell on holy Olympus saw him sneak the massive sickle into the hall, and under the draped table.

"What if another were to find it first?" Hermes asked in a low voice, barely above a whisper.

"Then it will be as you've told Lord Hades," Athena answered. "Tell everyone that you've brought the sickle back to Olympus to its rightful owner, for Kronos gifted it to Junia when she was a child. And now that she's come of age, so she ought to be reunited with it."

"And what will happen next?" Hermes continued.

"It would be best if I kept you ignorant of my plans," Athena said.

Hermes raised his eyebrow, unamused at the Virgin Warrior's answer. "Plausible deniability, eh?" he asked her. "I doubt that Zeus would be so easily deceived."

"None of this will matter once I've dealt with him," Athena replied with barely controlled pique. "And should you doubt my ability to challenge him, you may as well throw yourself at Hera's mercy at once, or become Junia's new favourite among the deathless gods who dwell on holy Olympus since she no longer cares for Apollo –"

Now there is an image I never cared to conjure.

"Surely you jest," Hermes retorted. "The wench hates me almost as much as Hera does."

"Then give her cause not to," Athena whispered, as the Cloud-gatherer made his imminent presence known in the usual manner, his footsteps shaking the ground as he made his way towards the banquet hall on starry Olympus.

"HERMES!" Zeus bellowed.

Hermes threw Athena a doubtful glance.

"No one knows anything yet," she whispered. "Remember, it is precisely as you've told Lord Hades. Leave the rest to me."

"Hermes!" Zeus repeated when he found his messenger behind the gift table. "Where the bloody hell have you been? We have a guest at the door!"

Once he fully understood the meaning of his father's words, Hermes suddenly took flight on winged sandals and headed towards the entrance to the banquet hall, the ichor all but drained from his features.

The Titans! I've completely forgotten about the Titans!

Nepheleid

Chapter Twenty-Nine

"HERMES!" Zeus bellowed from somewhere inside the banquet hall.

"Right away!" Hermes shouted as he sped across the vast room, his feet ostensibly hovering above the polished marble floor as he ran a direct course toward the exact spot where Junia stood.

"Hold on, I'll get it," Junia said, stepping aside and reaching for the door.

"Not so fast, child," Eris interjected, almost slapping Junia's hand away. She then grabbed the large iron hook and pulled open the door, narrowly missing Hermes' head by a hair.

Beyond the threshold stood Phanes, as beautiful in aspect as Junia remembered him from the previous evening's excursion. Yet, for reasons Junia did not fully understand, he appeared somewhat less imposing than he had when she found him in his own realm, ensconced in his Cosmic Egg. Junia then turned to glance at Hermes, who looked both relieved and confused for reasons that also eluded her. Only Eris, who stood sentinel by the large bronze door, seemed to fathom why the Eldest among the gods had come to Junia's coming-of-age celebration without a formal invitation.

After a moment, Hermes stepped in front of Junia and Eris and bowed respectfully before Phanes, then bade him to come inside, opening the door wider to allow for his wings.

"Who is it?" Zeus asked cantankerously from his seat on the other end of the banquet hall.

"Father, it is your ego," Eris answered before Hermes could speak.

Her words elicited a chuckle from Ares and Derek, who both dallied nearby, flanked by Paul, Hebe, and Herakles. The latter threw one another confused glances while Paul looked upon the scene with muted amazement.

"That word doesn't mean what she thinks it means," Junia heard Derek say to Paul. "It's actually a funny story. Hey, why do you look like you've just seen a ghost?"

"Dude," Paul replied fitfully. "That's –"

"God almighty squared," Junia muttered, finishing Paul's train of thought.

"Young ones," Hera said to the small assembly, seemingly materializing out of the very ether by the front doors of the banquet hall. "You ought to go listen to Apollo and the Muses sing. It is really quite lovely. Are you all right, Derek? My apologies, I did not mean to startle you."

"I'm fine," Derek answered, clutching his chest as he caught his breath.

Hera gave him a reassuring smile, then turned her attention towards Hebe. "Make certain that the mortals stay at the back," she told her, "Over there, by the gift table. And make certain that we are *not* interrupted."

"Yes, Mother," Hebe replied obediently.

"And keep an eye on this one," Hera told Eris and Ares, her gaze fixed on Junia.

"We will, Mother," Ares said, nudging Junia by the shoulder.

"And you," Hera said to Derek. "Deep breaths. On your feet. That's a good lad."

"Yes, ma'am," Derek managed to say as his heart slowly ceased to fibrillate.

"Come now," Eris told Junia, "that was an order, not a suggestion."

Junia frowned but complied, keeping pace with Ares, Hebe, Herakles, and Paul. Derek trailed behind, his gaze taking in his surroundings as if seeing the banquet hall for the first time. Eris poked him in the ribs, unsubtly bidding him to walk faster.

"Ow! Stop that!" Derek said. "I'm full of panini!"

Herakles laughed heartily. "You certainly are!" he said. "As is your friend!"

"So, I take it that Dionysus' brew has completely worn off?" Ares inquired, alluding to Derek's renewed sense of bafflement among the blessed gods who dwell on holy Olympus.

"I reckon it has," Eris answered while Hebe and Paul exchanged a knowing grin.

"Is the full bodyguard detail really necessary?" Junia asked. "I mean, it's not like everyone doesn't already know what I'm going to say when *Mr. Diaz* asks me about whether I want to stay or go…"

"You've just answered your own question, Stargazer," Ares replied.

"Huh?"

"Try again," Ares said.

"You think that Derek and Paul are in danger?" Junia answered tentatively. "Mom already made sure to stuff them to the gills with mortal food, so that they are not tempted to eat the food of the gods and get stuck here for all eternity, and then I don't choose to stay here out of guilt for trapping them on Olympus because of their mortal appetites."

"Not they," Ares said, "for I am certain that Father will send them back to the Nephele before the day is done. He is not so cruel as to keep innocent mortal men on Olympus as pawns, especially when one of them is clearly enamoured of Mother."

"Except for Ganymede," Eris interjected.

"Who was never given the chance to know a woman's touch, so he does not know better," Hebe said.

"Right," Ares agreed. "No, your mortal friends are not in danger, but I do believe that Father does not mean to play fair. I would not put it beyond him to have sent for Phanes to convince Mother not to follow you to the expanse beyond the Heavens –"

"Ha!" Junia shrieked. "So I was right!"

"We never told you otherwise, child!" Eris replied.

"Hold up!" Derek said to Paul. "Look! It's that weird, pretty blonde lady I told you about!"

Junia followed Derek and Paul's line of sight and saw golden Aphrodite enter the banquet hall, accompanied by silver-footed Thetis.

"So that is where she disappeared to," Hebe said. "Since when are those two friends?"

"That's the lady who kept making passes at you yesterday?" Paul asked. "Dude, no way! She's way out of your league! And so is that other babe."

"Hey, that's Thetis!" Derek said cheerfully.

"Thetis?" Paul repeated.

"Yeah, one of Dr. A's kids, one she took in as a stray," Derek answered. "Apparently, she does that sometimes. Yeah, Thetis went to get me my pants this morning in Dr. Archer's place, where I stayed last night. It was weird, I'll tell you later –"

"You were *mostly* correct, child," Eris told Junia, drawing the child's attention away from her mortal friends. "But I am afraid that our dear brother is mistaken. Father was not the one who sent for Phanes."

"Was it Thetis then?" Hebe asked. "That little tattletale! She simply cannot help herself, can she? Just like the whole sorry business with Briareus when Mother and Poseidon and Apollo led the insurrection against Father –"

"Oh, come now," Eris interrupted her. "Let's not speak of this dreadful event on the joyous occasion of our little sister's birthday!"

"All right," Hebe conceded. "But one has to wonder why Thetis has not yet learnt what happens when she meddles in Mother's affairs. It never ends well! And why is Aphrodite with her?"

"Why do you think?" Ares asked before catching Junia by the arm as she spun on her heels to make her way to the front of the hall.

"Fine!" Junia protested. "You know that just means I'll find another way to figure out what's going on?"

"That is what I am trying to prevent," Ares retorted with uncharacteristic calm.

"You do know that Mother and Father will blunt their voices from us all as they speak with Phanes, do you not?" Eris said. "They rarely do that, as they often prefer to make a spectacle of their quarrels for all to see. But they do have their means to keep their voices silent even from the ears of immortals. They learnt to do that long ago, when they were still in the habit of reconciling on mountaintops, even when Father hid them both in a shroud of golden clouds."

"Ew," Junia said.

"Their discussion with Phanes will be for their ears alone," Eris added. She then glanced at the golden maiden Galatea, who gave her a nod and made her way towards the more venerable gods at the front of the banquet hall.

"Paul, do you have your handheld terminal with you?" Eris asked after a moment.

"Of course!" Paul answered reflexively.

"May I?" Eris asked with undue politeness.

"Sure! Here, take it," Paul replied after pulling the small device out of his pocket and handing it over to Eris.

As Hebe and Herakles led Derek and Paul to a small array of couches next to the gift table at the end of the banquet hall, Eris busied herself with Paul's handheld terminal until she felt satisfied that it would yield the desired result.

"Why don't you join your friends for that hilarious game, the one with the black cards that they played earlier after they were fed?" Eris asked Junia.

"Mom won't let me," Junia answered. "She says I'm too young to play that card game."

"I doubt that very much," Eris retorted.

"She said it's all about gallows humour and sexual innuendo," Junia said.

"There is absolutely no innuendo, young one!" Herakles replied cheerfully to the amusement of Hebe, Derek, and Paul.

"Then go play it as your first grown-up deed for the occasion of your coming-of-age!" Eris said. "And look, Eileithya is joining them. Go on, with her at the table, you might even learn something new about anatomy!"

Nepheleid

"She is probably checking in on Derek," Ares said. "I think the boy might be infatuated with her ever since she rescued him from certain death at the hands of the Maenads... And she favours Mother in face and limb."

"That would do it," Eris chortled.

"I'd rather hang out with you two," Junia told Eris and Ares, sidling up to the latter in an annoyingly endearing manner.

"You are too young to hear what the ears of Hephaestus' golden maiden are about to reveal," Eris replied, shooing Junia away from the ground where she set down Paul's handheld device. "Now go on, go play with them, or go listen to Apollo and the Muses."

"They're not singing anymore," Junia whined, pointing towards the Archer as he made his way towards Eris and Ares. "And what are *you* doing here?" Junia asked Apollo with mild irritation.

"I've come here to make certain that this one," Apollo answered, pointing at Eris, "does not cause Derek's precious mind irreparable damage by confounding him any further now that the brew that Dionysus gave him has worn off. And also, to bear witness as you choose your fate at your coming-of-age celebration."

"Of course," Junia sneered.

"Aww," Hebe said, looking straight at her siblings.

"That does it," Eris declared. "I am turning on the magical mute function for anyone under three thousand years of age! That means you. Now go play with Hebe and Eileithya and the boys!"

"Ugh, fine," Junia said moodily, taking the hint from Eris and shuffling away from her and Ares and Apollo.

Once Eris' attention was no longer set on following her every move, Junia meandered towards the other side of the gift table. She then dropped to the floor and scuttled behind the thick white tablecloth, resolving to watch the live footage captured by Galatea's mechanical eyes and extrapolate its meaning through a combination of lip reading and telesthesia.

At last, Eris activated the three-dimensional broadcast on Paul's device and said, "Previously, on Housewives of Olympus!"

"That was clever," Ares said, "sending Galatea to attend to Mother and Father. They will think of her as part of the décor and pay her no heed.

"I do have my moments," Eris agreed.

Junia held her breath as the projected image displayed Hera and Zeus standing to Phanes' right and left, respectively, with Phanes looking unnaturally taller than the uncommonly stately King and Queen of Olympus. Though her body language emoted deference, Hera looked rather vexed as she looked up at Phanes and listened to his long-winded pontification about the sanctity of her, sacred marriage or some other nonsense Junia was genuinely glad not to hear. Junia felt an awkward gratitude towards Eris for shielding her virgin ears from Phanes' sanctimonious drivel, as well as a completely irrational, albeit momentary, pang of fear that Eris and other immortals she held dear might change their minds about joining her on the Nephele and the City-ships of its ilk yet to be made. Junia put this appalling thought out of her mind, determining that Phanes' recent incursion into her complicated world was the reason why her peace of mind and sense of home felt unduly threatened. She finally resolved that Phanes had to be dealt with in a decisive manner, albeit without resorting to violence, for Junia lacked the terrific weapon gifted to her by King Kronos upon their first meeting in the realm of Tartarus when she only a small child, a weapon she had failed to convince Eris to retrieve upon her return to starry Olympus.

Or perhaps *some* measure of violence could be justified. Phanes, like all the other gods who dwell on starry Olympus not bound for the Nephele, appeared to delight in meddling in Junia's affairs as well as those of her mother. Junia suddenly found it inordinately unfair that she was not yet strong enough to break through Eris' wall of silence and eavesdrop on Hera and Zeus' exchange with Phanes, even if Hera told her that her godly powers would grow in due time. Junia also found it supremely exasperating that *someone*, though not Zeus himself if Eris told it true, summoned Phanes to set Hera straight – even though Hera's cause to leave her extraordinarily awful husband was justified a thousandfold by any reasonable metric.

What are you going to do about it, child? she heard Eris say wordlessly inside her mind.

I will figure out who summoned Phanes here and why, Junia almost answered aloud, to which Eris answered with a brief wink before resuming her viewing of the spectacle broadcast before her by the mechanical eyes of Galatea.

It was Thetis, wasn't it? Junia asked Eris with her mind. The Harbinger of Chaos did not react at the mention of the Sea-nymph's name, even if Thetis intervening made the most sense. She usually meant well, even though her last intervention in the last epic quarrel between the King and Queen of Olympus ended with Hera having to swear fealty to Zeus after spending a night hanging from the Sky.

It is quite possible that she learnt her lesson well, Eris' voice echoed in Junia's mind.

Okay, so maybe it wasn't Thetis. Was it Aphrodite? Junia asked next, though this seemed quite unlikely. Junia knew Aphrodite as one who thought only of herself, whereas summoning Phanes to Olympus would constitute an act of altruism which no true narcissist was capable of undertaking.

Eris' countenance betrayed no reaction other than a wan grin as Junia's mind lingered on such thoughts. *You see her well for what she is*, Junia thought she heard Eris say within her mind, *And for all we know, Aphrodite might be the one responsible for other heinous trickery, such as your recent, albeit brief, infatuation towards Lord Apollo.*

Junia blushed at being reminded of her momentary foolishness in that regard, recalling all the times she heard Hera tell Klymene, Demeter, and others about her disapproval of her youngest daughter's blossoming love towards Leto's son. Of course, it made perfect sense that Aphrodite should use Junia as a pawn in such an insidious manner if only to supremely annoy Hera, for the Archer always had unhappy loves. Hera would never want Junia to end up like Cassandra, a princess of Troy who did not keep her part of the deal she made with Apollo when she asked him to teach her the art of prophecy in exchange for sexual favours. As a result of her impiety, no one believed her predictions until the day of her death at the hands of King Agamemnon's embittered wife, Clytemnestra. Nor would Hera want Junia to end up like the Sybil at Cumae, who, like Cassandra, spurned Apollo after learning the art of prophecy without granting her divine teacher his reward. Instead of dying young, the Sybil was given as many years of life as grains of sand she could scoop with her hands, however, as punishment for denying Apollo, the god refused to grant her eternal youth with her longevity.

Then there was Daphne, who escaped Apollo's advances by metamorphosizing into a laurel, which he then declared to be his sacred tree. Or Marpessa, who chose the mortal Idas, thinking that Apollo's love for her would wane as she aged and grew feeble in mind and limb. Or Coronis, mother of Asclepius, whom Apollo outright murdered with one of his golden arrows when a crow informed him that she ran off with a mortal man while pregnant with their child. The child survived his mother's death and was later raised by the long-dead Centaur Chiron, half-brother to Hera. Or the boy Hyacinthos, killed by a discus blow to the head when he and Apollo were training at the sport.

Right, but were they not all mortals?

And are you certain you are not? Eris retorted coyly, albeit tacitly.

Junia then remembered that none of it mattered, for she no longer loved Apollo in that way, or perhaps at all. Junia had sublimated her attraction for the Archer with righteous spite, warranting that Aphrodite would never get satisfaction in her endless campaign against Hera by corrupting the heart of her youngest daughter.

So Aphrodite is our enemy, then…

After giving it some thought, the possibility that Aphrodite would have been the one to summon Phanes to holy Olympus began to make the most sense, for Aphrodite was forever in league with the First-begotten amongst the gods. She always boasted of being Phanes' faithful servant, doing his bidding even to inveigle almighty Zeus against the latter's better judgement.

Did Zeus not take his revenge on Aphrodite once, by having her fall in love with the mortal Anchises, to whom she bore Aeneas, the sole Trojan survivor of the fall of Troy?

Junia agreed, unsure whether this notion came from Eris or from some long-buried memory of Klymene telling her of Aphrodite's notoriety shortly before Hera's forced return to Olympus a few years prior. Junia then resolved to find Aphrodite, so she could give her a piece of her mind –

"Don't worry, my dear," she heard a familiar, mellifluous voice say. "The imminent threat you saw in Elysium cannot prevail against the combined might of both Zeus and Lord Phanes…"

Nepheleid

Junia spun on her heels towards the source of the voice and spied Aphrodite nearby, smiling beatifically at a rather anxious-looking Thetis. The pair were strolling past Athena, who appeared exactly as morose as she had that very same morning when Paul arrived on his flying canoe.

Why the hell is she so sour? Was it the thing I said to her last night when we were in the Asphodel? That can't be it, because there is no way in Tartarus that she didn't know what Zeus did to Metis...

Athena seemed to pay no mind to anyone else gathered in the banquet hall, just as Thetis appeared to ignore Aphrodite's words. Junia then tried to probe Athena's thoughts but found herself incapable of breaching the Virgin Warrior's inner walls.

Ugh. Can I just grow up already so I can be strong enough to pierce the shields in everyone's heads?

Junia's own thoughts were interrupted by the silent shrieks emanating from Thetis' mind.

Okay, I take it back. Not everyone's mind needs probing. But what's wrong with Thetis?

As soon as Junia considered these thoughts, Thetis' mind closed itself, leaving nothing but echoes of the Sea-nymph's momentary terror. Remembering that Thetis possessed the prophetic gift, Junia followed Thetis' line of sight, finding that it lingered upon Athena's unflinching gaze, which itself pointed to the table behind which Junia hid.

Eris, do you think they saw me? Junia wondered loudly in her mind.

Well, did you hear any of them making a caustic remark about you hiding behind the gift table at your own coming-of-age party?

Right.

Deducing that there must be something peculiar hidden under the table, Junia lifted the nearest corner of the white tablecloth and found that which she had sought the previous evening when Eris took her on her adventure between the realms.

"Jackpot!" Junia clamoured, realizing only too late that she had uttered the last part aloud.

Athena gasped loudly, distracting Eris from her sustained effort to maintain the wall of silence around Junia.

With her head partially covered under the gift table, Junia overheard Phanes say, presumably to Hera, "I did not bring you to your bridegroom solely for the purpose of procreation, young one. You two were fated to be joined in a sacred union for the purpose of universal harmony and to put an end to the endless wars between the deathless races that dwell upon the broad-pathed Earth! If you forsake your love –"

Deciding that she had heard enough, Junia seized the sickle with both hands. She struggled to drag it from under the gift table, for it was too large and unwieldy for such a young godling, even if, in her mortal guise, she was stronger by far than the brawniest mortal athlete. Preoccupied with lifting the weapon without drawing too much attention to herself, Junia failed to notice that Eris, Ares, Apollo, Hebe, Herakles, Eileithya, and the mortal lads Derek and Paul were now on their feet, utterly baffled by what they were witnessing. At last, Junia lifted the sickle off the polished floor, balanced it against one of her shoulders, and leveraged the weapon's weight as she lunged towards Phanes at the other end of the banquet hall on high Olympus.

Aphrodite yelped in surprise. Noticing the direction in which Junia ran, she leapt towards the maiden to intercept her in her flight. Ares also sprang to his feet to join Aphrodite, but when Junia suddenly tripped over an unseen obstacle, the child let go of the mighty weapon, which landed straight in the middle of Ares' cuirass chest plate. With a look of utter disbelief, Ares collapsed onto his back while the blade sliced through the stone floor, pinning him where he lay, as Aphrodite and Junia both ran to his side.

"Ares!" Junia cried, her mien a vision of abject distress. "I'm so sorry!!! Say something! Ares!!!! Ares, why did you do that? ARES!!!!"

Thetis shielded her eyes while Apollo calmly walked towards Ares and knelt beside him to examine his wound. Eileithya knelt behind Ares to cradle his head on her lap. Hebe and Herakles took Paul and Derek aside to shield them from the gory spectacle. Derek hesitated, as if unsure of what he saw, while Paul complied unquestioningly as if he knew exactly what had come to pass.

Only Athena remained motionless, her eyes wide with foreboding as the ichor completely drained from her features.

Nepheleid

A thunderclap rended the confusion in the banquet hall, nearly rupturing Junia's eardrums. She immediately covered her ears and looked up at her mortal friends, whose own ears were preemptively covered by Hebe and Herakles' hands, as if the pair already knew that their father would announce his presence in this manner. Everyone turned their gaze in the direction of the front of the banquet hall, whence Hermes appeared shortly before Zeus, Hera, and Phanes, with Galatea trailing behind.

Hermes glanced at Ares, then at Athena, as the ichor also drained from quickly his countenance.

"What in the name of Ouranos' castrated bollocks is going on here?" Zeus said imperiously while Hera stood beside him, her eyes fixed upon their wounded son and the sobbing child kneeling beside him.

"Oh dear," the Queen said softly, then turned towards Galatea. "This will require specialized assistance," she added serenely as if speaking to someone unseen standing behind or beyond the golden maiden. "Please hurry."

Chapter Thirty

"Ares, I'm so sorry," Junia wept as Eileithya gently pulled her off Ares so that Apollo could better remove the ichor-stained cuirass to inspect the wound. "It was an accident!"

"What did you do?" Aphrodite cried out, trying to push Junia away from the impaled god of war laying between them. "And don't you roll your eyes at me!" she told Eileithya. "I saw exactly where she was headed with that thing. That blade was meant for me!"

"I doubt it," Eileithya replied calmly, helping Apollo unfasten the buckles that held the cuirass in place. She shook her head, annoyed at Aphrodite's inflated sense of vanity in the face of her lover's grievous injury, even if Ares was in no danger of perishing from his wound.

"ENOUGH!" Zeus bellowed, drawing the attention of everyone gathered in the banquet hall on starry Olympus to himself.

"What happened?" Hera asked with unnerving serenity, looking at Apollo, Aphrodite, and her daughters encircling her injured son. "Start at the beginning, please."

"Well, Mother, clearly I've been stabbed," Ares jested weakly. "Though why, I cannot say. You've never fumbled before, Stargazer. Why start now?"

"I... I... tripped," Junia managed to say between her sobs.

"Where, child?" Eris asked, eliciting a surprised stare from Eileithya and all the others crowding Ares, as it was very much unlike Eris to abstain from amplifying her twin's facetiousness with a witty repartee of her own.

Junia lifted her gaze towards Eris, then pointed to a spot on the floor which held no crack or obstacle of any kind that could have made her lose her balance in her sprint.

Nepheleid

"Why were you carrying Kronos' sickle, Kitten?" Hera asked. "And why did you stab your brother with it?"

"I didn't mean to!" Junia sobbed. "Oh crap, Ares, I'm so sorry. Does it hurt bad?"

"Only when I laugh, Stargazer," Ares answered flippantly.

"Oh, for Heaven's sake," Aphrodite retorted. "Someone get her off him before she finishes what she started!"

Apollo caught Junia's fist as soon as he saw the flash of anger in her eyes, while Eileithya held her at arm's length with the uncommon strength which all of Hera's trueborn children possess until Eris peeled Junia off the floor and enfolded her in a bear hug.

"Really?" Eileithya softly scolded Ares, who was wise enough not to reply, for he knew that his midwife sister found his bravado foolish at the best of times.

Ares probably already knew that Eileithya thought him especially daft for imperilling his virile body to defend the goddess of love, who once cursed him after he slew Aphrodite's mortal lover, Adonis, in a fit of jealous rage. In Eileithya's estimation, Ares' present gallantry was as purposeless as that of women who, in centuries past, died in childbirth in great numbers, knowing full well that their offspring's only purpose was to become cannon-fodders, or the producers of such cannon-fodder, for an uncaring and self-interested State. Unless, as Eileithya hoped, Ares meant to protect young Junia from Aphrodite's wrathful retaliation for thinking herself the maiden's target, given that Aphrodite often believed that all that came to pass under the Heavens pertained to her somehow. If this were the case, then Ares' bravery was as noble and true as Mother hoped it would eventually become. Since Ares' motivations were often difficult to ascertain, in this instance, Eileithya charitably gave her brother the benefit of the doubt.

"He will be all right, child," Eris reassured Junia. "He cannot die, remember?"

Eileithya threw Eris a sharp look, drawing her sister's attention towards the mortal boys flanked by Hebe and Herakles beyond the fray.

"Oh, come now, they cannot hear us," Eris protested. "They are less than three thousand years old, remember? And they're mortal!"

"Then why isn't your sound barrier working on me?" Junia asked, her sobs slowly receding with every breath.

"Because you broke her concentration with this," Ares replied, gesturing at the giant blade of legendary renown protruding from his chest.

"Please, hold still," Apollo told Ares, effectively thwarting Eileithya from scolding the god of war any further for making fun of his own predicament. Apollo then looked up at Zeus and Hera, as well as Phanes, who stood behind the royal pair, and said, "the scope of Ares' injuries is beyond anything I can do for him here on Olympus. He will need to be taken to the Nephele, where I can have a full surgical team at my disposal. But first, we must cut the blade above and below him so he can be transported without raising anyone's suspicions."

"And how will you do that?" Aphrodite asked. "Hephaestus is on the Nephele. He is the only craftsman skilled enough to cut the sickle!"

Eileithya turned her gaze towards Galatea, who followed in Phanes' wake. The golden maiden nodded in assent as if confirming receipt of an unspoken message from high above starry Olympus.

"Can Herakles not help us lift up the blade off the ground?" Eileithya asked. "Until we find a way to take Ares to the Nephele?"

"Herakles is minding the mortals," Eris answered, nudging her head towards Hebe and Herakles, who continued to keep Derek and Paul distracted from the rather gory spectacle of Ares' skewering.

"Right," Eileithya conceded, glad that Derek's fragile mind was kept distracted and that Paul was playing along as if he knew not what was happening in the hallowed halls of starry Olympus.

"We will have to find a way," the Archer said, "otherwise Ares will be stuck to this floor for a very long time."

"It's not so bad," Ares quipped. "Well, no worse than the time Hephaestus ensnared Mother upon her golden throne. At least for now, I can lie down –"

"Oh, do be quiet, Ares," Hera retorted, trying to suppress a grin. "And save your strength for your transport. Crossing the atmospheric barrier absent the gentle motion of the Hub can be rather gruelling!"

"Are your children in the habit of impaling each other at parties with the mighty weapons of their forefathers?" Phanes asked Zeus and Hera, jarring all the immortals gathered in the banquet hall with the otherworldly timbre of his voice.

Zeus turned his gaze towards his Queen as if wordlessly denouncing her as the one at fault in this absurd situation.

"No, they are not," Hera answered casually before turning her gaze once again towards Junia. "And who brought you Kronos' mighty sickle?" Hera asked once more, her tone noticeably less gentle than before.

"I... I found it under the table..." Junia stammered. "I swear, it was there, and I found it, and... and..."

"And you ran towards me to stab me with it!" Aphrodite said sharply.

"No, you got in the way!" Junia protested. "Then Ares got in your way, and then –"

"Where were you running to with King Kronos' sickle, Zoe?" Zeus asked with thinly masked annoyance.

"It's my sickle," Junia whined. "Kronos gave it to me. It's mine!"

"That does not matter," Hera snapped. "I made it abundantly clear that the sickle was not to leave its hiding-place in the Underworld until *you* were old enough to wield it responsibly. So, one of you lot fetched it against my orders," she continued, looking at the others gathered in the banquet hall. "And I would very much like to know which one of you is responsible for my son getting impaled at my daughter's coming-of-age celebration!"

No one dared to speak, prompting the Queen to look straight at Eileithya, her perennial collaborator and truth-teller. Of course, Hera never suspected her midwife daughter of bringing the sickle to Olympus, for Eileithya never cared much for warfare nor for the weaponry of the ancient race of Titans who ruled before her parents took the throne of Heaven from wily Kronos and rich-haired Rhea. Nor would Hera suspect fractious Eris of this particular instance of mischief, for the Harbinger of Chaos preferred to wage war upon the minds, instead of the bodies, of her foes. Within the span of a mortal heartbeat, Eileithya discerned that the culprit Hera sought must have been in possession of a more unequivocal, masculine animus, as well as enough ill will in their heart against the rulers of Olympus to bring to the abode of the gods the very first weapon of revolution ever forged in the bosom of the broad-pathed Earth. Glimpsing beyond the tip of the sickle jutting out of Ares' chest, Eileithya noticed the lingering look of horror on Hermes' countenance, mirrored by the dispassionate, impassive mask of shock on Athena' waxen features.

There you are.

Remembering that the Virgin Warrior had seemed rather peevish of late, without anyone – save perhaps for Hermes and Eris – knowing why, Eileithya deduced that Athena must have had a hand in bringing the sickle to Olympus for ill intent. Oddly enough, Eileithya cared not for Athena's motivation for doing so, for she always considered her eldest half-sister as the worst of sycophants – far worse even than swift Hermes. Athena often sided with Zeus' judgements... not because of the righteousness of his decrees, but because of her loyalty to her father. This loyalty towards the Cloud-gatherer became unquestioning after he spared her from punishment following the failed insurrection against his supremacy shortly before the Trojan War. Since then, Athena had done everything in her power to endear herself to Zeus, often at Hera's expense. And yet, though there were times in centuries past when Eileithya herself had to betray Hera's confidence and spy on her mother at Zeus' behest, she did so on pain of expulsion from starry Olympus, for her father thought it wise to weaken his Queen by alienating her closest allies until the gods fell from favour when the Nazarene took their place in the hearts and minds of mortals.

You were always Father's favourite. You always had a choice, whereas I never did.

"I see," Hera said, following Eileithya's line of sight and finally setting her gaze upon the Virgin Warrior.

"You see what, exactly?" Zeus asked, failing to discern the subtleties of his Queen's mental machinations.

"Is there something you would like to confess?" Hera said aloud to no one in particular, though her gaze alternated between Athena and Hermes. "You do remember that I offered safe passage to those who would like to join my crew on the Nephele, regardless of what may or may not have transpired between us, do you not? And obviously, whoever brought the sickle to Olympus never meant to have Junia use it against Ares. That was a dreadful accident that will soon get sorted out. So, which one of you would like to confess that they brought the sickle here, where Junia could find it and possibly maim herself or others with it? Be quick to unburden your conscience, for I will withdraw my generous and merciful offer after Junia and some among you leave Olympus with me tonight."

Eileithya bit her lip, slightly annoyed at her mother's insistence at giving unquestioning amnesty to anyone and everyone on high Olympus - except for Dionysus and Aphrodite. Perhaps Hera could do worse than to allow Dionysus passage to the Nephele where he could serve as a bringer of comfort to the forlorn, as Derek disclosed earlier in that moment of clarity induced by the brew he consumed when left unsupervised. As for Aphrodite, lover of smiles, women of her ilk have long found themselves useful in the service of rulers, whether for good or ill, as trusted confidantes and spies. Perhaps rich-haired Rhea told it true. Perhaps golden-throned Hera, for all her cleverness, possessed for more courage than sense, and saw enemies where there were none to be found, and allies among those most likely to betray her in the end.

"And why is that, precisely?" Zeus asked Hera with displeasure. "You don't suppose this whole sordid affair is any indication that Zoe is old enough to make her own decisions regarding her future, do you? You said it yourself. She is far too young to wield Kronos' sickle responsibly. Therefore she is far too young to choose her fate. That settles it. With Lord Phanes as my witness, I command you and Zoe to remain on Olympus. Ares, you may go, if only to remove that thing in your chest. And take the mortals lads with you. They have no further business here. Ganymede can finish the plumbing work the clever one started. Everyone else stays."

"But Father," Apollo said, "I must go as well to the Nephele to extract the sickle from Ares' chest!"

"Then summon the learned team of physicians here to help you take care of it," Zeus retorted. "And bring back Hephaestus if you must. The rest of them can stay there with Prometheus for all I care."

"That would be most ill-advised," Apollo replied. "If mortals knew that some among us can survive an injury of this magnitude, then they will start to ask questions, for which we are not yet ready to disclose the answers!"

"Then let Hermes spin them a tale with his silver tongue," Zeus retorted crossly.

"How could he," Apollo said, "if he is without breath for a full year, for having failed to keep his Oath to Lord Hades, by which he would never suffer to see Hera and Junia kept prisoner on Olympus against their will?"

Eileithya smiled, impressed at Apollo's boldness. Centuries ago, the Archer would never have bothered to defend his Queen's interests in her sempiternal war of words with Zeus, yet in recent years Apollo's attitude towards Hera became inexplicably favourable, as if he had grown inordinately fond of his father's wife. Had Hera, in forsaking her King, inadvertently done the impossible and caused Apollo, the eternal youth and bachelor, to progress in his views pertaining to the female sex?

Wonders never cease.

"Right," Hera agreed triumphantly. "There is that whole business to consider. And also your part in causing Junia to impale her brother with Kronos' blade."

"What in Tartarus are you going on about?" Zeus asked irritably.

"Obviously," Hera said, "you got Hermes and Athena to bring the damned thing up here, otherwise they would not look as do mortals who have just seen a ghost. Which, in my understanding, they have seen several, having spent part of the night in the Underworld doing who knows what! So yes, I am accusing you of sending them to bring the sickle here and of provoking the ire of an adolescent girl so that she would make enough of a fool of herself so that you declare her mentally incompetent! And how *did* you fumble, Kitten?" Hera continued, turning her gaze towards Junia. "As Ares said, you've never before missed your targets in training, why start now?"

"Ask him!" Junia answered, pointing at the space where she lost her balance.

"Is that true, Brother?" Hera asked the void beside Junia and Eris. "Did you cause Junia to trip and fall?"

At once, Hades removed his helmet and revealed himself, eliciting gasps from everyone gathered except for Hera, Junia, and Eris. "It is," he said calmly, as if his presence on Olympus were a normal occurrence, instead of the most uncommon of events.

"Were you there the whole time?" Zeus asked Hades incredulously.

"What, you didn't know?" Hera and Junia retorted almost in unison.

Ares laughed, then groaned in pain.

"Please hold still," Eileithya whispered to him, her eyes fixed on the Lord of the Underworld. She then wondered how Ares, for all his dauntless bombast, would ever belong in the temperate, rational world that Prometheus and Hera's learned mortals were to create in the expanse beyond the stars if Zeus were ever to let Hera and Junia leave of their own accord. Once freed from his impalement, would Ares be fulfilled in his duties as head of security on the Nephele or other City-ships of it silk yet to be built? Once the children of the Nepheleids dropped anchor on new worlds, would he then remain as a protector of women and children, and flocks and fields, as the ancients of Old Rome once knew him?

And how would Eileithya, a masterful midwife, fit into a world of women spacefarers who would find themselves forced to delegate the fertility of their wombs to mortal-made machines? At times like these, Eileithya wished she could sidestep her mother's ever-watchful gaze and speak of such matters to her grandmother, the Titan-Queen Rhea, who now dwelt in Elysium with Kronos, her newly freed Consort, as well as the rest of his Court.

"And what, pray tell, are you doing here, dear Brother?" Zeus asked Hades, jolting Eileithya from her contemplation.

Before Hades could answer, a knock resounded at the large bronze doors at the front of the banquet hall. Eris threw Eileithya a knowing glance. Mouthing the words, 'Be careful what you wish for', Eris then looked towards Ganymede as he sped towards the front door, for Hermes, in an aberrant display of fretfulness, had remained transfixed throughout the duration of Ares' predicament.

"Who is it now?" Zeus asked his Cup-bearer, who promptly shrieked, then fainted with the daintiness of a sack of rocks.

Eris released Junia from her grip and flew towards the entrance of the banquet hall.

"What the hell is going on?" Zeus griped as he spun towards the open front doors behind Phanes.

The First-begotten obliged and stepped aside from Zeus' line of sight, revealing Eris standing before a very peeved-looking Kronos, his Queen Rhea, and the Titan-Court exiled from Elysium.

After a moment, Eris said, "Father, it's your id, Shall I let them in?"

Nepheleid

Chapter Thirty-One

"Hermes... look alive!" Hades whispered, nudging the messenger god out of his torpor and back to the present moment.

In the span of a mortal heartbeat, Hermes realized that he had not moved a muscle since young Junia found the sickle under the gift table, nor had he been his usual, loquacious self since Kronos' mighty, Sky-sundering blade found itself lodged into Ares' chest, pinning the god of war to the floor of the banquet hall. Also, Hades had somehow just materialized out of thin air, and now there was talk of Titans at the door. Was this Eris' idea of a joke, or had the minx somehow defied the long-established laws of space and time and smuggled the progenitors of the blessed gods to holy Olympus to mercifully distract her heavyhearted younger sister from her remorse for impaling their brother? As with all matters pertaining to Eris, Hermes believed that any combination of possibilities could be true.

"Did you bring them here with you, Uncle?" Hermes asked Hades, half in jest.

"I did not," Hades answered. "They came on their own."

"And you allowed it?" Zeus asked warily.

"I was unaware that they were here until this very moment," Hades replied. "Remember, Brother, that the Titans are no longer prisoners dwelling at the bottom of the pit of Tartarus, nor am I their jailer any longer. And as rulers of Elysium, it is their prerogative to return to the living Earth whenever they so choose, just as it is with the mortal shades of the Mighty Dead over which they reign. I could not thwart them from coming here even if I wanted to."

"When exactly did you get here, Brother?" Hera inquired.

"When it was brought to my attention that the sickle formerly belonging to our Father was no longer hidden in my Kingdom," Hades answered,

Nepheleid

his gaze fixed upon Hermes.

"Then why remain hidden from us all?" Hera asked, raising an eyebrow. "We would have welcomed you as an honoured guest!"

"I wanted to join the festivities, truly I did," Hades continued, "however my main reason for coming here was to ensure that no one did anything foolish with the sickle –"

"You're a bit too late for that, Uncle!" Ares interrupted with a soft chuckle, then winced in pain from laughter.

"Ares, do shut up!" Hera, Apollo, Eileithya and Aphrodite scolded him almost in unison, eliciting another chortle from the god of war, followed by a predictable, pained grunt.

"All right then," Hermes said as he spun on his heels and made his way toward the front of the banquet hall. "Let us see what other fresh hell this blessed day has in store for us!"

As soon as Hermes reached the heavy bronze doors, white-armed Hera leaped ahead of him to find her grandsons Anicetos and Alexiares flanking the Titan-Court outside the front steps, looking rather at a loss for words. Hermes then remembered that stalwart Herakles and fair Hebe's progeny had never before met the Titans. The previous Winter, when it seemed as though all of Olympus gathered in the Garden of the Hesperides to find Hera bound at her Tree, the lads had stayed behind to guard the ramparts of the heavenly Citadel while their elders witnessed the miracle of yet another, albeit short-lived, reconciliation between their King and Queen. This time, Anicetos and Alexiares gazed awkwardly upon Ganymede's limp form sprawled upon the floor, not daring to open the door any wider lest they nudge or bruise their royal grandfather's favourite pet.

Without much ceremony, Hera instructed the boys to mind the still-unconscious Ganymede, in the event that he was actually awake and playing dead out of sheer dread of the forefathers of his Olympian masters. Once Anicetos and Alexiares dragged Ganymede out of the way, Hermes opened the doors wider and greeted the venerable callers with gracious words of welcome. Hera stood behind him, her gaze fixed upon the Heavens, scrying the firmament for a sign from her kin on the Nephele.

"Grandfather Kronos, Grandmother Rhea, and to all the Titan-Court

278

who reigns upon blessed Elysium," he said decorously. "To what do we, the gods who dwell on high Olympus, owe the pleasure of your visit?"

"Well," Kronos said with an amused half-grin, "since the lot of you young ones could not shut up about Junia's coming-of-age celebration, coming to visit us in Elysium at the wee hours – yes, Hermes, I always know what time it is on every corner of the broad-pathed Earth – we Titans decided to come here to give my favourite granddaughter our very best. Ah, there is my beautiful daughter –"

Hermes turned around and noticed that Hera now stood directly behind him at the threshold of the bronze doors, with Eris at her left.

"Will you not let us in?" the Titan-King continued, looking vexed all of a sudden. "Why are you looking up at the Heavens, Daughter, we are right here! Were you expecting someone else? Someone more airborne?"

"I would gladly let you in, Father," Hera replied, "however, there has been an incident –"

"And your timing could not have been worse had you stabbed Ares yourself!" Zeus told the Titans snidely, having also seemingly materialized out of the ether at the front doors instead of waiting inside the banquet hall with the others.

"Don't put your tunic in a twist!" Hera retorted caustically. "Help is already on the way!"

"Did you invite the Titans to Olympus?" Zeus asked Hera. "Really? On this day of all days?"

"I invited no Titans," Hera answered, "other than Okeanos and Tethys, but they seldom leave their abode at the boundaries of the Earth. Although, I am glad to see Klymene here. Hello Darling! Do come inside. As for these Titans, you ought to ask this one," Hera continued, staring straight at Hermes, "as he apparently spent the entire night visiting them in Elysium, talking endlessly about Junia's party."

Zeus threw Hermes a sharp look. "You look guilty for some reason. What the hell did you and the others do all night?" he asked in a manner that imparted his sheer indifference about the actual nocturnal comings and goings of his messenger.

"Will you let the rest of us in?" rich-haired Rhea asked Zeus.

Nepheleid

"Do you promise to behave?" Hera replied with enough bravado to elicit a startled glance from both Hermes and Zeus. "Very well, do come in," she continued. "You remember Lord Phanes, do you not?"

As soon as Hera uttered these words, the Titan-King and his Queen, as well as the entire Titan-Court, halted their steps to gaze upon the eldest and most powerful being in the Cosmos standing before them, his massive size blocking the grisly spectacle of Ares' predicament at the back of the banquet hall.

"And here I thought the lot of you would have been well acquainted by now," Hera quipped with such verve that Hermes almost wondered whether Eris had been the one to give voice to such thoughts.

As for Kronos, all traces of his earlier amusement completely vanished from his features. After a moment, he said, "It is an honour to greet the First-begotten among our deathless kind." He then bowed respectfully, then Rhea and the rest of his retinue followed his example.

"And I am also honoured," Phanes replied tentatively, as if the Titans' presence made him also ill at ease, "to greet the five Pillars of the Cosmos, who sundered Heaven from Earth and have since sent the Cosmos on its skyward course, ever onward at great speed, away from the broad-pathed Earth."

The strange spectacle of Phanes and the Titans' mutual discomposure piqued Hermes' curiosity, for he would never have imagined that anyone or anything in the Cosmos could unsettle the eldest among the race of immortals. After a moment's reflection, Hermes recalled overhearing a physics lecture back at the CARINA school at Borealis during the year when Zeus decreed that Hermes ought to remain on Turtle Island with his Queen so long as she persisted in her voluntary exile from Olympus. During the lecture, Mnemosyne, the Mother of the Muses, explained to the pupils how Chaos was a necessary precondition for Life, for in a completely ordered system, all Life would cease to exist.

And now you understand that Phanes, the Source of all Life, unmatched in power, is a being of pure Chaos, for in presiding over the Chaos of primordial procreative union, he obeys no laws but his own. Much more so than I, if you can imagine. Now, think of what the Titans are, and that which they have done…

Hermes turned around and noticed Eris staring straight at him, her usual sardonic smile gracing her full lips. Though the messenger truly despised it when Eris intruded upon his thoughts, this time, he had to admit that she was right. As much as Phanes was the first to emerge from the primordial Chaos at the moment when the universe came into being, the Titans were ultimately the first to impose Order upon the Chaos of the newly created Cosmos by interrupting the unceasing, perpetual union of Gaia and Ouranos, thus severing Heaven from Earth, and appointing the cardinal directions, the procession of the Seasons, and the rule of Time upon the world.

And don't forget that they eat babies. Just ask Dionysus' previous incarnation, Zagreus, born of the unholy, chaotic union between Zeus and his daughter Persephone. For all of Zeus' boasts of succeeding the Titans in being the bringer of Order upon the Cosmos, he certainly is susceptible to the allure of Chaos, even at the best of times... Do you not see it? Do you not see that Dionysus is also pure Chaos in his own way? Is it any wonder that Hera hates him so?

Hermes paused, pondering Eris' wordless disclosure in the confines of his mind. He had always wondered why Hera, the reigning Queen of Olympus and the wife of the victor against the Titans, would remain allied to her King's former foes long after their defeat. Now Hermes realized that Hera perceived the Titans, flawed though they may be, as the primordial heroes, the first to bring Order upon the Cosmos and to keep the more destructive excesses of Chaos at bay. Yet in doing so, the Titans, and especially their King, eventually became a force for evil by imposing an excess of Order upon the world, as evidenced by Kronos' refusal to let his five eldest children – who, like all children, remain nuggets of Chaos until they come of age – live outside the confines of his belly.

Kronos was once the King who reigned over the Golden Age of mortals, yet in his deposal he let the world fall into the hands of a languid lecher who let the world turn to shit on his watch.

Though he did not fully disagree with Eris' stern estimation of their father's reign, Hermes considered such thoughts trivial at the moment, for the Titans were now following Hera to the back of the banquet hall, after many among their number inevitably noticed a rather large sickle sticking out of a massive, albeit handsome, god's chest. As could well be expected, many Titans expressed astonishment at the misuse of their King's celebrated sickle, for among their kind, this object represented the very embodiment of the long reign of their race upon the broad-pathed Earth.

Nepheleid

By the time Hermes, Hera, Eris, and the Titans made their way back to where Ares lay, the Charites were busying themselves with cordoning a perimeter around Ares with garlands of yellow flowers. Predictably, this sent the god of war into a painful laughing fit, prompting Aphrodite to scold her handmaidens with the ill timing of their otherwise brilliant display of whimsy. At some point, Hebe and Herakles had released the mortals, Derek and Paul, from their protective custody. The boys were now assisting Anicetos and Alexiares in assessing Ganymede's state of consciousness, far from the judgmental gaze of loud-thundering Zeus. Junia had also joined them, as did Klymene, perhaps on Apollo's orders to keep the maiden from fretting any further about Ares' predicament. On second thought, Hermes surmised that it was more likely that Junia stepped away from Ares' vicinity of her own initiative to stay out of the line of fire when Hera and Zeus would inevitably resume interrogating their fellow gods about how and why the sickle found its way on starry Olympus.

"What is this?" Kronos asked Hera as he gestured towards his sickle and its victim pinned underneath.

"That would be the incident I was referring to earlier," Hera replied causally.

Kronos gave his daughter a strange look, then turned his gaze towards Junia. "You must not use a sickle as you would a spear, Moppet," he told her gently. "You must cut with a sweeping motion, and aim *low*."

At these words, Kronos' four Titan brothers chuckled while their wives shook their heads and rolled their eyes in embarrassment.

"It was an accident!" Junia protested.

"We know!" the other blessed gods who dwell on holy Olympus replied in concert.

"So, the oaf was not your target?" Kronos asked Junia, who answered with a shake of her head. Kronos grinned, then turned to look upon rich-haired Rhea, whose own look of shock and disbelief appeared to amuse Ares a great deal.

"If you don't stop this," Apollo told Ares in a stage whisper, "I will have to blindfold you."

"That will only encourage him more," Aphrodite replied, then clasped her hand over Ares' mouth to stop him from howling in laughter.

"What do you think?" Kronos asked Rhea. "I do agree that our little Moppet has truly come of age, even if her aim leaves a lot to be desired?"

"Zeus was not her target either," Hera said before Kronos could answer, "so perhaps you ought to calm yourself."

"No, it was me!" Aphrodite interjected. "She ran towards me, and my dear, unfaltering Ares protected me from the brat!"

"Seriously, Aphrodite! Not everything is about you!" Hera said with an emphatic roll of her large, beautiful eyes. "Besides, what cause would she have to harm you since you will not be joining us on the Nephele?"

Aphrodite gasped, then looked straight at rich-haired Rhea. "Did you hear that?" she shrieked. "She would ban me from her City-ship, all because I've told her that I would not stand idly by as she turned her learned mortals into sexless geldings!"

"What on Earth is she going on about?" Rhea asked Hera.

"They have womb machines on the Nephele!" Aphrodite continued.

"Yes, we have artificial wombs," Hera conceded. "So what?"

"Sister," Aphrodite told Rhea, "Hera plans to use these false wombs so that she can have mortals reproduce without the act of love! She claims that it is to change them and make them more resistant to the rigours of microgravity or some nonsense, but I don't believe a word of it!"

Kronos quavered visibly at Aphrodite's words, then threw Rhea a knowing look, as if both the Titan-King and his Queen were already aware of this technology aboard the Nephele and City-ships of its ilk yet to set sail towards the stars. Hermes then pondered whether the Titans had any designs for such devices once the Nephele was out of reach from the broad-pathed Earth.

"Interesting as this may be," Zeus said with a hint of boredom in his voice, "there remains the matter of that sickle sticking out of this one's chest!"

"I'm all right, thank you for asking!" Ares retorted caustically.

Junia covered her face with the palm of her hand.

Nepheleid

"He will be fine," Klymene assured Junia. "Back in the day when wars were common, Ares used to get stabbed or shot all the time! He has not died yet, nor could he even if he wished it!"

"Exactly!" Eris agreed.

"I don't care a whit who Junia targeted when she picked up the sickle!" Hera told Zeus exasperatedly. "I want to know *who* put the sickle here, where she could find it in the first place! And *you* ought to be more concerned about who *their* target was! Wouldn't you agree, Brother?" she added, addressing Hades. "Perhaps you could enlighten us on the matter?"

"It was not I, Sister, who brought the sickle to Olympus," Hades answered. "Though I must confess that I was the one who thwarted Junia from doing something foolish with the blade."

"And a fine job you did!" Ares countered facetiously.

"I meant to stop her in her momentum," Hades explained. "I did not mean for her to trip and skewer you like shrimp on a brochette. For that, I do apologize."

"Eh, these things happen," Ares said.

"See?" Eris told Junia. "It was all Uncle Ninja's fault that you fumbled."

"Of course, it wasn't you who brought the sickle here!" Hera retorted. "I already know it was Hermes, for he is still sopping wet from his dive into one of the Rivers in your Kingdom. Only the Rivers in the Underworld can keep an immortal soaked for longer than is otherwise natural! I was giving him an opportunity to admit it so that we could get to the bottom of the matter!"

Hermes felt his breath halting in his throat. How in the world did he not remember being sopping wet in the midst of all this lunacy? "Yes, it was I who brought the sickle to Olympus," he managed to stammer after realizing that his silence would further incriminate him. "I did it because I wanted to bring Junia a worthy gift for her coming-of-age."

Zeus gave Hermes a cold, hard stare. "Really?" he said. "The sickle?"

"Well, yes," Hermes continued. "I believed it constituted a thoughtful gesture at the time. Junia and I did get off on the wrong foot, and I was there in the Underworld on the day she received it as a gift from Kronos when she was a small child –"

"And a child she must remain, at least for the time being," Zeus declared.

"Oh, bloody hell," Hera protested.

"No, I cannot accept her as having come of age on this day," Zeus explained, "for her first deed as an adult was to stab her brother unintentionally –"

"And, if she'd done it on purpose, would you have decreed otherwise?" Hera asked Zeus in annoyance.

"Well," Zeus replied, gesturing at Ares.

"Oh, fuck off!" Ares retorted.

"It was an accident, you loud-thundering twat!" Junia cried out to Ares' pained amusement.

"Do not speak to your father this way!" Rhea scolded Junia.

"Oh, come off it!" Hera told Rhea. "She is right, and he is being a stubborn tyrant, threatening to keep her here against her will, only to annoy me! And you raised him to be this way! You know as well as anyone that your idiot son had no business being your chosen in the first place! You know, more than anyone else, that had he not swallowed his first wife, he would have become even more of a slothful brute." She searched the banquet hall for a moment, then pointed a finger at Dionysus. "Than this one!"

"You knew?" Athena said in a low voice that carried marvellously through the stunned silence in the wake of Hera's diatribe.

"We all did, Pallas," Hera answered. "But justice never came for your mother, as Zeus then quickly set out to marry Themis, who was the goddess of Laws and Justice when my father was still King, just so he could avoid facing any kind of retribution!"

"That was not why I wed Themis, I'll have you know!" Zeus protested. "I was – and still am – quite fond of her."

"Why did you not tell me?" Athena asked Hera.

Nepheleid

"Because I was afraid something like this would happen," Hera replied, gesturing at Ares.

"That's fair," Ares said.

"You held your tongue for my sake," Zeus told Hera, with his gaze fixed upon Phanes. "And yet you claim to no longer love me. Perhaps you will miss at least some part of me should you somehow leave aboard the Nephele and set sail across the vast Cosmos?"

"Oh, piss off!" Hera retorted. "Not everything under the Heavens is about your cock!"

"But is there not truth in his words, Hera?" Phanes asked. "Do you not still love your King?"

"How could I?" Hera answered, "when he would compromise my daughter's future for the sole purpose of spiting me! He would wager the fate of the entire race of mortals aboard the Nephele and City-ships of its ilk yet to be built, because Junia made a daft mistake, as all young people have always done and will always do! Never mind that he, in his so-called wisdom, would have made this one King," she added, pointing again at Dionysus. "He had him sit on the throne of Heaven as an infant when he was still the son of Persephone, and yet once he grew to manhood, he and his gaggle of drunken tarts have committed far worse atrocities in the throes of intoxication, without the excuse of youthful guilelessness! For all his boasts of keeping Order upon the Cosmos, Zeus would have crowned his unholy bastard King just so he could live out his endless existence as the indolent knave that he is!

"You," she said, turning and addressing the Cloud-gatherer, "are the *worst* hypocrite to ever have reigned within the hallowed halls of holy Olympus! Was it any wonder that so many among your former lovers and your innumerable children joined Poseidon, Apollo, and I in our failed rebellion against you centuries ago? Is it any wonder that today, most of the blessed gods who dwell on starry Olympus have already chosen to follow Junia and I to the Nephele? Even Artemis, and her own mother Leto, my former rival, if you can imagine it! And can you honestly tell me that you could not anticipate that the day would come when Athena found out the truth about how her mother met her end, a truth you've kept hidden from her for her entire life, just as you've kept from me the truth about the fate that befell Eurymedon, my first husband, and the father of Prometheus, my firstborn? As for you, Lord

Phanes, you have much to answer for in that regard, but I'll get to you in a moment. But yes, Zeus, tell me, are you truly surprised that Athena has finally learnt the true extent of your depravity and plotted with Hermes to cut you down where you stand, Oath of Fealty be damned? Today might not have been the day Junia came of age, no, but at least *someone* did. And her mother would be proud."

Despite his best efforts to keep his composure, Hermes felt his jaw slacken and drop, while Athena's fair features reddened with rage. Hermes was unsure against whom she was angriest. Meanwhile, Kronos tried his best to keep his lips from twisting into a half-smile while the rest of the immortal gods, Titans, and the two mortal lads gathered in the banquet hall on holy Olympus remained silent.

"You may as well admit it," Hera told Athena after a long, uncomfortable interlude. "And yes, I've already decided to grant you asylum among my crew on the Nephele."

"What about Hermes?" Junia asked in an oddly confident tone.

"Hermes?" Hera repeated, taken by surprise. "Hermes will stay here on Olympus with Zeus as his messenger, as he's always done!"

"No," Junia replied.

"What did you say?" Hera retorted, astounded by Junia's bravado.

"No, Hermes must come too," Junia said flatly. "He will come with us on the Nephele and be my protector while Ares heals from his wound."

"Kitten," Hera said with a soft, yet stern, voice, "you will have no need for a protector once the Nephele unmoors and takes flight. And look at what his plotting has done! He had his role to play in… this!" she added, gesturing towards Ares.

"That wasn't Hermes' fault, no matter how much you want it to be," Junia said. "I was the one who picked up the sickle, I was the one who lunged, then tripped, then fell, then dropped it on Ares. I didn't mean to do it, but it was definitely me. If Hermes has to stay here, then so will I!"

"What?" Hera said, somewhat dumbfounded.

"I'll stay here," Junia continued, "unless you reverse your position on Hermes not being allowed to go above the Hub. I'll stay, and I'll *marry* him, and do the sex and everything, and –"

"I've heard enough," Zeus said, appalled and amused in equal measure. "And what do you have to say about this?" he asked Hermes, whose mouth still lay agape.

"I think I'm having an aneurysm," was all he managed to say.

"Junia, you are being silly," Hera said.

"You know, young one," rich-haired Rhea said, though Hermes could not discern to whom exactly she was speaking. "Defying one's father and mother is how our kind has always come of age."

"And she admitted her own fault in wounding Ares," august Themis said, voicing her thoughts for the first time since the evening's absurd chain of events began. "That alone takes integrity and courage."

"Perhaps more courage than sense?" Rhea said, obviously addressing Hera this time.

Hera pinched the bridge of her nose in annoyance. "All right," she conceded, "Hermes can come too. But you are *absolutely not* marrying him."

"Excuse me!" Zeus interrupted. "There is still the matter of Athena and Hermes' attempted treachery! I want them to admit who their true target was!"

"Oh, for Heaven's sake!" Hera protested. "We all know it was you! Be grateful they did not carry through with their plan, even though they clearly have grown to hate you as much as I do! Do you really want the lot of us to stay here with you, now that you know? Think about it. Take all the time you need but be mindful that we plan to leave here before sunrise tomorrow."

"It appears that you have reached a stalemate, Brother," Hades said, reminding everyone that he was still in their midst.

"Then what do you suggest?" Zeus retorted. "And where the hell is Poseidon? He should be here too! Not that he can ever be bothered to come to Olympus anymore. Does he hate me also?"

"I am sorry to be the one to break the news," Hephaestus said as he limped through the front doors into the banquet hall, his long parachute and cables trailing behind him. "But Poseidon and his Sea-Court, all save for Thetis, his ambassador on Olympus, have already taken temporary residence on the Hesperides Autonomous Station, where they will be briefed until they are ready to settle aboard the Nephele. Now…" he added, pulling a light blow torch from one of the many pockets in his CARINA-issued flight suit. "Where is that idiot brother of mine?"

Nepheleid

Chapter Thirty-Two

"Please tell me you did not jump from low Earth orbit like your sister did last Winter?" white-armed Hera asked Hephaestus, the mirth in her voice tempered with annoyance, as the smith god limped gingerly towards the far end of the banquet hall where the others were gathered.

Trust Hera to scold her son like a child even when coming to her rescue of sorts, Zeus thought grudgingly, unsure whether to be pleased or peeved at Hephaestus' fortuitously-timed arrival among his deathless kin. As was his custom, the Cloud-gatherer sought Metis' acquiescence to his passing thought in the confines of his mind, but the Oceanid remained uncharacteristically silent at his prompting.

"Rest assured, Mother," Hephaestus answered as he untethered himself from his parachute and cables, while a half-dozen of his golden mechanical handmaidens followed in his wake, folding the thick fabric and rolling up the cables after having done the same with their own landing equipment. "We leaped from the Henokhie when we were well within acceptable skydiving range. Your shuttle should be landing soon," he added, turning his head towards the open doors, through which all could see the aircraft making its descent as it pierced the clouds above holy Olympus.

"You see, Kitten?" Hera said with good humour. "When you follow proper landing protocol, your clothes do not get burned up on re-entry due to atmospheric friction!" She then bit her lip, remembering that Ares was in a particularly jocular mood despite having been impaled by the only weapon ever known to depose a former ruling Sky-King. Luckily for Ares, Apollo covered both his ears before Hera said anything as the Archer had grown accustomed to anticipating his Queen's attempt at levity in the midst of even the most egregious quandary.

That one has grown far to close too our bride than I would like, Zeus prodded Metis again, hoping that his constant mind companion would share her thoughts about what Zeus believed to be Apollo's protracted yet burgeoning interest in Hera's wit and considerable charms.

Nepheleid

"So," Hephaestus said as he reached the place where Ares lay pinned under the Titan-forged sickle, surrounded by Apollo, Aphrodite, Eileithya, and many others. "I see you got yourself trapped even worse than the time I caught you and this one under a golden net!" he added, careful not to mention his wife by name, even if golden Aphrodite sat right between Ares and Hephaestus.

Without anyone uttering a single word, Hephaestus' golden maidens simultaneously pulled their folded parachutes out of their backpacks and began cushioning and covering Ares with the fireproof fabric, wrapping several layers around the blade as their master lit up the blow torch and motioned to begin his cut above Ares' chest.

"Wait!" Eris interjected. "We should avoid severing the blade if we can help it at all. It would be best to move it – and Ares – all in one piece onto the shuttle."

"Why?" Apollo asked, somewhat taken aback by Eris' suggestion.

"Ares could bleed abundantly," Eris answered. "And strange things are born from the ichor of immortals when it is spilled upon the ground... And there are mortals here. At least one of whom has no idea what is happening. As for the other one..."

"All right," Hephaestus conceded as he put out the torch. "Have it your way, but we need to lift Ares and the blade off the ground all at once."

"Herakles!" Hera called out.

"Make way," stalwart Herakles said to his fellow immortals crowding Ares, with Hebe at his side and their strong sons behind them. "The boys and I will lift the blade. Hebe, Eily, and Aphrodite can lift Ares on my count..."

"Halt!" Zeus thundered, interrupting the proceedings. "There is still the matter of resolving the wager that Hera and I made. No one leaves Olympus until the consequences of Zoe's aborted coming of age are addressed!"

"Are you being serious right now?" Hera asked incredulously, stepping between Zeus and Ares' entourage. "Forget about the wager, our son is grievously injured! Not that you ever cared about him!"

"For all I know," Zeus replied, "this was all an elaborate ruse of yours to smuggle Kronos' sickle aboard the Nephele. Do not think for a second that we do not all know what that blade can do! We all saw what happened when Zoe opened a portal from the Kingdom of Hades to the Garden of the Hesperides with one stroke of the blade!"

"An elaborate ruse? Did the voice inside your head tell you this?" Hera retorted as if deliberately attempting to trigger a heightened emotional response from Athena, who had wisely kept her peace since Hephaestus' arrival on starry Olympus. "No, of course not. Even *she* is not so daft as to suggest that I would have my own son stabbed by his little sister to smuggle a blade that is already hers." Turning to face Hephaestus and the others, she added, "Again, this time on my count."

"SILENCE!" Zeus bellowed, to which Hera responded with a dumbfounded glower.

As if emboldened by Hera's umbrage, the Titans and their children who dwell on starry Olympus began closing ranks around Hera: first Iapetos, the Pillar of the East, and his Consort Klymene, followed by Junia; then Kreius, the Pillar of the South, and his wife Eurybia, daughter of Gaia and Pontos, the wine-dark Sea, as well as Hyperion, the Pillar of the West, and his wife Theia. Then came Koios, the Pillar of the North and axis of Heaven, with his bride Phoebe and their daughter, the dark-robed Leto, and finally Kronos and Rhea, joined by Hestia, Hades, and Demeter, though the goddess of the grain made a show of standing a few paces away from the Lord of the Underworld. Meanwhile, Apollo, Aphrodite, and Eileithya rose to their feet, flanked by Eris, Hebe and Herakles, and their sons Anicetos and Alexiares. The nine Muses formed a line behind Apollo, though they let fleet-footed Artemis pass through to stand by her twin. Behind them stood Athena and Hermes, unmoving but otherwise making a show of having joined the immortals rallying around Hera. Only Dionysus and his Maenads stood apart from the caucus, as well as august Themis, ever Zeus' loyal advisor, who remained by Phanes' side as if to shield the First-begotten from the unpleasantness that would surely follow. The mortal boys Derek and Paul also stood apart from the crowd, however Zeus assumed that they, along with a very harried and pale-looking Ganymede, were left intentionally out of the fray for their own protection.

Standing in the midst of the gathering of immortals, Hephaestus turned to face the Thunderer, holding his blow torch in his right hand, while the other fingered a large, ancient hammer that had been his constant companion for as long as Zeus could recall. Hephaestus limped a few paces to Hera's side, then stood still, as if waiting for Zeus to make a move.

"You too?" Zeus asked Hephaestus, somewhat disappointed that the smith god once again failed to learn his lesson about intervening on his mother's behalf in her quarrels with her King.

"Yup," the smith god replied in the causal manner of the mortals of Turtle Island. He then turned his gaze towards the open front doors of the banquet hall, where the Henokhie came into full view after landing within the ramparts of the heavenly citadel.

From the open side door of the shuttle, Iris, Mnenosyne, and Asia emerged and made their way up the outer steps leading inside the banquet hall. Oddly enough, Prometheus was not by Asia's side. Zeus surmised that he might have been the one piloting the craft, and likely elected to remain within to avoid an unnecessarily ugly confrontation with his old foe. As soon as Mnemosyne crossed the threshold of the open doors of the banquet hall, the nine Muses gathered around their mother while Iris and Asia stayed a few paced behind them, as if keeping the way to the exit unencumbered.

I suppose I've lost them as well, Zeus pondered gloomily.

In the corner of his eye, the Cloud-gatherer noticed that winged Iris, though clad in CARINA-issued aviator attire, was carrying a weapon of sorts under the fold of the sleeve of her flight suit, though Asia and Mnemosyne appeared unarmed. Zeus then recalled that the last time Iris was seen among the blessed gods, he had threatened her with his thunderbolt for persisting in her refusal to reveal Hera's whereabouts, until Apollo intervened just in the nick of time, allowing the messenger goddess to escape. Iris had not set foot on Olympus since. Zeus then turned his glance towards Apollo, noticing that the Archer had taken hold of his golden bow, which he had earlier set down on the floor while attending to Ares. As for Artemis, she now stood behind her twin, her silver bow at the ready, with an unflinching gaze set upon the Thunderer.

If I try to prevail with force alone, then all that we hold dear will be lost, Zeus thought, hoping that Metis would finally rouse and provide him with wise counsel on how to gain victory against the overwhelming unpopularity of his position among his fellow immortals.

Have I lost you too, dear one? Or are you disappointed that our daughter failed to deliver you from your prison the way we rescued my brothers and sisters from the prison of Kronos' belly? Have you also grown to despise me, the way all the other blessed gods have evidently grown to hate me?

"My King," august Themis said, mercifully breaking the tense silence within the banquet hall. "Perhaps there is a way to end this stalemate once and for all."

Zeus turned towards the Titanide with a look of utter despondency. "What counsel have you for me, dear Themis?" he asked in an uncharacteristically soft voice.

"Perhaps it would be wisest to leave this matter in the hands of an impartial third party?" Themis replied.

"Of course!" Zeus agreed, his voice swelling with renewed vigour. "That is an excellent idea! Let the mortals decide!"

"Wait! My King-" Themis retorted with some alarm, as the rest of the crowd gazed upon the Father of gods and men with astonished incredulity.

"He did not just..." Zeus heard Hermes whisper to Athena, to which the Virgin Warrior replied, "Yes, he absolutely did."

"Wait for it," Hera told them both, though loud enough for even the mortal lads to hear.

"You, blond one!" Zeus addressed Derek. "You must decide if it is just, from your professional standpoint, whether it is right for –"

"Mr. Diaz," Derek interrupted. "I really can't be of any help right now. I'm not qualified yet to provide you with the weapons-grade level of therapy that you clearly need. And I think I might still be on drugs..."

Zeus furrowed his brow, though he graciously abstained from rending the very air with thunderclaps to show his displeasure and imperil the boys' tender mortal flesh. He turned towards the son of Turtle Island, whose mind appeared unclouded.

"Nope!" Paul answered in a well-rehearsed monosyllable before the king of Olympus could even address him.

Zeus sucked in a breath, then reminded himself of the grief he would have to face later from white-armed Hera should he retaliate against one of her clever mortals bound for the Nephele. He then set his gaze upon Ganymede, sweet, loyal Ganymede, who threw him the most spiteful glance he had ever seen upon his lovely features.

"Is this a *fucking* joke?" the Trojan-born prince shrieked, as though intent on meeting his final fate.

Hera gasped, then stifled a laugh, unaccustomed to hearing the otherwise impeccably mannered Cupbearer use foul language for the very first time in the august presence of the blessed gods who dwell on holy Olympus. "Yes, we can keep him," Zeus heard her say, presumably to Junia, though Zeus could not be certain at the moment.

"This is *precisely* how my homeland came to be razed to the ground!" Ganymede spat out, his previous terror now sublimated into righteous anger.

"Oh, will you people ever let that go!" Eris whined. "It's been three and a half thousand years already!"

"My King," Themis said diplomatically. "Perhaps we ought to leave this matter in the hands of one who is far older than these mortals, and wiser."

Zeus turned to face her. "I hope you are not referring to –"

"Yes, my King," Themis agreed, charitably interrupting the Cloud-gatherer to soften the blow. "That is precisely who I meant. The First-begotten is a most befitting arbiter of the matter at hand."

"You would have the son of Chaos be my judge?" Zeus asked dejectedly.

"We would," Mnemosyne answered in her sister's stead, "have your cause be judged by one who would favour an outcome favourable to the preservation of Earthly Life and the Memory of our deathless kind, wherever we immortals are fated to roam."

Zeus turned his gaze towards Hera, whose amusement quickly gave way to disquietude.

"And you would accept Phanes' judgment?" Zeus asked his Queen. "Whatever it may be, and even if you do not find it favourable to your cause?"

Hera pondered these words, seemingly unaware of the glances that Junia exchanged with Kronos who, unbeknownst to the Queen of Olympus, had taken a few steps towards Ares and the Titan-forged blade still protruding from the god of war's chest. Zeus furrowed his brow at his father, then produced a thunderbolt which he kept on hand to remind others of his lingering might despite his current opprobrium among the Olympian Court.

"I would," Hera said finally, as Junia took a step towards Kronos. "Though only if you swear to accept his ruling should you also find it distasteful to your position. Then, and only then, do you have my word."

"Very well," Zeus replied. "I swear by the Oath of the Holy River Styx that I will accept Lord Phanes' judgment, whatever it may be. So it is decided. "Lord Phanes, the fate of Olympus is in your hands. We await your judgment."

"I've already decided," Phanes said, far sooner than anyone had anticipated.

"Now, do not be hasty," Zeus said tentatively. "This is a matter of grave importance."

"I've considered the matter since long before this one came to visit me in my realm last night," Phanes replied, throwing a furtive gaze at Eris. "For Eris to come visit me twice in the span of a day on the broad-pathed Earth is enough cause for alarm at the best of times, and it seems that matters are dire indeed, for the Queen of Olympus to have found once again common cause with her old foes against her King. The Trojan prince tells it true, such strife has transpired before in the past, but this time, your contention imperils more than the survival of one City-State in one strategically important place in the mortal world. This time, the quarrel between the lovers who once celebrated their union in the Garden of the Hesperides for three hundred years threatens the very preservation of Life upon the broad-pathed Earth!

"Gods of Olympus and of the realms across the worlds of the living and of the dead! Do not think that I am blind to all that transpires in your worlds below from my own faraway realm! Queen Hera, do not think that I am ignorant of all the terrible things that have come to pass between you and your King since I drove your bridal chariot and brought you to your bridegroom! You have grown at times cold and pitiless towards those whose plight you should have understood better than any other. You have grown to realize far too late that your anger was misdirected for too long, and this has left you broken and embittered, even as you continue to strive to restore your former purpose as the Mistress of all Life. You wish to sow Earthly Life among the vast Cosmos, and for that, I commend you. However, you cannot succeed if your heart does not fully mend from its brokenness, despite your immeasurable strength. It is your strength that has kept you deliberately broken at times, for in your pain and anger you have found splendid purpose.

"Though it is my ruling that you and the Princess of Olympus shall leave with your learned mortals and any immortal that chooses to come with you on your journey and take flight on your City-ship above the Heavens, I also rule that loud-thundering Zeus shall accompany you in your voyage across the stars. As will golden Aphrodite, my loyal servant born of the Seafoam, and Dionysus, who brings joy to mortals, as well as anyone else you may despise but who also wishes to aid you in your most worthy endeavour.

"Wait, what?" Hera stammered, unsure whether Phanes' ruling constituted genuine praise or insincere adulation. "You cannot expect me to bring him!"

"You must," Phanes replied. Turning his gaze towards Zeus, he added, "And you, do not think that I have failed to notice how your absolute power has degraded your character into one of immoderate indulgence, even when rightfully challenged by your unfaltering and gracious Queen! You will accompany Hera to the Nephele as her Consort, but you shall never rule as King again until you prove yourself worthy of her trust and her love, without malice or coercion. Have you anything to say about the justness of my ruling, or would you suffer the penalty of those who perjure themselves against the Oath of the Holy River Styx?"

"I accept your ruling, Lord Phanes," Zeus said sedately after a moment. "Though if my Queen will allow it, it may take more than a few days to prepare for the journey."

Hera's lovely features turned an alarming shade of red as all eyes turned to gaze upon her, awaiting her reply.

"You have a fortnight," she told Zeus at last. "Junia and I will leave in the morning with the mortals, as soon as Paul Red Buffalo finishes his task in your palace and sends his conveyance on its way. Now, if the lot of you are quite done, Ares needs to be transported to the Nephele *at once!* If you are not going to help us, then please kindly get out of the *fucking* way!" To Phanes, she added, "And this matter is far from done, mark my words. I told you that I would get back to you with regards to the egregious injustice you have committed against me and my sovereignty."

Phanes smiled at Hera, then vanished from the banquet hall on holy Olympus before the Queen could finish her diatribe. Taking the First-begotten's exit as an opportunity to act, Hephaestus, Apollo, Herakles, Hebe, Eileithya, Aphrodite, Anicetos and Alexiares, and Eris promptly lifted Ares and the sickle off the ground in concert, as Hephaestus' half-dozen golden maidens rushed to their side to take the sickle from them. Galatea joined them to carry Ares with soft, even motions so as not to injure him further. Apollo followed the golden maidens as well as Iris, Asia, Mnemosyne, and the nine Muses aboard the Henokhie, then took one last look at his fellow immortals on starry Olympus.

"I will see you all very soon," he told them. "Please, take no offence if I do not greet you on the Hesperides as you get briefed, as I will be quite busy with Ares over the next few days."

Zeus nodded at Apollo, then watched as Iris slid the side door of the Henokhie shut before the shuttle took flight towards the Nephele, shining high above holy Olympus like a multifaceted jewel against the darkening Night.

Nepheleid

Epilogue

As had come to pass ten thousand times since the end of the last Ice Age, October came to the Northern Hemisphere of the broad-pathed Earth. It was a polychromatic display of brightly dying vegetation, all in exquisite russet and sunset-coloured tones, and other such beautiful nonsense that makes mortal poets go mad with lust at the changing of the Seasons. Such was the spectacle that Junia had whined about hoping to behold from the Nephele, high above the Earth, on the occasion of her tenth birthday, had she not been compelled to relocate to the abode of the gods with white-armed Hera when Zeus found a loophole in his recalcitrant bride's convoluted divorce plan. But today, on the day of Junia's actual fourteenth birthday since she was hatched from the prototype of whatever unholy contraption Hera and her learned mortals devised to liberate female spacefarers from the dangers of pregnancy and childbirth, Eris sat beside her young charge, glad that her efforts to bring their mother and the intact Olympian Court to the Nephele finally came to fruition.

For reasons likely pertaining to looming adolescence and the general unpleasantness that is sure to follow, Junia sat moodily on the senior management deck of Hesperides Station, where six months prior, Prometheus found her sulking as she regretted her Earth-dive to starry Olympus. This time, Eris sat beside Junia on the upper deck, watching the seemingly endless stream of immortals filing in through the Hub, feigning space sickness and other mortal afflictions as instructed for the benefit of the mortal staff at the reception terminals.

"If you're waiting to spit on Zeus when he comes in," Eris said, "then you'll be terribly disappointed. He got here last night to be briefed personally by Prometheus and Hera, all six of the Titanides, and Okeanos himself, about the role they have carved out for him on the Nephele. It sort of makes you wish you were a fly on the wall when it happened, does it not? Or perhaps not, as Zeus might have swallowed you whole!"

Junia made a sour face.

Nepheleid

"Too soon?" Eris asked.

"The Titanides are loyal to their husbands," Junia replied, her frown subsiding somewhat. "Most of whom are Titans. What you say makes no sense."

"The Titanides have always favoured peace," Eris retorted, "and this time is no different from any other time. Remember, the Titanides remained neutral in the war that Zeus and his brothers waged against the Titans, which is why they were never confined to gloomy Tartarus. This time, they want their brothers and husbands to remain free, and they warned Zeus about the Titans' designs for the future of spacefaring humanity so that the mistakes of the past are not repeated in the stupidest way imaginable."

"Then, you, Prometheus, and Asia and everyone else *meant* for Zeus to come along the whole time? Just to keep the Titans in check?" Junia asked incredulously. "Wasn't this whole exercise a way for Mom to get rid of him forever?"

"And she has, in a way," Eris answered.

"No, she didn't!" Junia said in exasperation. "Phanes said he had to stay with her and be her Consort! That's just a fancy word for husband. She gained nothing by having him board the Nephele!"

"Phanes decreed that Zeus ought to remain with Hera as her Consort but not her King," Eris corrected her. "He cannot rule as King unless he proves himself worthy. And absent the support of Athena and Hermes at the moment, that might prove difficult!"

"They're still not speaking to him, huh?" Junia asked. "I guess they can't, if they're hiding out in Witness Protection."

"There is no need for that, as Mother absolved them both of their attempted Metis-ectomy," Eris replied. "As a result, Athena is now haunting the Nephele's command tier with Prometheus and Asia, while Hermes is working comms. Because, of course, he is."

"Of course," Junia agreed with a weak, albeit genuine, laugh.

"Though they might as well have succeeded," Eris continued, "as it appears that Zeus has not heard Metis' wise counsel inside his head since your first fourteenth birthday party. Which brings me to my next question: why aren't you up there on the Nephele, celebrating your *real* birthday with your school friends? You will still have this glorious view of the autumn colours from up there. You may as well enjoy it, as you will not see this any longer once the City-ship unmoors next week."

"Ugh," Junia groaned. "I'm not really in the mood to celebrate."

"Because of Ares?" Eris asked. "Apollo said he was recovering quite well, especially since you kindly donated those umbilical stem cells growing out of your navel, which no one is supposed to know about, and which will render the entire population of the Nephele and City-ships of its ilk nigh-invulnerable to space sickness and radiation in the long haul amid interstellar space."

"I know he'll be fine," Junia agreed. "I saw him this morning. He no longer needs a jesus-ton of painkillers to numb him like he did at first because he's a ginger."

"Is it because you are not allowed to carry knives on your person until you are thirty?"

"No," Junia laughed. "But that sucks. And apparently, the cake is coming pre-cut at my party because Mom doesn't want any sharp objects at the venue. As if everyone at school didn't already think I was overprotected!"

"Well, you can never be too careful," a familiar male voice said from behind the two sisters.

Eris spun around and spied Apollo by the entrance of the lift, decked in his medical officer's uniform, absent the ichor stains from his long intervention with Ares over the past few days.

"My prince," Eris greeted him half in jest.

"My princess," Apollo replied in an equally teasing manner.

"Cut it out, you two," Junia whined. "This was only funny the first ten thousand times. You two sound like you're engaged or something!"

"It will never not be funny that Mother has chosen us both as her second-in-command at ALSESTIS," Eris replied.

"Yeah, but Phoebus is number one when she's awake," Junia said, "and you when and only when she decides to take to the sleeping chambers for months at a time so as to not arouse anyone's suspicions about our inability to age."

"Well, I do my best work when Mother is taking long naps," Eris retorted.

"I'm surprised to see you here," Apollo said, looking straight at Junia. "Your friends are waiting for you up there. I think it would be rude not to attend your own party, especially since Derek finally decided it was safe to go, as he will be the oldest pupil there along with Paul."

"I'm sure Eileithya being there to supervise everyone doesn't hurt," Junia retorted.

"Artemis is there to chaperone the lot of them as well, I'll have you know," Apollo replied. "There is no chance he'll come out of there as your brother-in-law anytime soon!"

"So, Derek finally came out of hiding, then?" Eris chuckled. "And here I thought he would be the one to need weapons-grade therapy."

"It took some convincing," Apollo explained, "but now he no longer believes that we are, in fact, extraterrestrials bound for our home world at the far end of the galaxy. I've since convinced him that his stay on Olympus was all part of a simulation, an experiment of sorts to gauge how well some pivotal future crew members such as himself would react were we ever to encounter previously unknown intelligent entities on worlds yet to be discovered."

"And it worked?" Eris asked.

"It worked well enough," Apollo said. "So far, Derek agreed to work with me to integrate some of these concepts into a framework we could further develop in a few years within the CARINA fleet."

"And here I thought you had almost ruined a perfectly good mortal with psychobabble and other such nonsense," Eris replied.

"What about Paul?" Junia inquired.

"Paul is faring well," Apollo answered. "No damage control needed at all on his account."

"That's not a surprise," Eris said. "That boy has antifreeze in his veins!"

"The Buffalo Calf Maiden must have told him and his people who we were," Apollo explained, "long before the Hub was completed and the Nephele was fully built. By then, the gods of Turtle Island already knew your mother well, and some even gave her a name by which she is known only among their kind."

"Sky River Woman," Junia whispered.

"A lovely name, and oddly fitting, don't you think?" Apollo asked Junia.

"I guess?" Junia replied, a bit confused at Apollo's meaning.

"What you don't know," Apollo continued, "is that even before Hera knew about Prometheus' designs for the future of humankind, she dreamt of setting sail upon Rivers across the Cosmos, broadening the boundaries of the Great River Okeanos into the expanse between the Stars. I witnessed it with my own eyes, on the night you came to be."

"Ew," Junia whinged, eliciting raucous laughter from Eris.

"Eris," Apollo said, "I would like to speak with Junia in private."

"I'm not sure that's allowed," Eris replied. "Seeing that she did not, in fact, come of age on starry Olympus..."

"Suit yourself," Apollo retorted. "You might actually prove of service in answering some questions."

"Oh, boy! This should be fun!" Eris said, moving aside to allow Apollo to sit next to Junia on the floor of the upper deck.

"We haven't spoken in some time," Apollo told Junia, "and I was worried about your state of mind."

"The whole sickle thing was an accident –"

"We all know this," Apollo interrupted. "I wanted your assurance that you will not try something like that again, now that Zeus is aboard the Nephele as Head of Human Resources."

"And that was my idea," Eris snickered, as if endlessly amused at this turn of events.

"It's not even a real position!" Junia protested. "There's no real Human Resources department since staffing concerns are dealt with directly by the heads of each Division within the CARINA fleet."

"He's not here to manage mortals and the staffing needs of the City-ship," Apollo retorted.

"Nor is Dionysus *actually* the manager of the wellness centre, even if that's the title he's been given," Eris added. "Though Aphrodite is *really* assigned to the Aquatic Biolab on the decks below, as Mother thought it fitting that she remain where she could do the least harm, and because seeding oceans worlds with Life falls well within her purview."

"Then Zeus is not here to pretend to manage humans?" Junia commented. "Why the hell is he here then, other than being commanded to stay here by Phanes."

"Prometheus knew that he would need Zeus to keep the more destructive side of both Chaos and Order at bay," Apollo said, "just as Prometheus always meant for Hera to join the ALSESTIS Division to neutralize excessive and oppressive Order with her constant, albeit inadvertent, habit of setting events into motion with far-reaching consequences across the vast Cosmos."

"My Mom is not a harbinger of Chaos," Junia protested. "That's Eris' job!"

"Chaos is good," Eris countered. "Chaos fosters Life in all its glorious diversity, and Mother is the Mistress of all Life!"

"Well, that's only true to the extent that Chaos, more specifically, allows for enclaves of Life to form in a Cosmos moving towards a state of entropy," Apollo explained.

"That's what I said," Eris countered.

"And you," Apollo told Junia, "almost became a partisan of entropy, or destructive Order when you decided that you ought to cut down Phanes with Kronos' sickle."

Junia's eyes grew wide in shock, but she did not reply.

"And now you know that even the gods can make grievous mistakes," Apollo continued, "as all of us have done in the past. As have I, on so many accounts. Just as you now know that, although Ares came to no lasting harm, you will always have done this injury to him, even if a far worse outcome would have unfolded had he failed to stop you from your murderous schemes. Far be it for me to understand what was going through your mind then, but I know how upsetting Phanes' power can be for those among us who favour a more rational outlook. And though I was never properly a child, having tasted nectar and ambrosia on the day I was born, causing me to grow to manhood all at once, I can somewhat understand why you do not feel comfortable with the degree of Chaos that Phanes has brought to your world. But just as Derek now understands his ordeal on Olympus to be a test of how the human mind can accept certain levels of Chaos to assimilate enormities, you need to make peace with an enormity of your own – your coming-of-age and all the Chaos down below that your blossoming into maidenhood will bring."

Junia blushed, her silence betraying her lingering, yet poorly suppressed infatuation towards the Archer.

"I know I've given you much to think about," Apollo said. "But know this, whenever mortals of all the nations of the world have tried to suppress the Chaotic madness that Phanes kindles in the hearts and loins of all living beings as the most primal urge to preserve Life, terrible crimes have been committed, and most of its casualties have been women, for their very ability to create Life within their wombs. So, think on that. And go join your school friends on the Nephele. Go enjoy the few moments of childhood you have left, such is a luxury some of us never had."

Junia bit her lip and slowly rose to her feet, throwing Eris a questioning glance.

"Just go, you little space cadet! Have fun!" Eris commanded. "And don't run with scissors!"

Junia nodded, then leaned over to give Apollo a quick embrace before running into the lift.

"Well, that was pleasantly unexpected," Apollo told Eris.

"You mean, you did not see that coming, O Lord of the prophetic arts?" Eris jested.

"I must admit, I did not," Apollo replied. "Even those blessed with the prophetic gift cannot always accurately predict the consequences of others' thoughts and actions. There are too many moving parts, too much *Chaos* for there to always be a clear outcome beyond a few precise parameters. That is precisely why neither I nor Hera could have ever foreseen the convoluted way you and Prometheus arranged to smuggle

Kronos' sickle aboard the Nephele, by using Ares as a sheath!"

"You thought that was us?" Eris protested. "Are you seriously regurgitating Zeus' hypothesis against Prometheus and Mother right now?"

"It was all a little on the nose, don't you think?" Apollo asked. "And even absent Metis' counsel, Zeus can be correct about some things some of the time. Now, tell me the truth. You and Prometheus wanted the sickle aboard the Nephele for its wondrous Space and Time-sundering properties, did you not?"

"The outcome was desired, that is true," Eris avowed. "Though I must admit that the execution was a complete surprise."

"Thank Heaven for little girls?" Apollo quipped.

"Thank Heaven for hormonal rage," Eris replied. "And Thetis' perpetual meddling for reminding us that the Titans cannot be trusted to rule over free-thinking and enlightened minds. And, of course, the filial impiety of one who just found out that she was not a motherless daughter after all."

"Speaking of unforeseen outcomes," Apollo said, "how do you think Hera will fare now that Zeus is already among us on the Nephele? I cannot have her undergo any more fugue states like the ones she experienced over the last few months she spent on Olympus."

"Hera has no time for such foolishness," Eris answered. "She has an entire City-ship full of learned mortals to keep alive!"

"But knowing that you would be at the helm should she take a long rest in the sleeping chambers," Apollo said, "I fear that she will choose to never sleep again and drive herself mad for good measure!"

"Not unless Zeus lulls her to sleep with at least one of his remaining redeeming skills, other than keeping the Titans on their toes. For all we know, Hera and Zeus are christening each other's separate sleeping quarters right now as we speak, while the rest of us are about to brief this fresh crop of immortals from starry Olympus."

"Still," Apollo said, "I doubt this was her preferred outcome."

"Her preferred outcome was that the Earth remains in good hands in the care of the gods of Turtle Island and others of their ilk while our kind sets forth to sow Earthly Life among the stars," Eris replied.

"With Titans on board, ready to render the descendants of these learned mortals into simpletons," Apollo said.

"For all her strategic brilliance, Mother can be blind at times to the looming treachery of even her closest allies," Eris agreed. "Even the children – and wives – of the Titans know not to trust the motives of deposed, long-ruling Kings when they all too willingly offer their help to bring Order to the unknown expanse beyond the known Cosmos. That is most likely the true reason why Phanes commanded Zeus to remain at Hera's side. It's quite brilliant, really. Having Zeus and the Titans on this City-ship is akin to neutralizing destructive Order with slightly less destructive Order, with Hera thrown in the mix to move things along when entropy takes hold."

"Under the purview of Human Resources?" Apollo asked, a sombre sad smile taking hold of his handsome features.

"Well, we had to make this funny somehow, did we not?" Eris retorted. "Oh, don't be like that! There is a good chance that Zeus will annoy Hera like he always does, and she will choose to take to the sleeping chamber for some time. Then, after the Nepheleids find a newly discovered wanderer with the right conditions to sow the seeds of her sunset garden, on a world bathed in the perpetual golden light of a red dwarf star, perhaps there Hera will take another bridegroom once she grows truly weary of the current one, as she awakens from another long nap."

"At the dawning of the Aeon of Eris?" Apollo asked, "where your talents of sowing Chaos will provide the essential conditions for Life to run amok on an unsuspecting world until the Titans clean up the mess?"

"I have no intention of compromising the intellectual prowess of the mortals under our care to these grey faces," Eris replied. "I will be a kind, compassionate despot, in that I will burden them with the freedom to do as they will, with all the unspeakable responsibility that true self-governance entails."

Apollo smiled at her words. "May Hera never slumber again!" he said finally as they both rose to their feet to greet the newcomers below.

Nepheleid